The Storm in the Barn

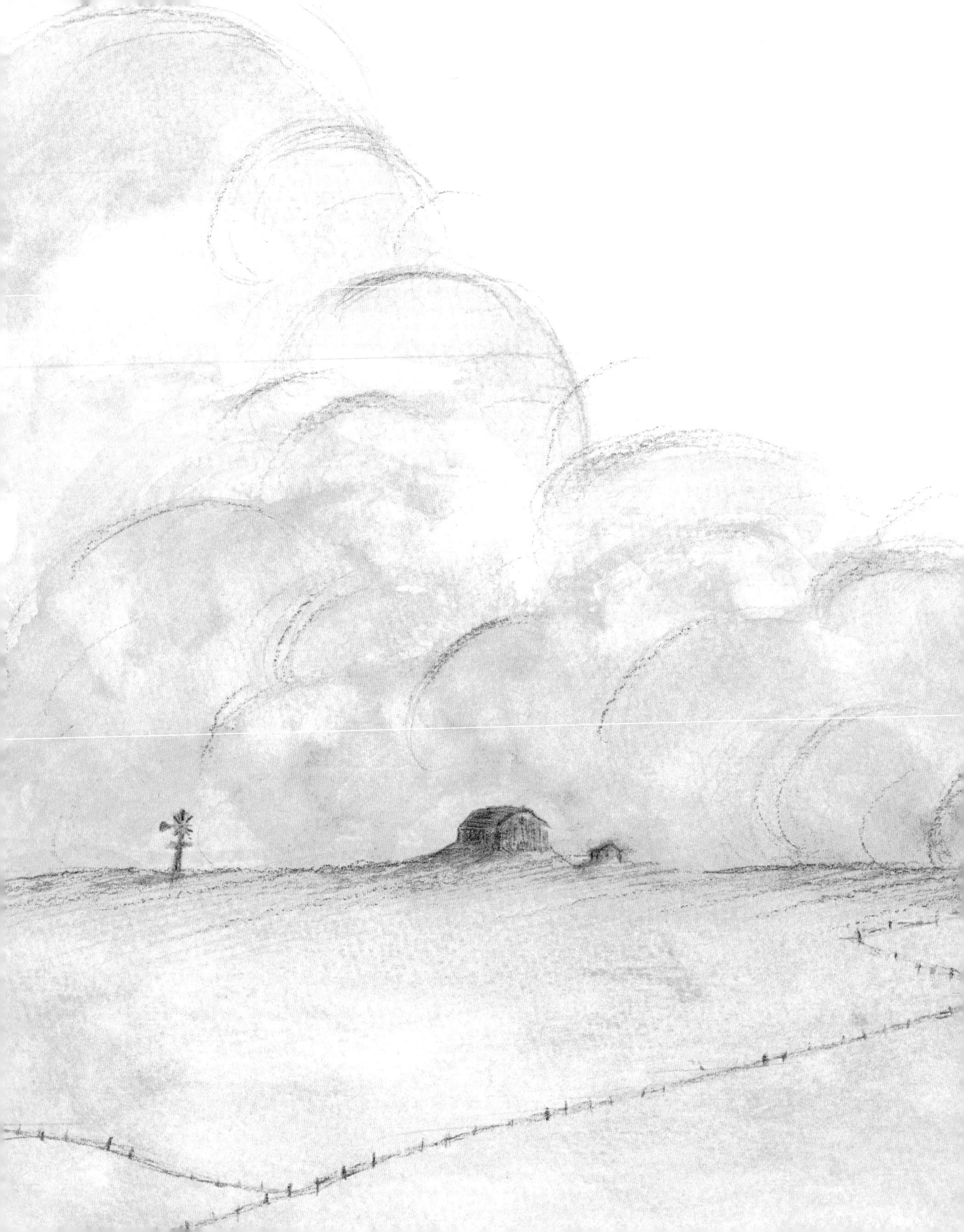

The Storm in the Barn

MATT PHELAN

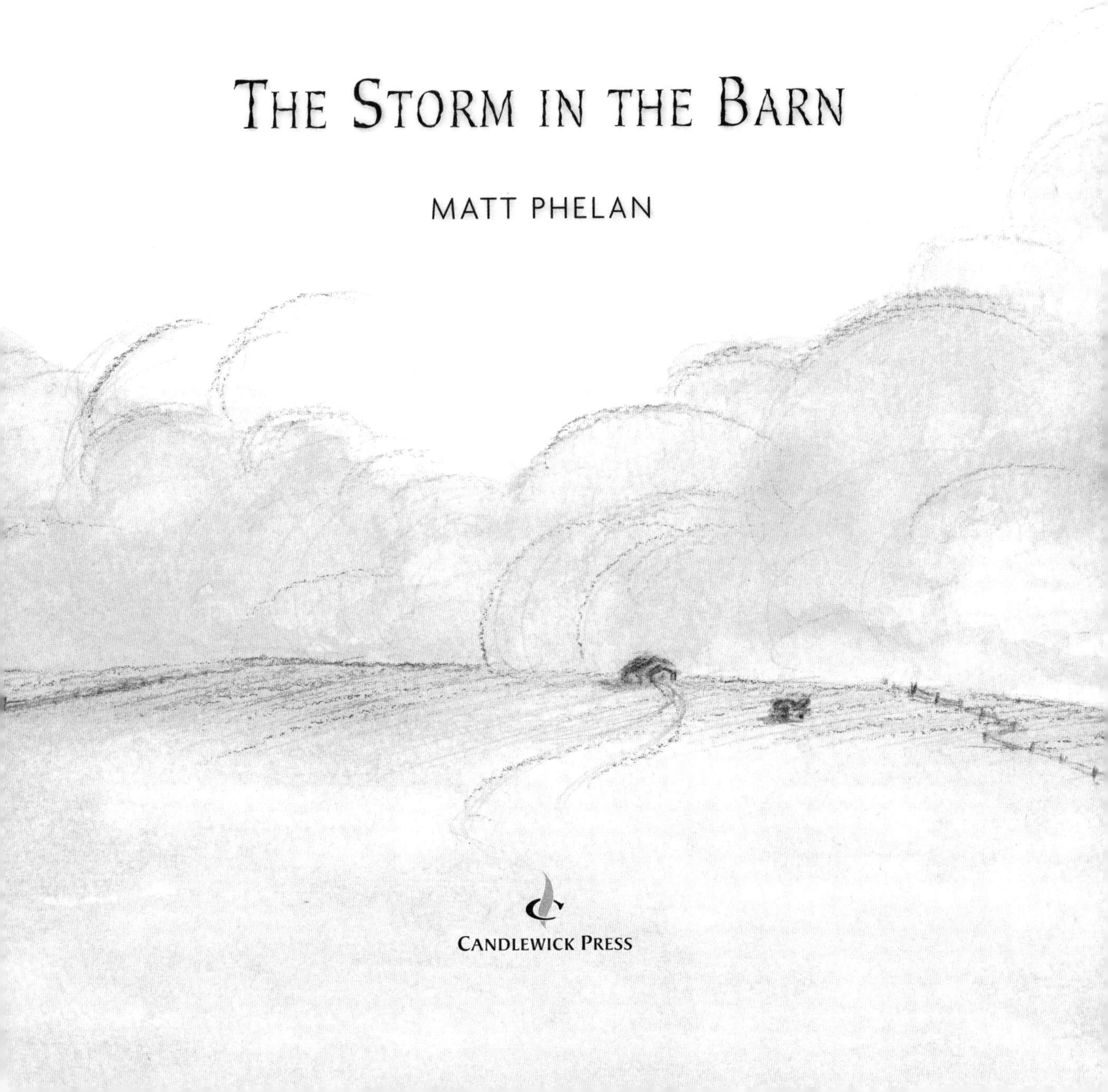

Candlewick Press

This is a work of fiction. Names, characters, places, and incidents are either products of the author's imagination or, if real, are used fictitiously.

First edition 2009

Library of Congress Cataloging-in-Publication Data is available.

Library of Congress Catalog Card Number 2008938396

ISBN 978-0-7636-3618-0

2 4 6 8 10 9 7 5 3 1

Printed in China

This book was typeset in Agenda Light Italic.
The illustrations were done in pencil, ink, and watercolor.

Candlewick Press
99 Dover Street
Somerville, Massachusetts 02144

visit us at www.candlewick.com

For my dad,
who shared his love of stories

Every theory of the course of events in nature is necessarily based on some process of simplification of the phenomena and is to some extent therefore a fairy tale.

— Sir Napier Shaw, *Manual of Meteorology*

KANSAS, 1937

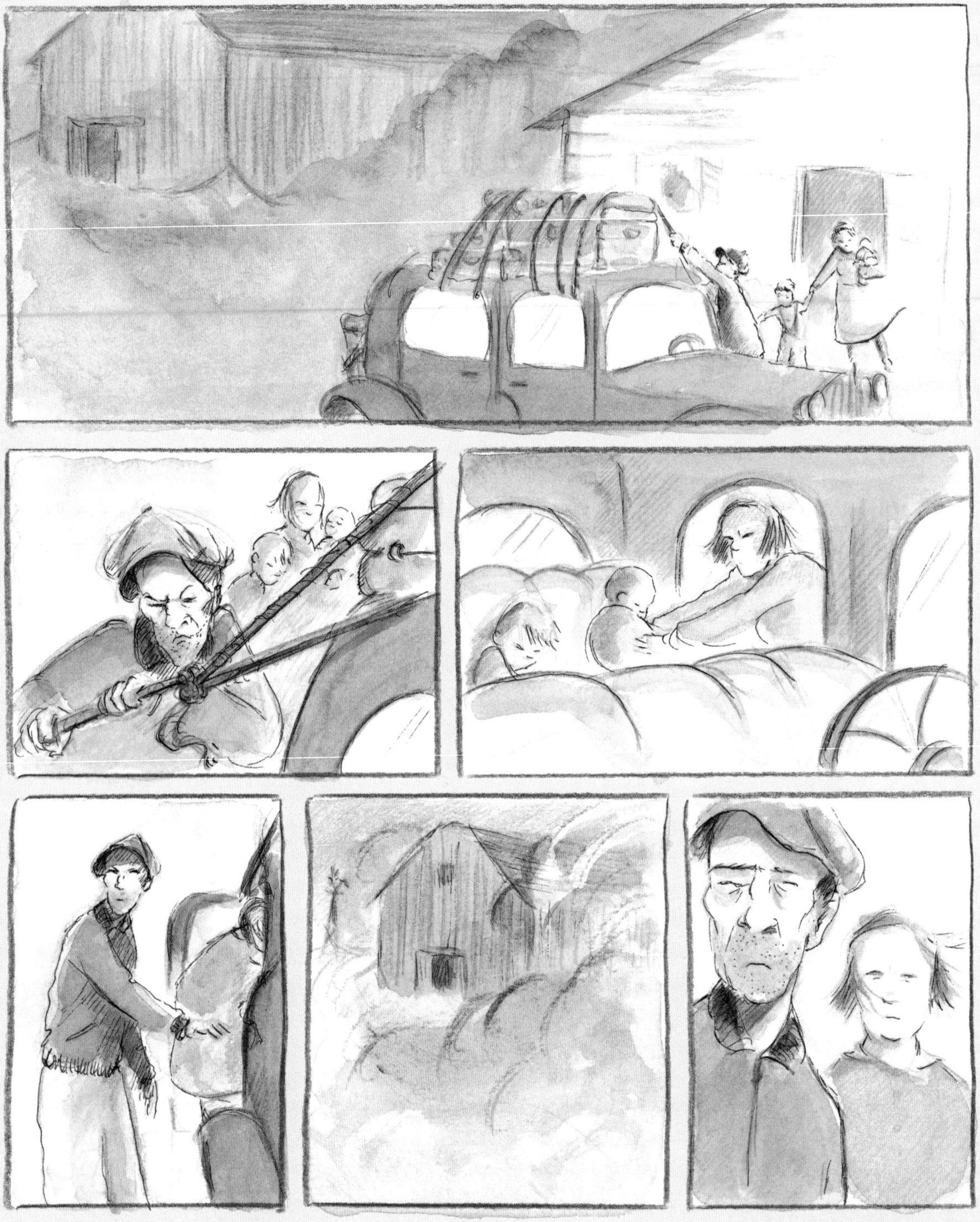

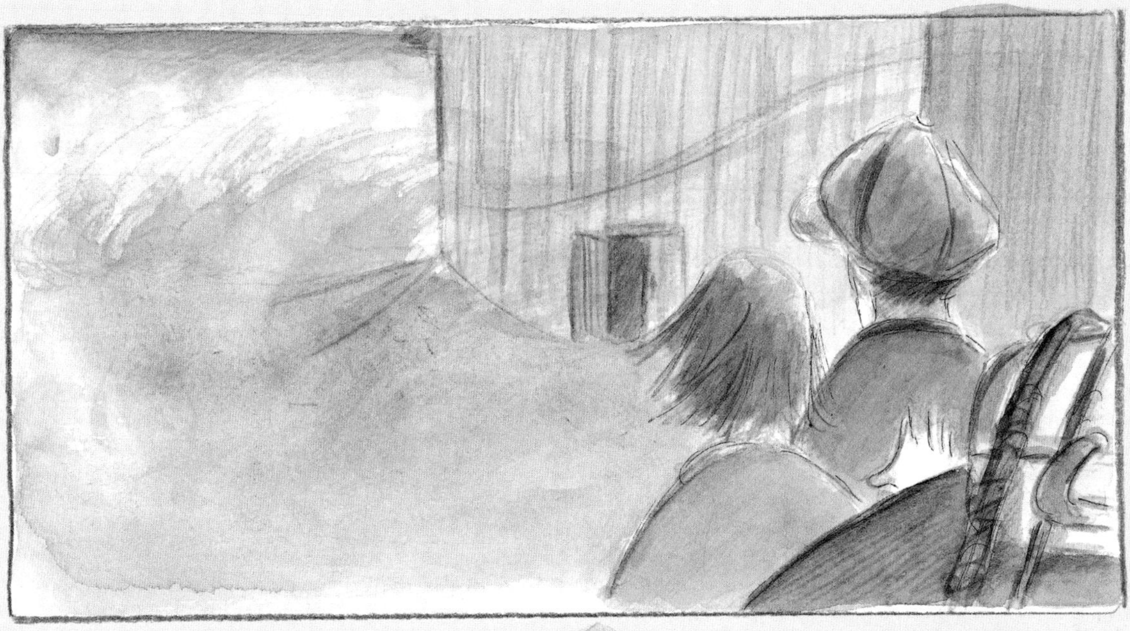

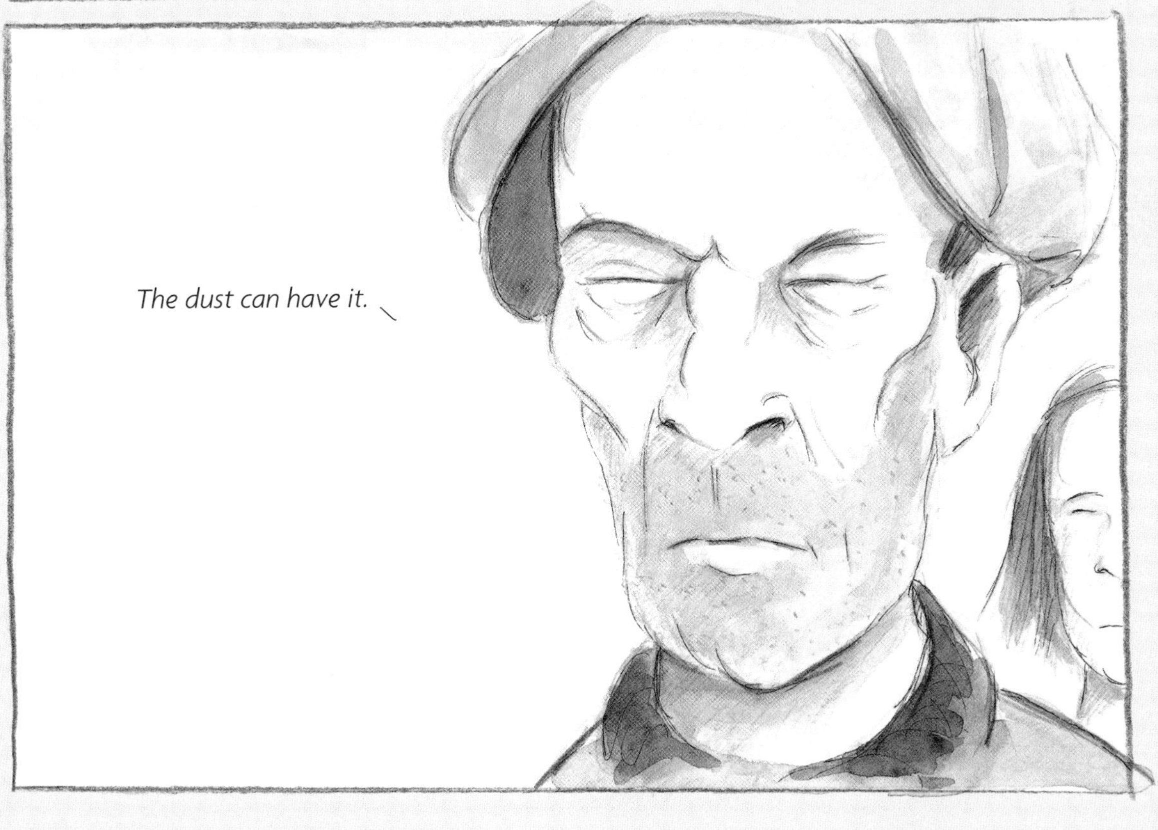
The dust can have it.

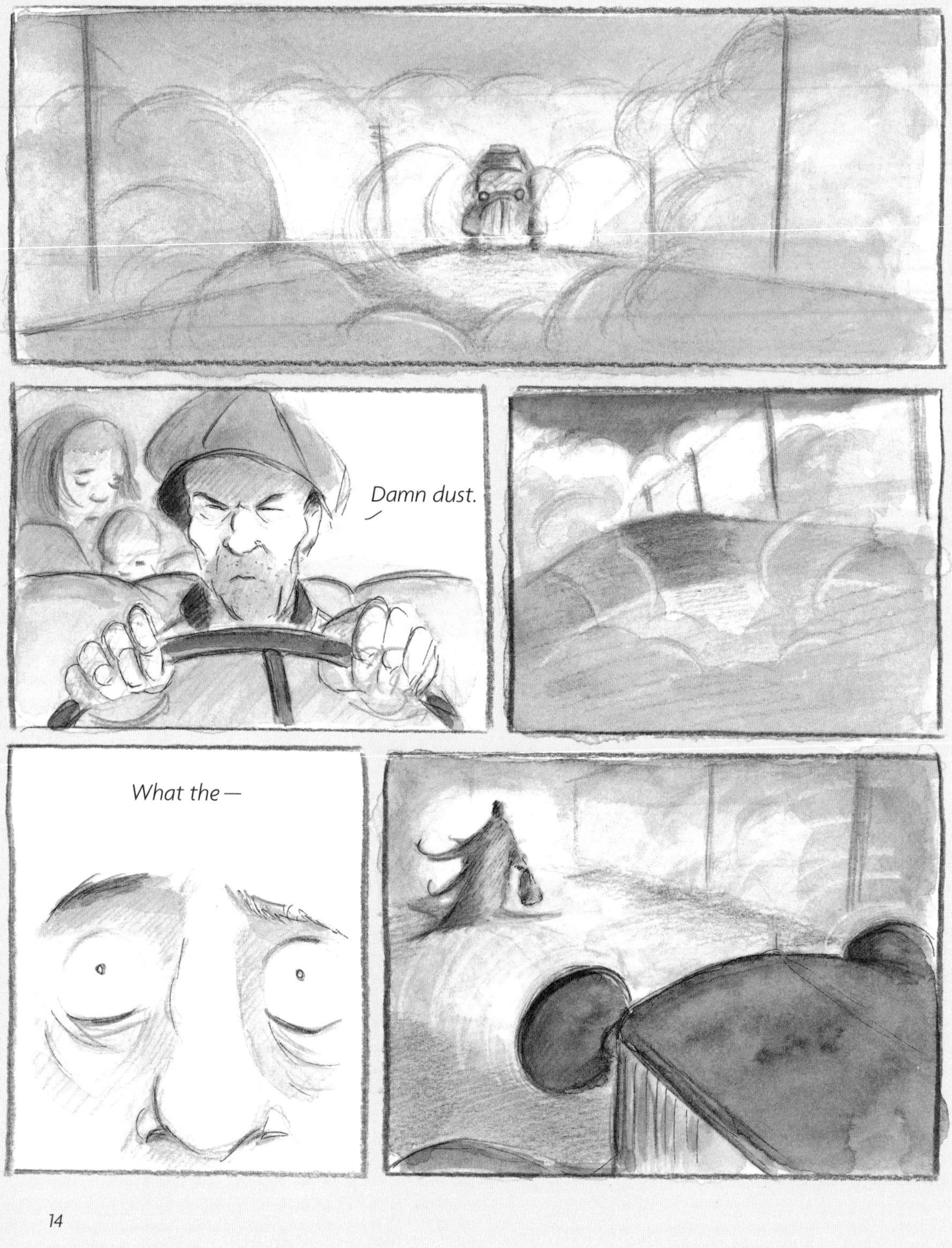
Damn dust.
What the—

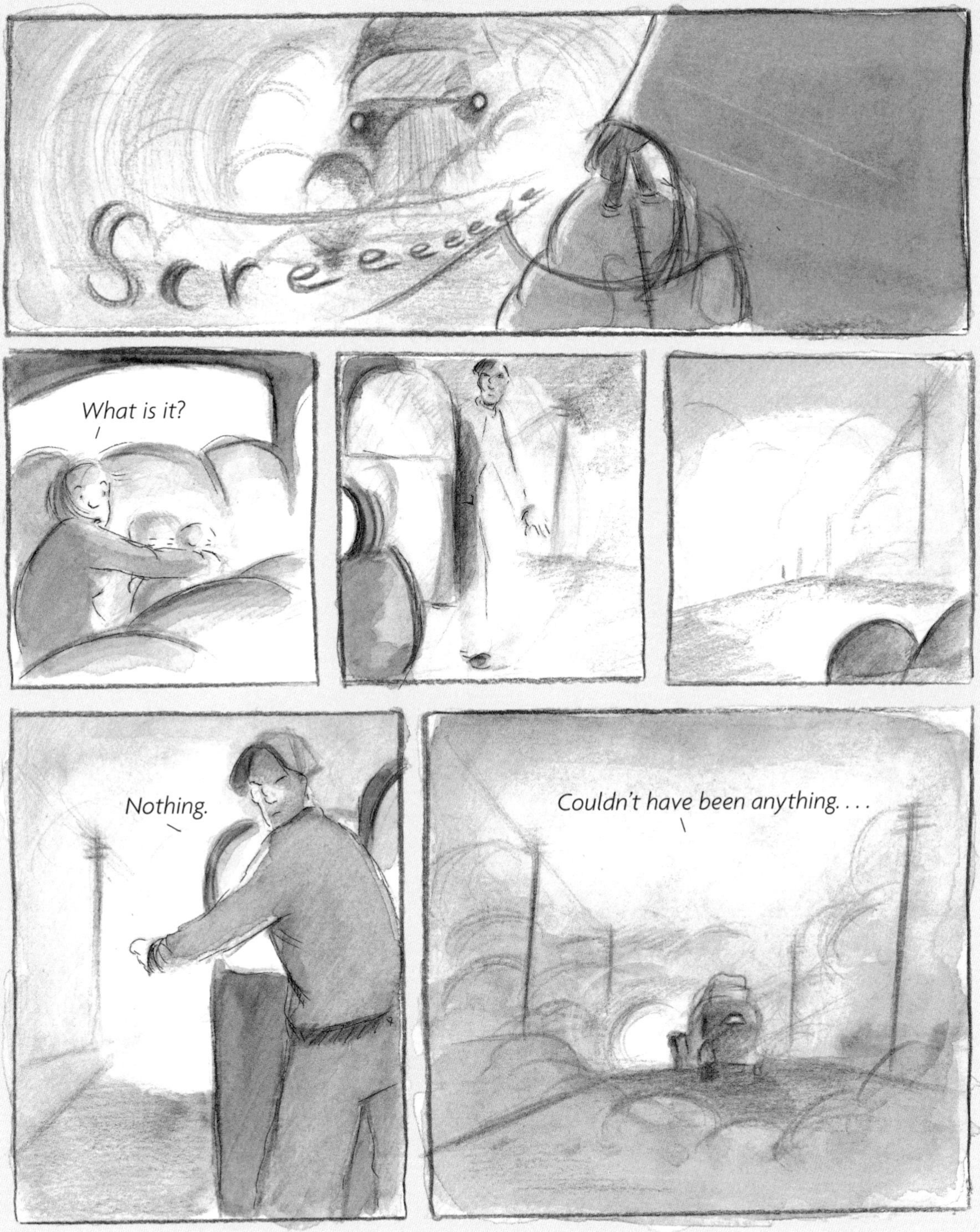
Screeeeeee
What is it?
Nothing.
Couldn't have been anything. . . .

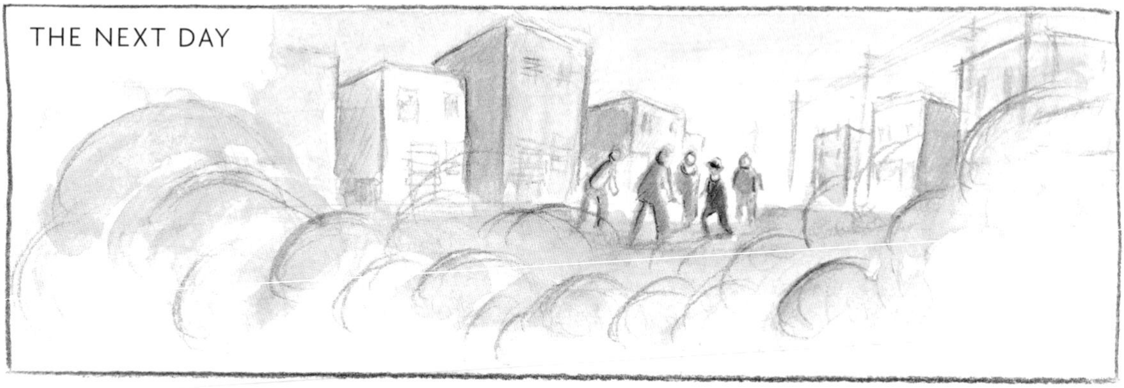
THE NEXT DAY

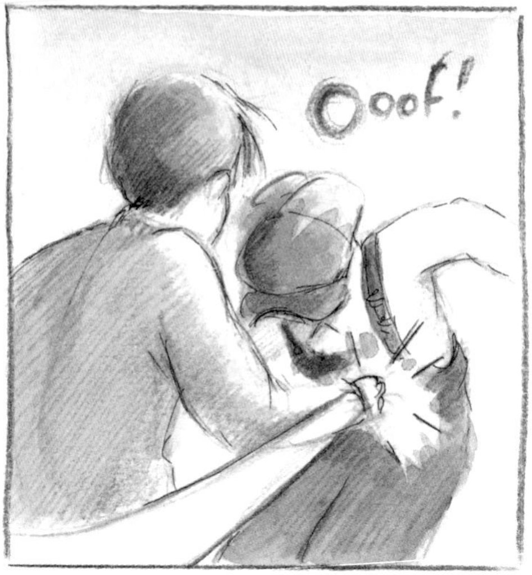
Ooof!

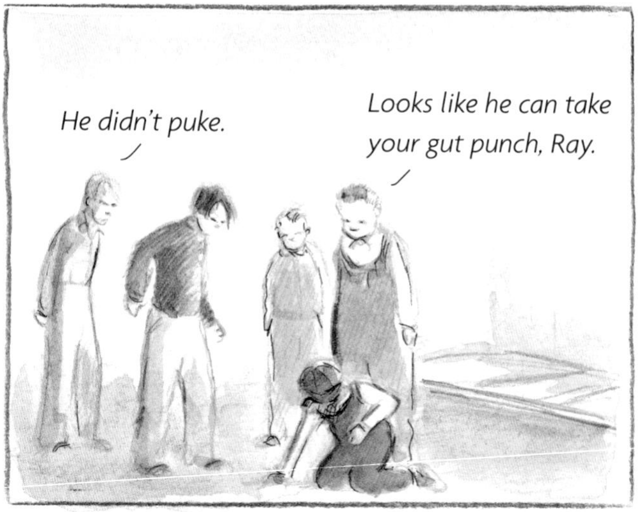
He didn't puke.
Looks like he can take your gut punch, Ray.

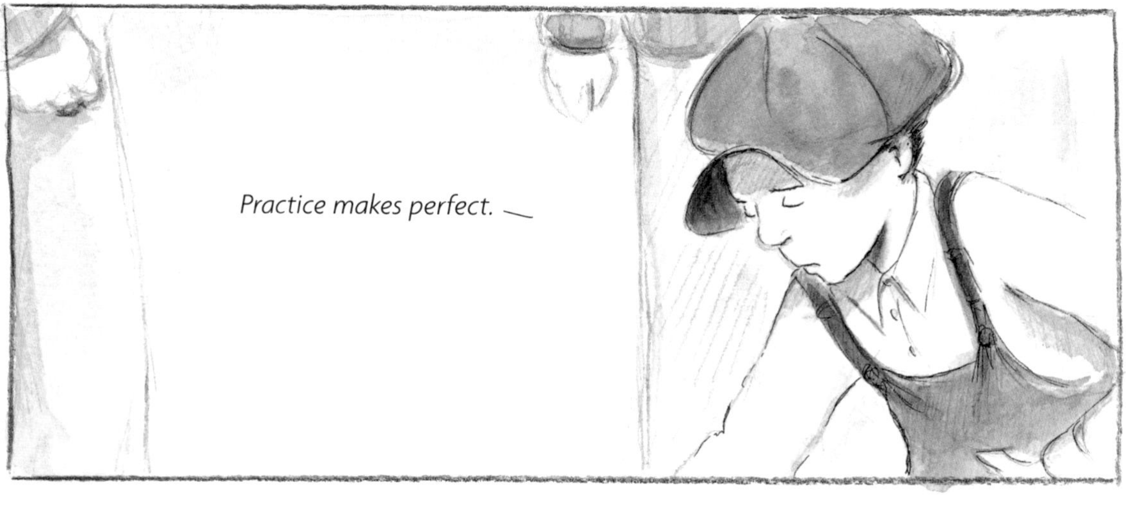
Practice makes perfect.

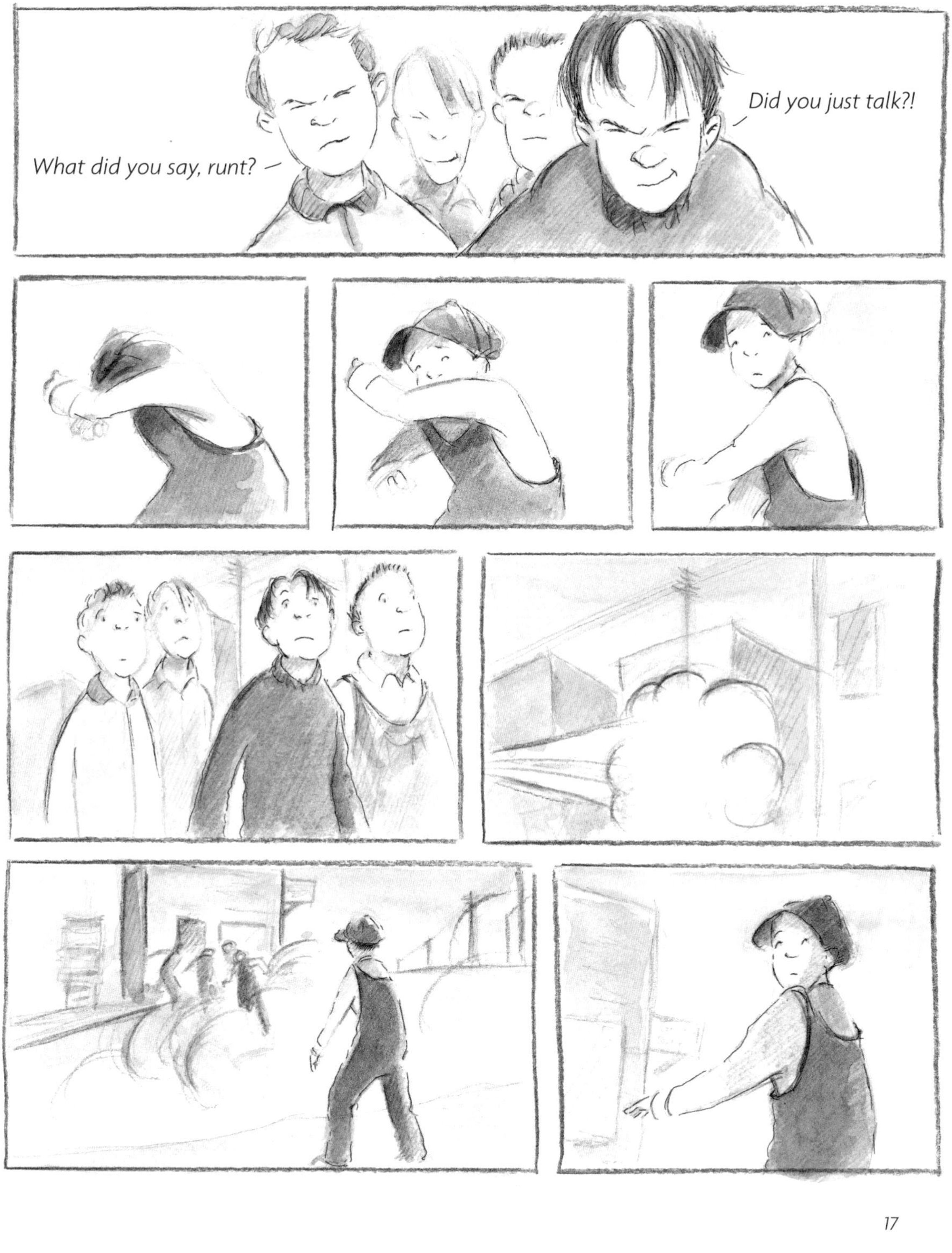
What did you say, runt?
Did you just talk?!

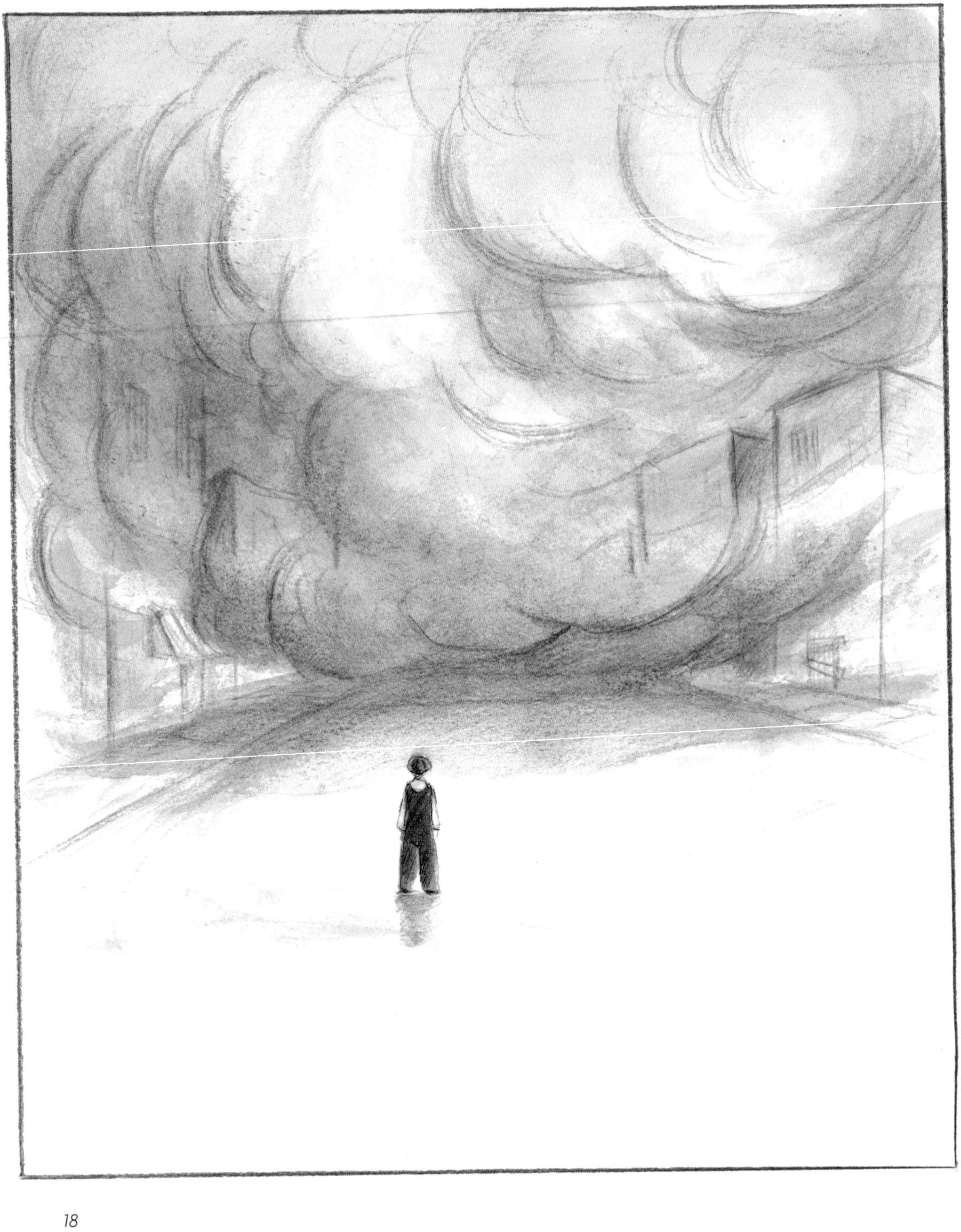

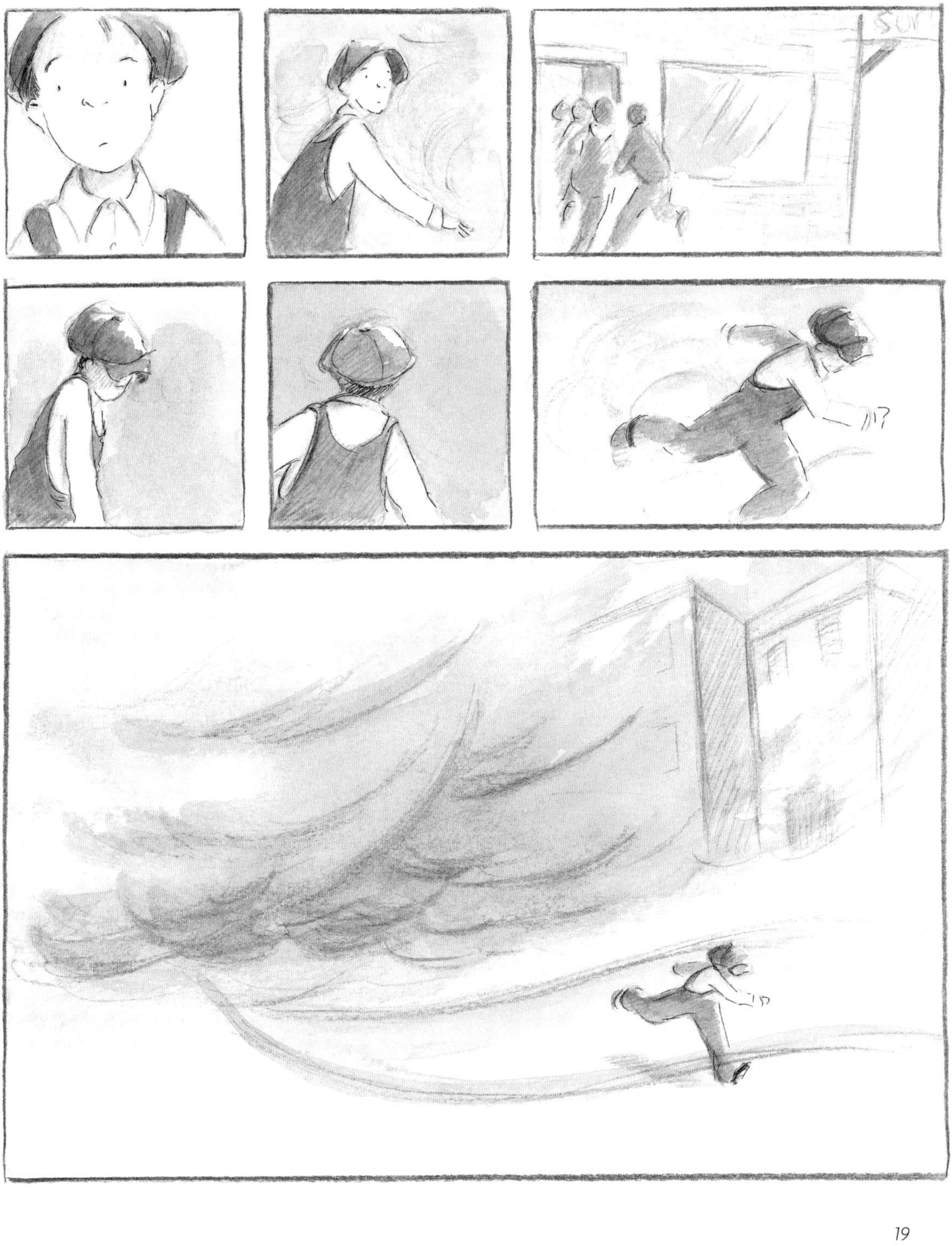

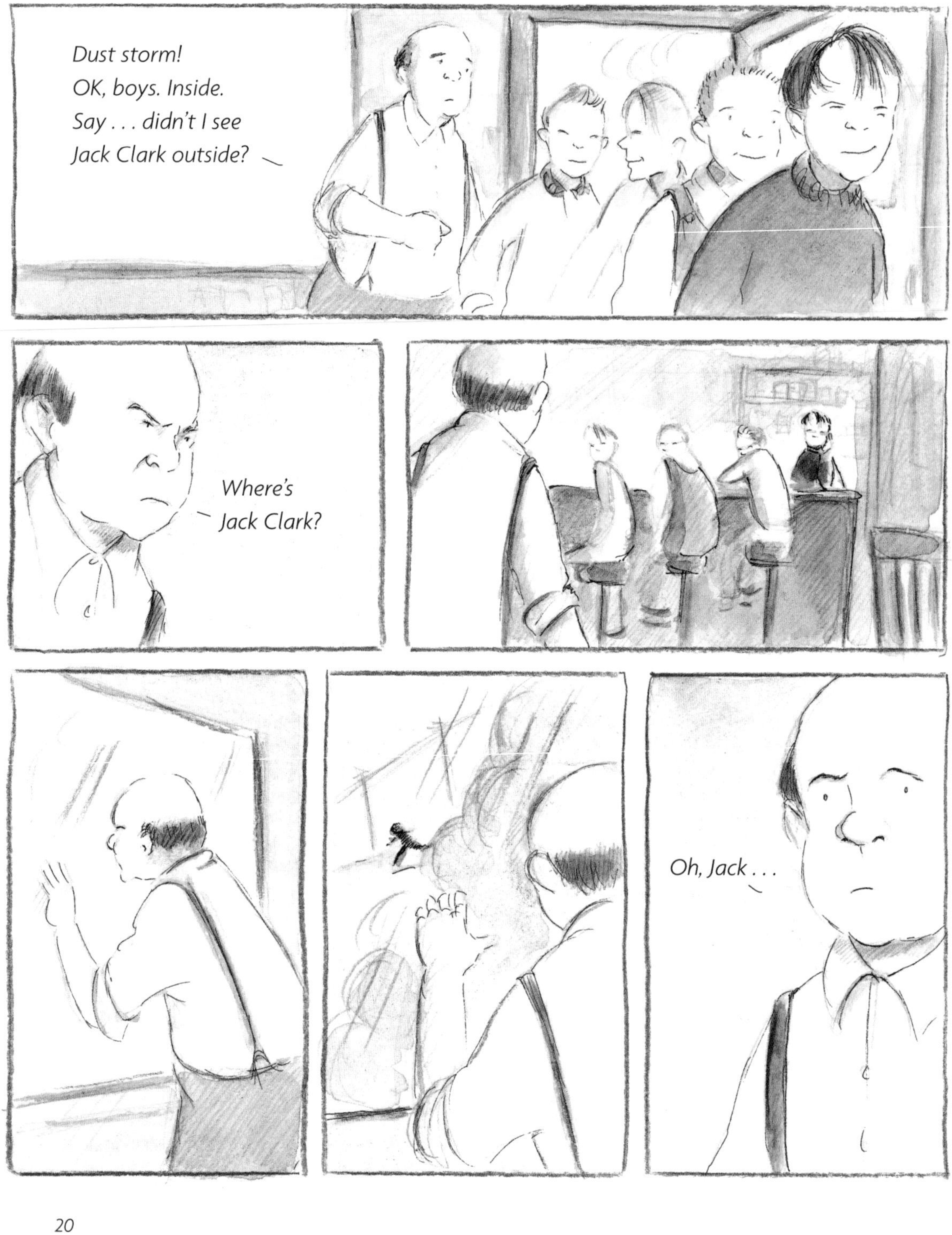
Dust storm!
OK, boys. Inside.
Say . . . didn't I see
Jack Clark outside?
Where's
Jack Clark?
Oh, Jack . . .

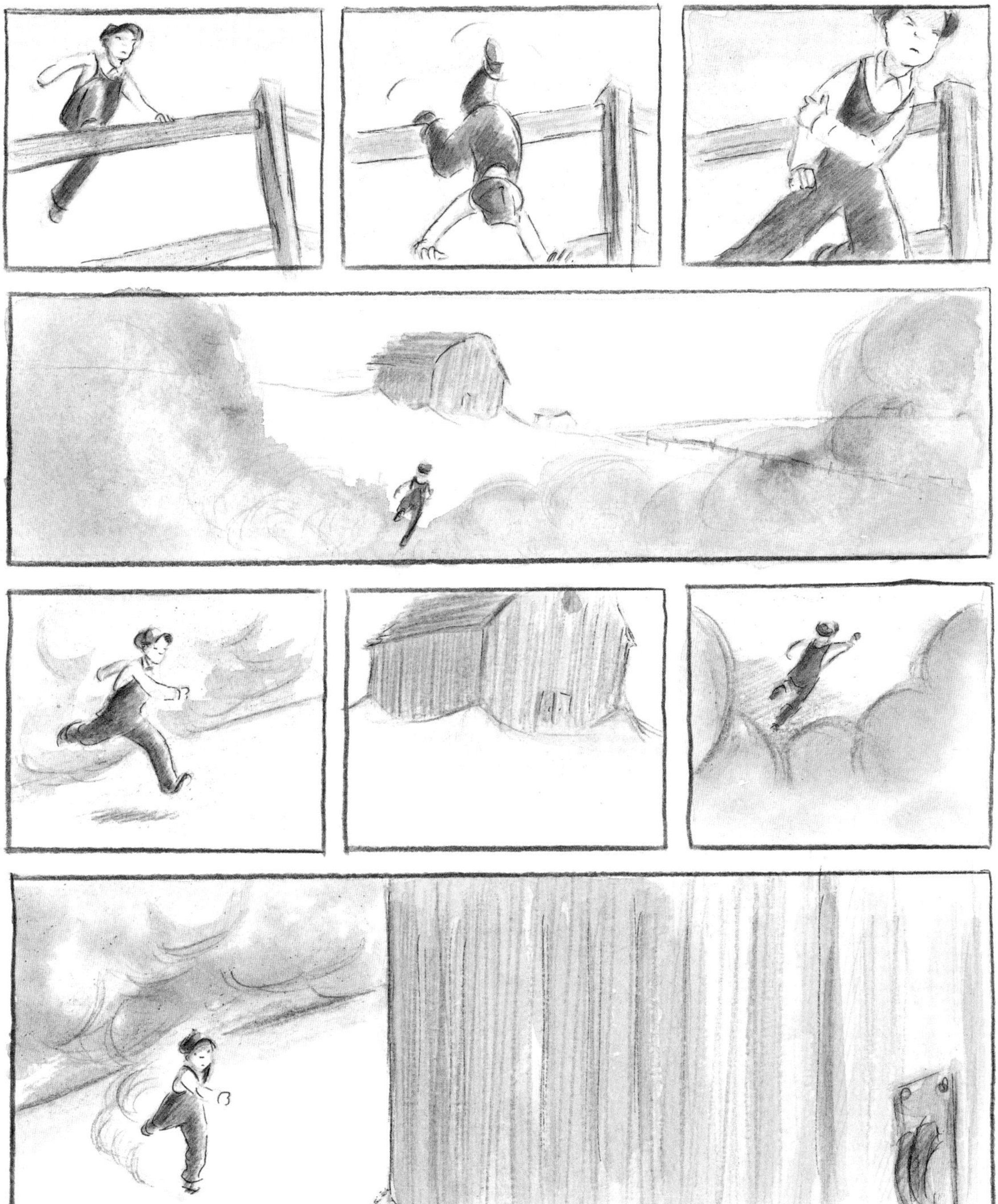

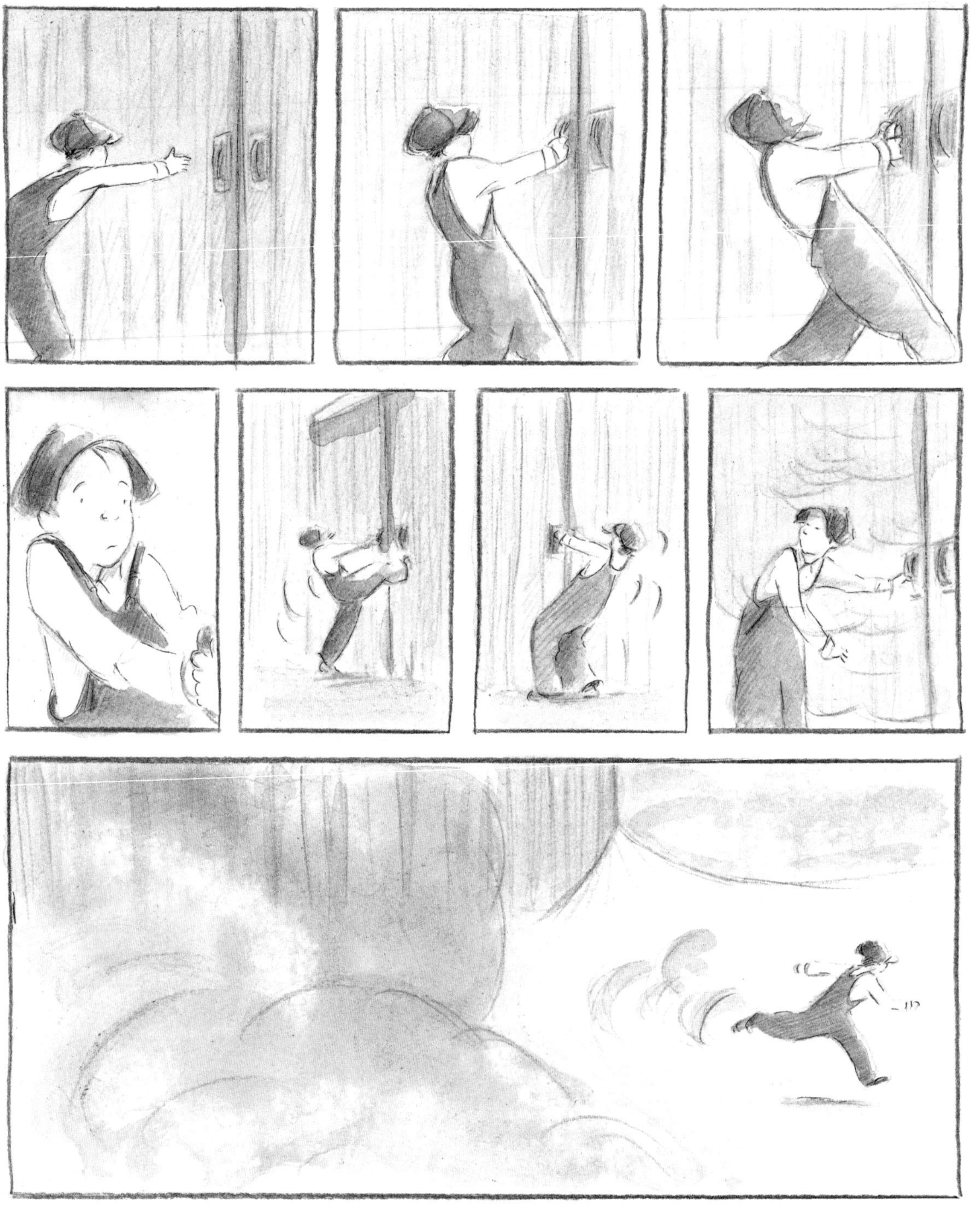

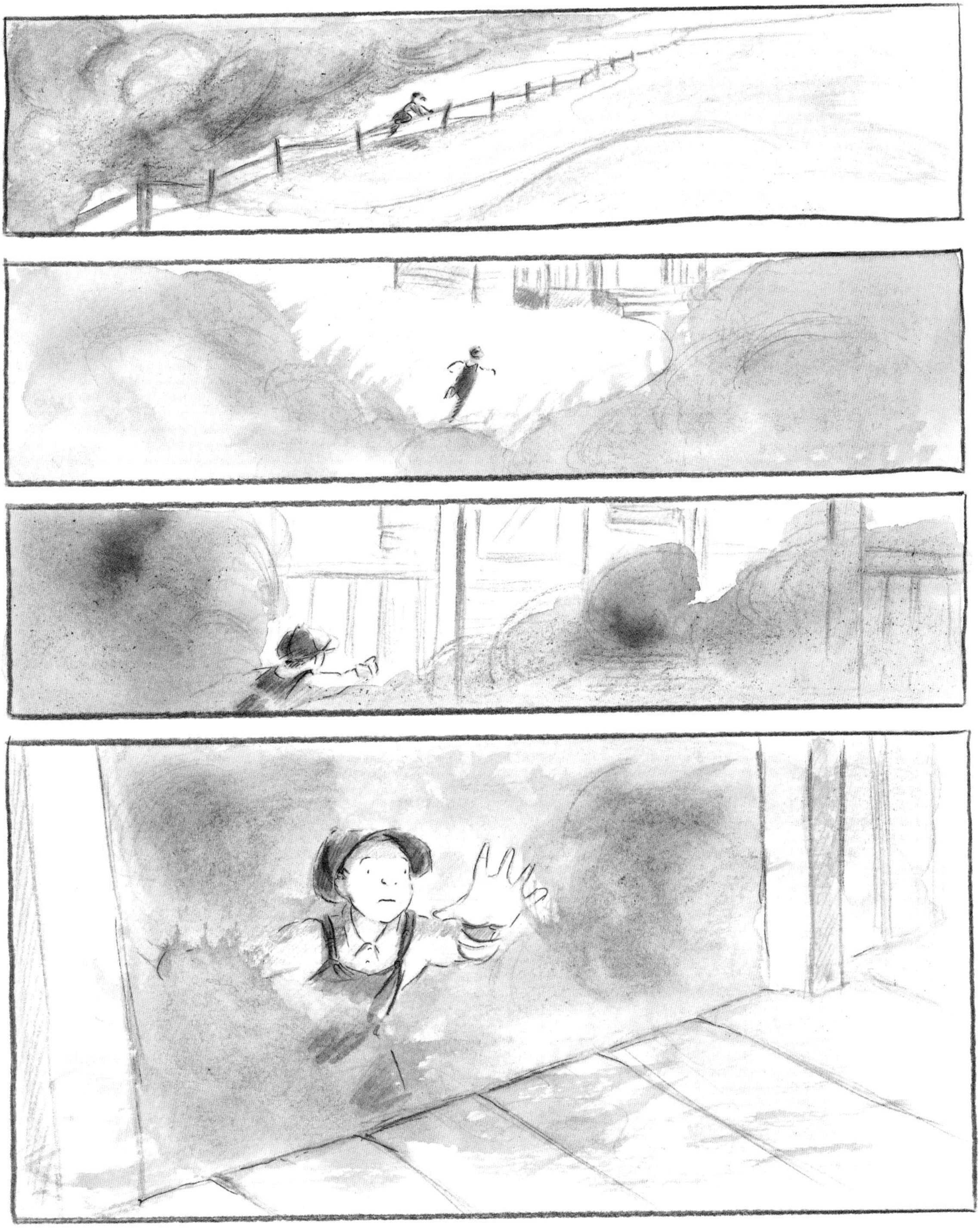

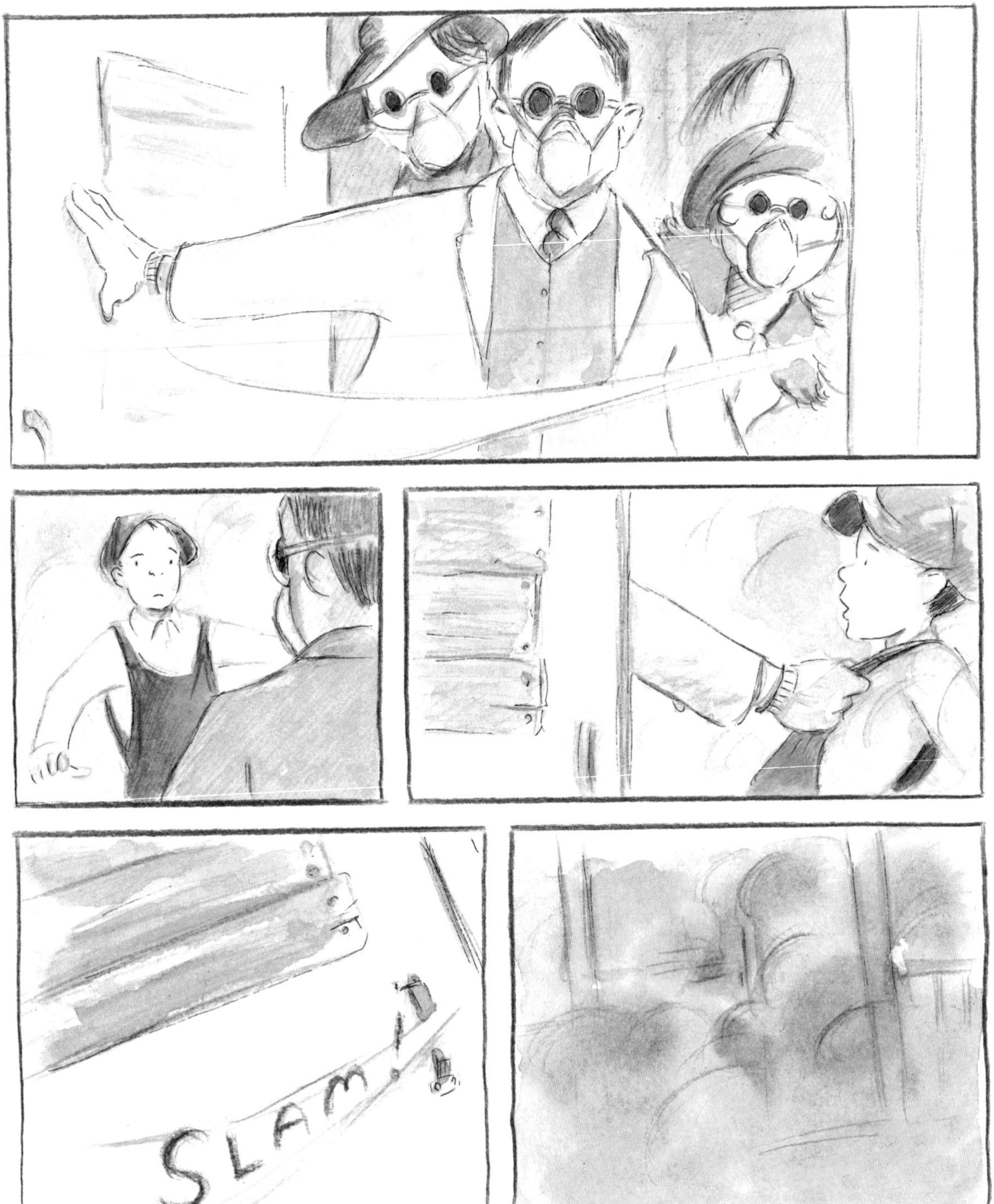
SLAM!

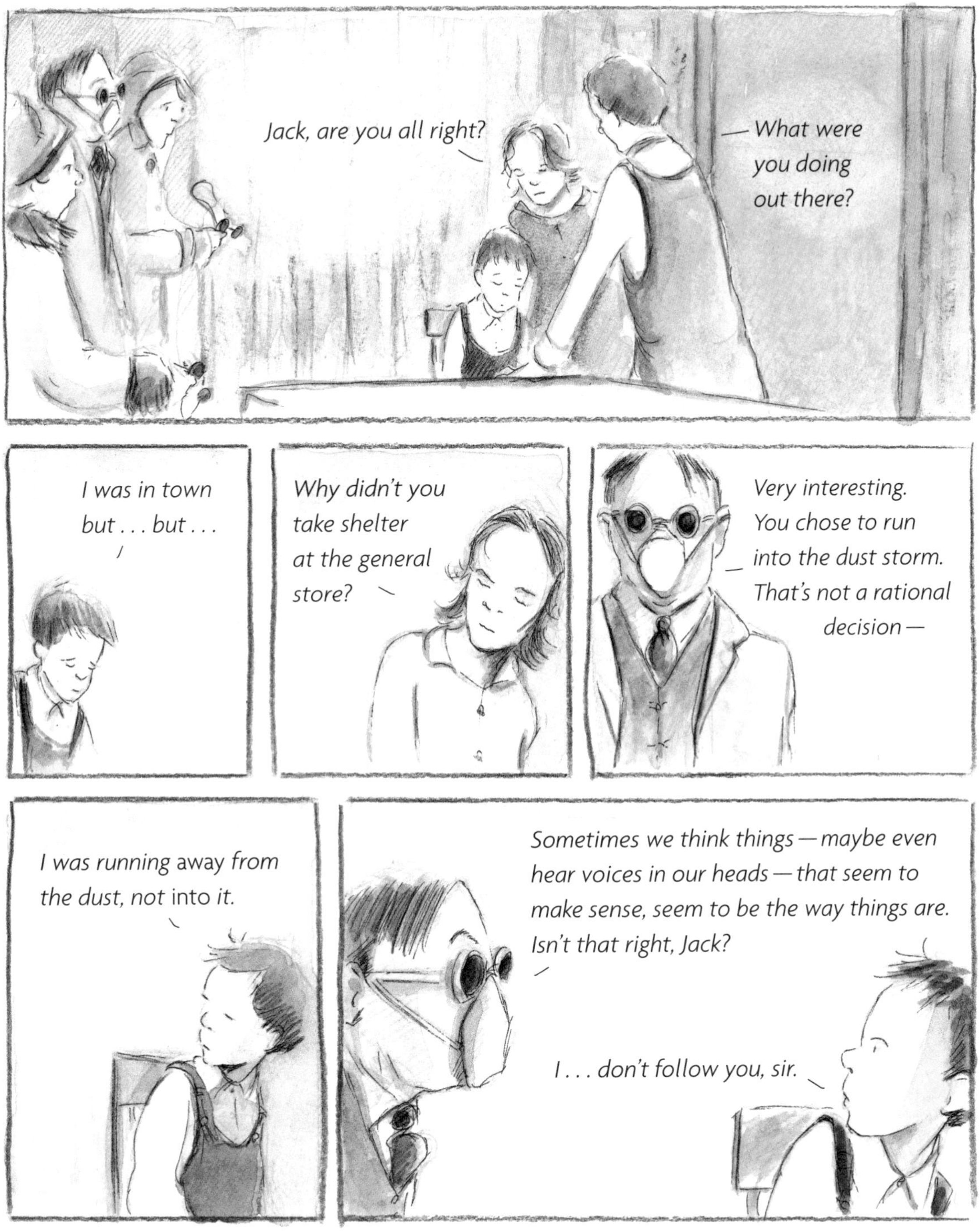
Jack, are you all right?
What were you doing out there?
I was in town but . . . but . . .
Why didn't you take shelter at the general store?
Very interesting. You chose to run into the dust storm. That's not a rational decision—
I was running away from the dust, not into it.
Sometimes we think things—maybe even hear voices in our heads—that seem to make sense, seem to be the way things are. Isn't that right, Jack?
I . . . don't follow you, sir.

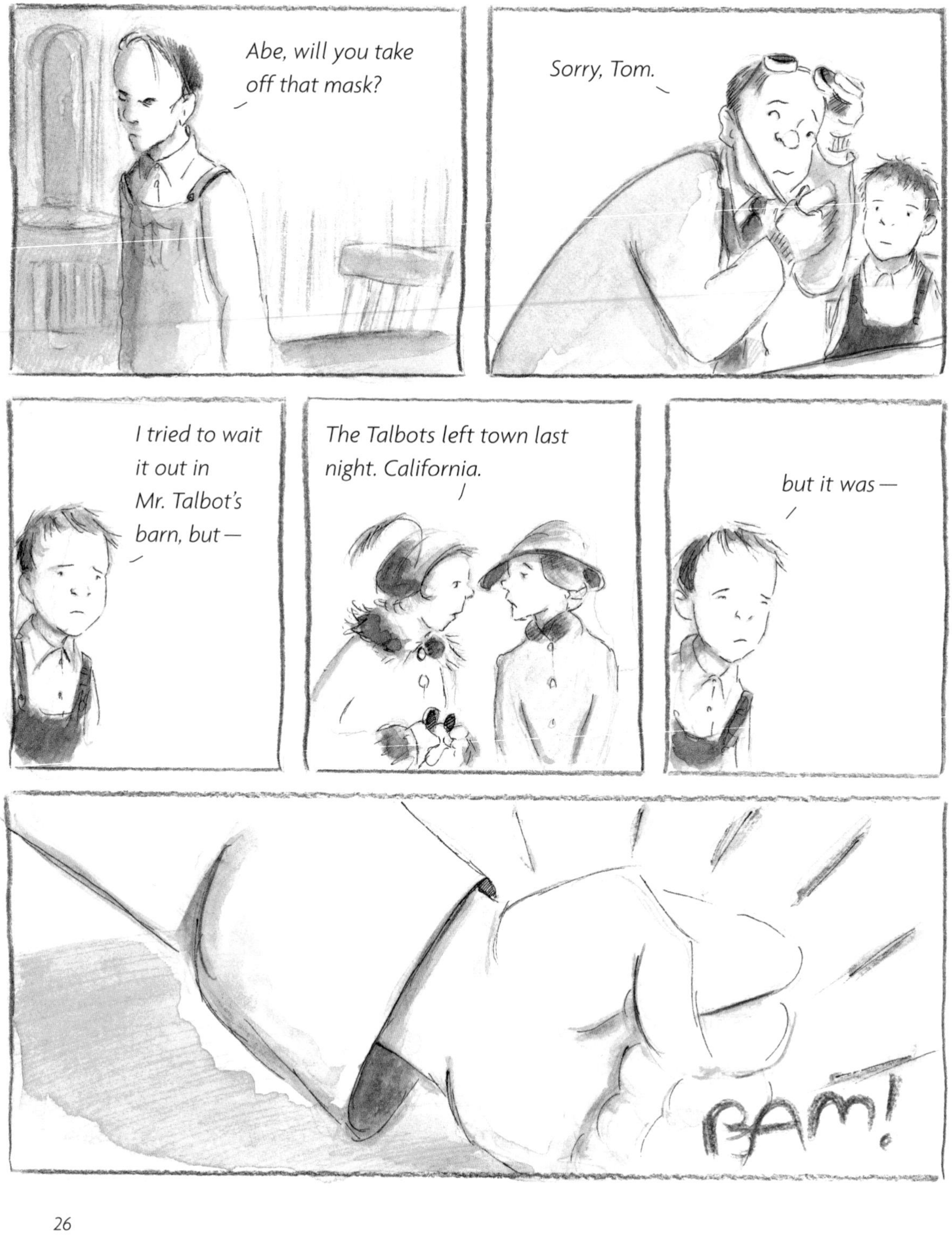
Abe, will you take off that mask?
Sorry, Tom.
I tried to wait it out in Mr. Talbot's barn, but—
The Talbots left town last night. California.
but it was—
BAM!

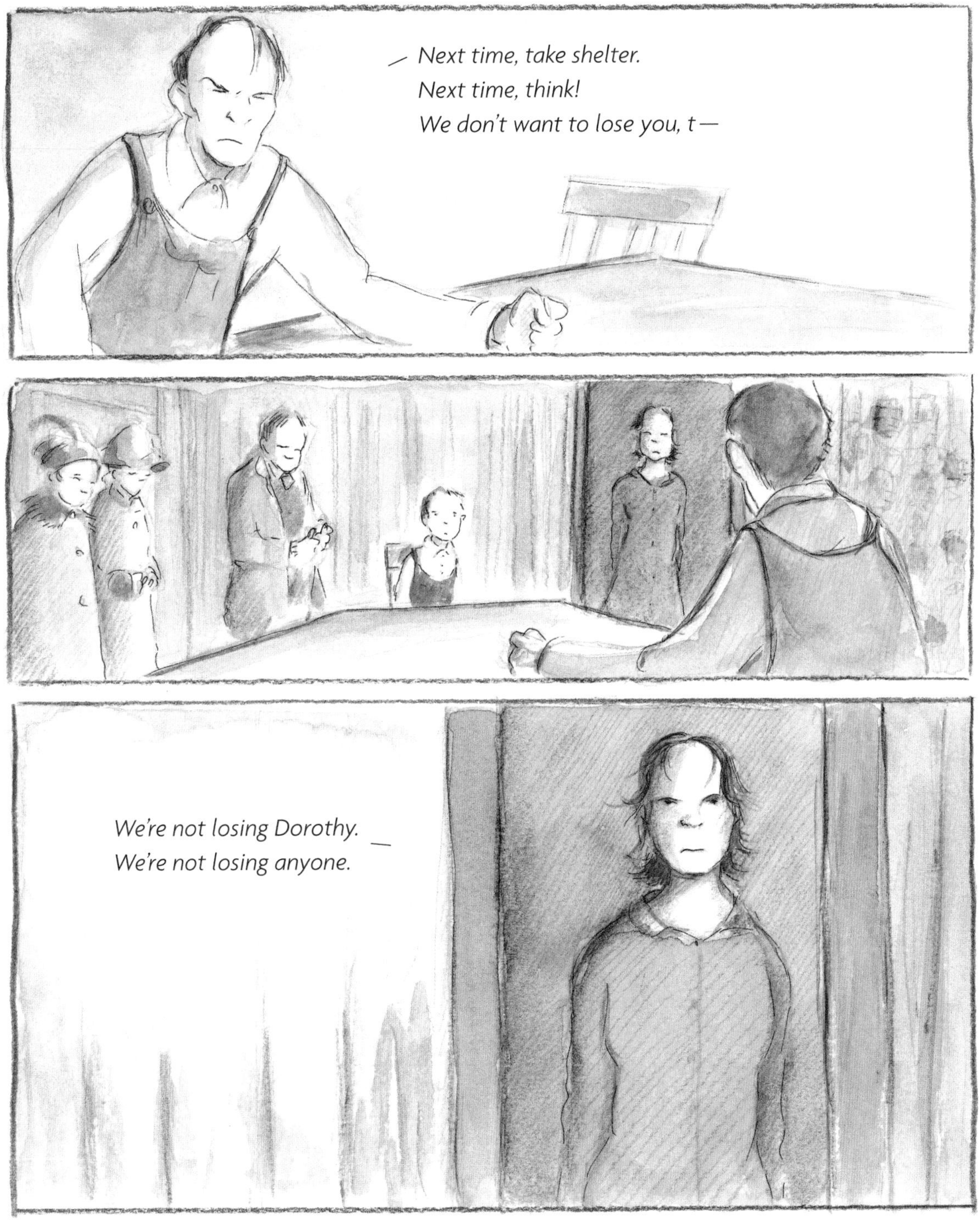
Next time, take shelter.
Next time, think!
We don't want to lose you, t—
We're not losing Dorothy.
We're not losing anyone.

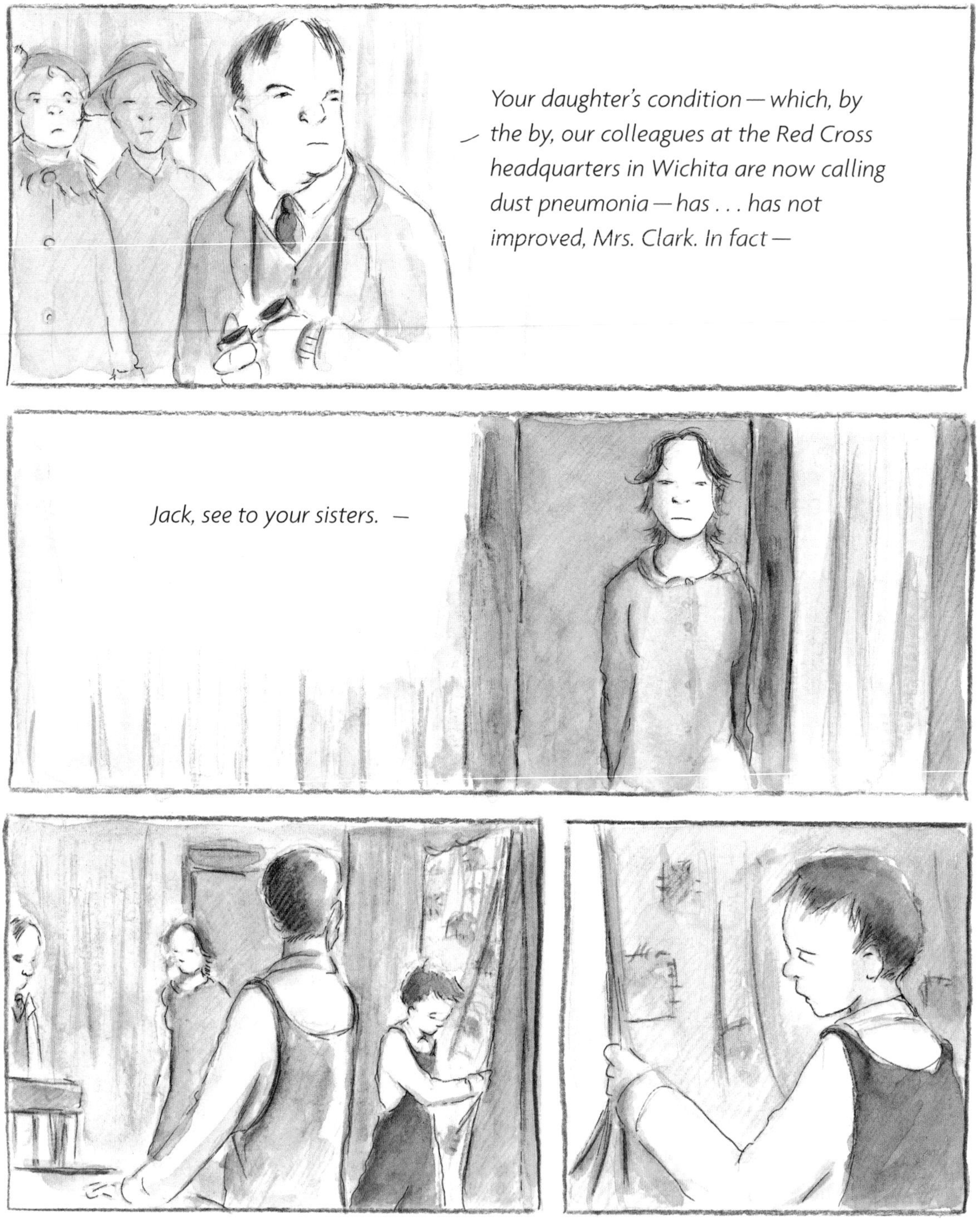
Your daughter's condition — which, by the by, our colleagues at the Red Cross headquarters in Wichita are now calling dust pneumonia — has . . . has not improved, Mrs. Clark. In fact —
Jack, see to your sisters. —

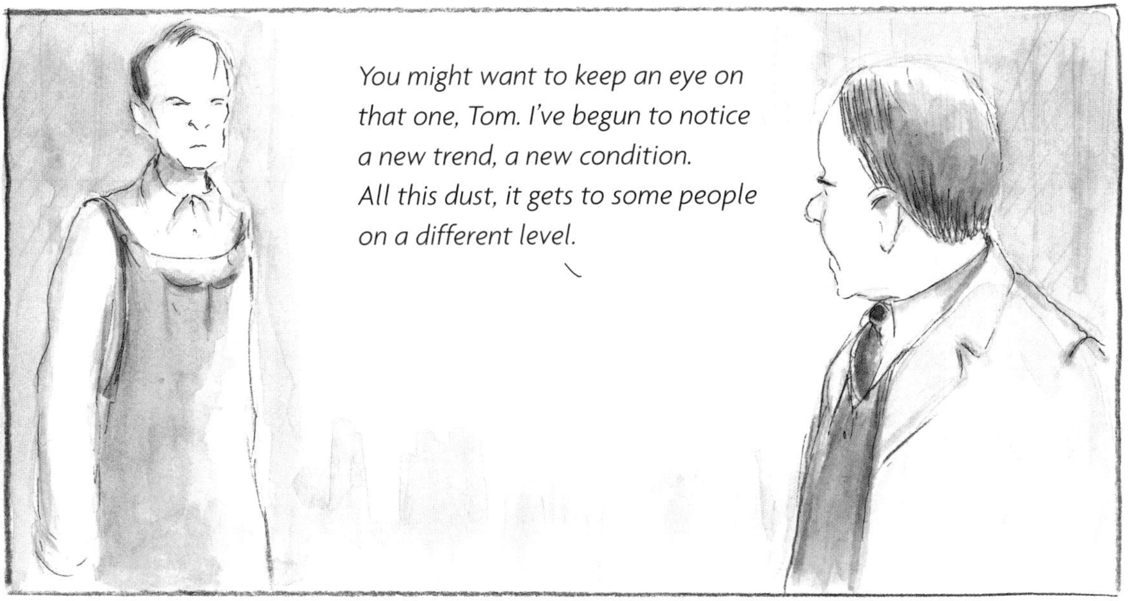
You might want to keep an eye on that one, Tom. I've begun to notice a new trend, a new condition. All this dust, it gets to some people on a different level.

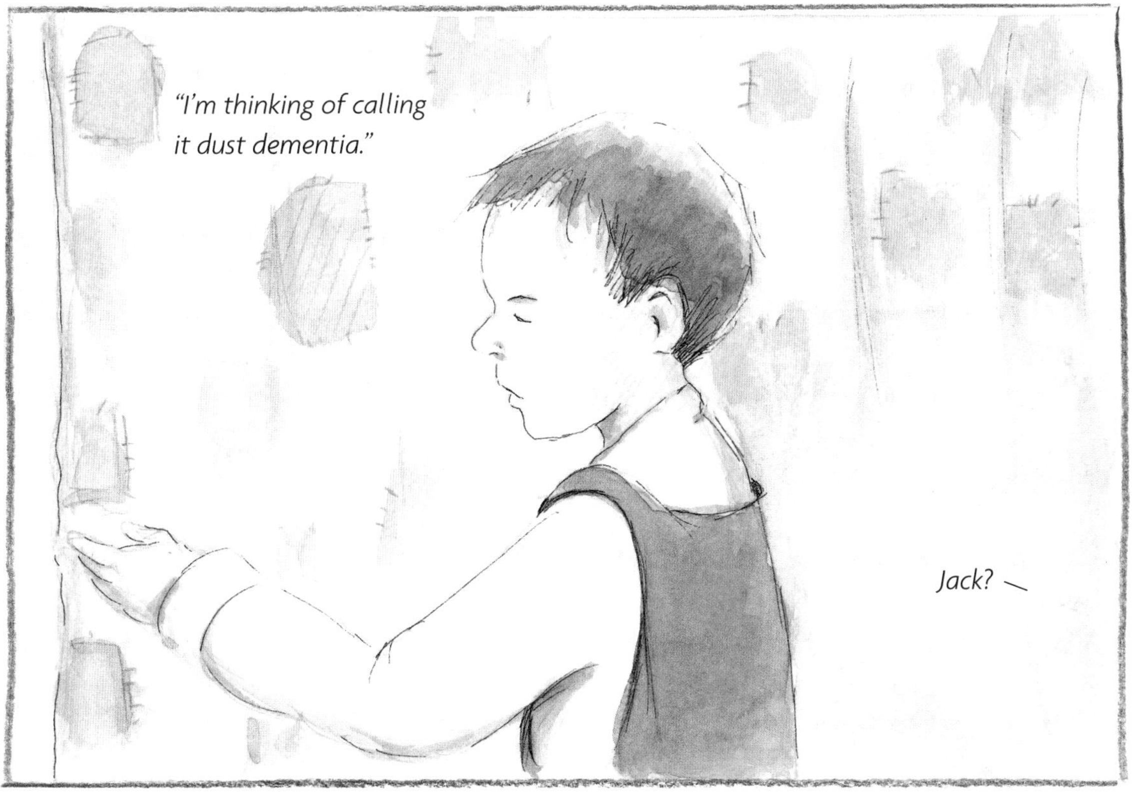
"I'm thinking of calling it dust dementia."
Jack?

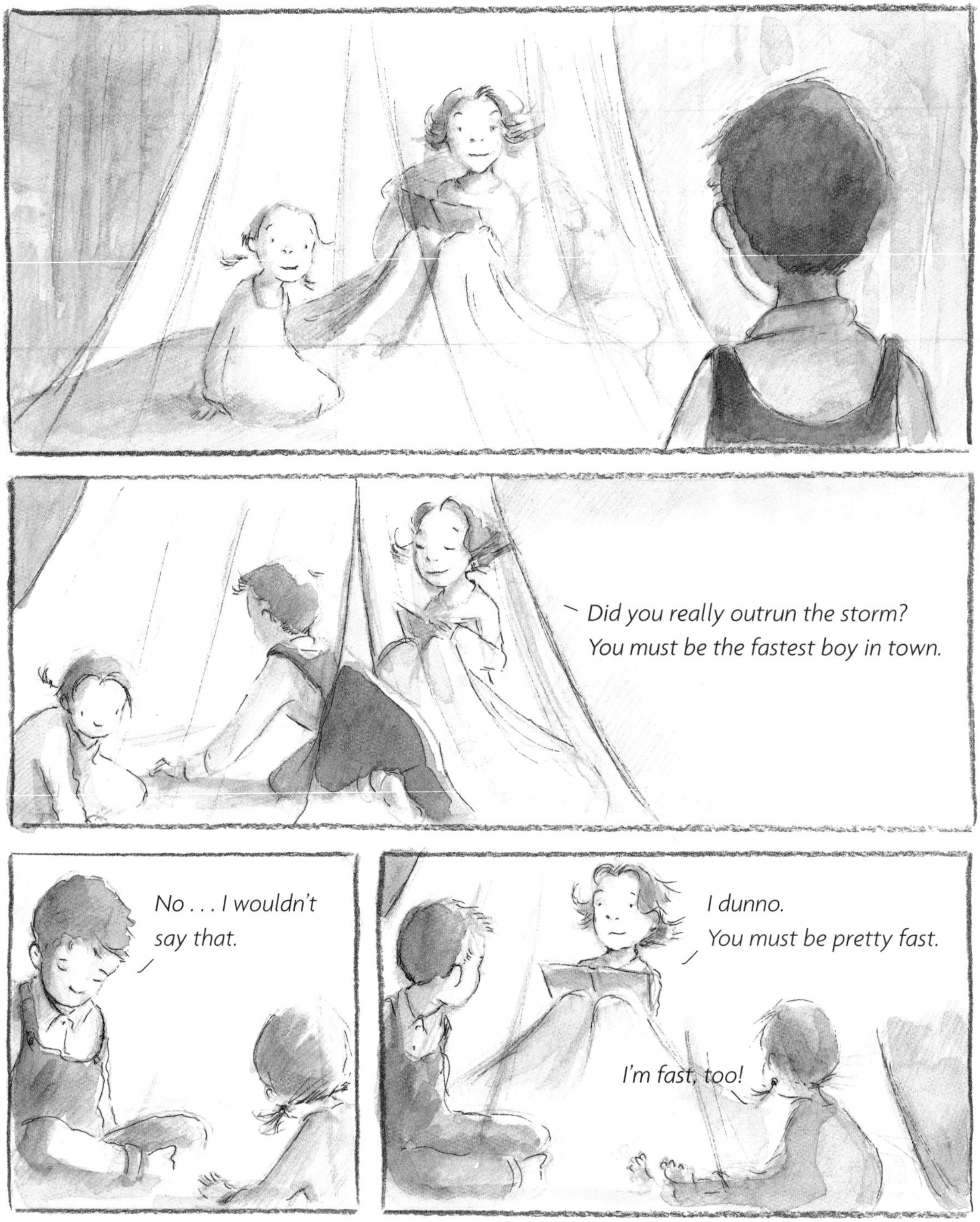
Did you really outrun the storm?
You must be the fastest boy in town.
No . . . I wouldn't say that.
I dunno.
You must be pretty fast.
I'm fast, too!

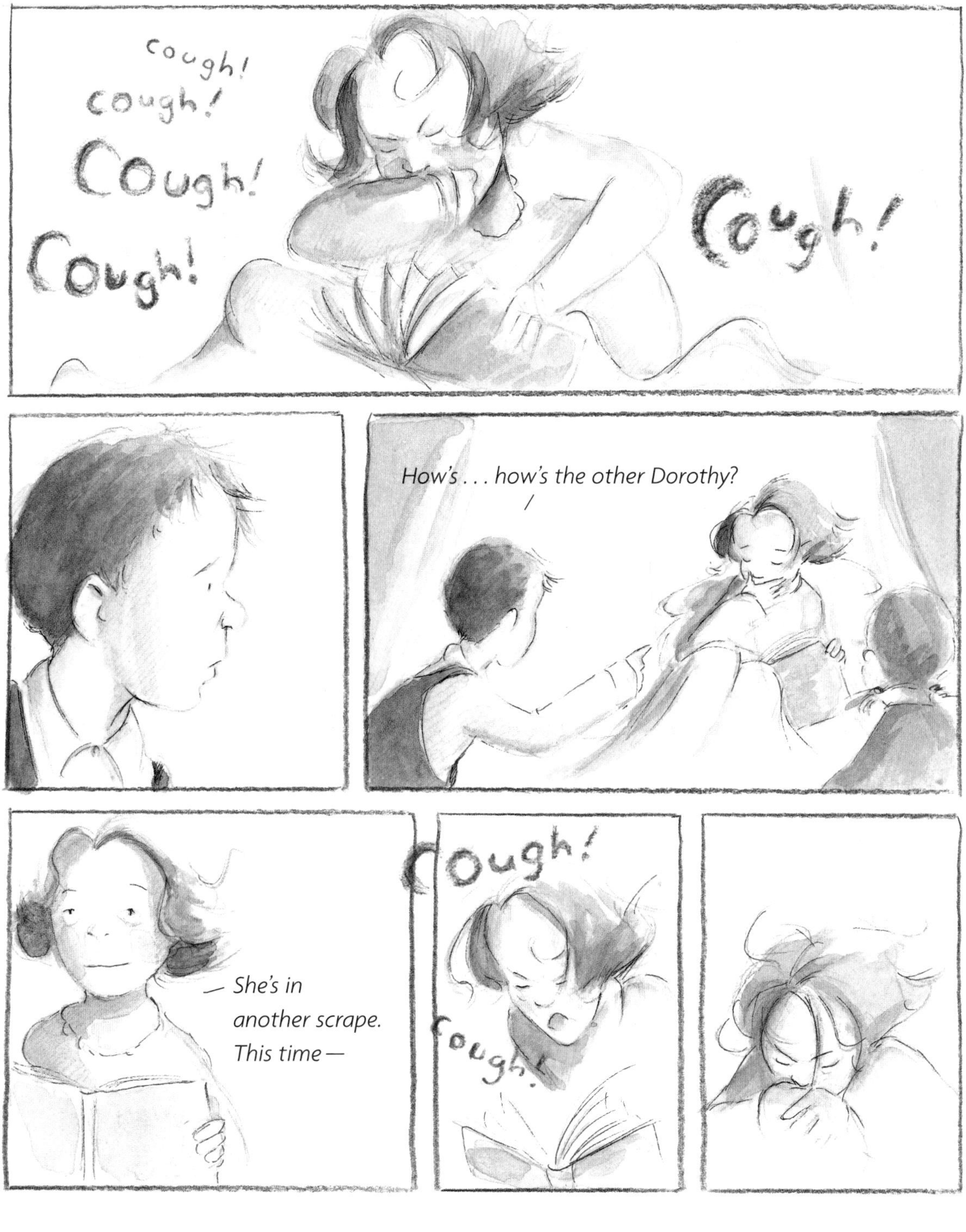
cough!
cough!
Cough!
Cough!
Cough!
How's . . . how's the other Dorothy?
She's in another scrape. This time—
Cough!
cough!

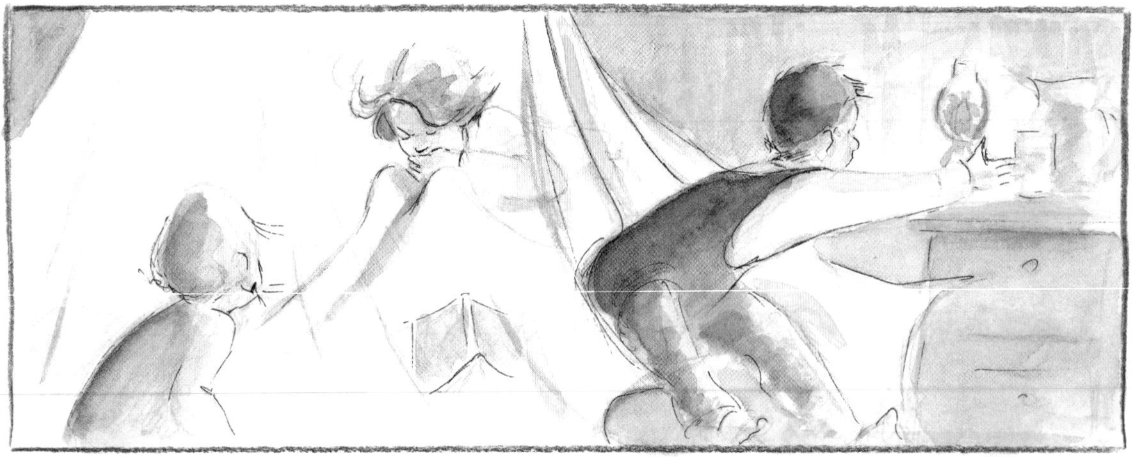

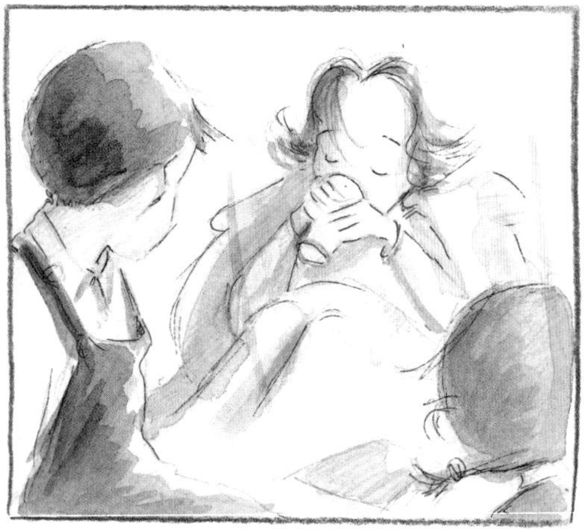

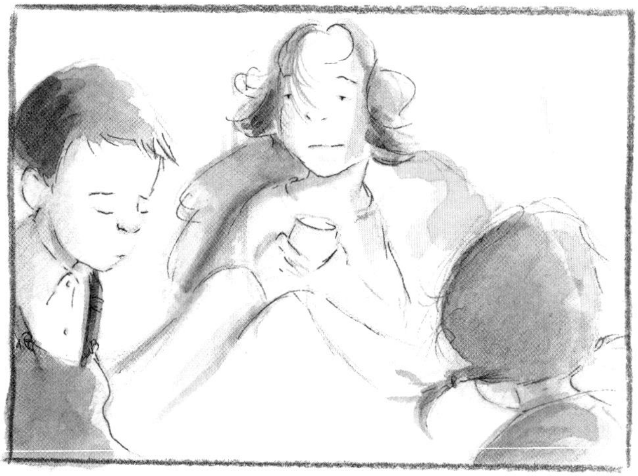

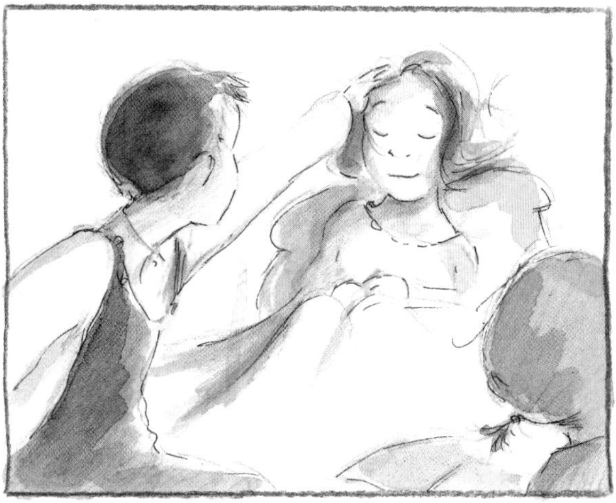

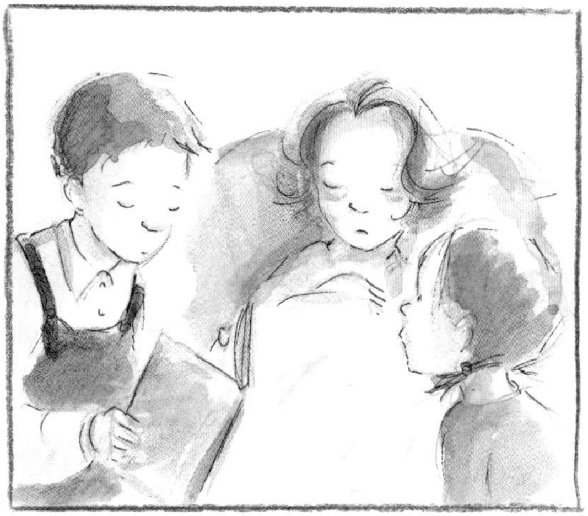

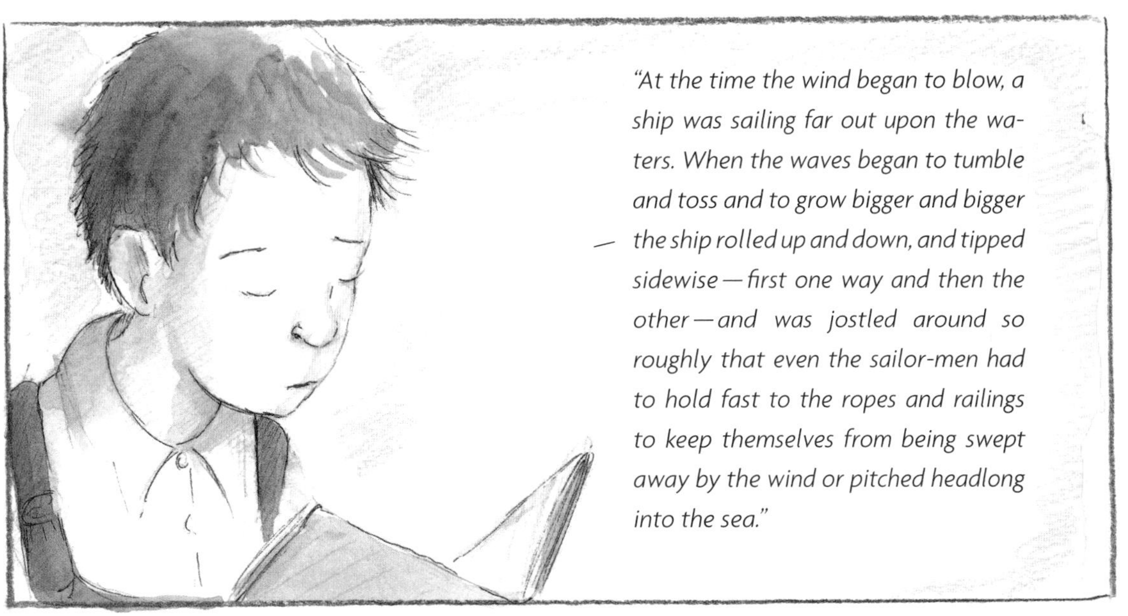

"At the time the wind began to blow, a ship was sailing far out upon the waters. When the waves began to tumble and toss and to grow bigger and bigger the ship rolled up and down, and tipped sidewise—first one way and then the other—and was jostled around so roughly that even the sailor-men had to hold fast to the ropes and railings to keep themselves from being swept away by the wind or pitched headlong into the sea."

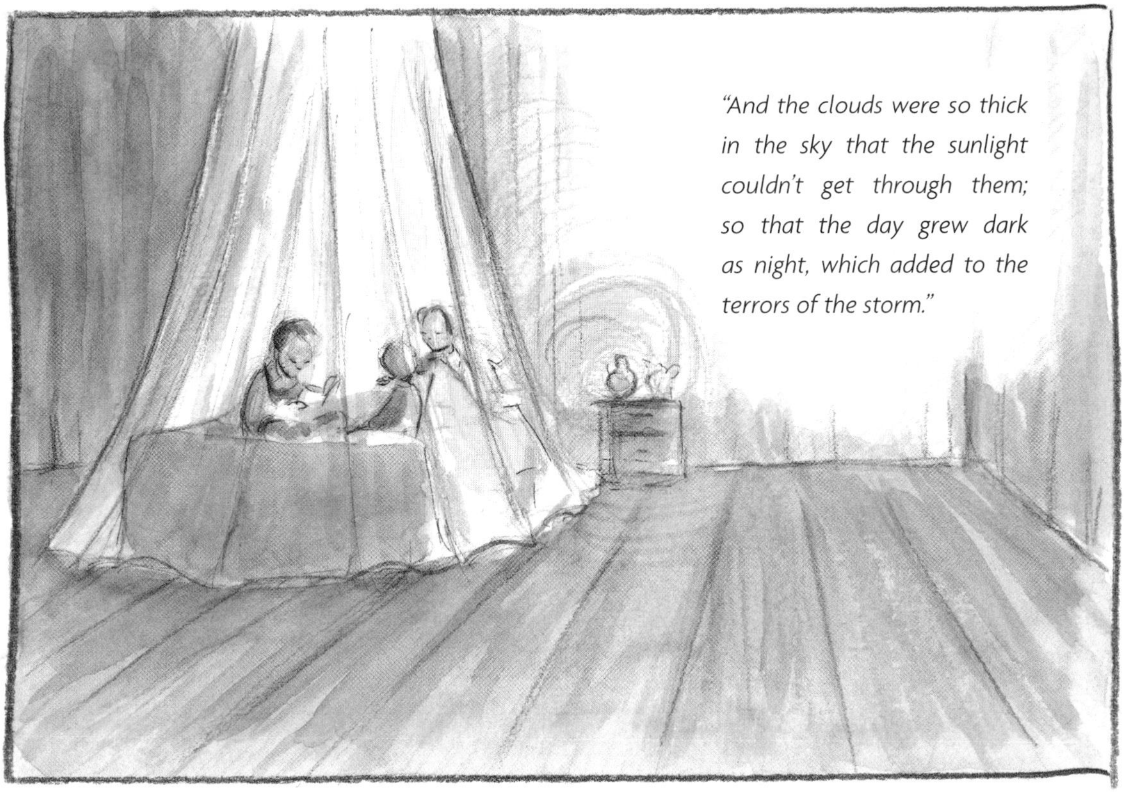

"And the clouds were so thick in the sky that the sunlight couldn't get through them; so that the day grew dark as night, which added to the terrors of the storm."

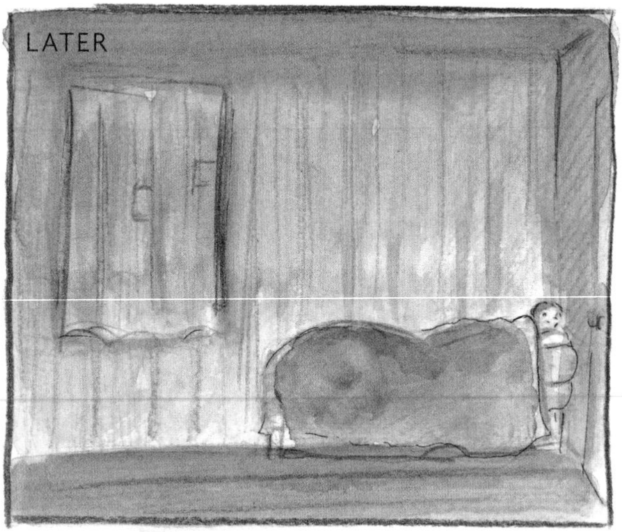
LATER

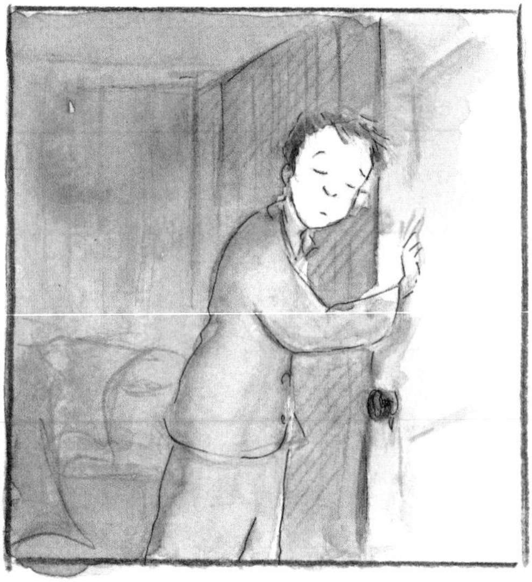

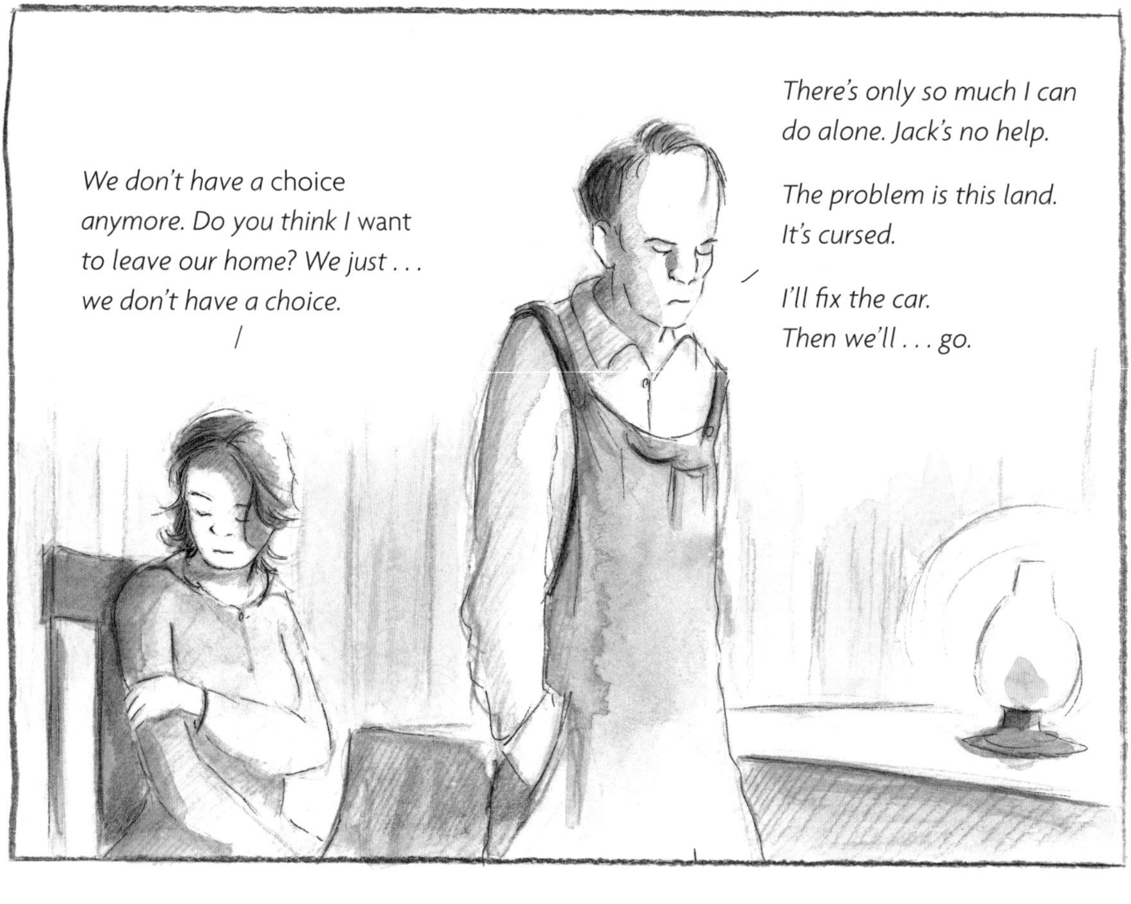
We don't have a choice anymore. Do you think I want to leave our home? We just . . . we don't have a choice.
There's only so much I can do alone. Jack's no help.
The problem is this land. It's cursed.
I'll fix the car. Then we'll . . . go.

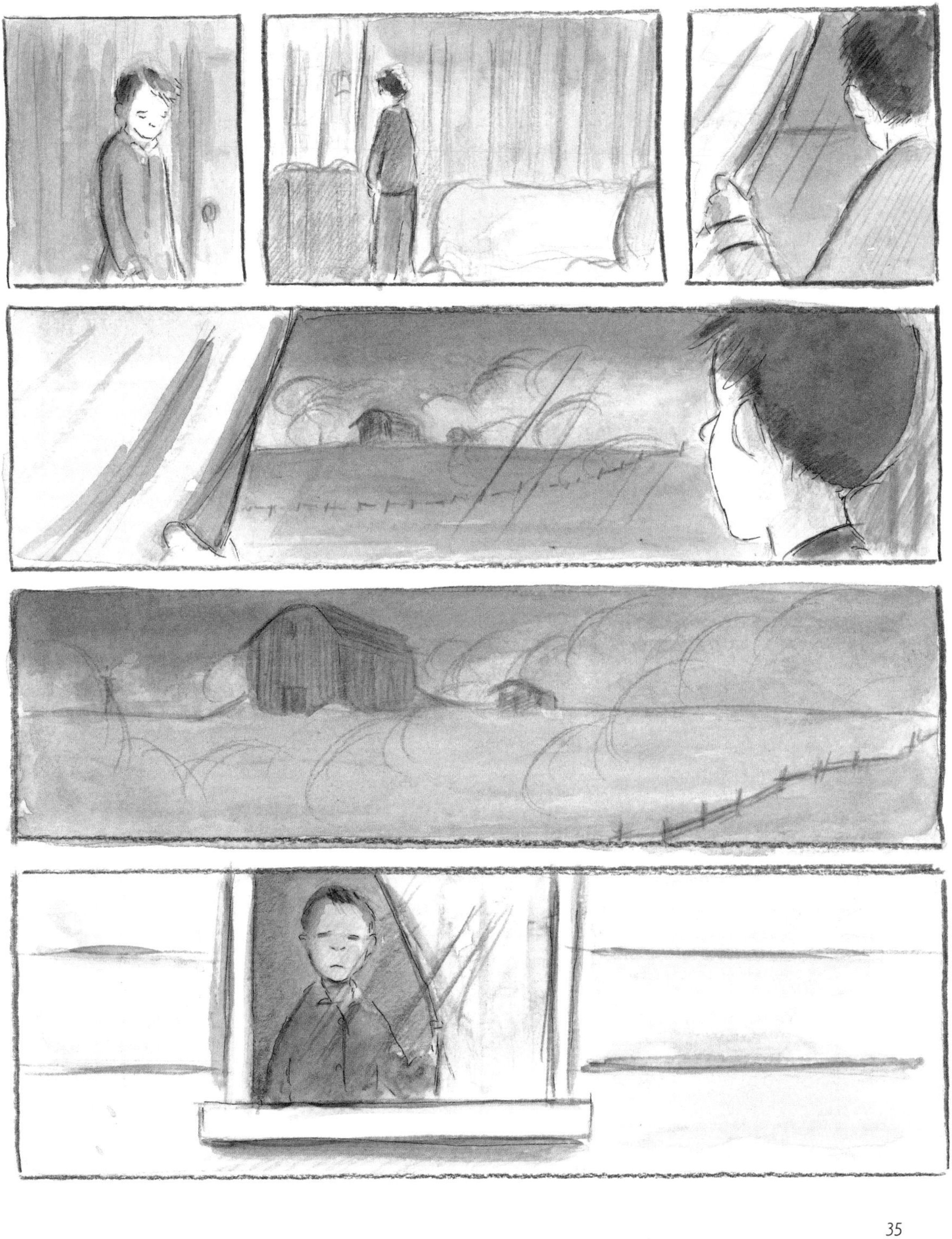

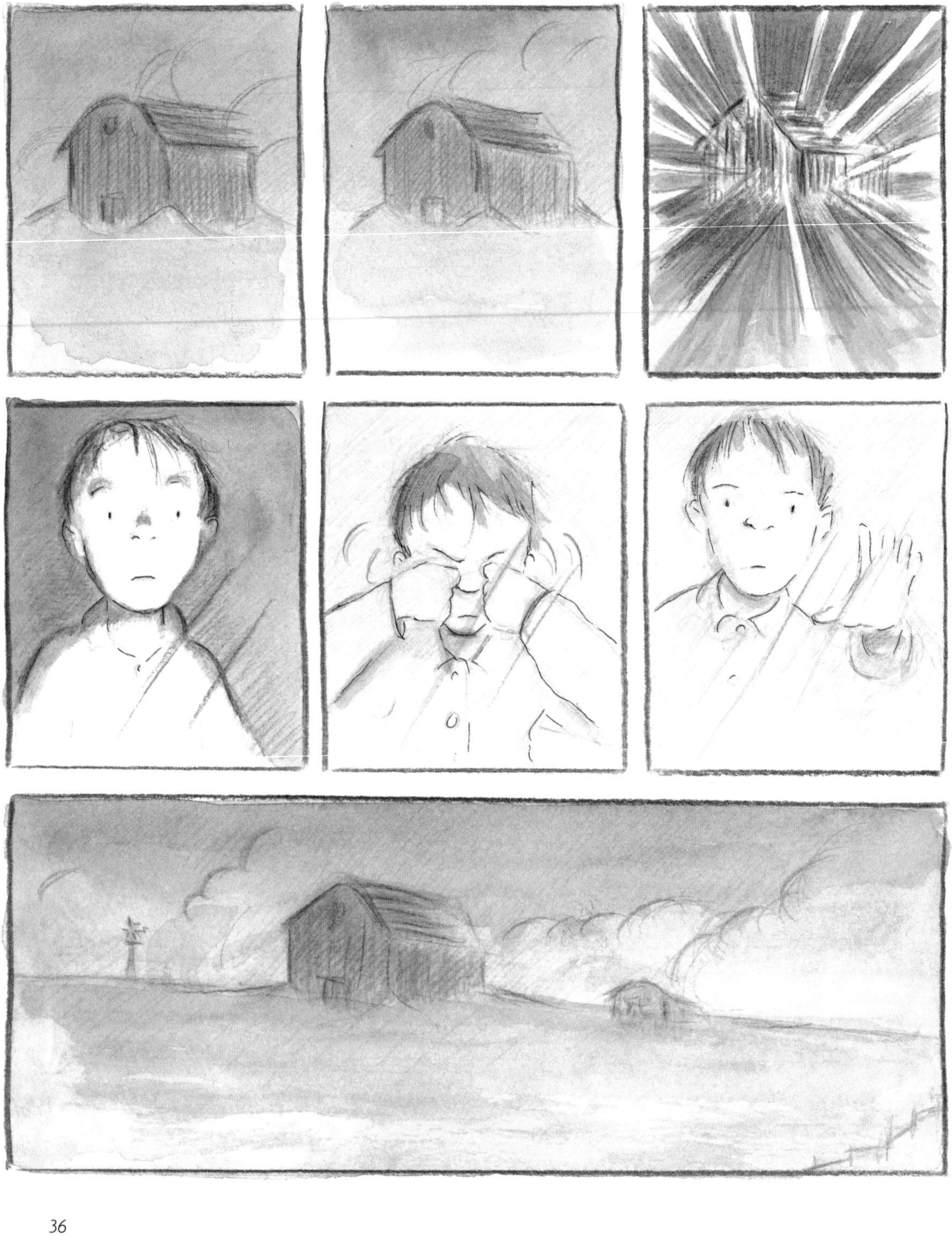

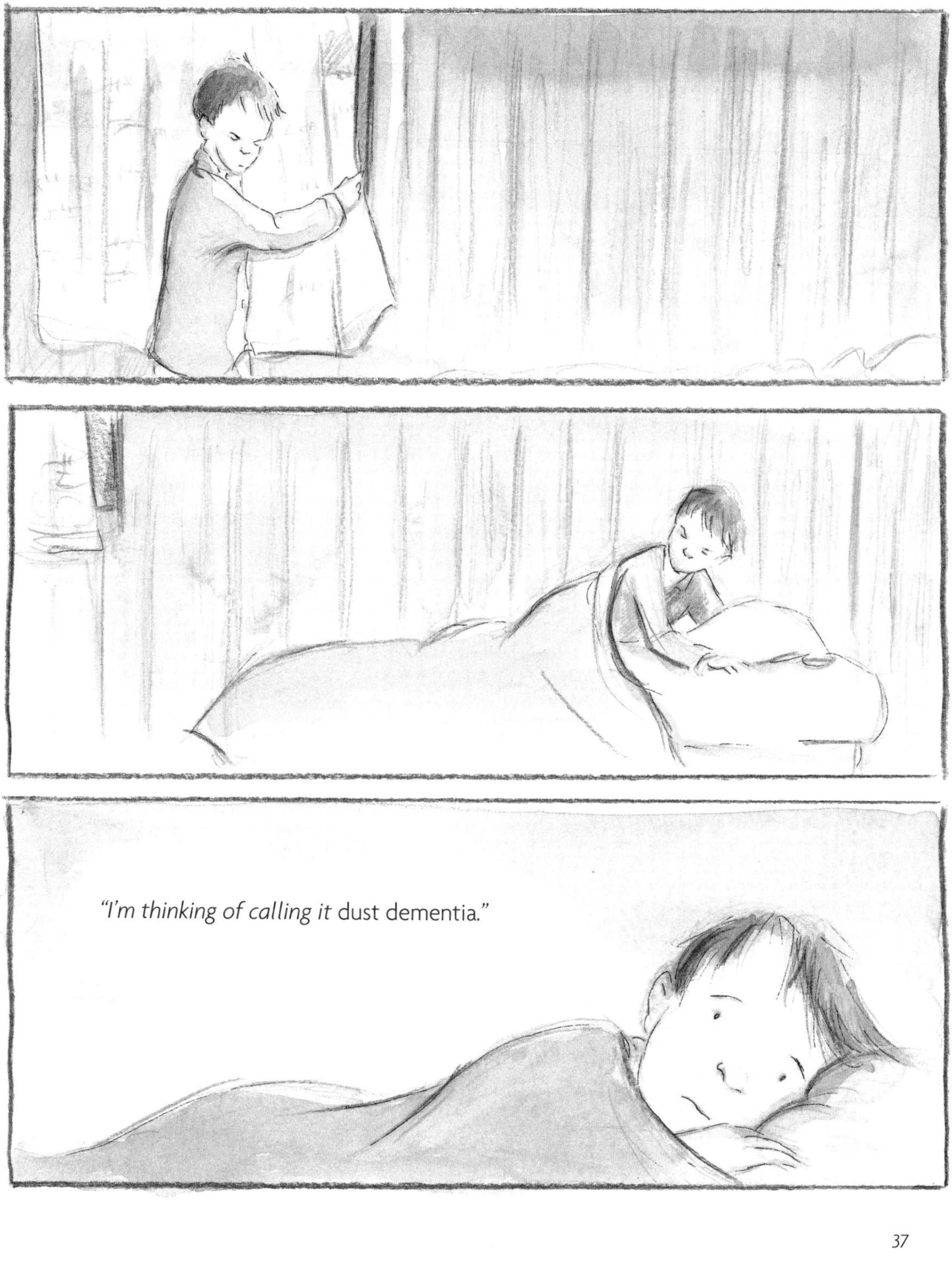
"*I'm thinking of calling it* dust dementia."

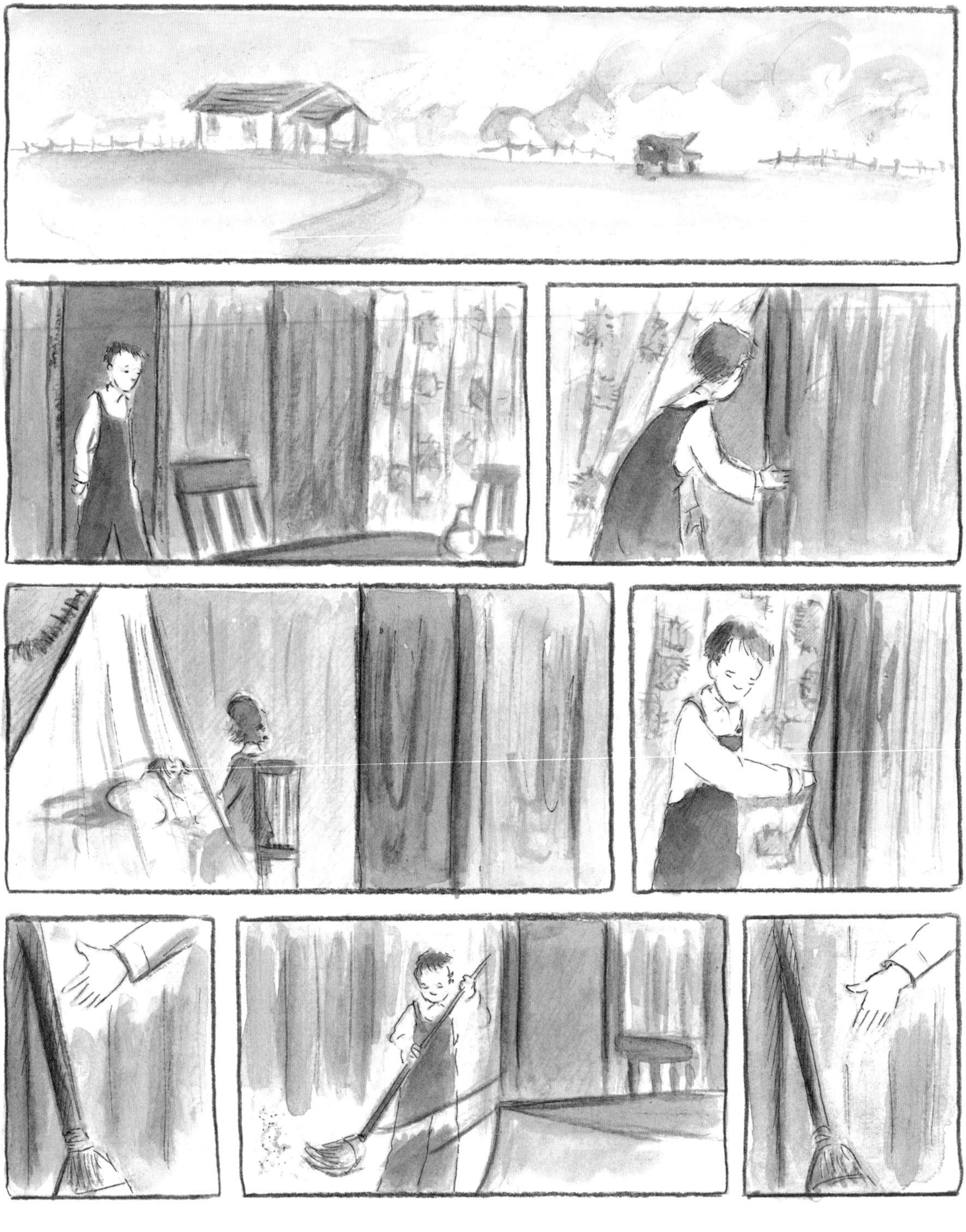

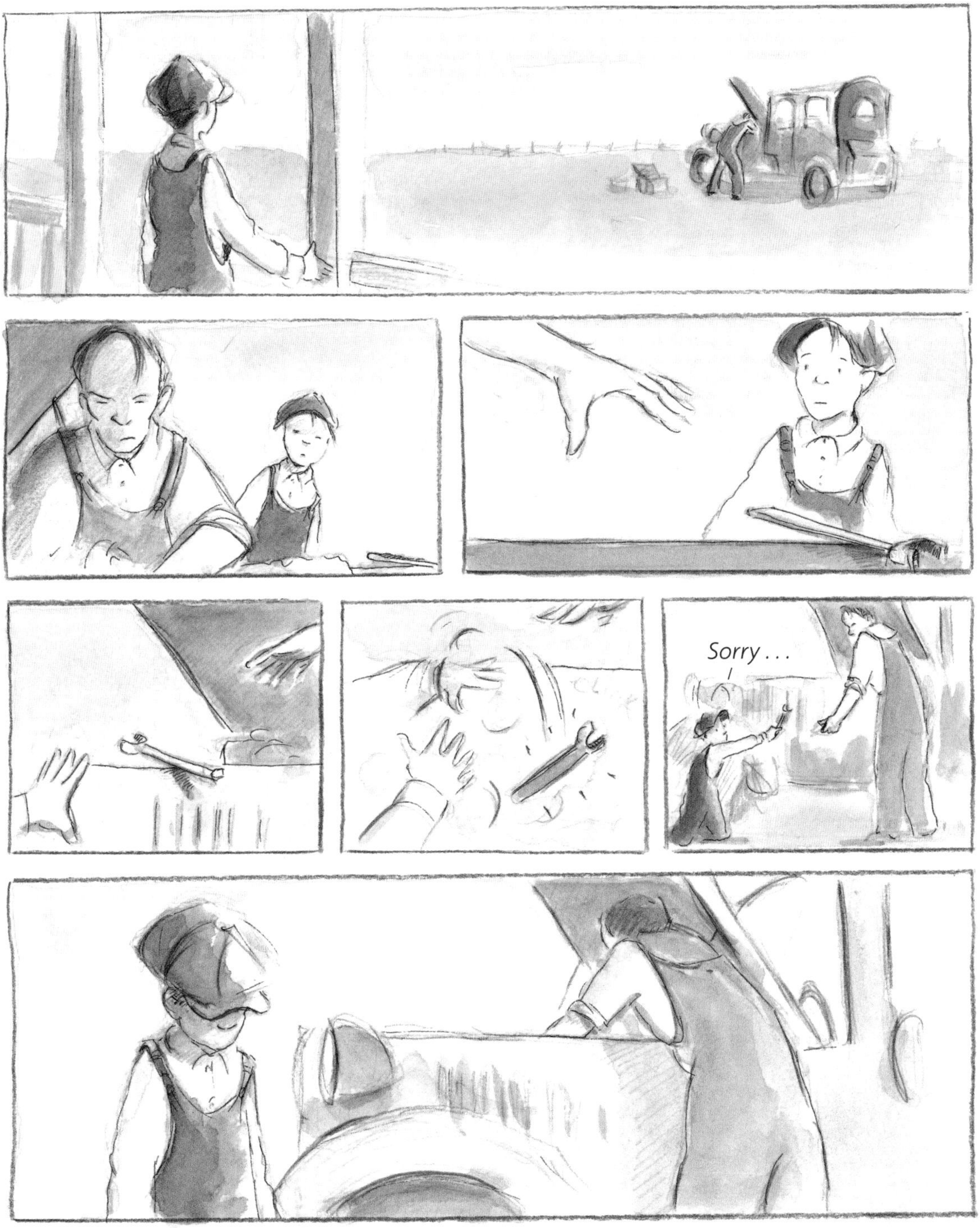
Sorry . . .

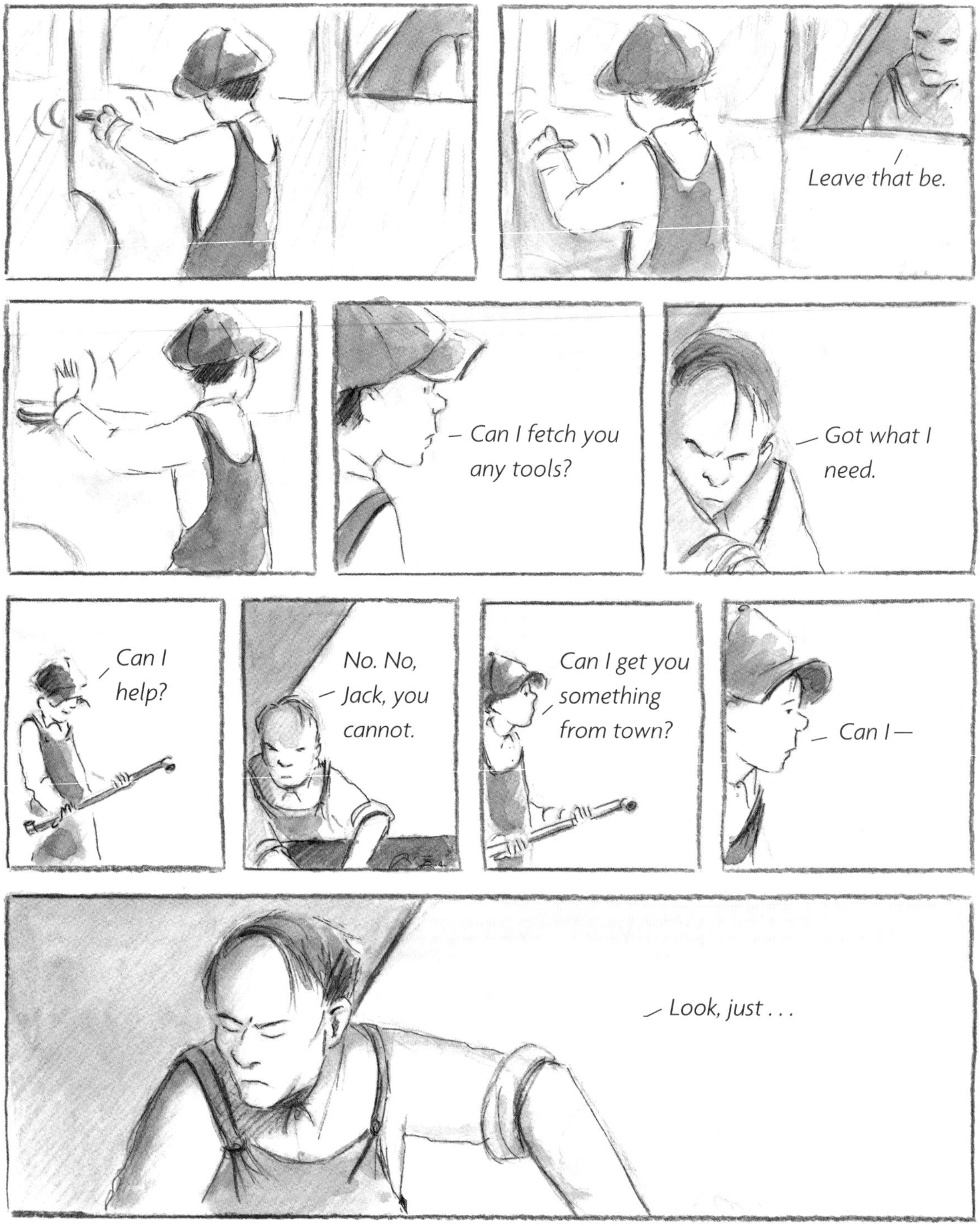
Leave that be.
Can I fetch you any tools?
Got what I need.
Can I help?
No. No, Jack, you cannot.
Can I get you something from town?
Can I—
Look, just . . .

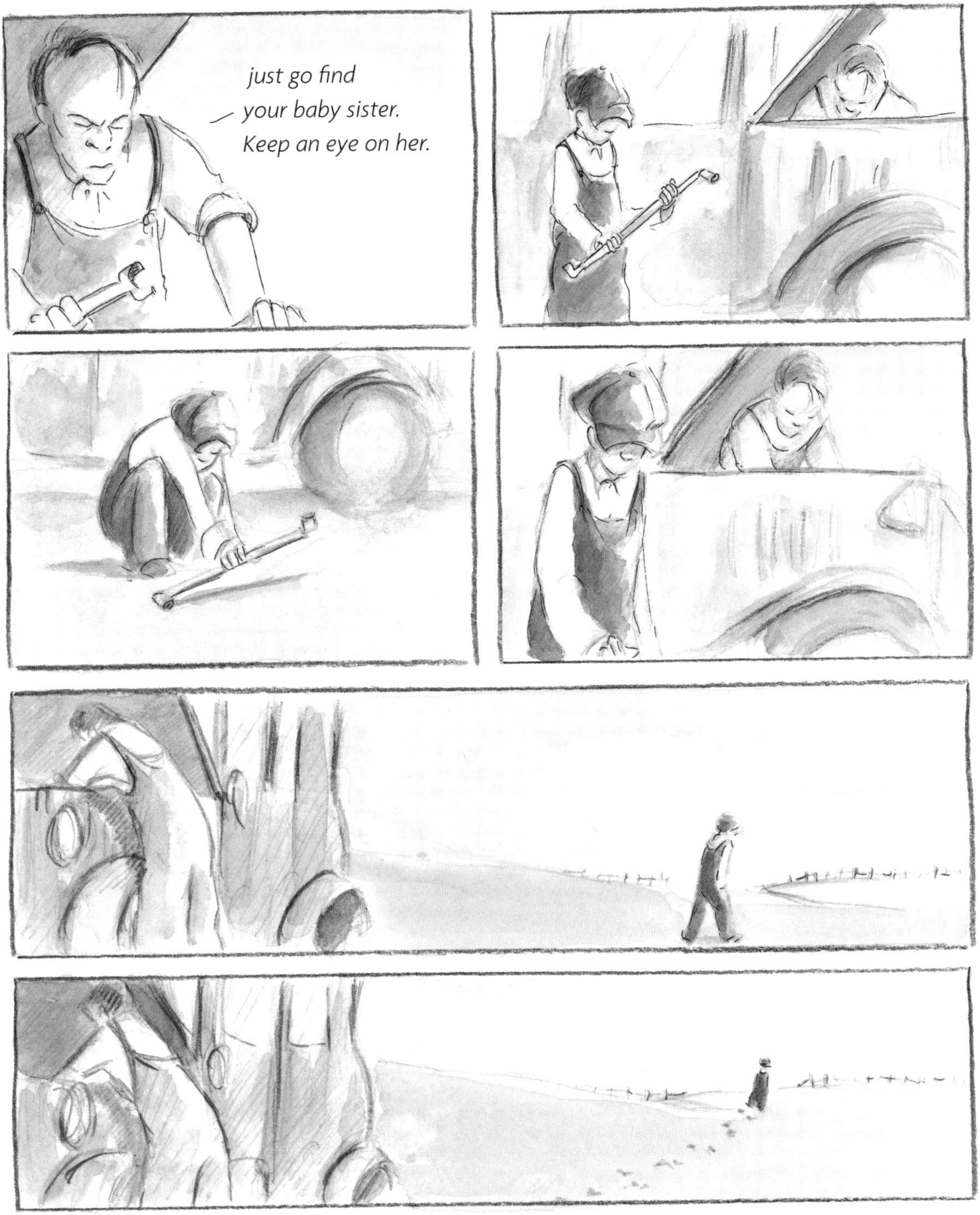
just go find
your baby sister.
Keep an eye on her.

rain rain go away

come again another day

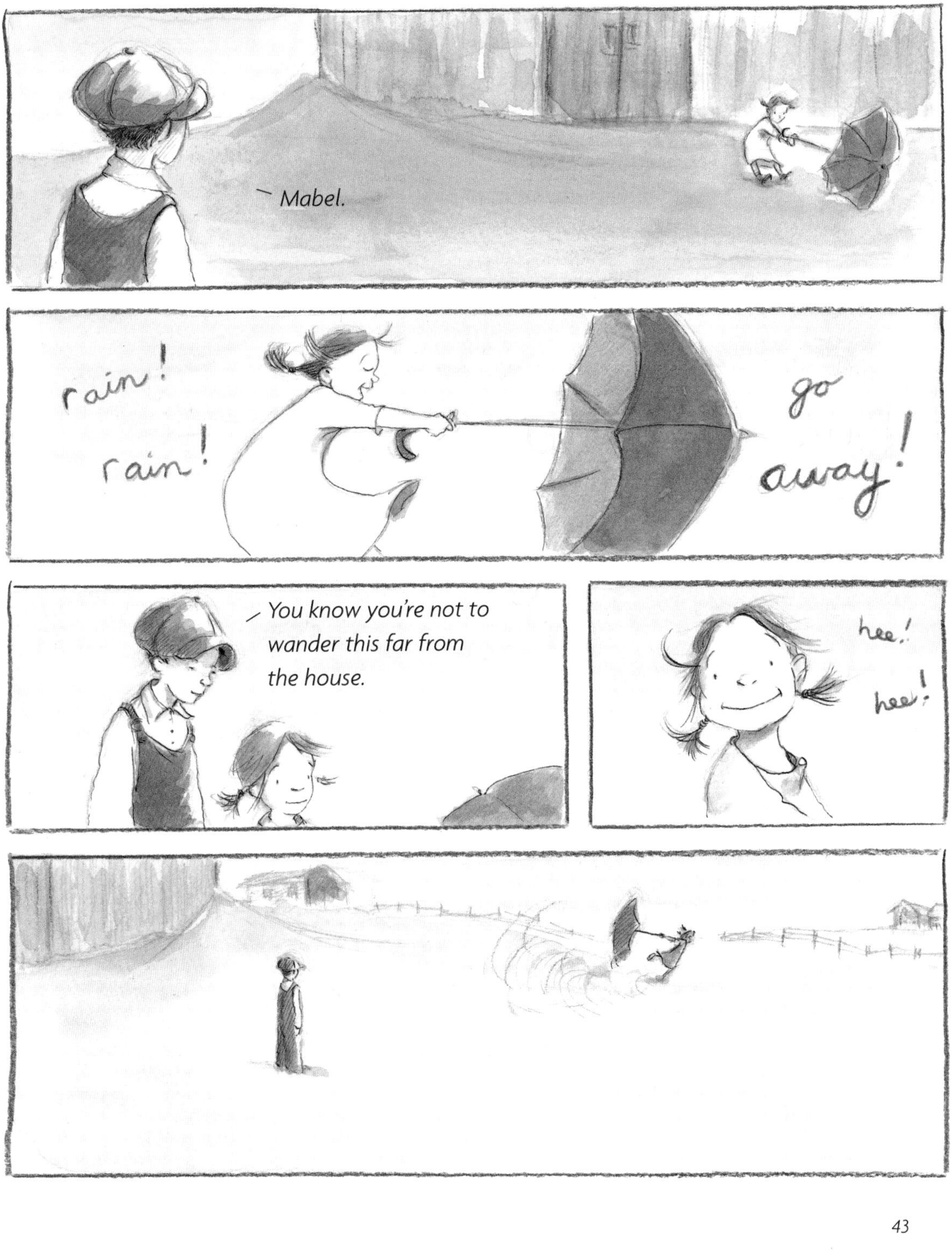
Mabel.
rain! rain!
go away!
You know you're not to wander this far from the house.
hee!
hee!

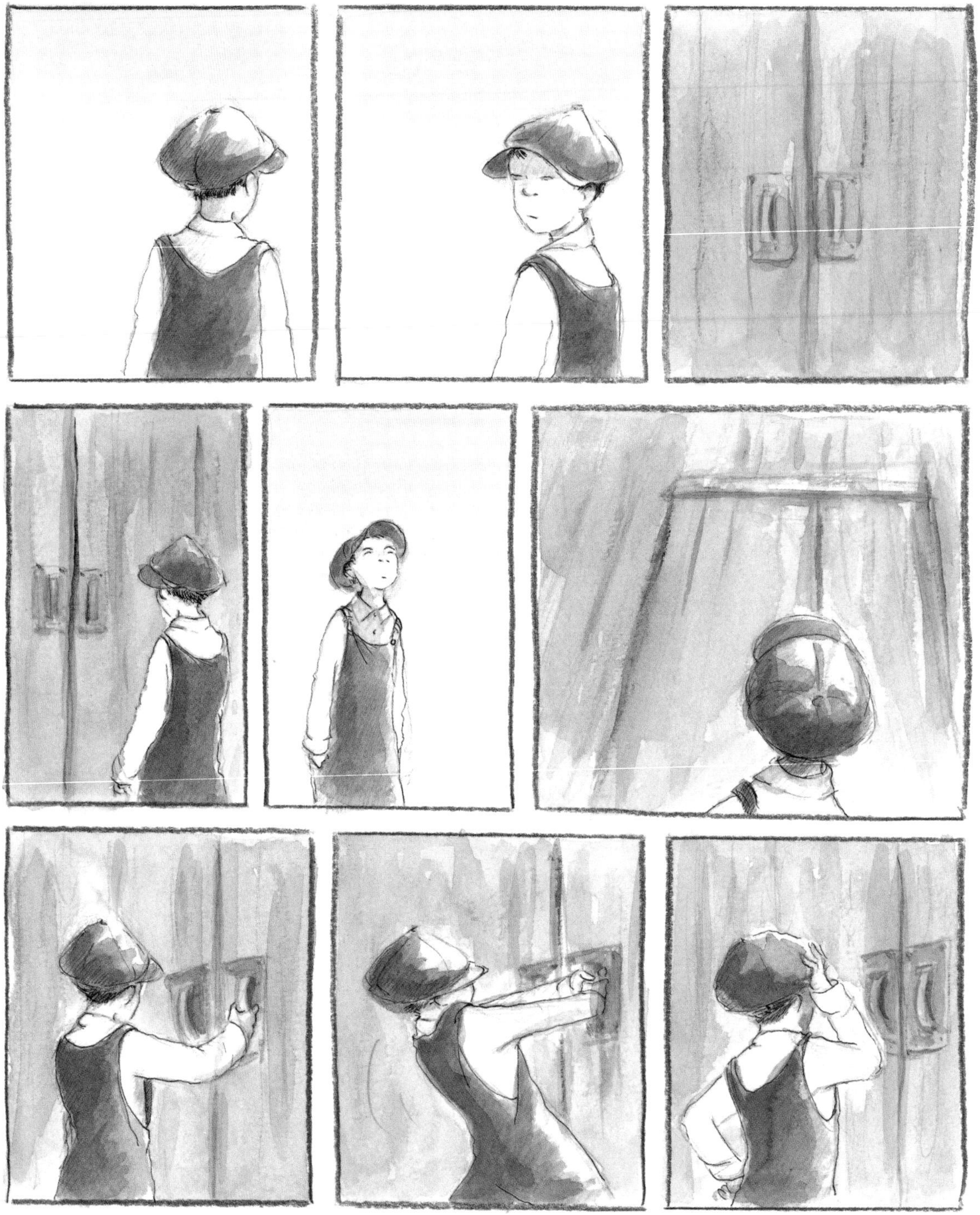

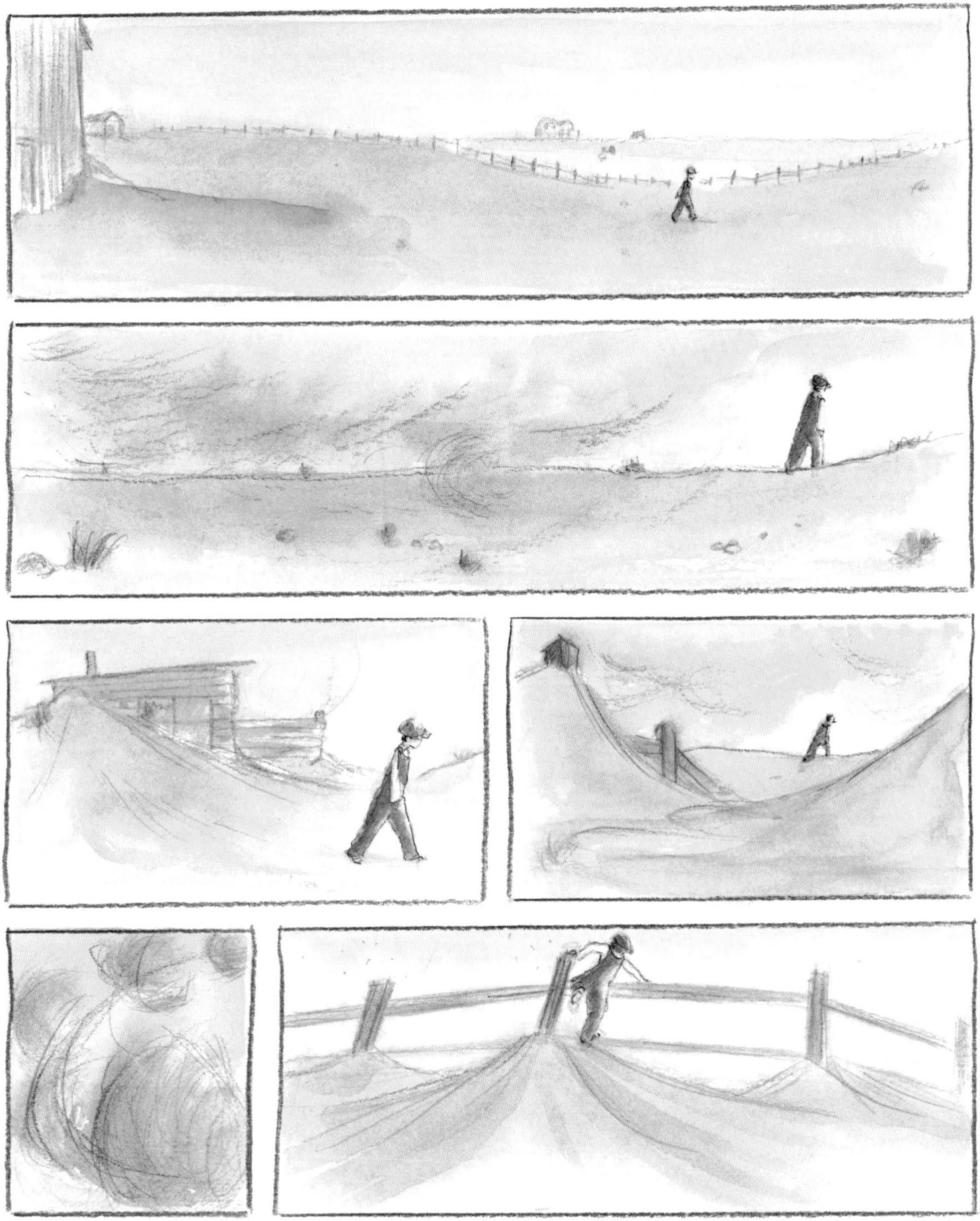

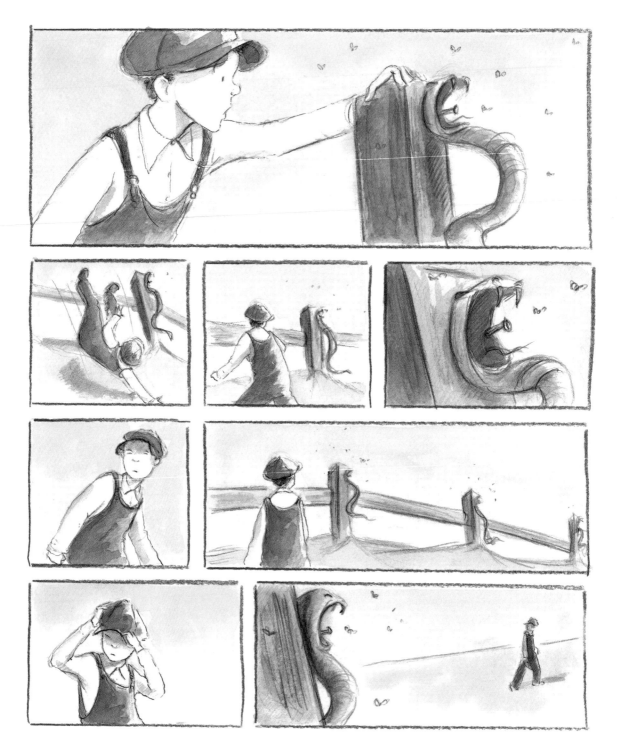

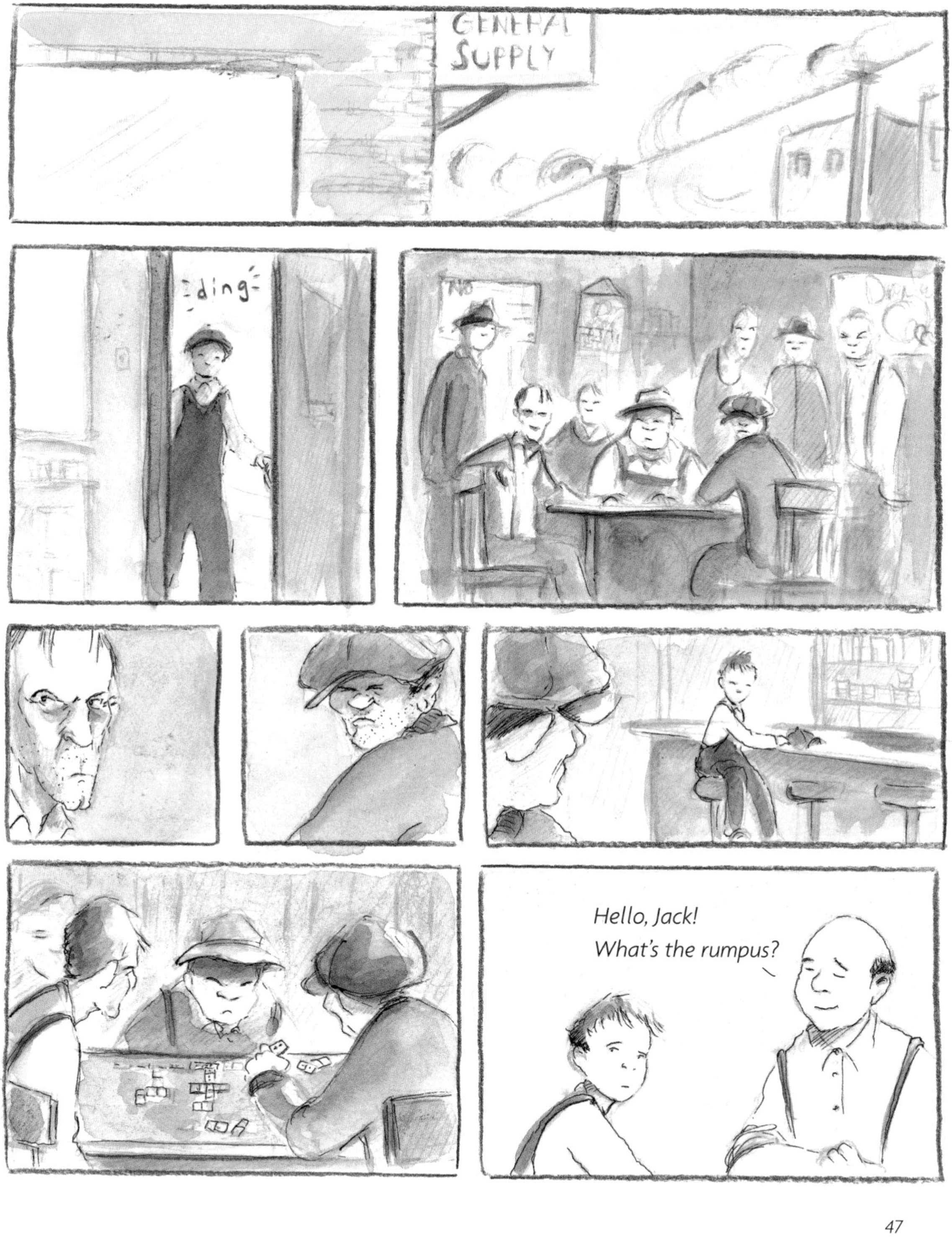
GENERAL SUPPLY
ding
Hello, Jack!
What's the rumpus?

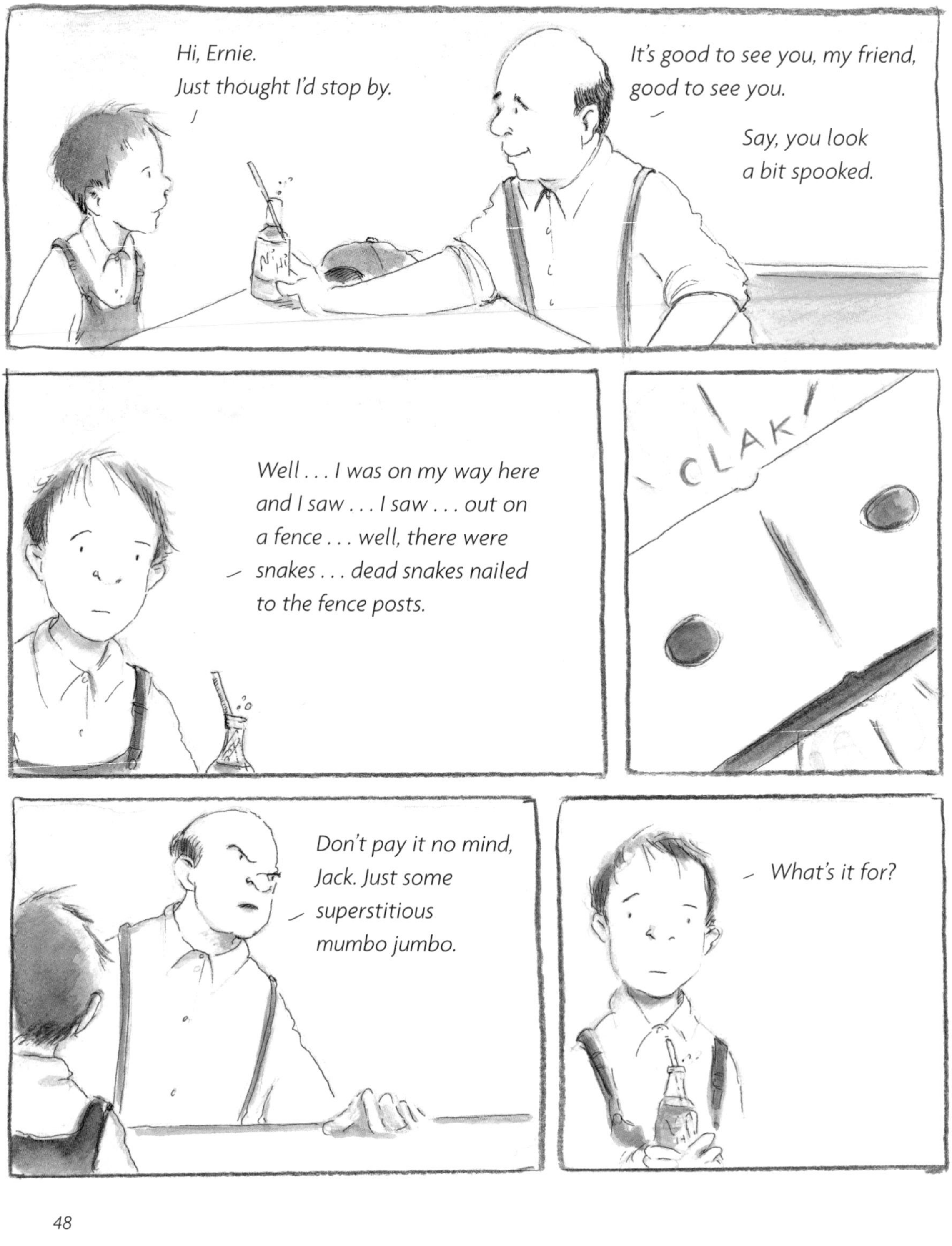
Hi, Ernie.
Just thought I'd stop by.
It's good to see you, my friend, good to see you.
Say, you look a bit spooked.
Well . . . I was on my way here and I saw . . . I saw . . . out on a fence . . . well, there were snakes . . . dead snakes nailed to the fence posts.
CLAK!
Don't pay it no mind, Jack. Just some superstitious mumbo jumbo.
What's it for?

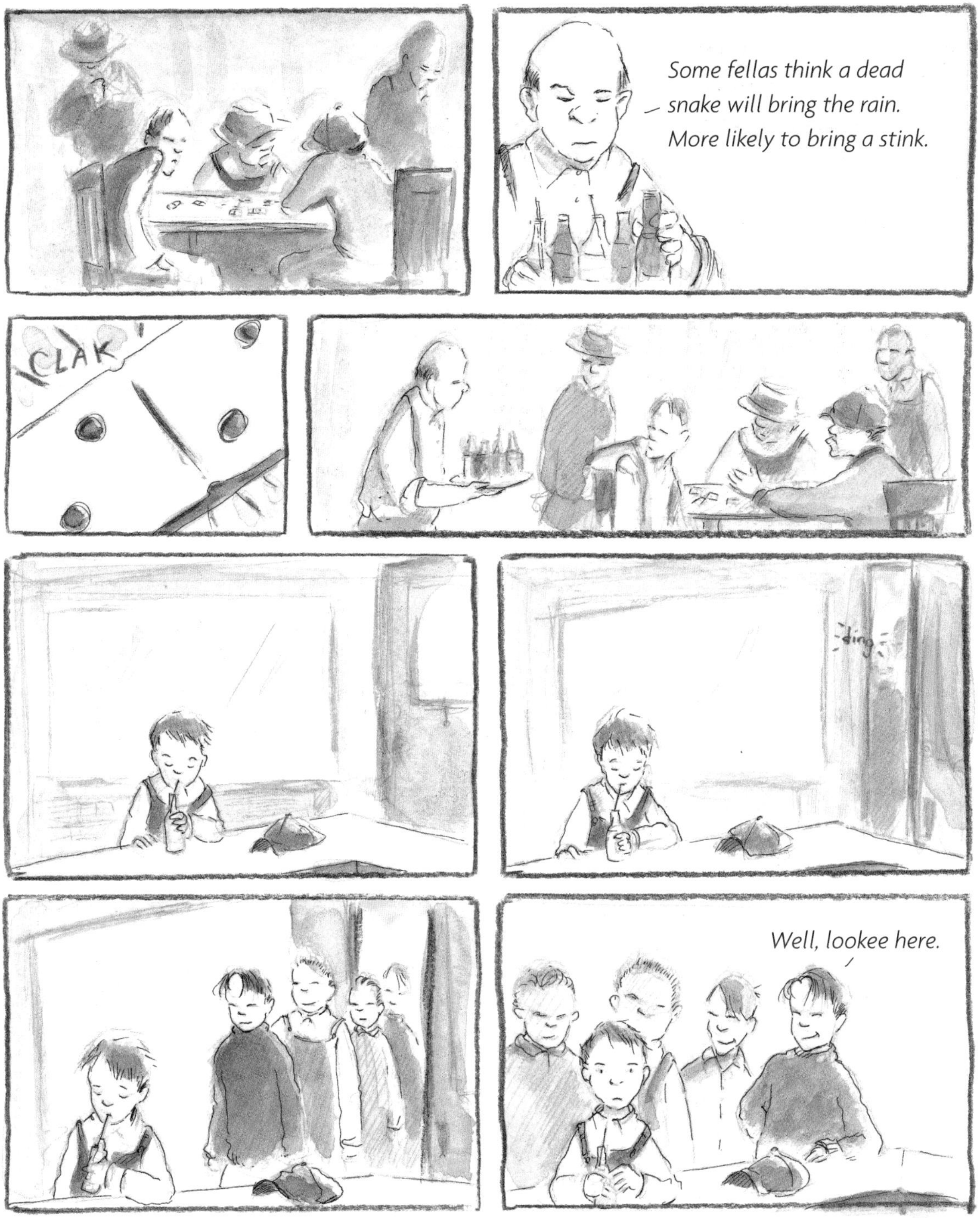
Some fellas think a dead snake will bring the rain. More likely to bring a stink.
CLAK
ding
Well, lookee here.

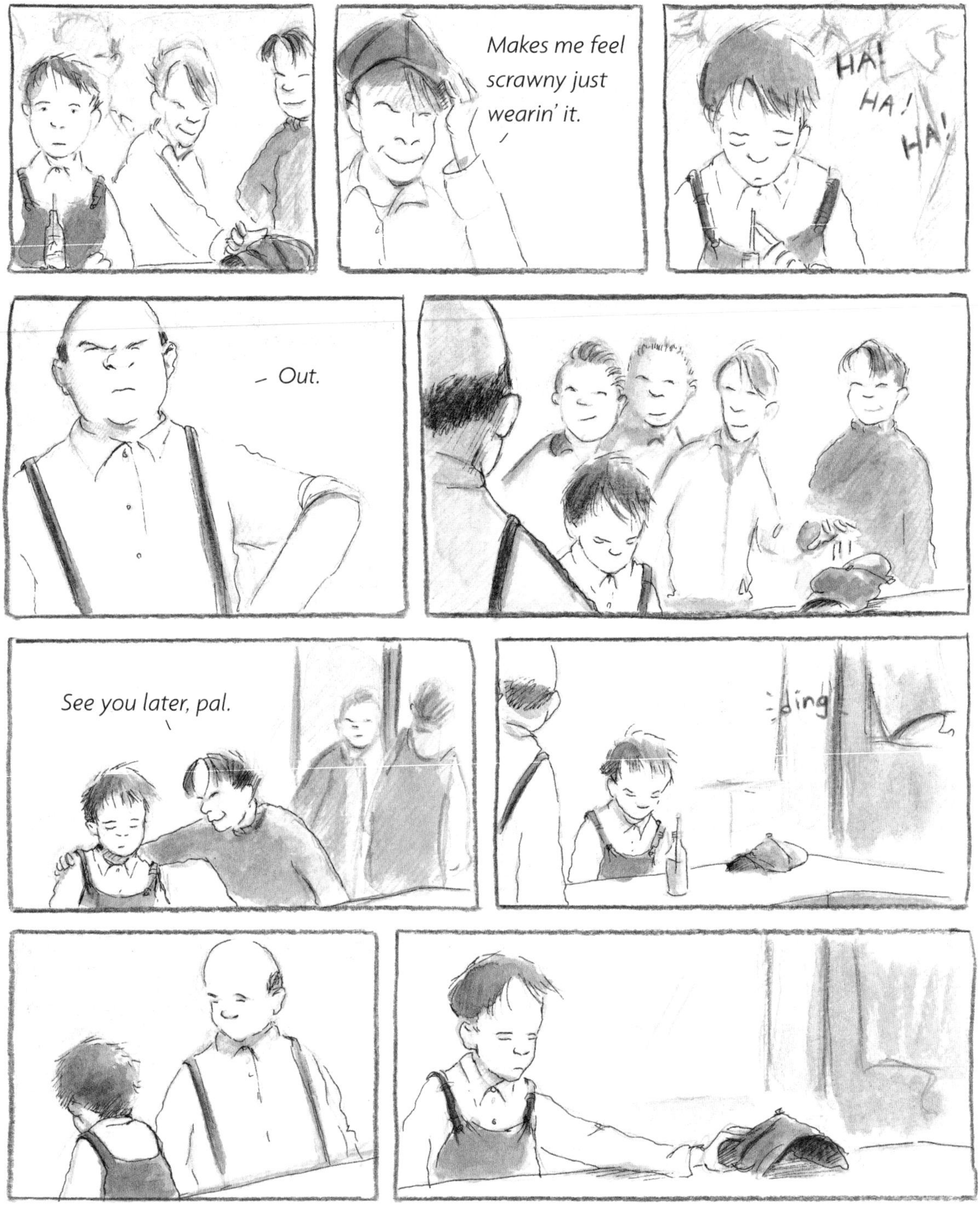
Makes me feel scrawny just wearin' it.
HA! HA! HA!
Out.
See you later, pal.
ding

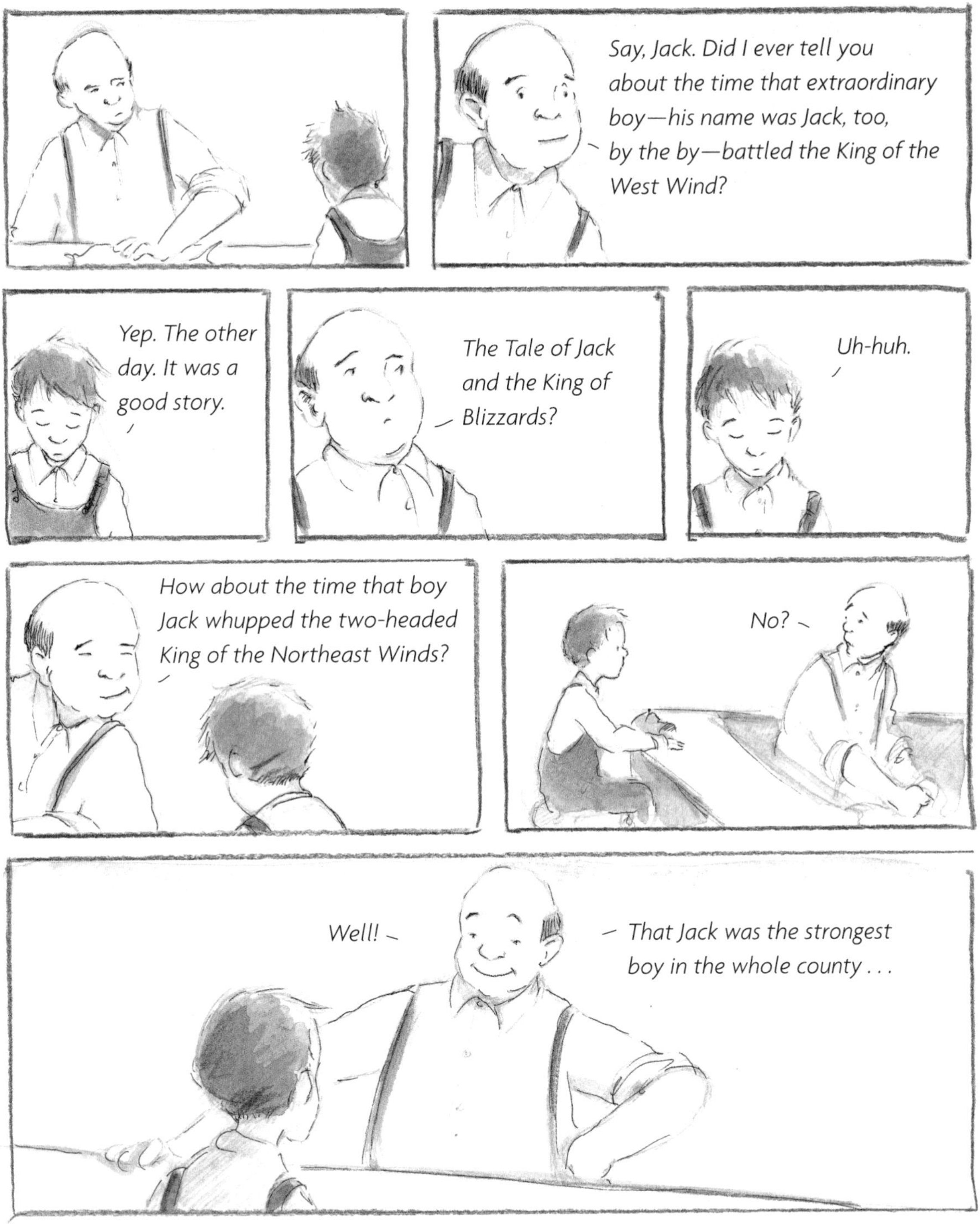
Say, Jack. Did I ever tell you about the time that extraordinary boy—his name was Jack, too, by the by—battled the King of the West Wind?
Yep. The other day. It was a good story.
The Tale of Jack and the King of Blizzards?
Uh-huh.
How about the time that boy Jack whupped the two-headed King of the Northeast Winds?
No?
Well!
That Jack was the strongest boy in the whole county . . .

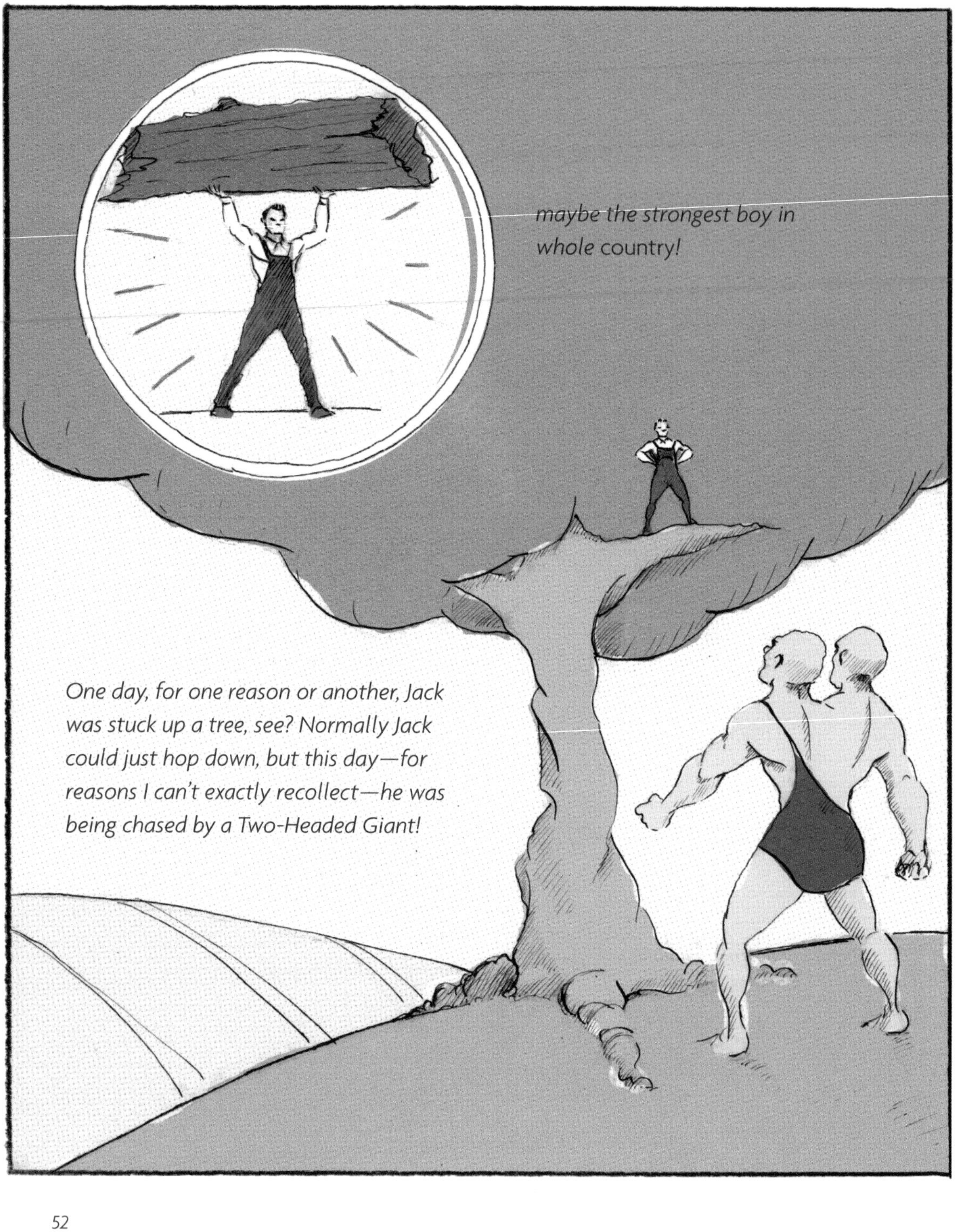
maybe the strongest boy in
whole country!
One day, for one reason or another, Jack
was stuck up a tree, see? Normally Jack
could just hop down, but this day—for
reasons I can't exactly recollect—he was
being chased by a Two-Headed Giant!

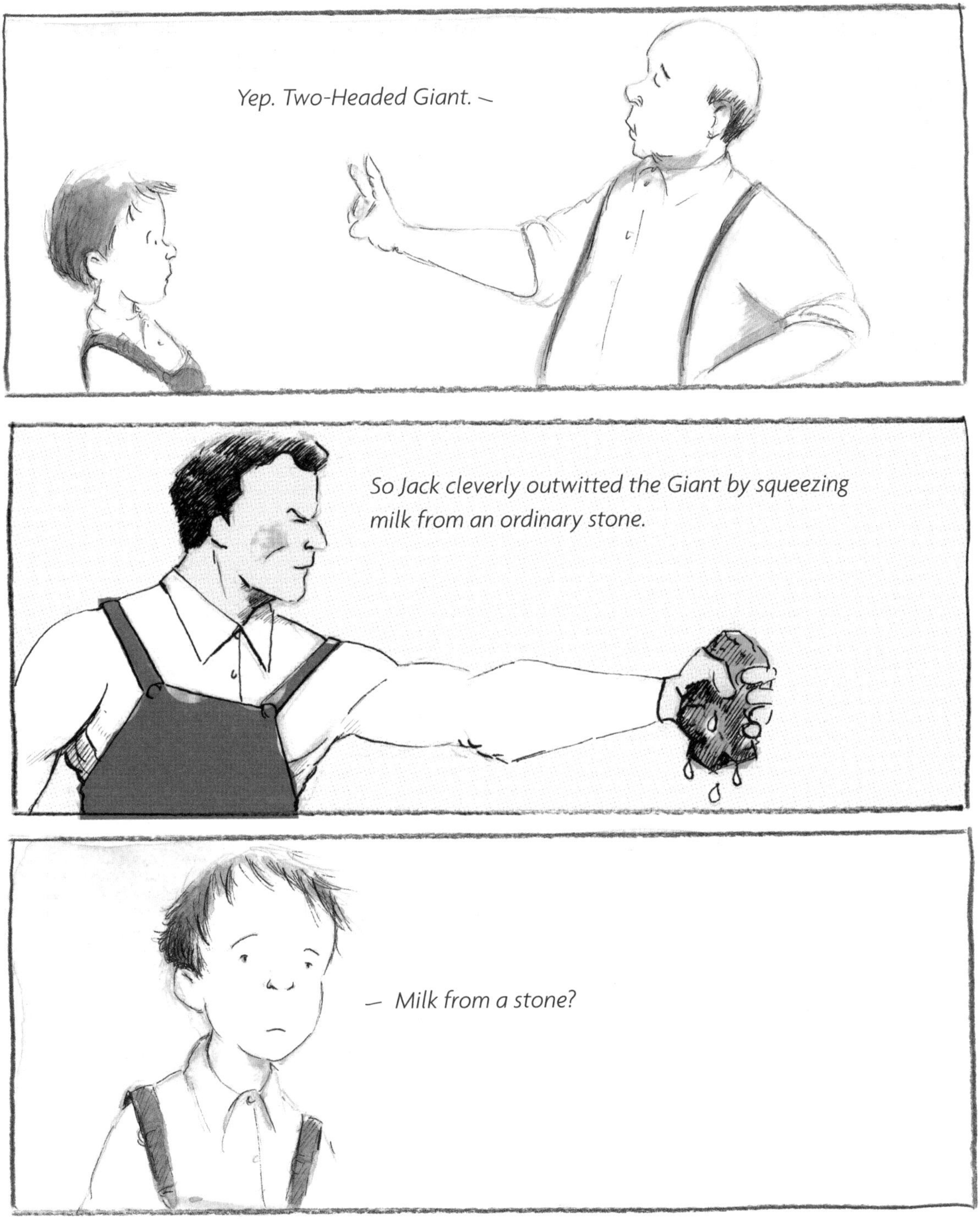
Yep. Two-Headed Giant. –
So Jack cleverly outwitted the Giant by squeezing milk from an ordinary stone.
– Milk from a stone?

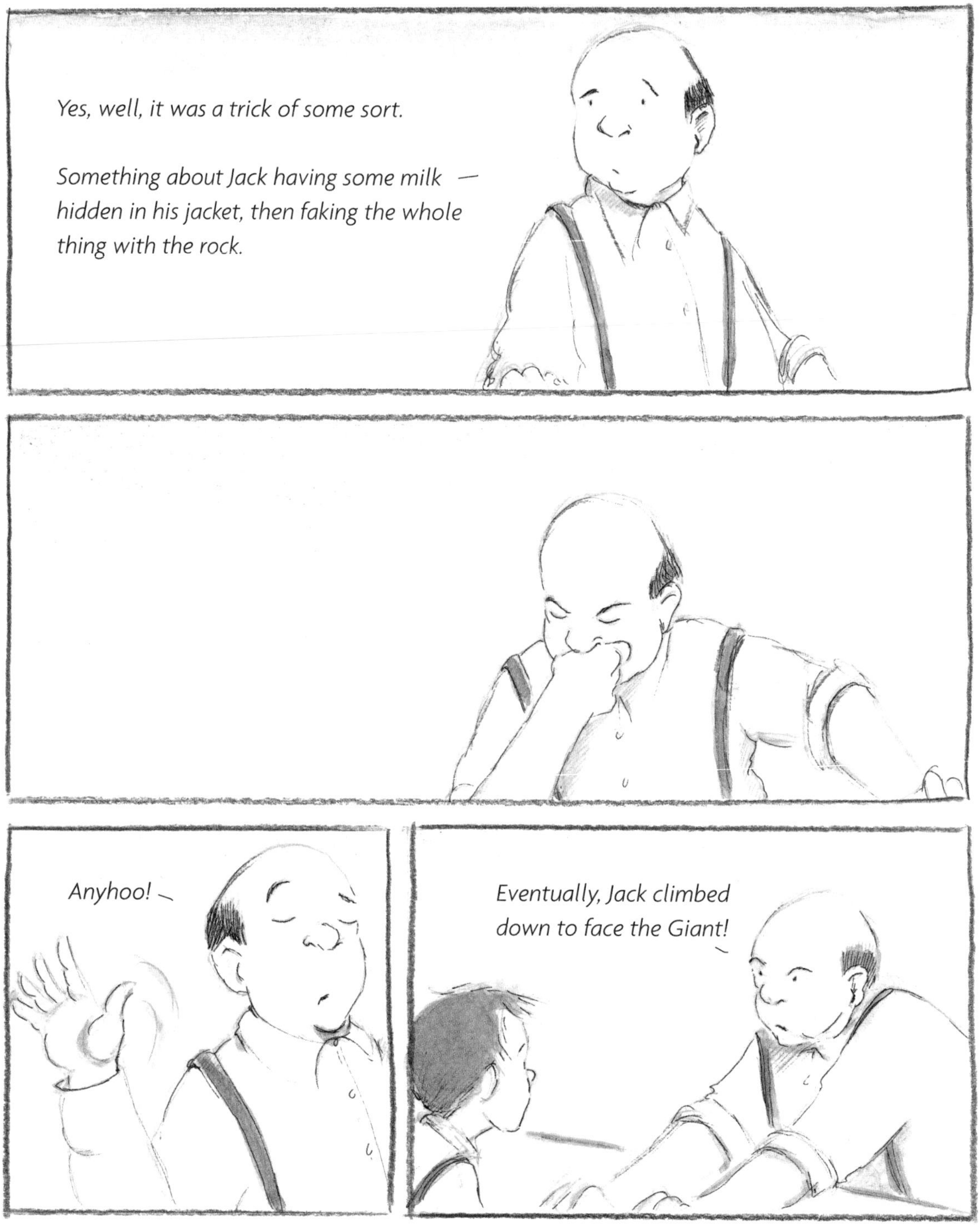
Yes, well, it was a trick of some sort.
Something about Jack having some milk —
hidden in his jacket, then faking the whole
thing with the rock.
Anyhoo!
Eventually, Jack climbed
down to face the Giant!

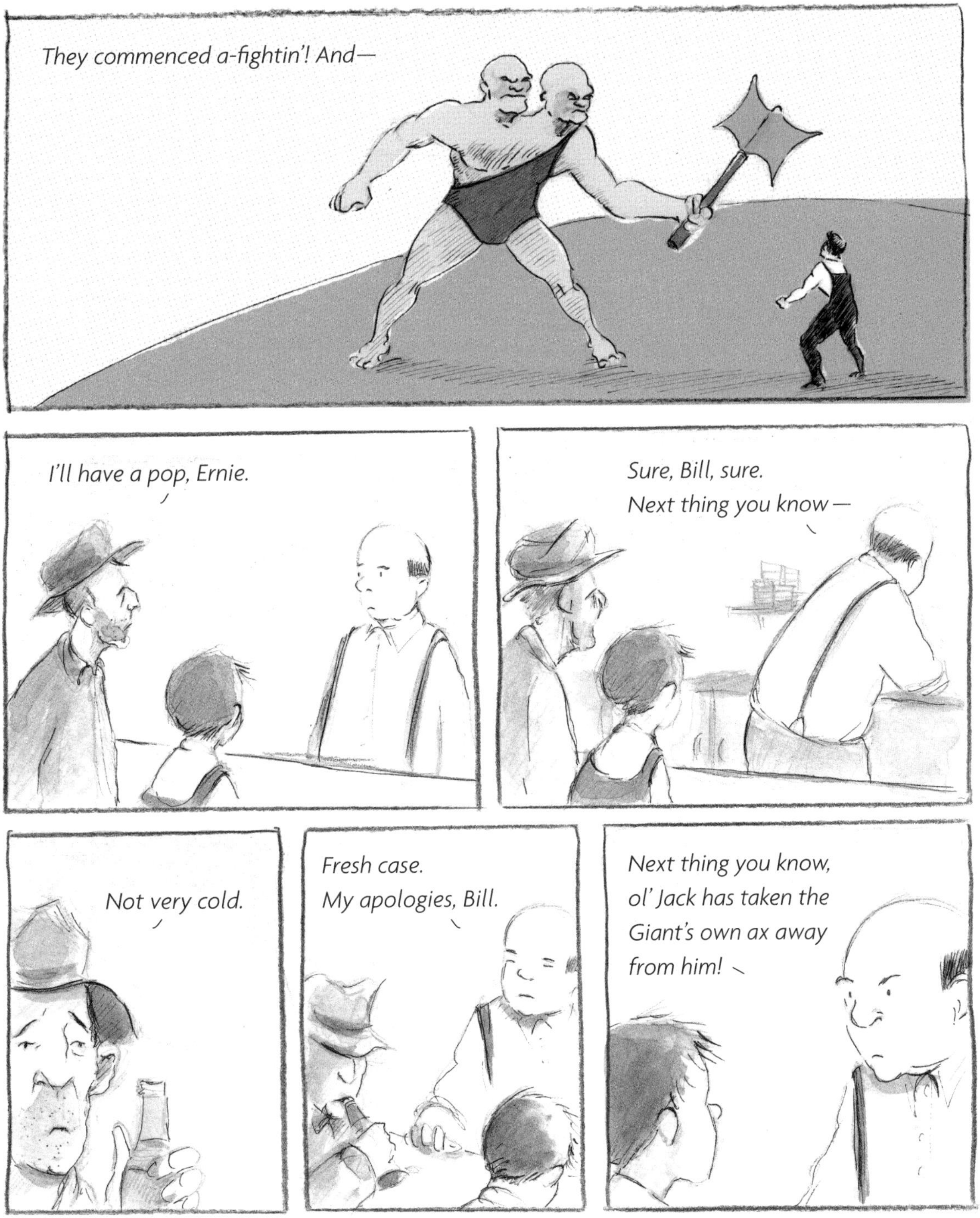
They commenced a-fightin'! And—
I'll have a pop, Ernie.
Sure, Bill, sure.
Next thing you know—
Not very cold.
Fresh case.
My apologies, Bill.
Next thing you know, ol' Jack has taken the Giant's own ax away from him!

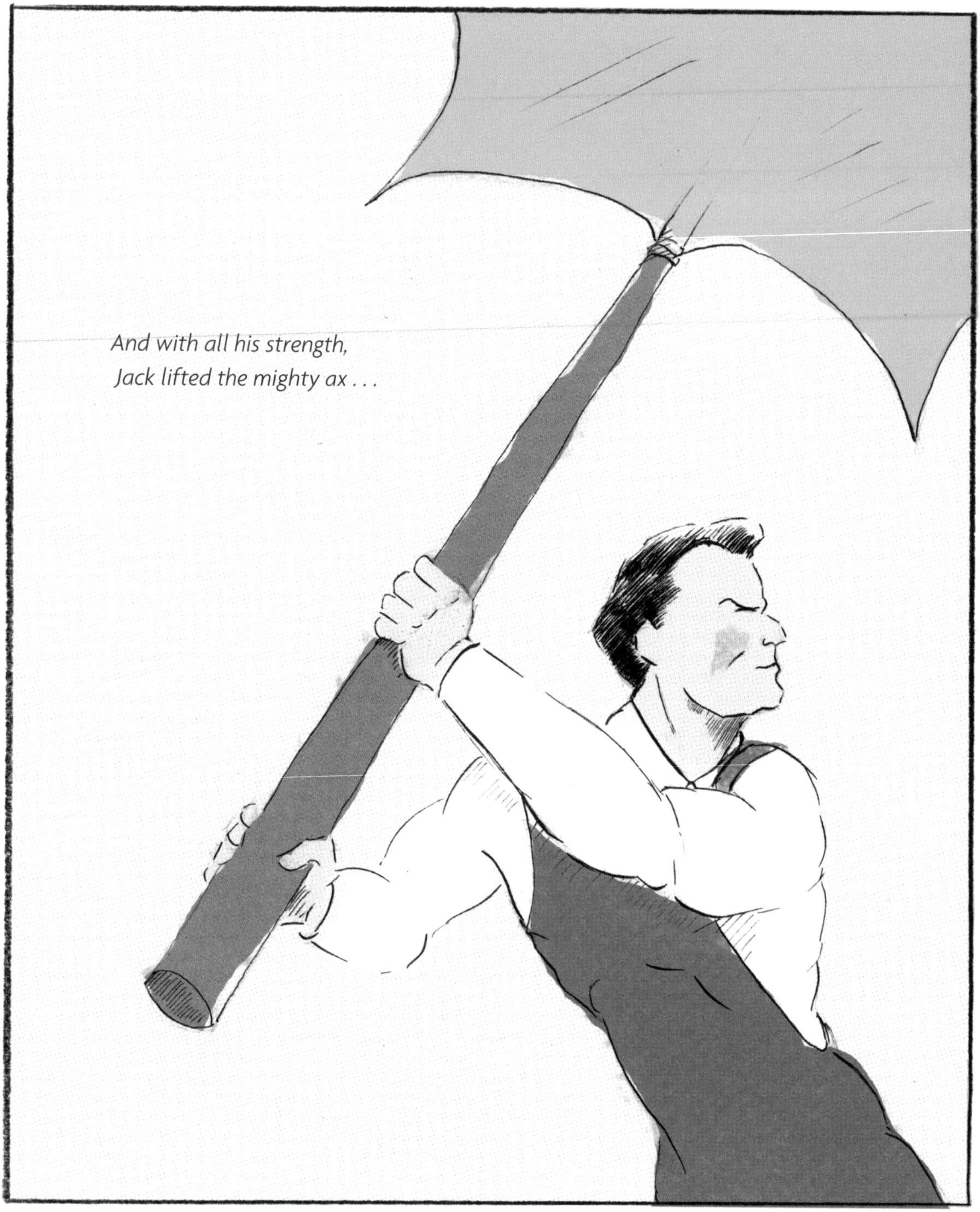
And with all his strength,
Jack lifted the mighty ax . . .

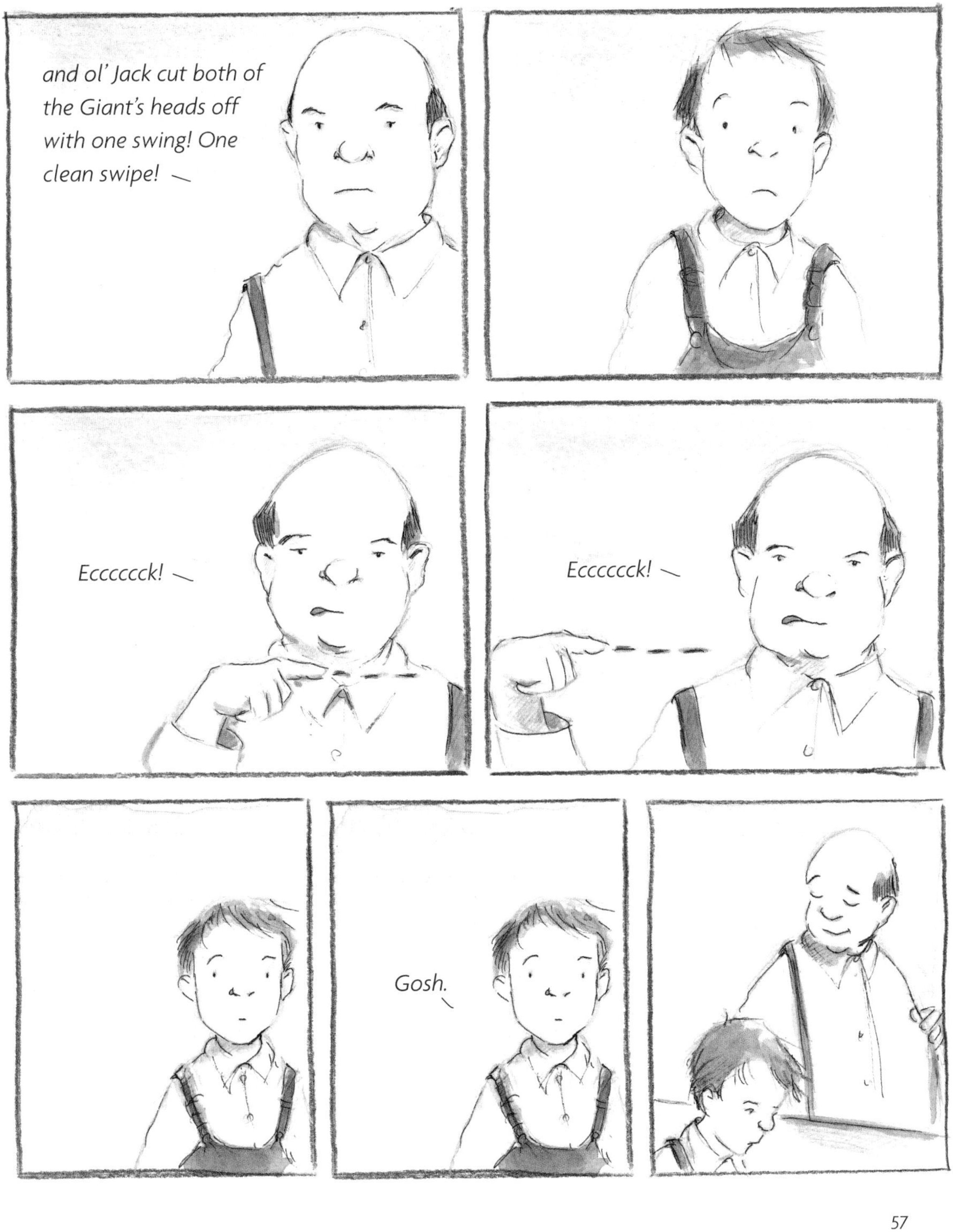
and ol' Jack cut both of the Giant's heads off with one swing! One clean swipe!
Eccccccck!
Eccccccck!
Gosh.

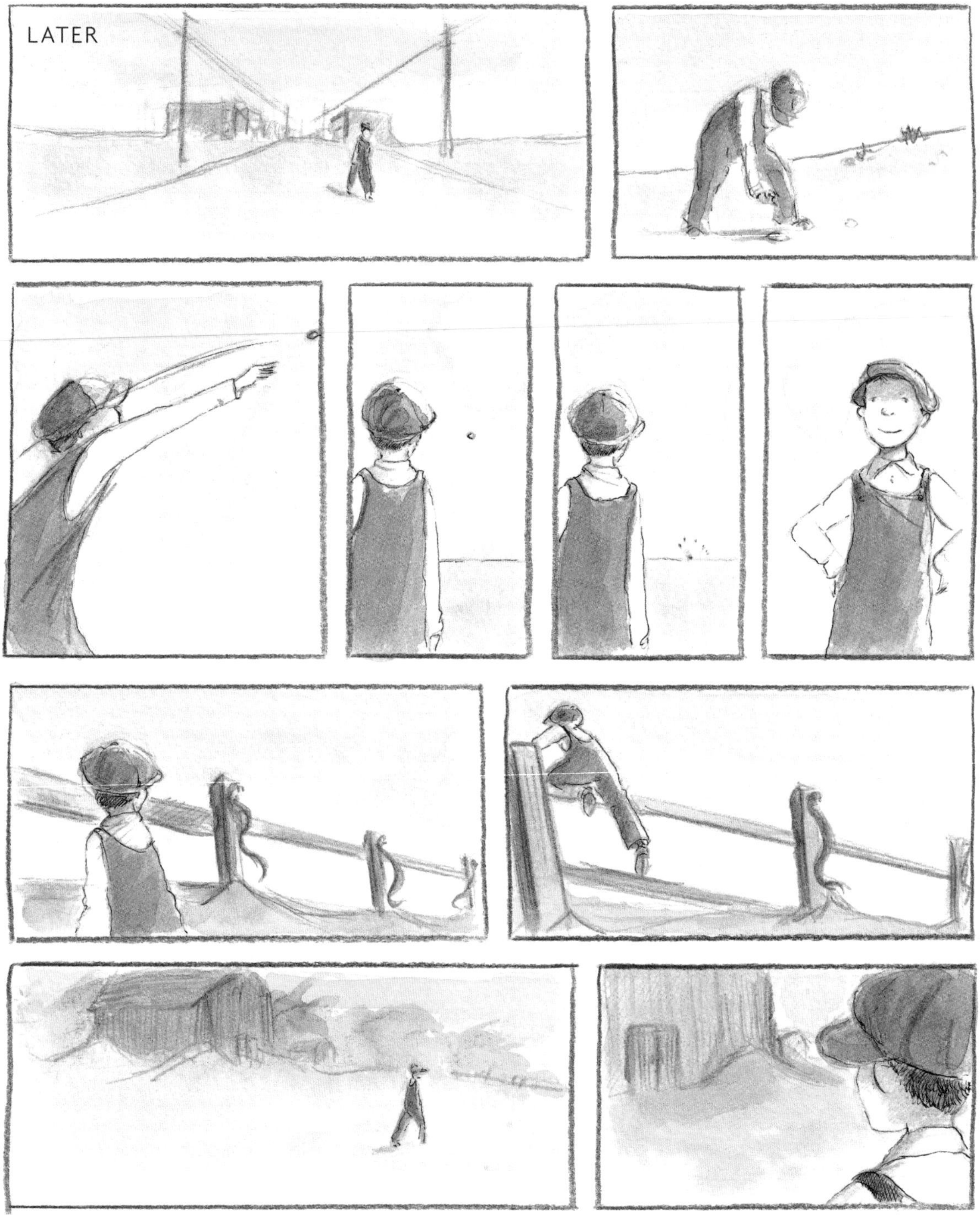
LATER

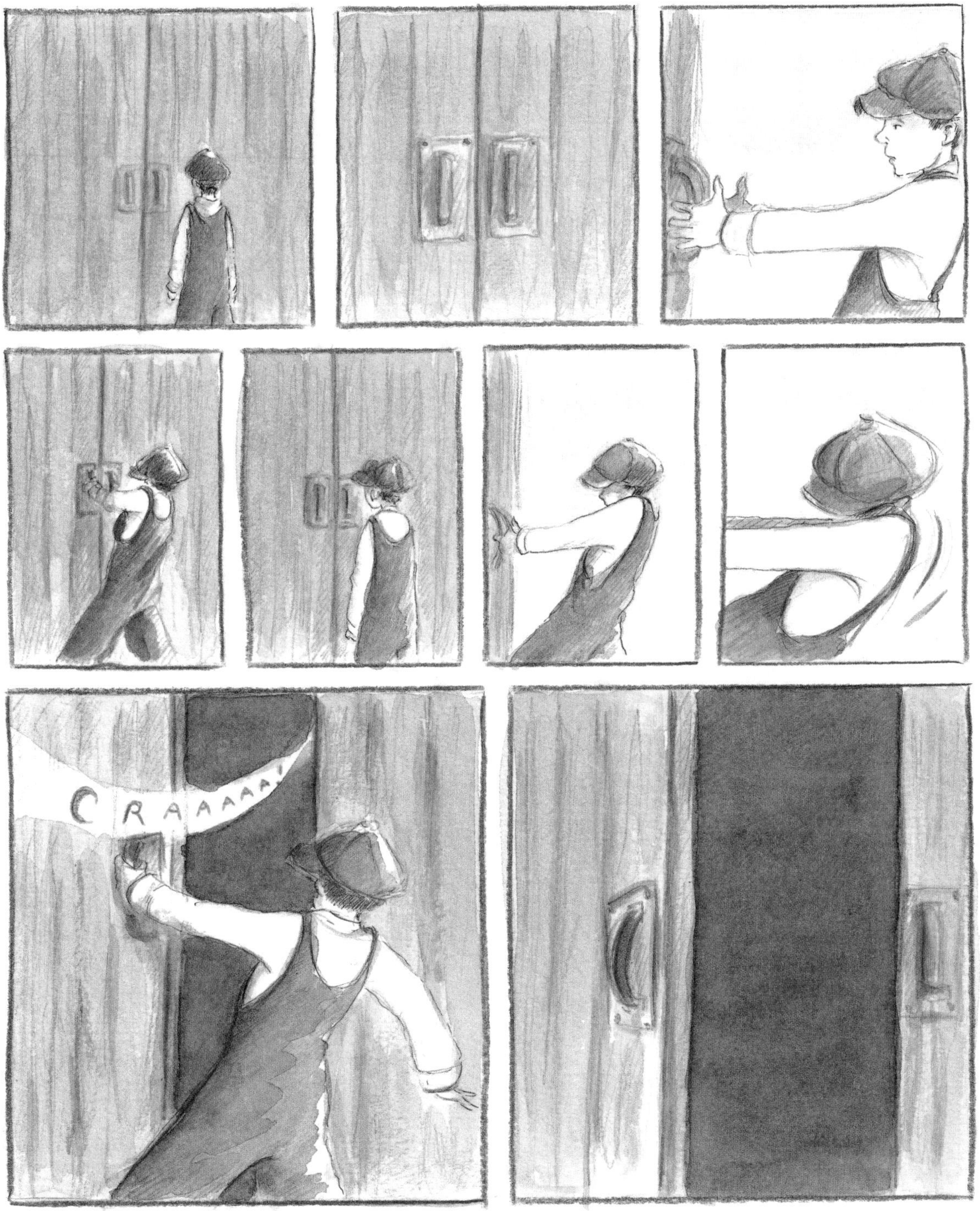
CRAAAAA!

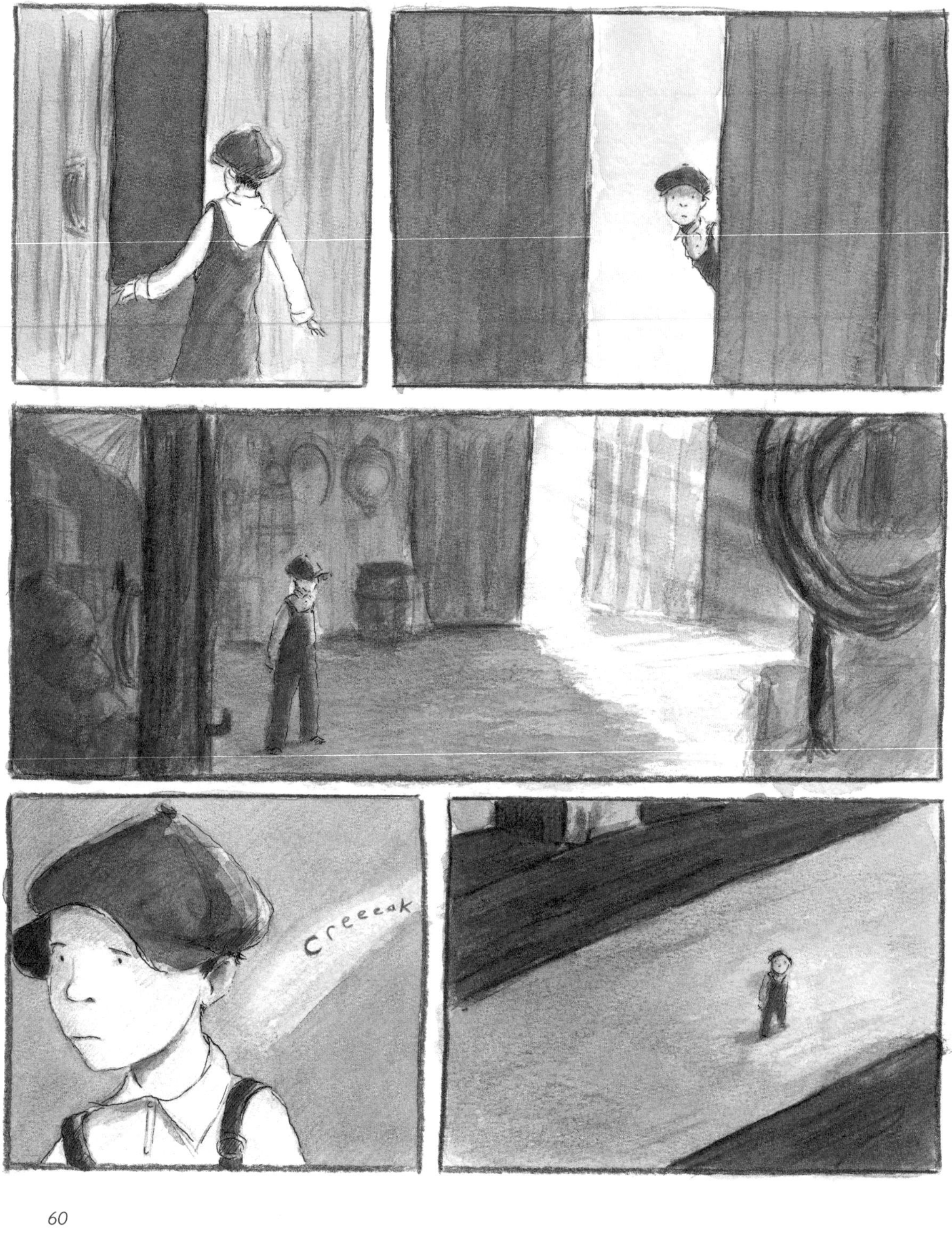
creeeak

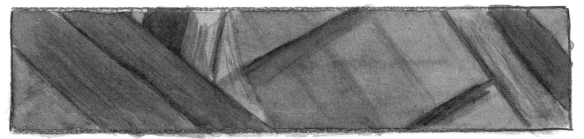

splish

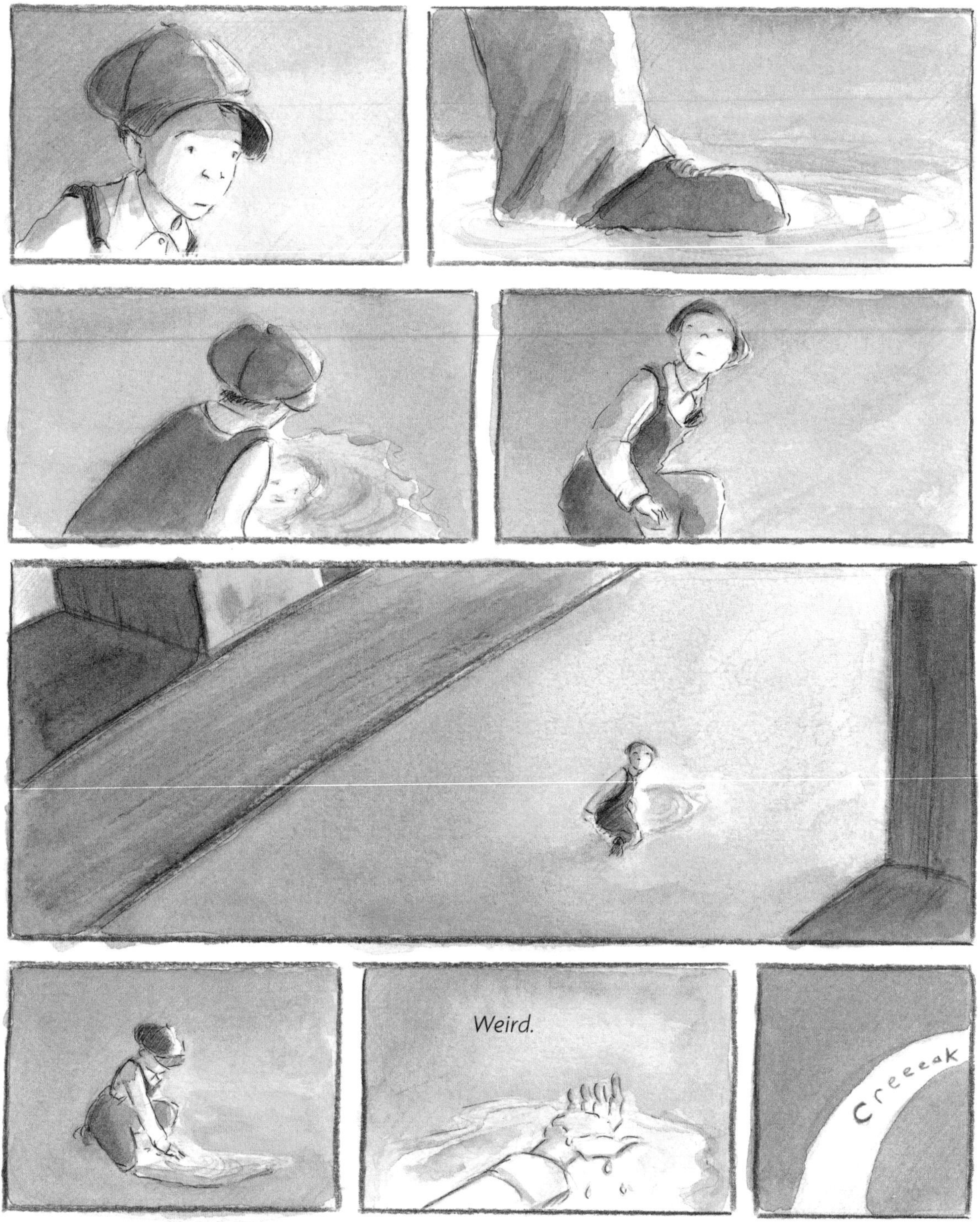
Weird.
Creeeak

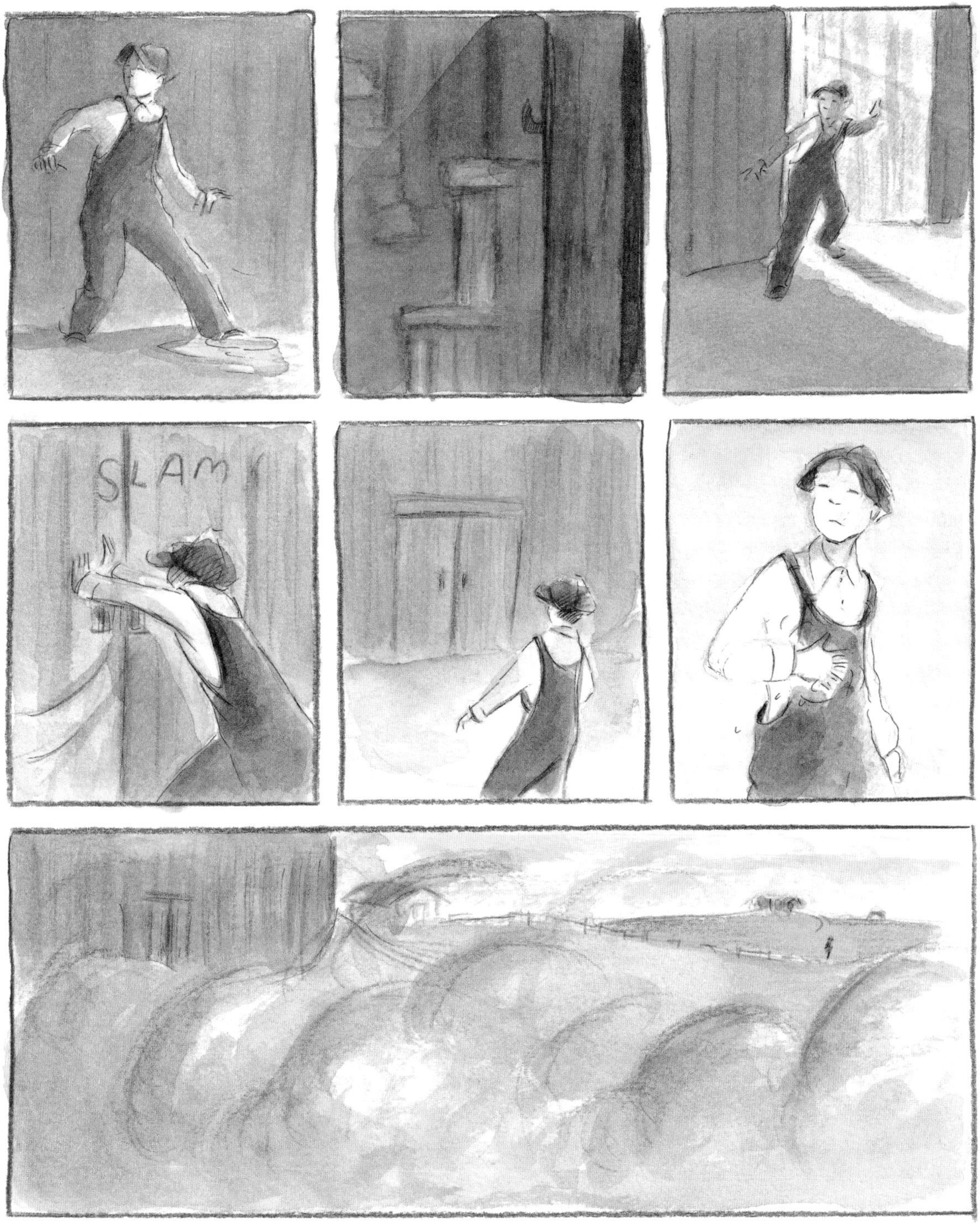
SLAM!

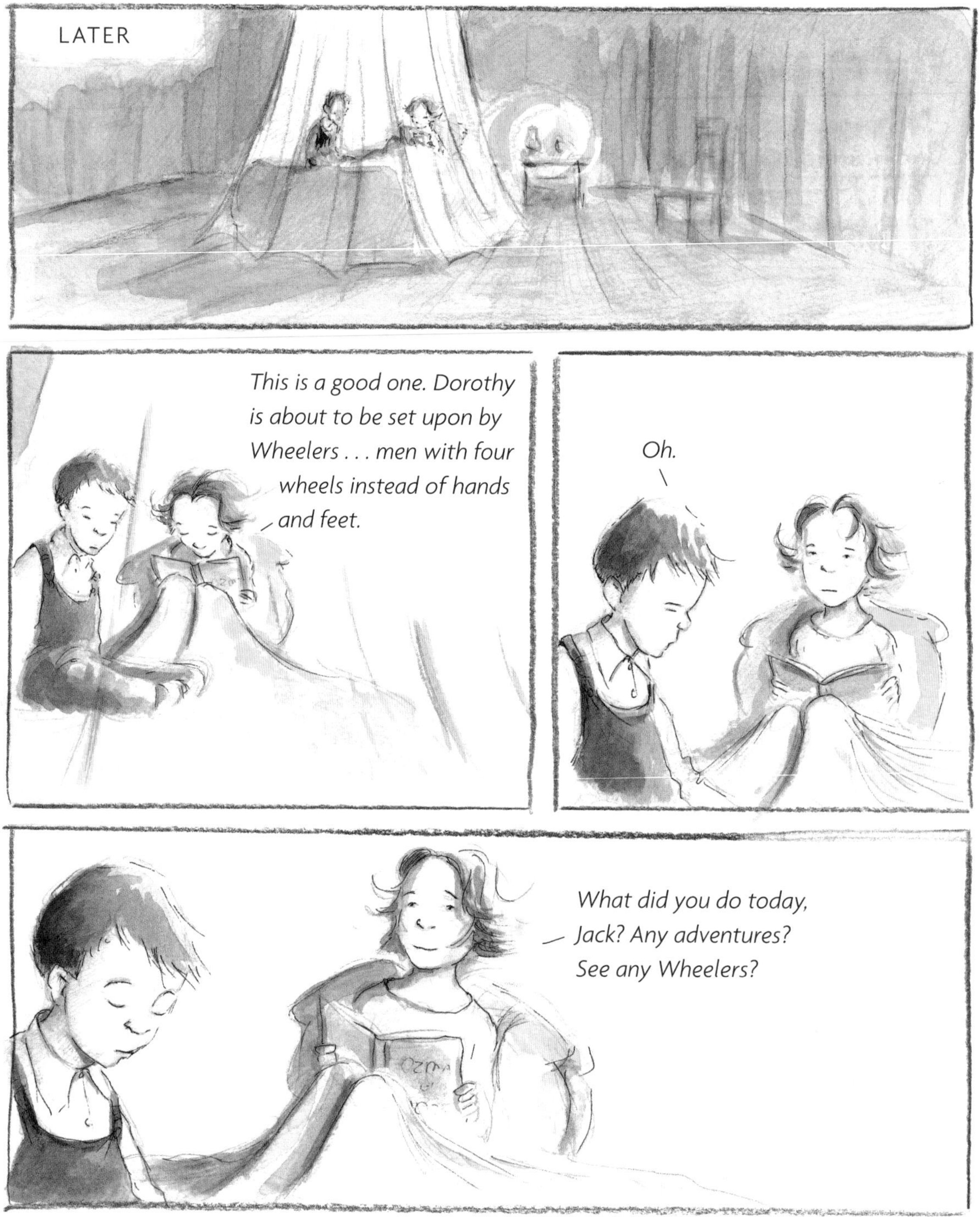
LATER
This is a good one. Dorothy is about to be set upon by Wheelers . . . men with four wheels instead of hands and feet.
Oh.
What did you do today, Jack? Any adventures? See any Wheelers?

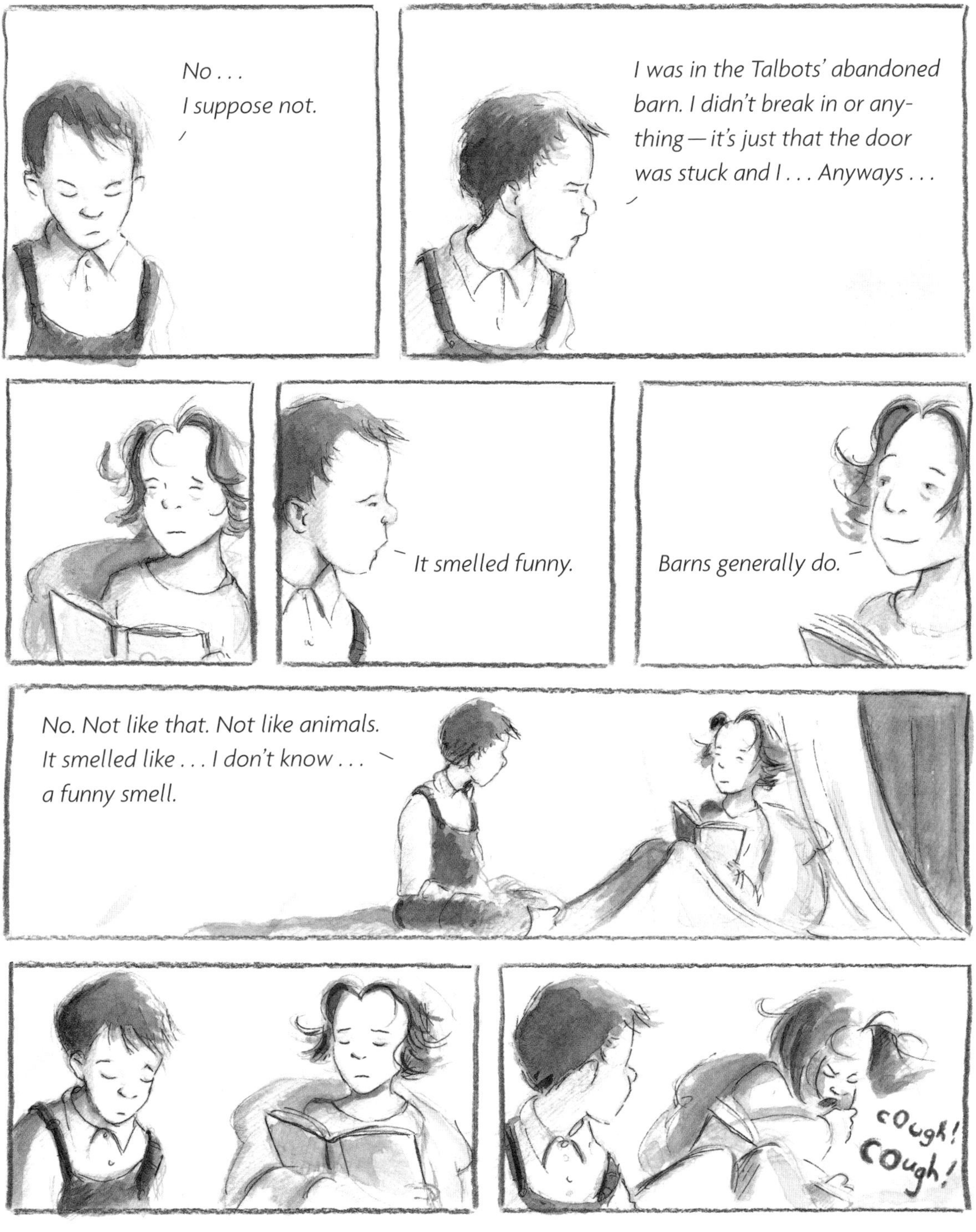
No . . .
I suppose not.
I was in the Talbots' abandoned barn. I didn't break in or any-thing — it's just that the door was stuck and I . . . Anyways . . .
It smelled funny.
Barns generally do.
No. Not like that. Not like animals. It smelled like . . . I don't know . . . a funny smell.
cough! cough!

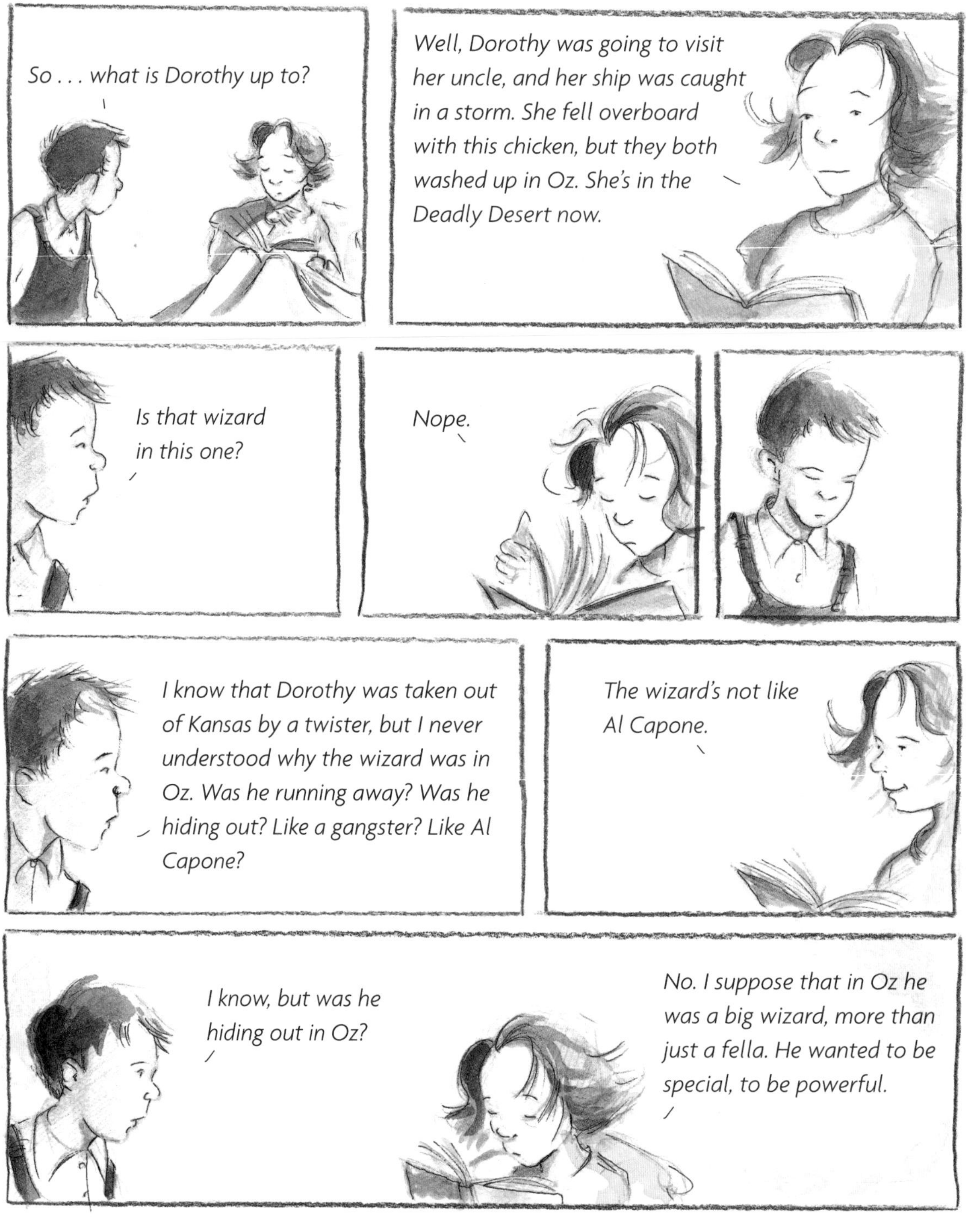
So . . . what is Dorothy up to?
Well, Dorothy was going to visit her uncle, and her ship was caught in a storm. She fell overboard with this chicken, but they both washed up in Oz. She's in the Deadly Desert now.
Is that wizard in this one?
Nope.
I know that Dorothy was taken out of Kansas by a twister, but I never understood why the wizard was in Oz. Was he running away? Was he hiding out? Like a gangster? Like Al Capone?
The wizard's not like Al Capone.
I know, but was he hiding out in Oz?
No. I suppose that in Oz he was a big wizard, more than just a fella. He wanted to be special, to be powerful.

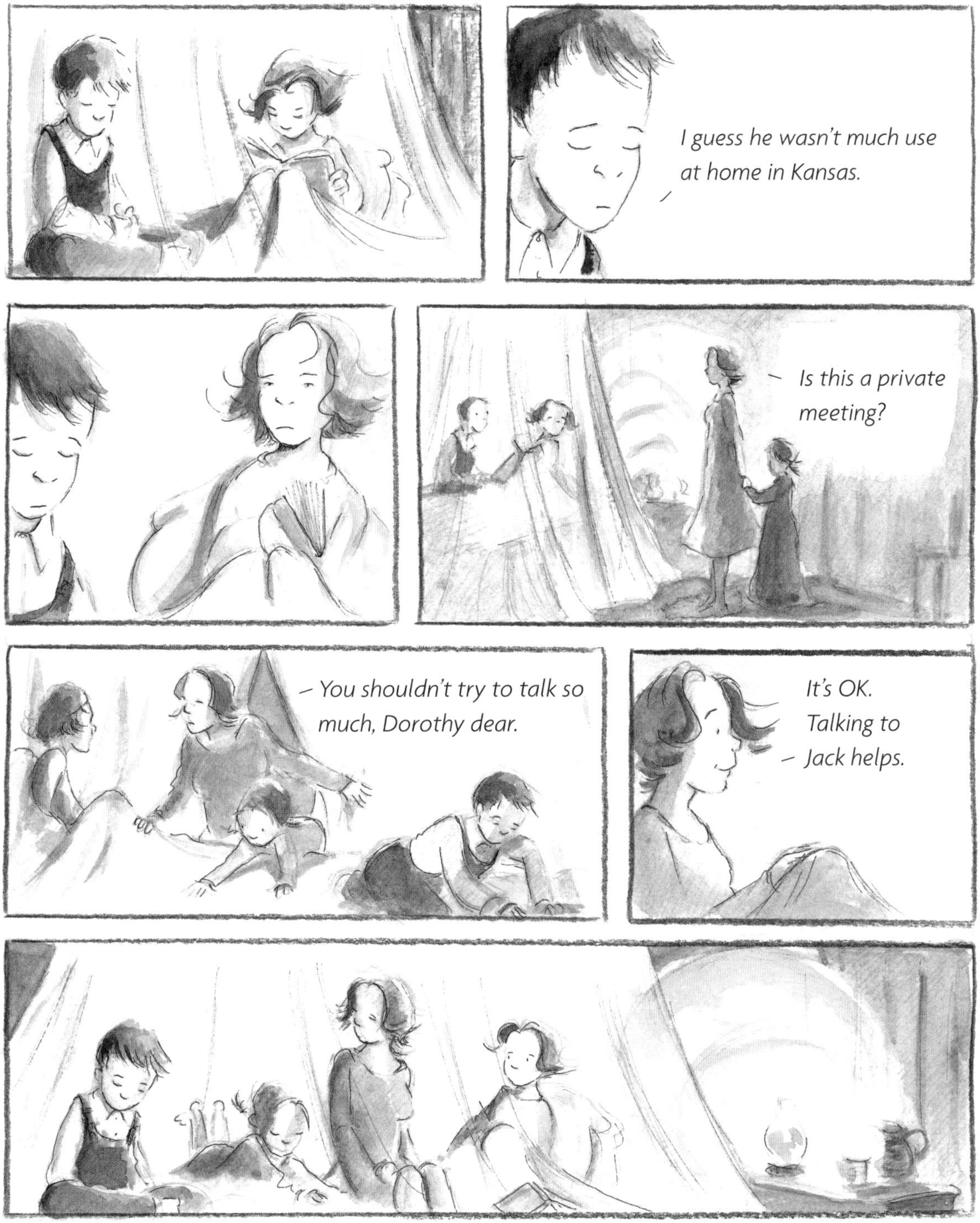
I guess he wasn't much use at home in Kansas.
Is this a private meeting?
You shouldn't try to talk so much, Dorothy dear.
It's OK. Talking to Jack helps.

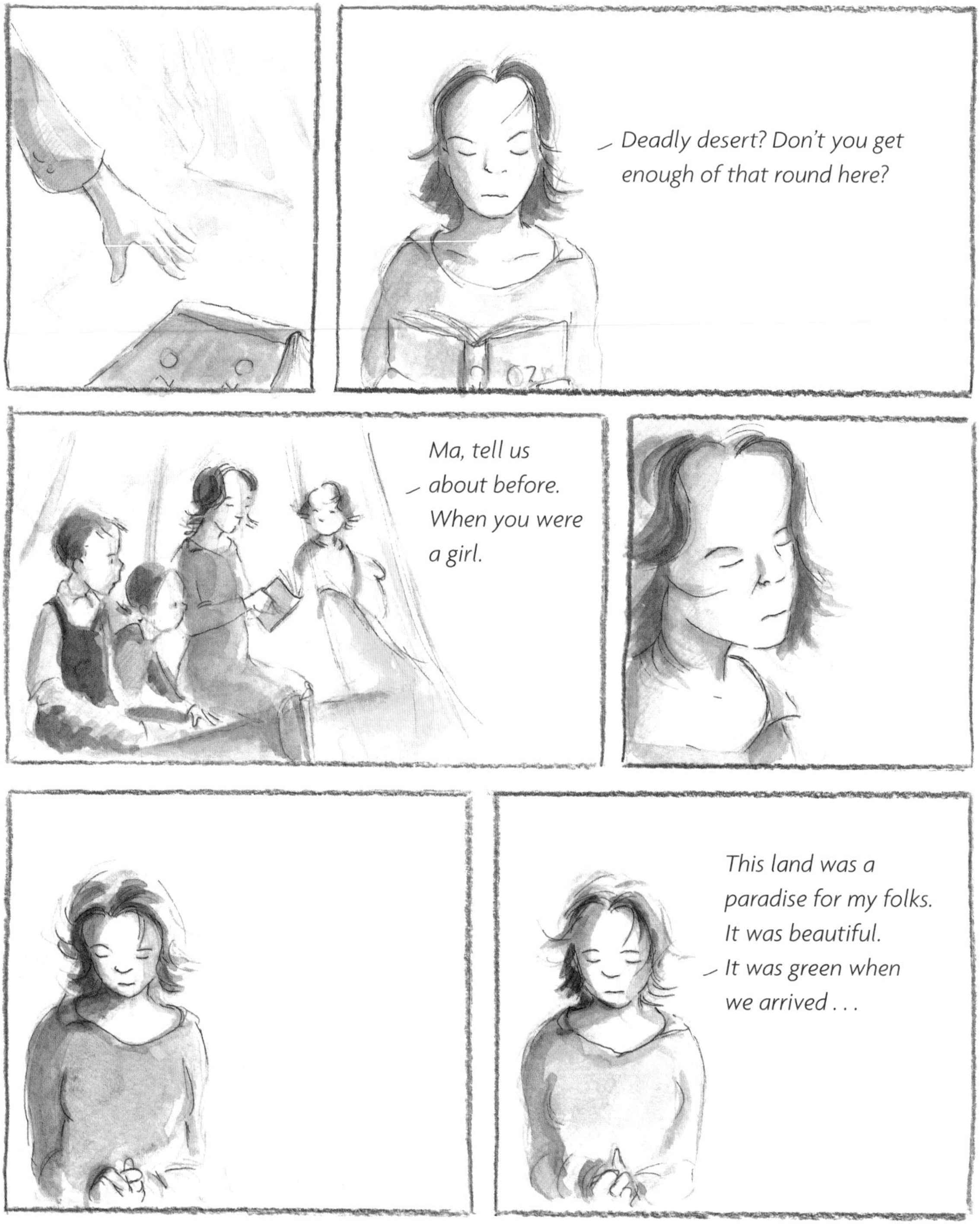
Deadly desert? Don't you get enough of that round here?
Ma, tell us about before. When you were a girl.
This land was a paradise for my folks. It was beautiful. It was green when we arrived . . .

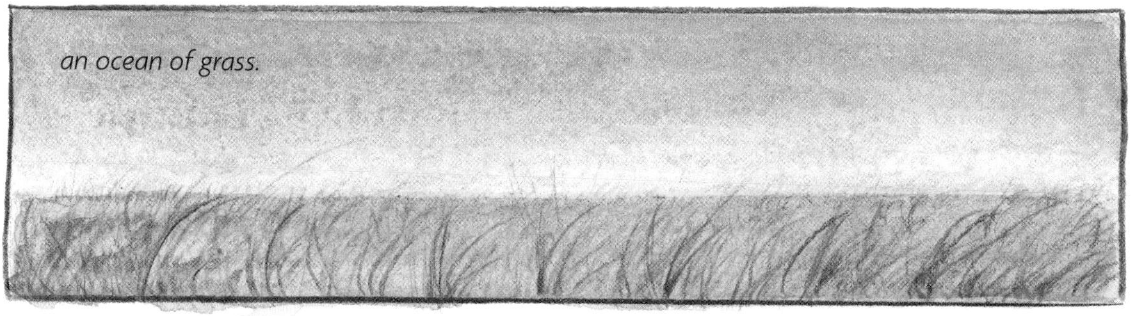
an ocean of grass.

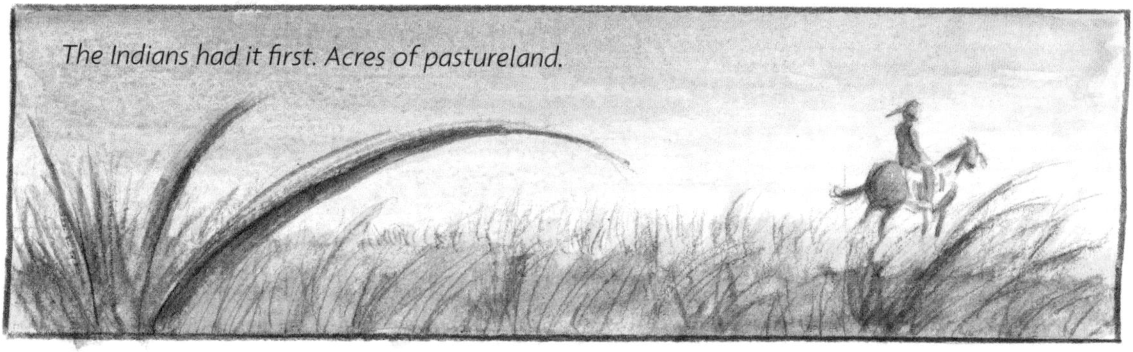
The Indians had it first. Acres of pastureland.

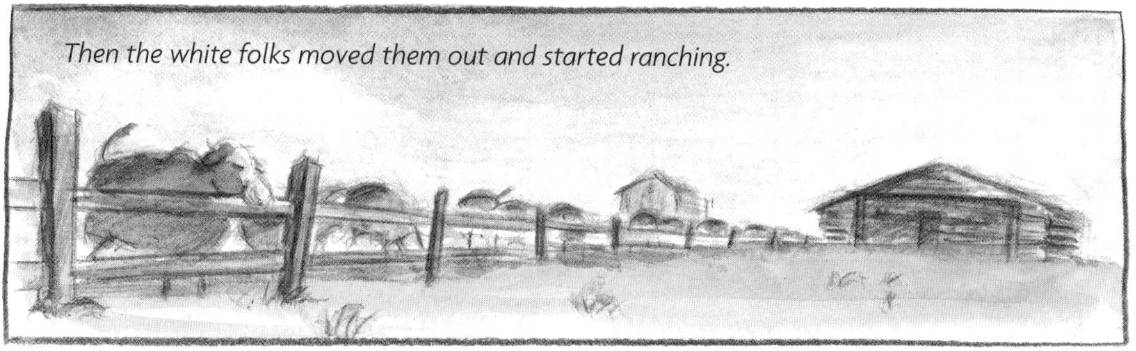
Then the white folks moved them out and started ranching.

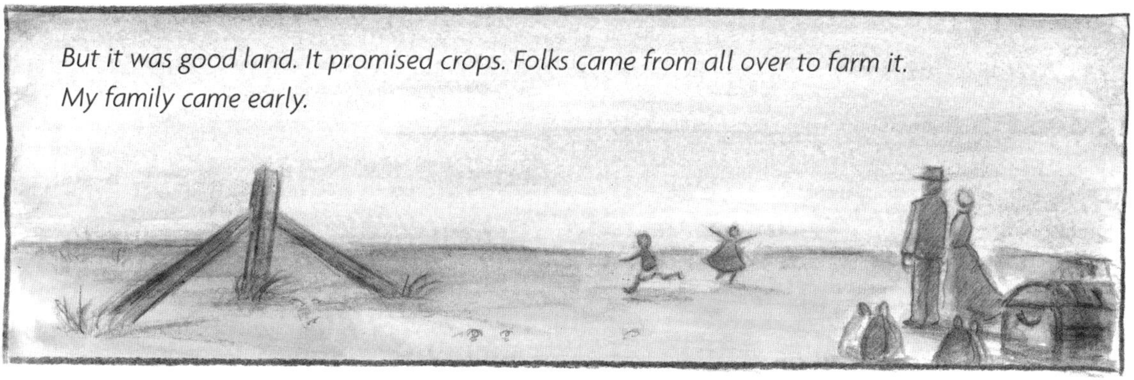
But it was good land. It promised crops. Folks came from all over to farm it.
My family came early.

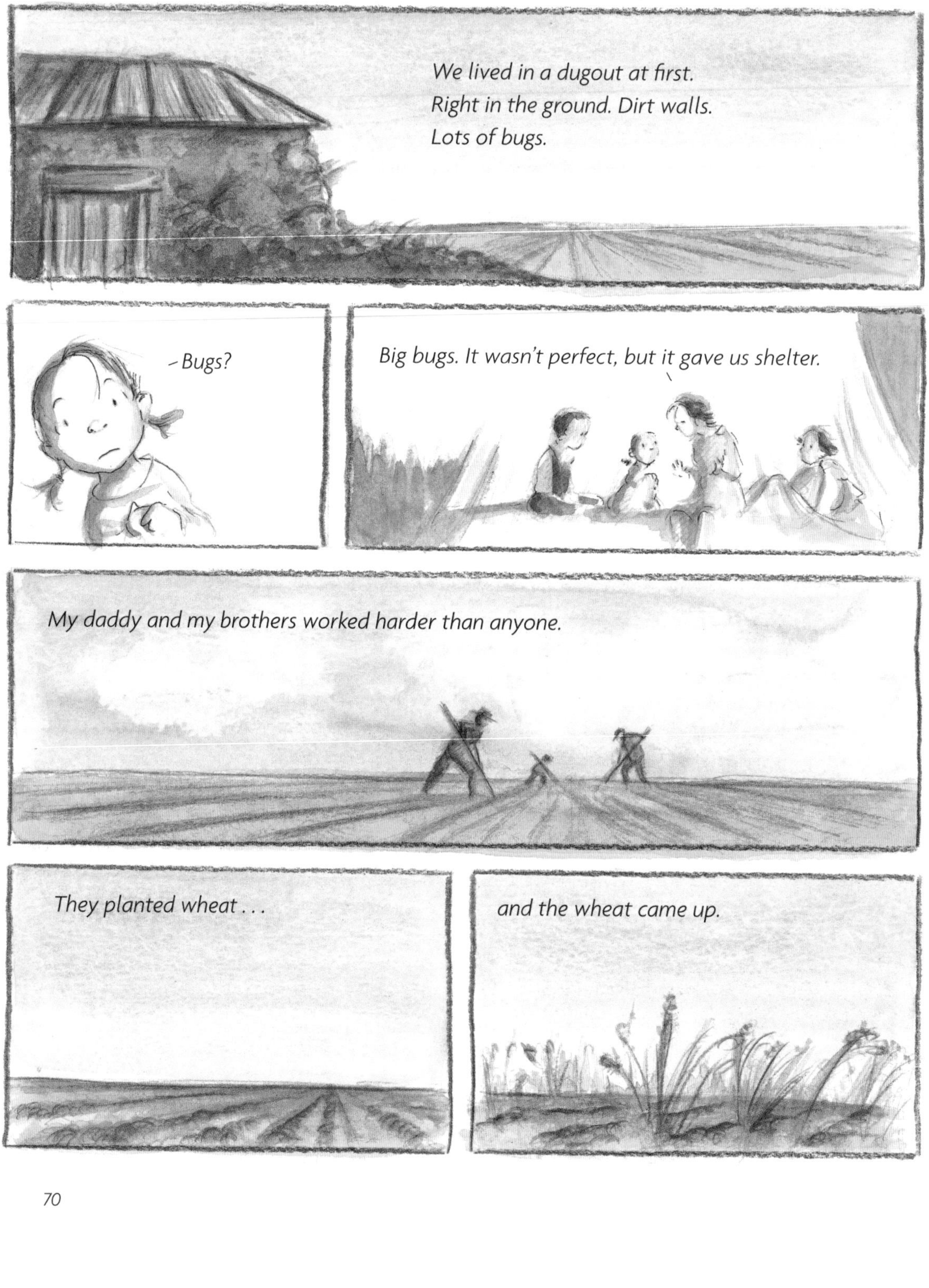
We lived in a dugout at first.
Right in the ground. Dirt walls.
Lots of bugs.
Bugs?
Big bugs. It wasn't perfect, but it gave us shelter.
My daddy and my brothers worked harder than anyone.
They planted wheat . . .
and the wheat came up.

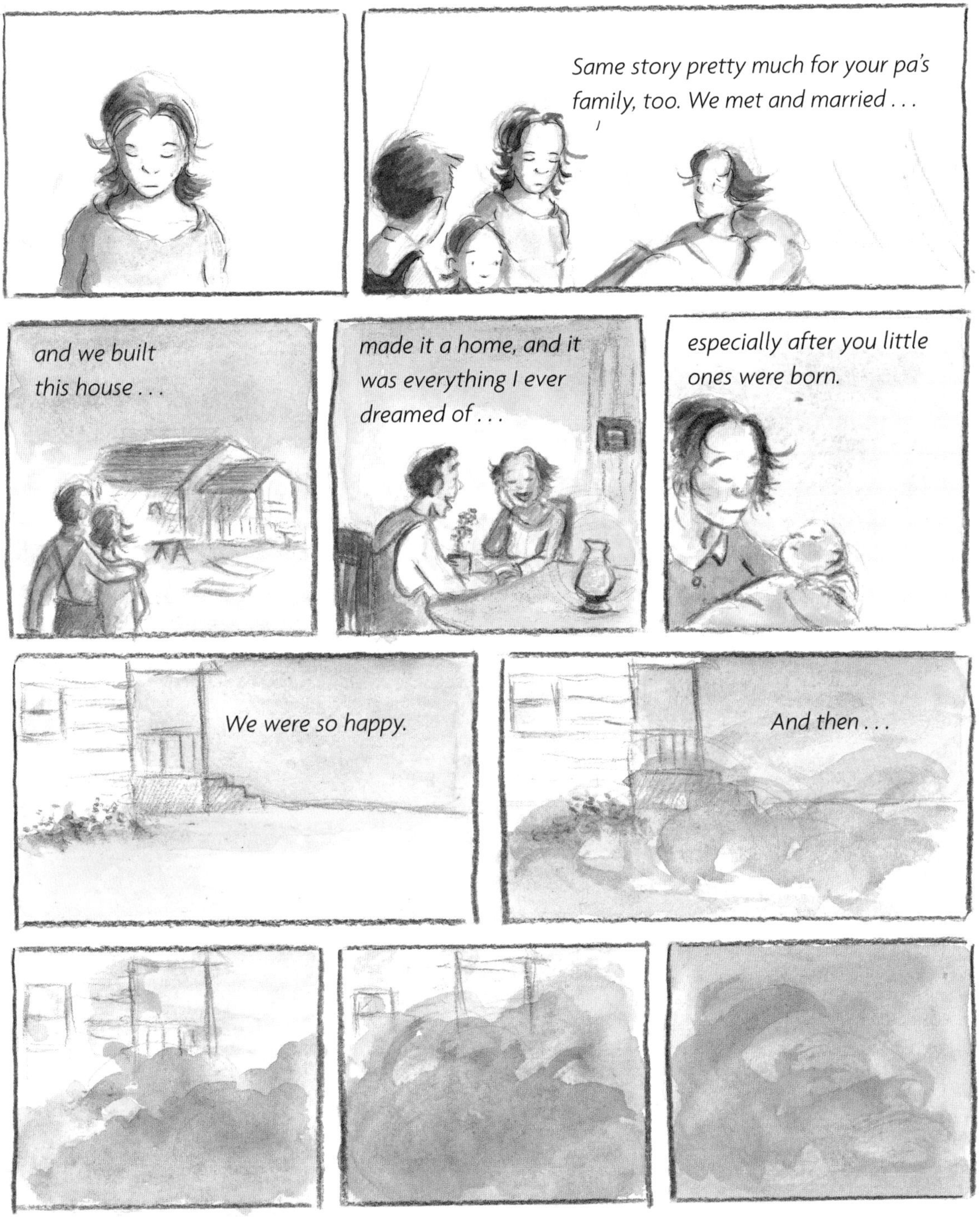
Same story pretty much for your pa's family, too. We met and married . . .
and we built this house . . .
made it a home, and it was everything I ever dreamed of . . .
especially after you little ones were born.
We were so happy.
And then . . .

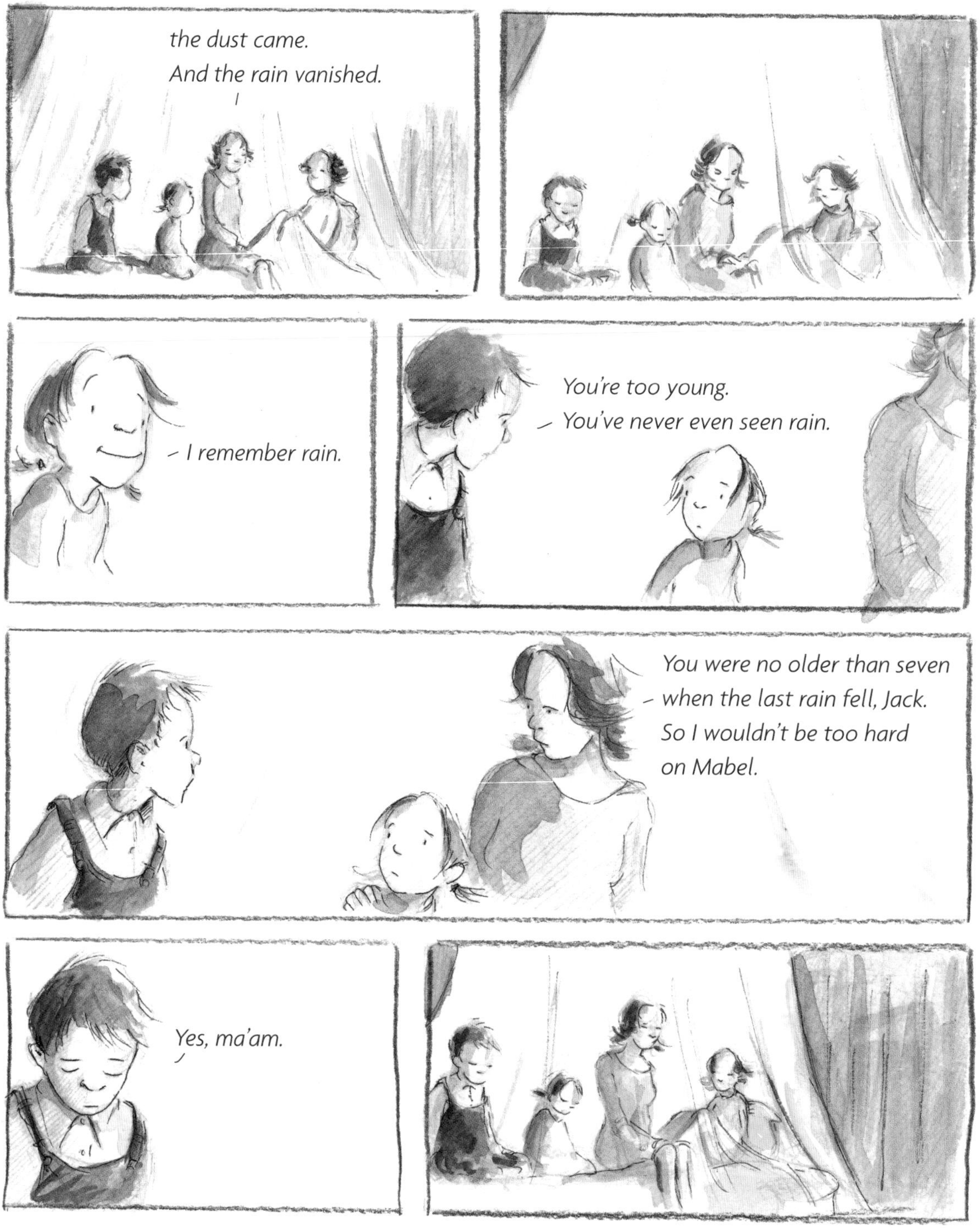

the dust came.
And the rain vanished.
I remember rain.
You're too young.
You've never even seen rain.
You were no older than seven when the last rain fell, Jack. So I wouldn't be too hard on Mabel.
Yes, ma'am.

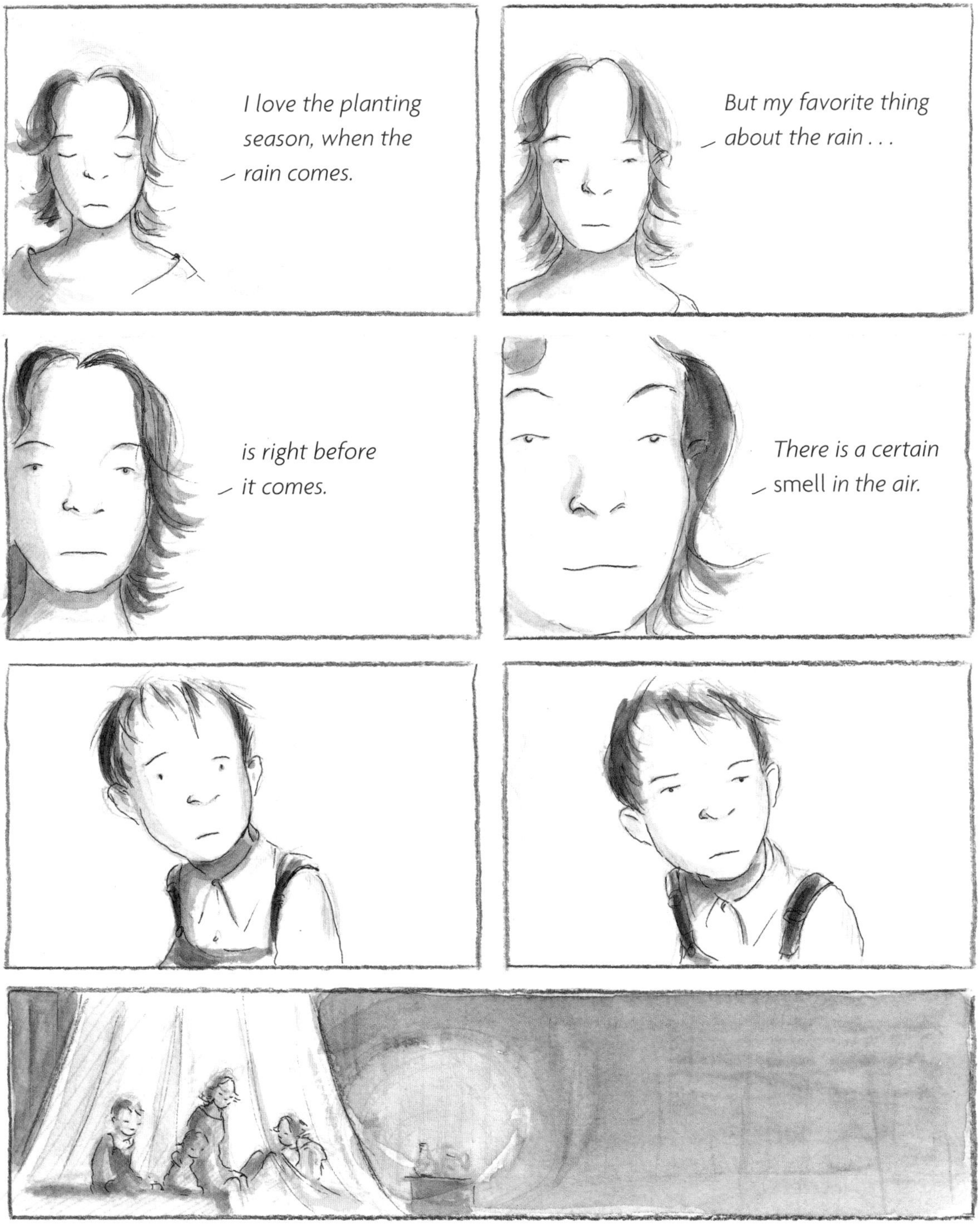
I love the planting season, when the rain comes.
But my favorite thing about the rain . . .
is right before it comes.
There is a certain smell in the air.

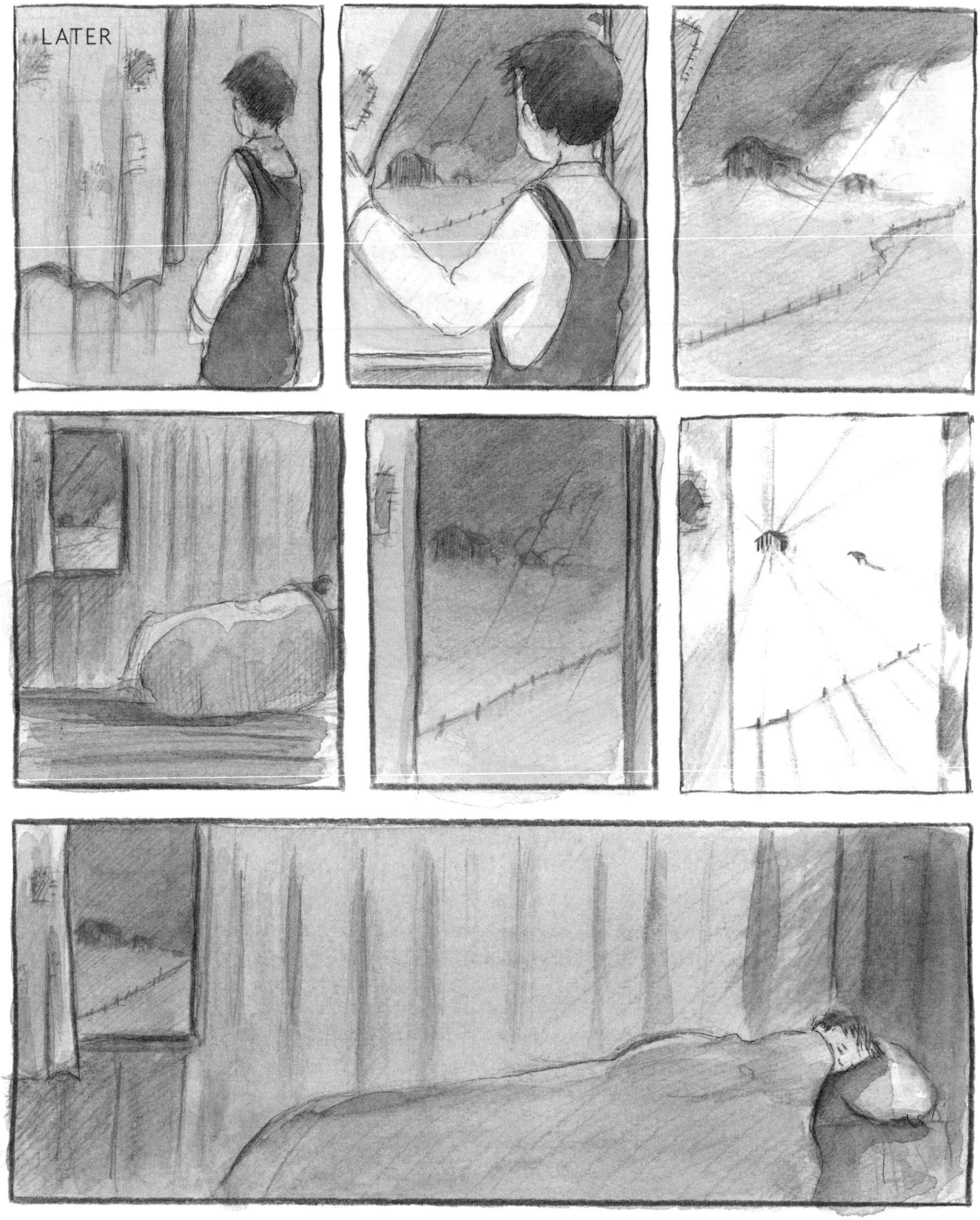
LATER

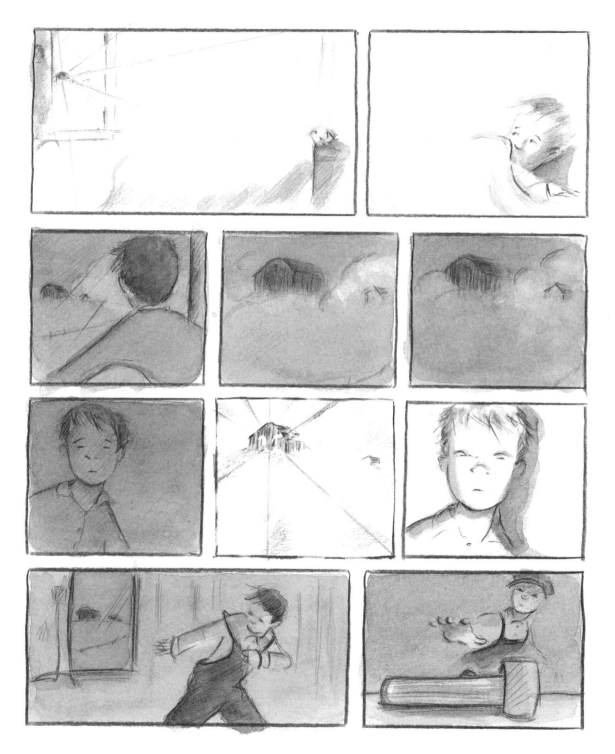

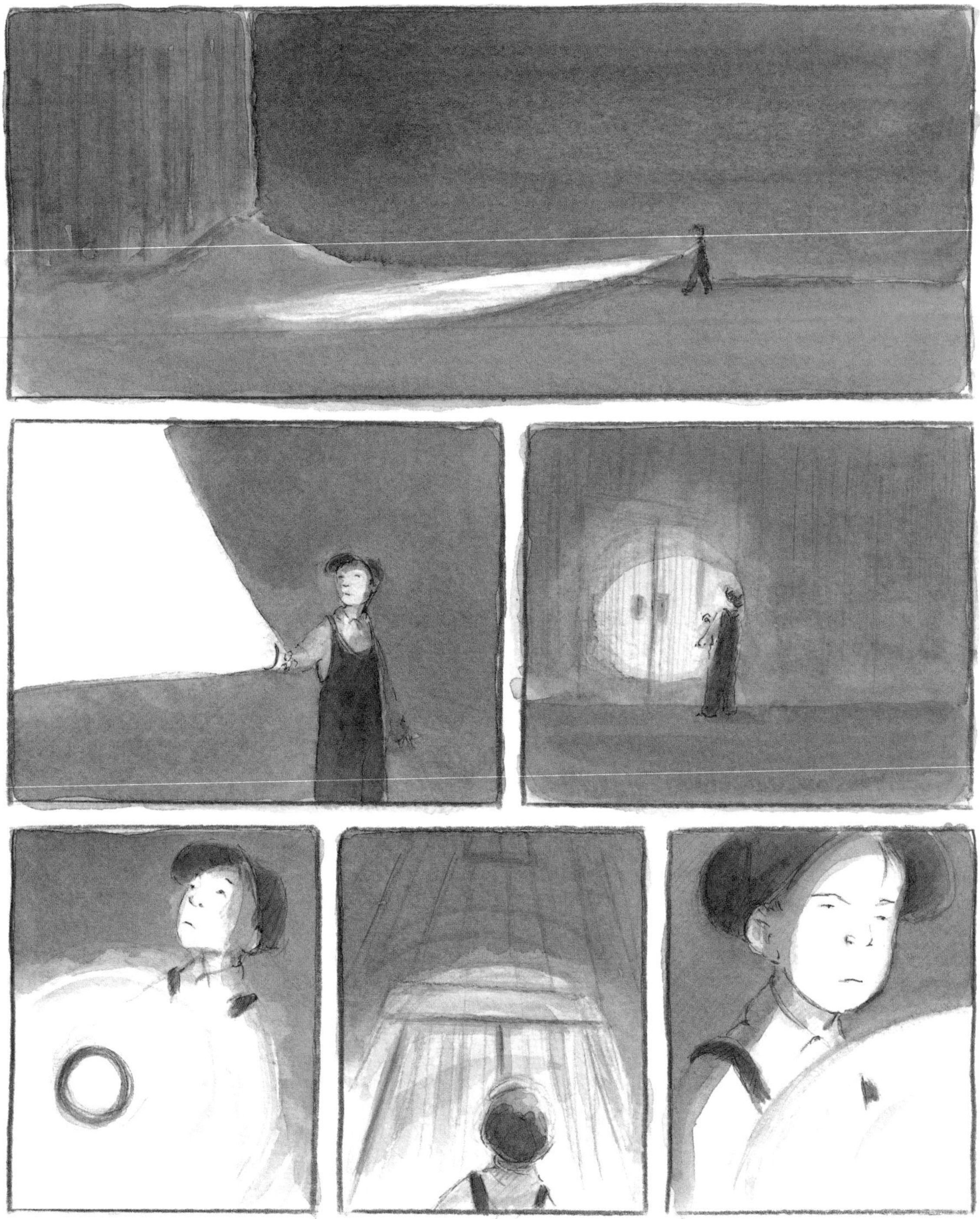

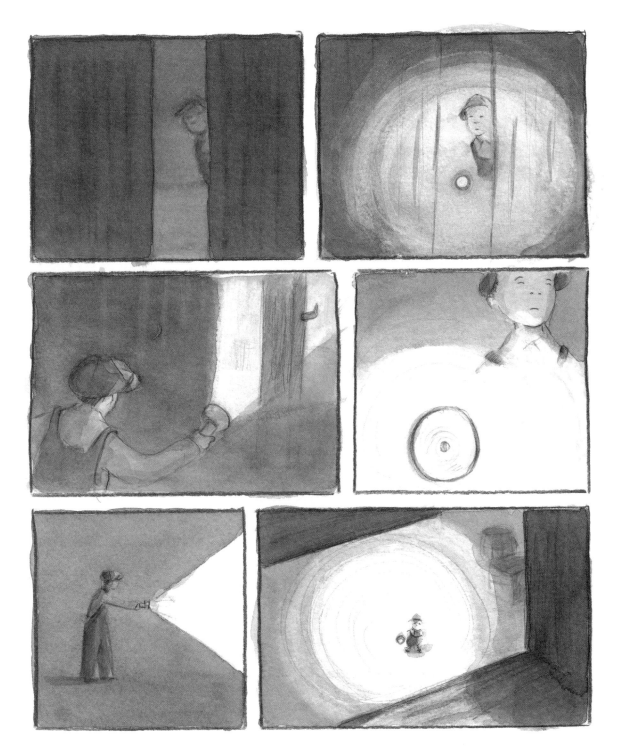

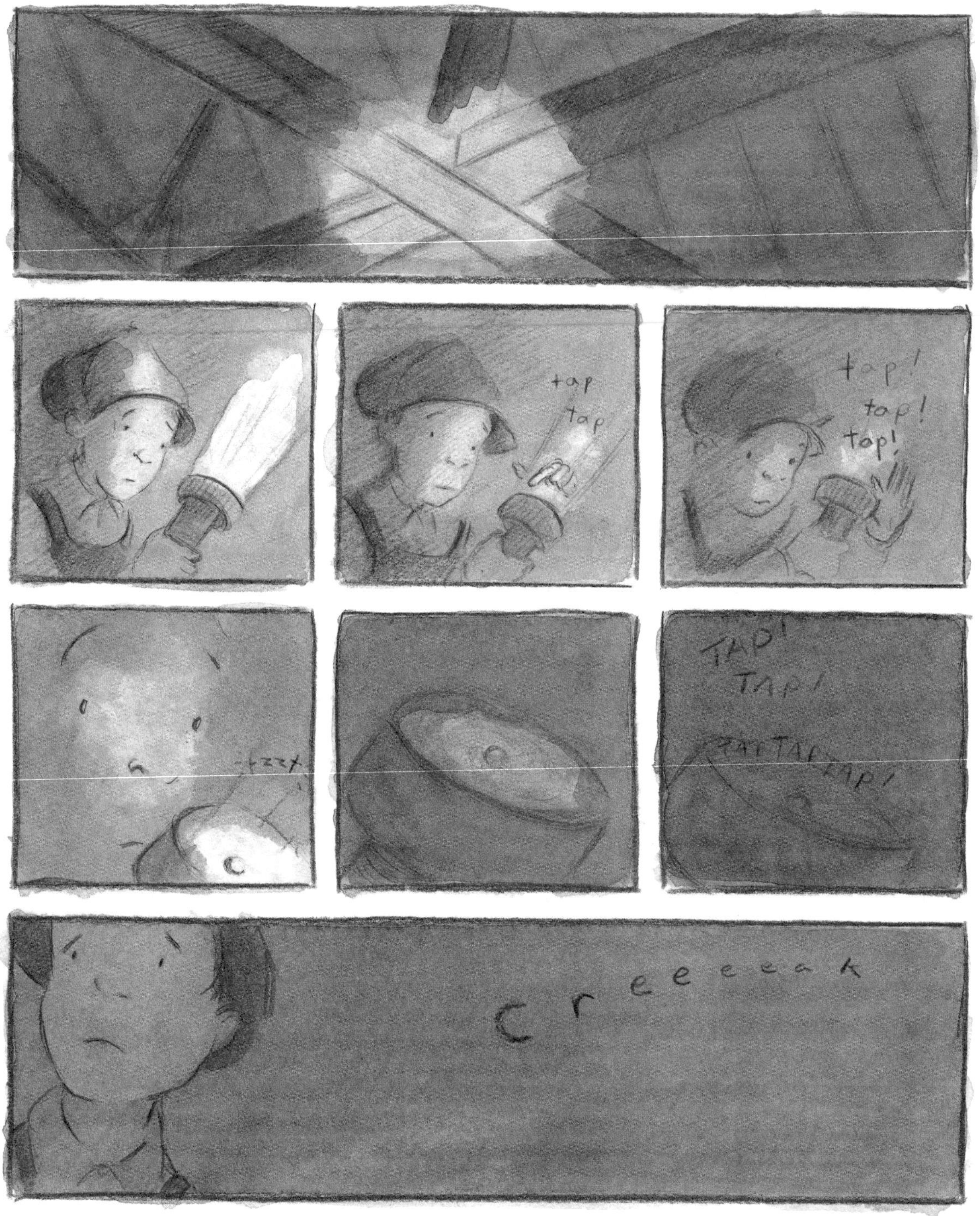
tap
tap
tap!
tap!
tap!
-fzzt-
TAP!
TAP!
TAPTAPTAP!
creeeeak

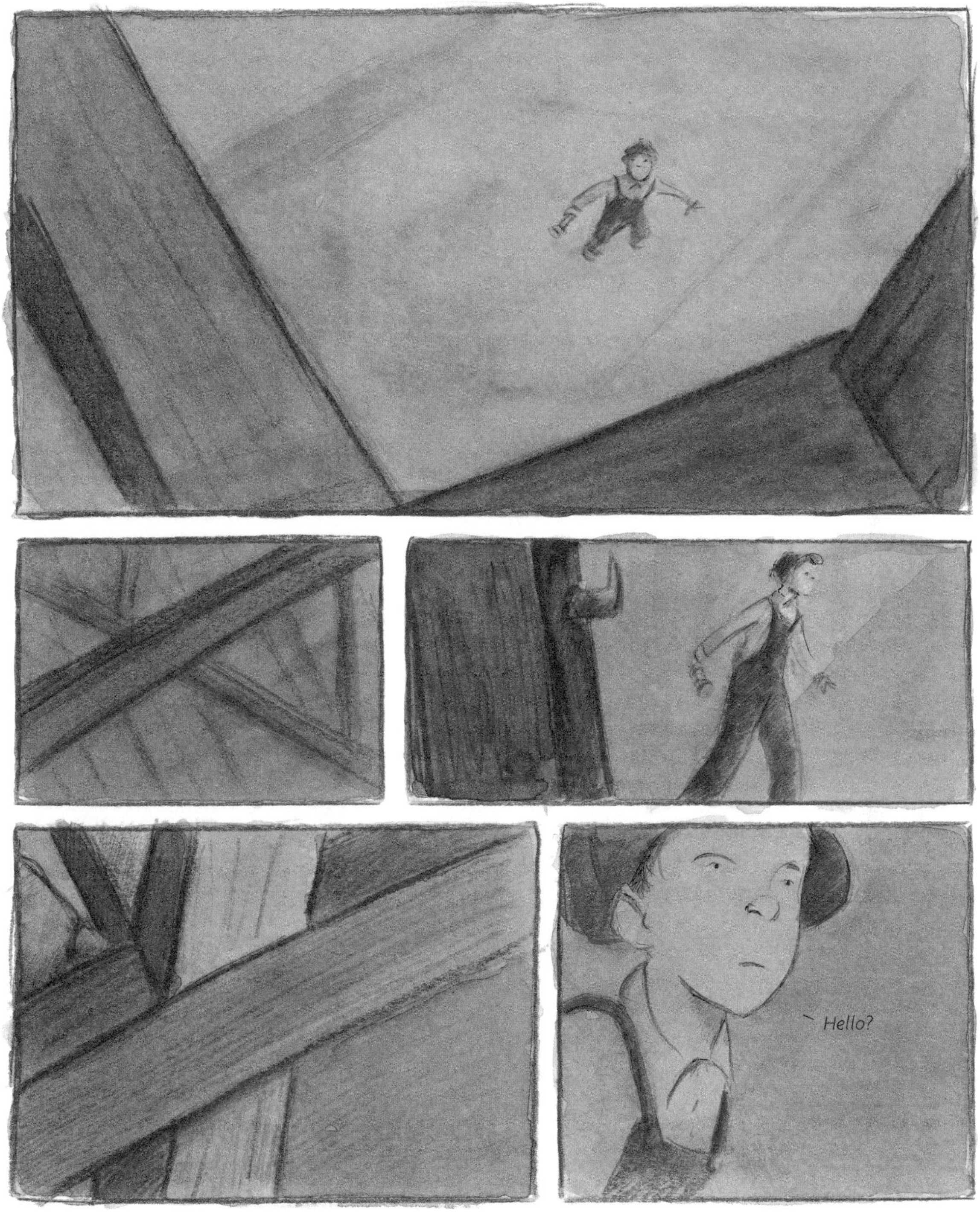
Hello?

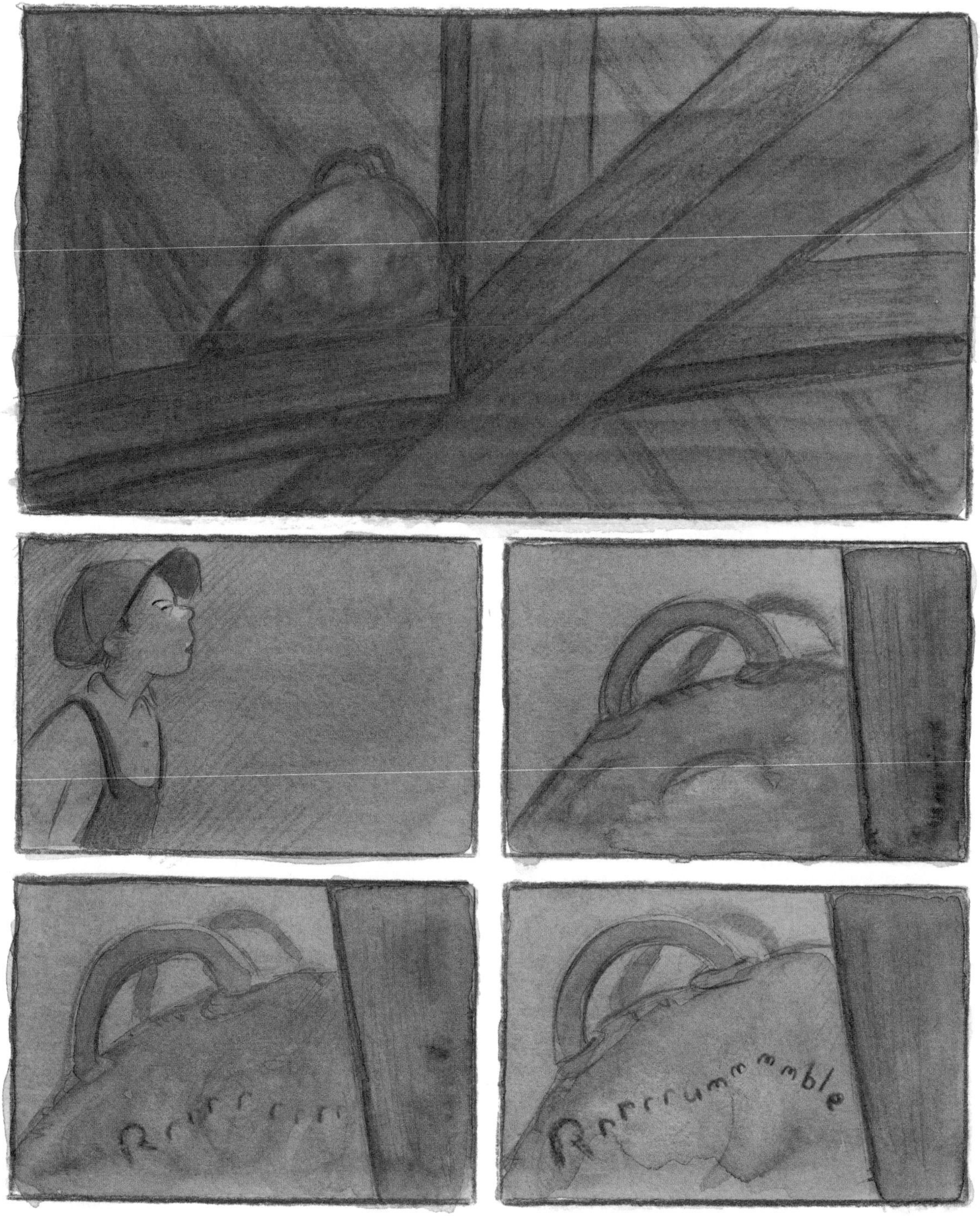
Rrrrrrrr
Rrrrrrummmmmble

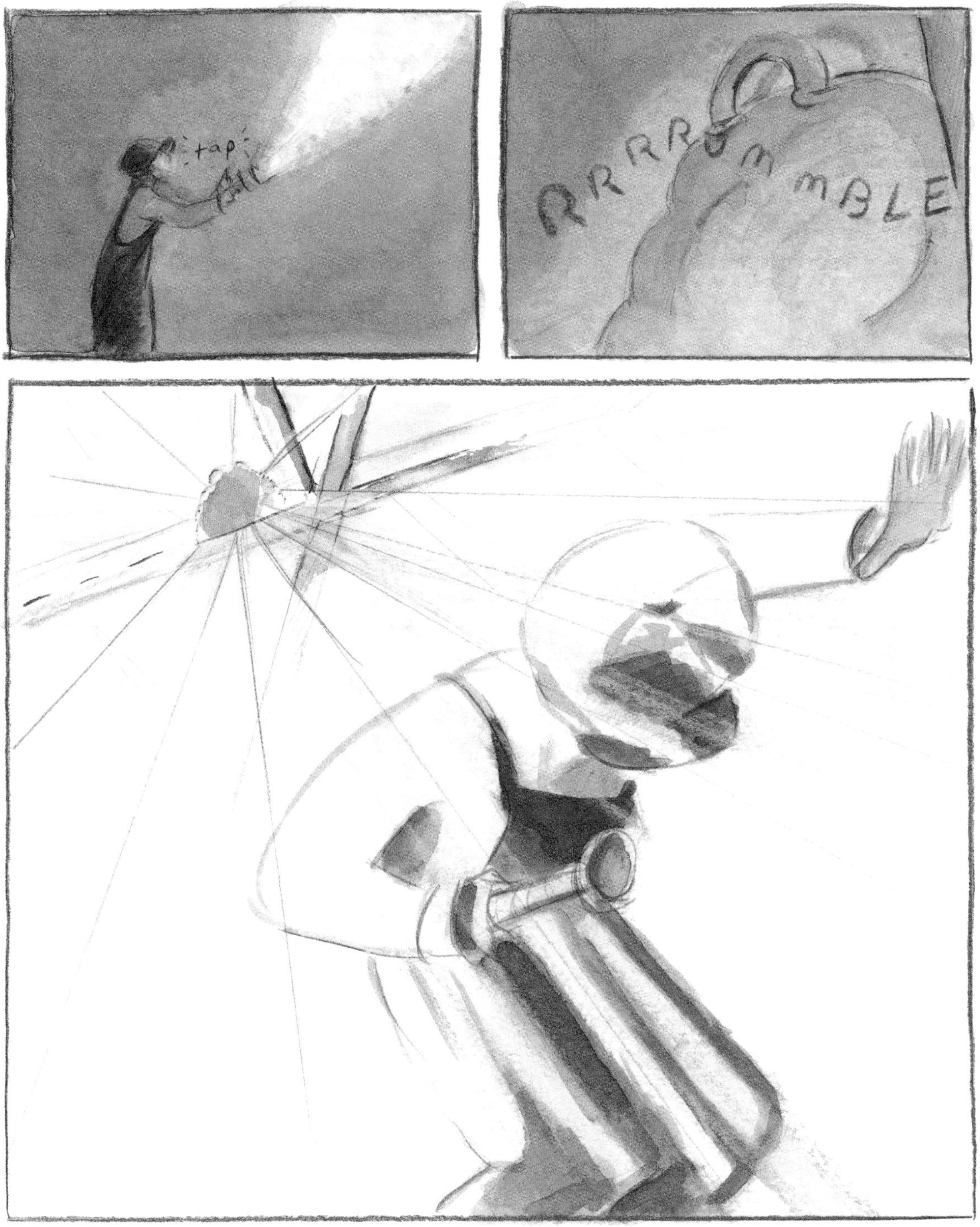
tap
RRRRummBLE

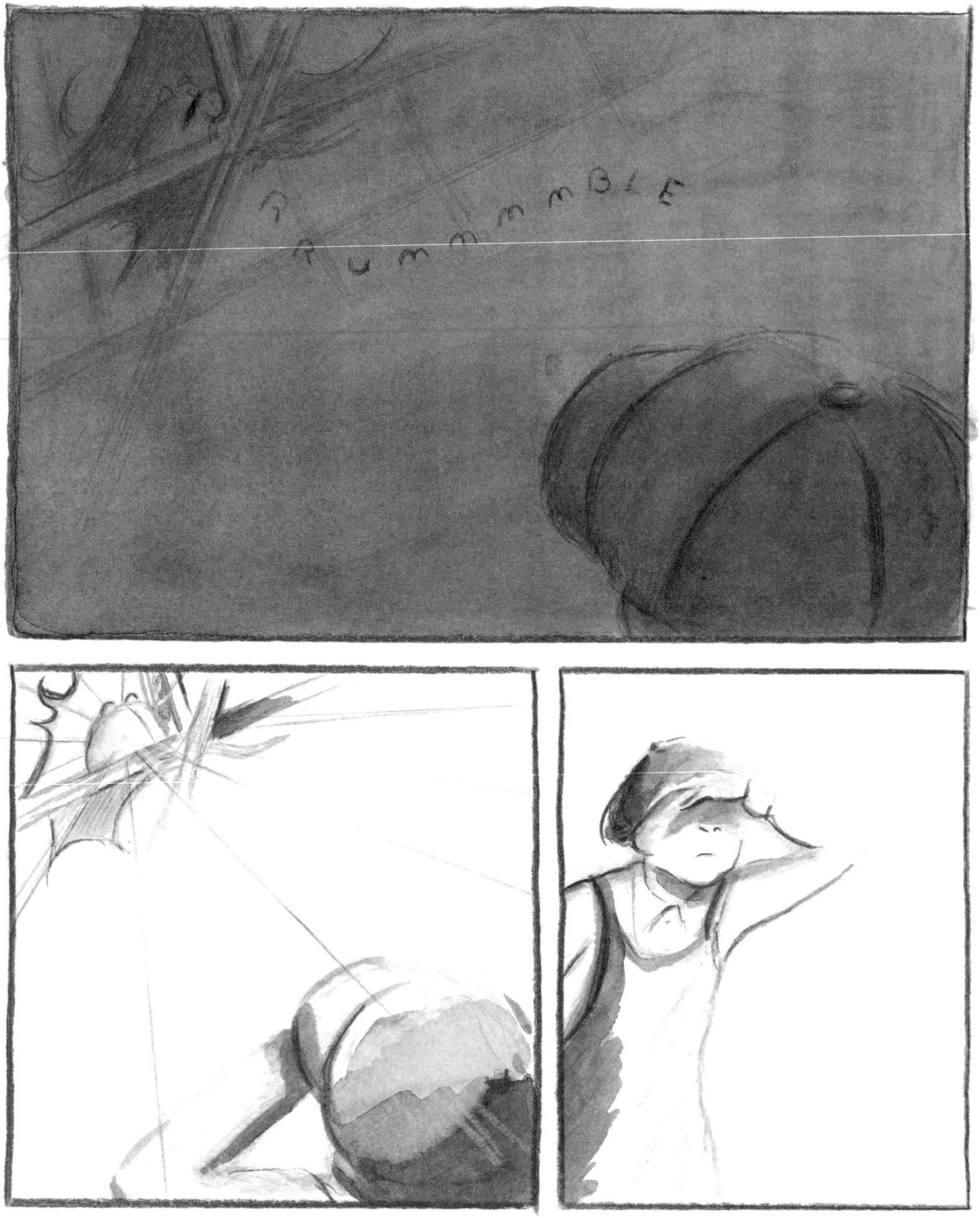
RRUMMMMBLE

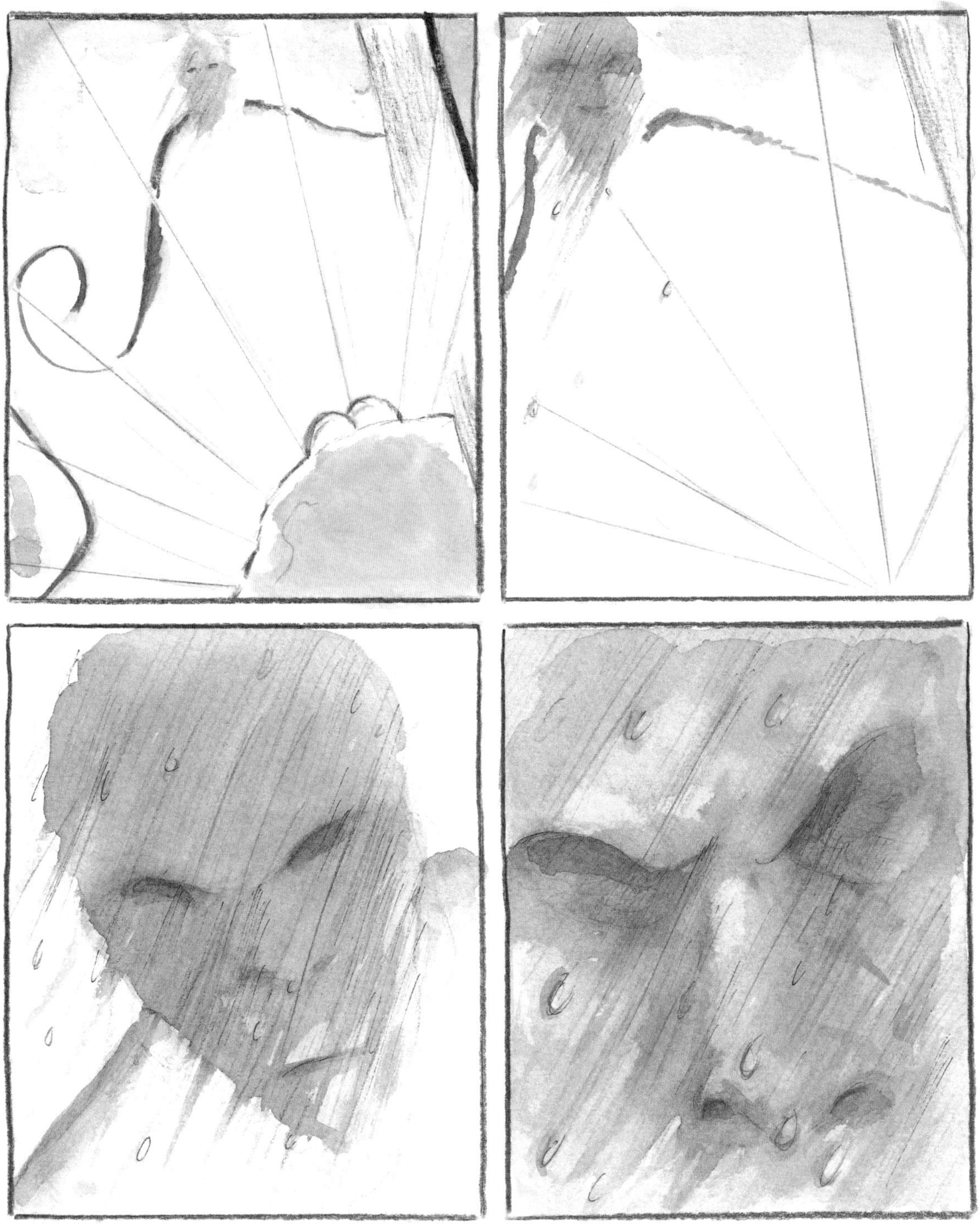

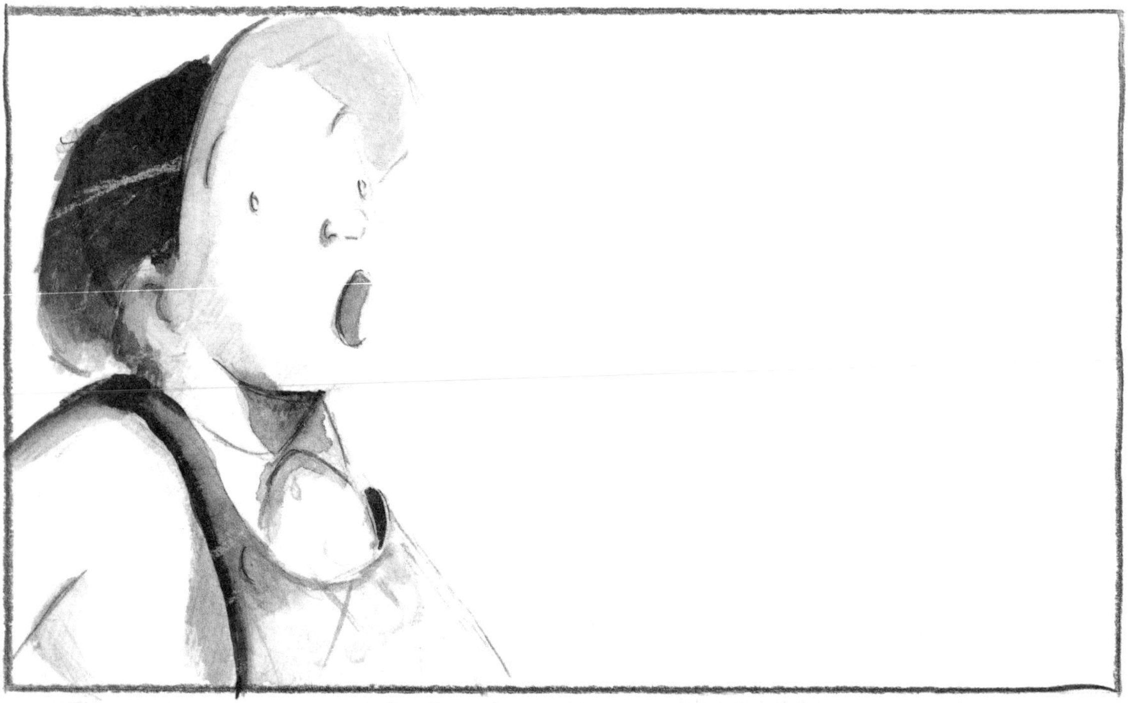

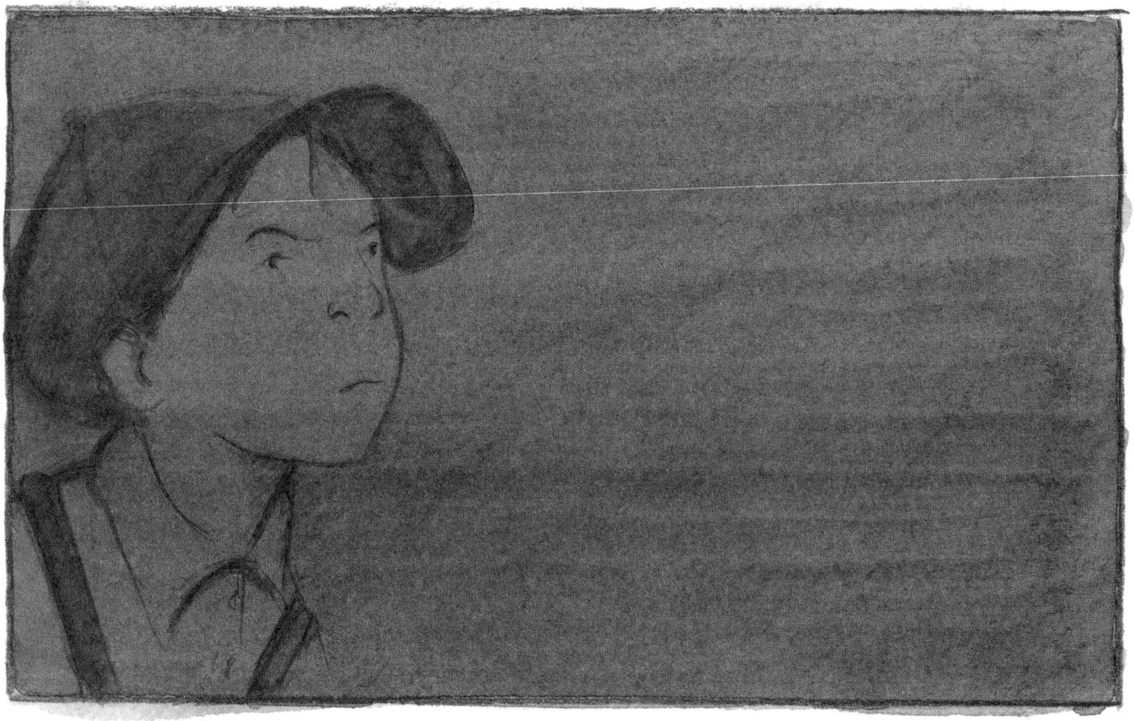

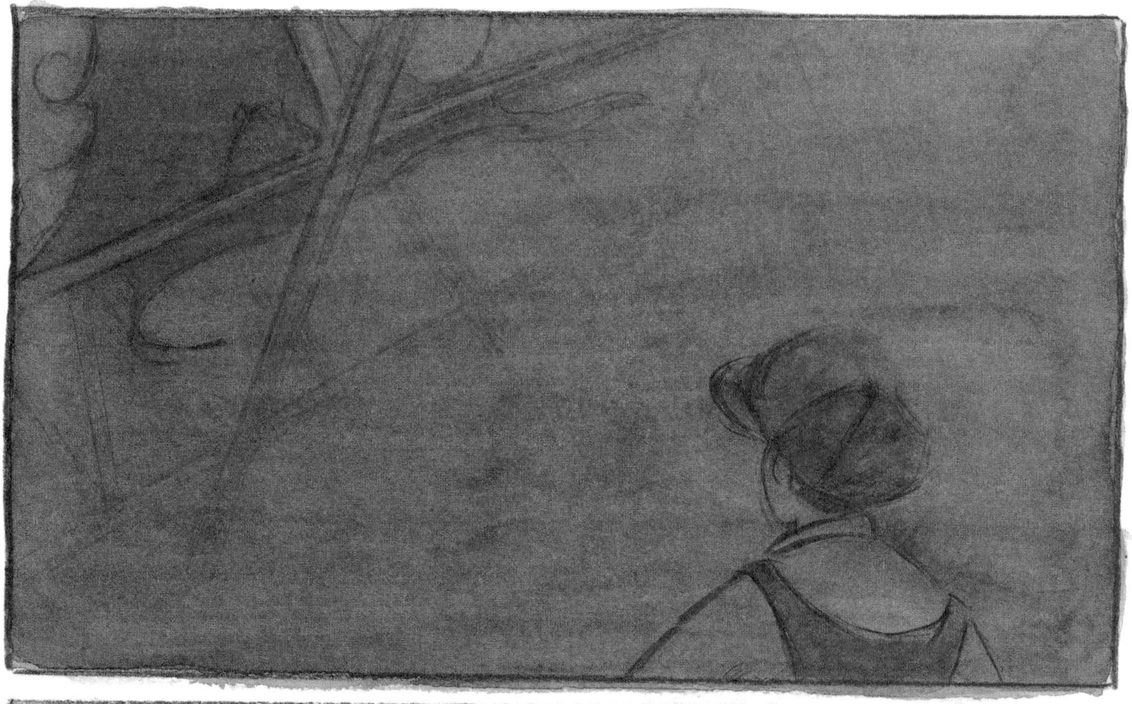

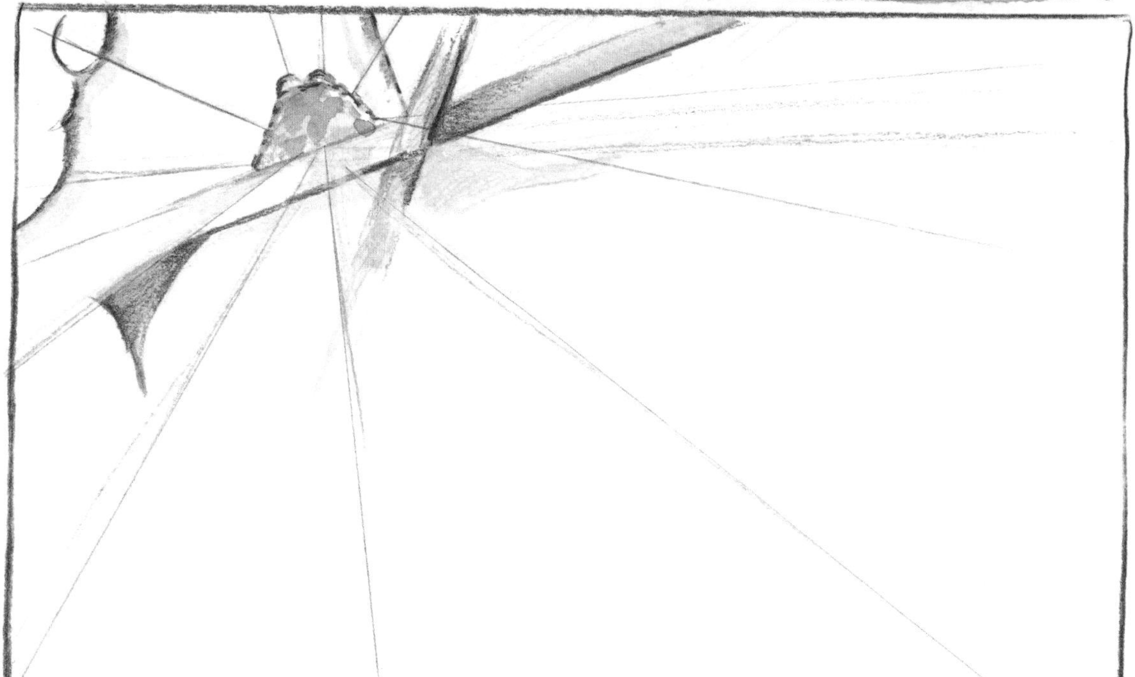

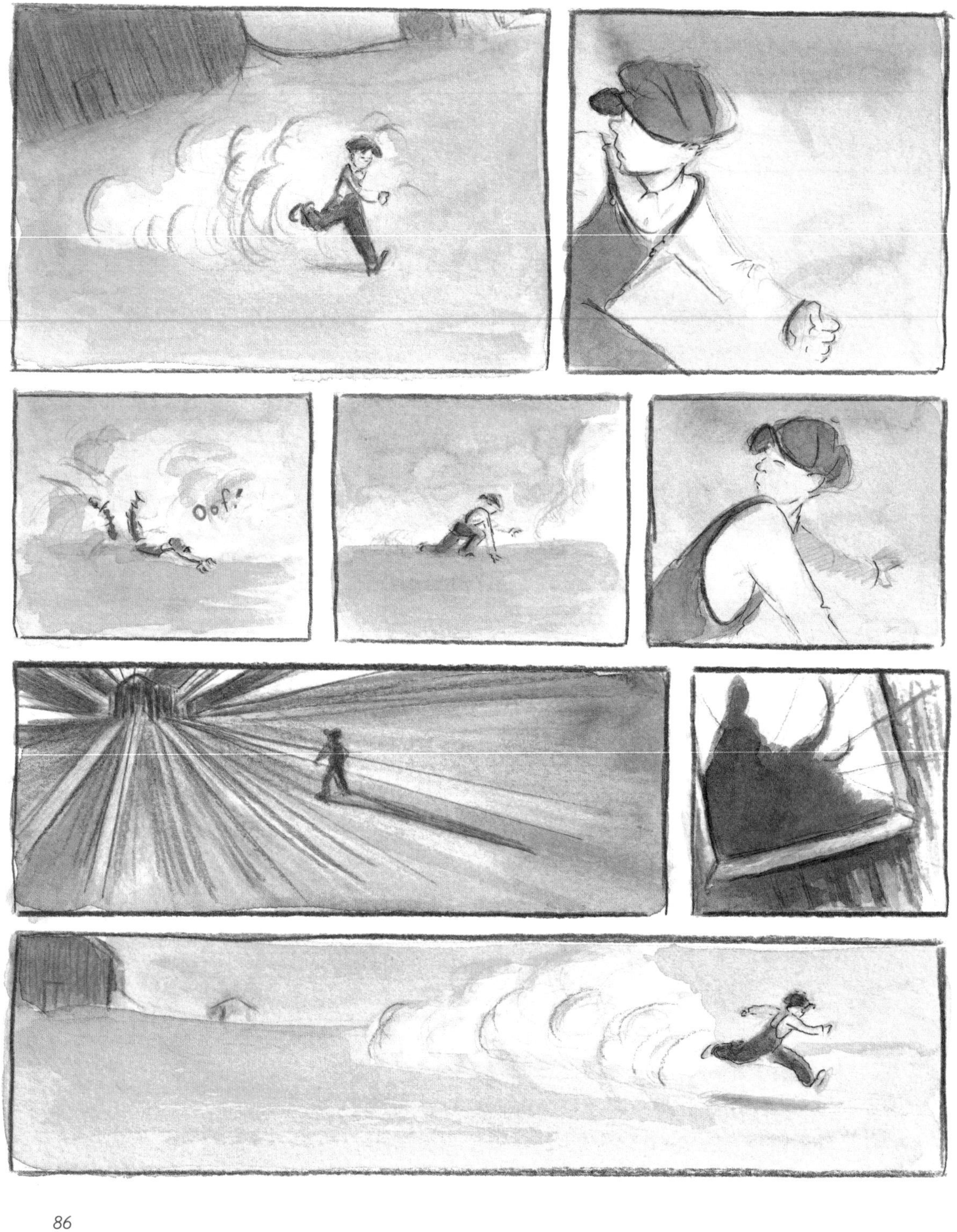
Oof!

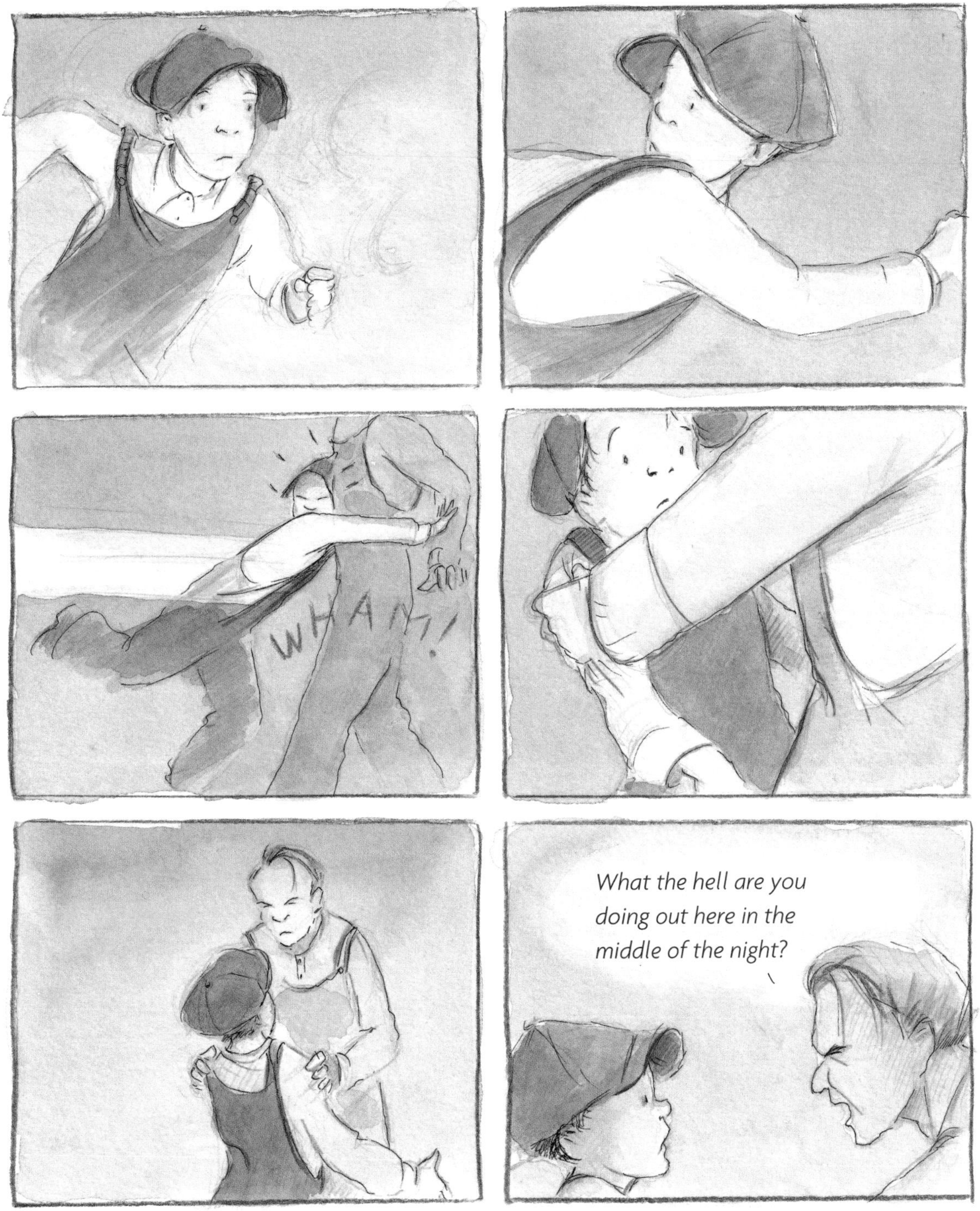
WHAM!
What the hell are you doing out here in the middle of the night?

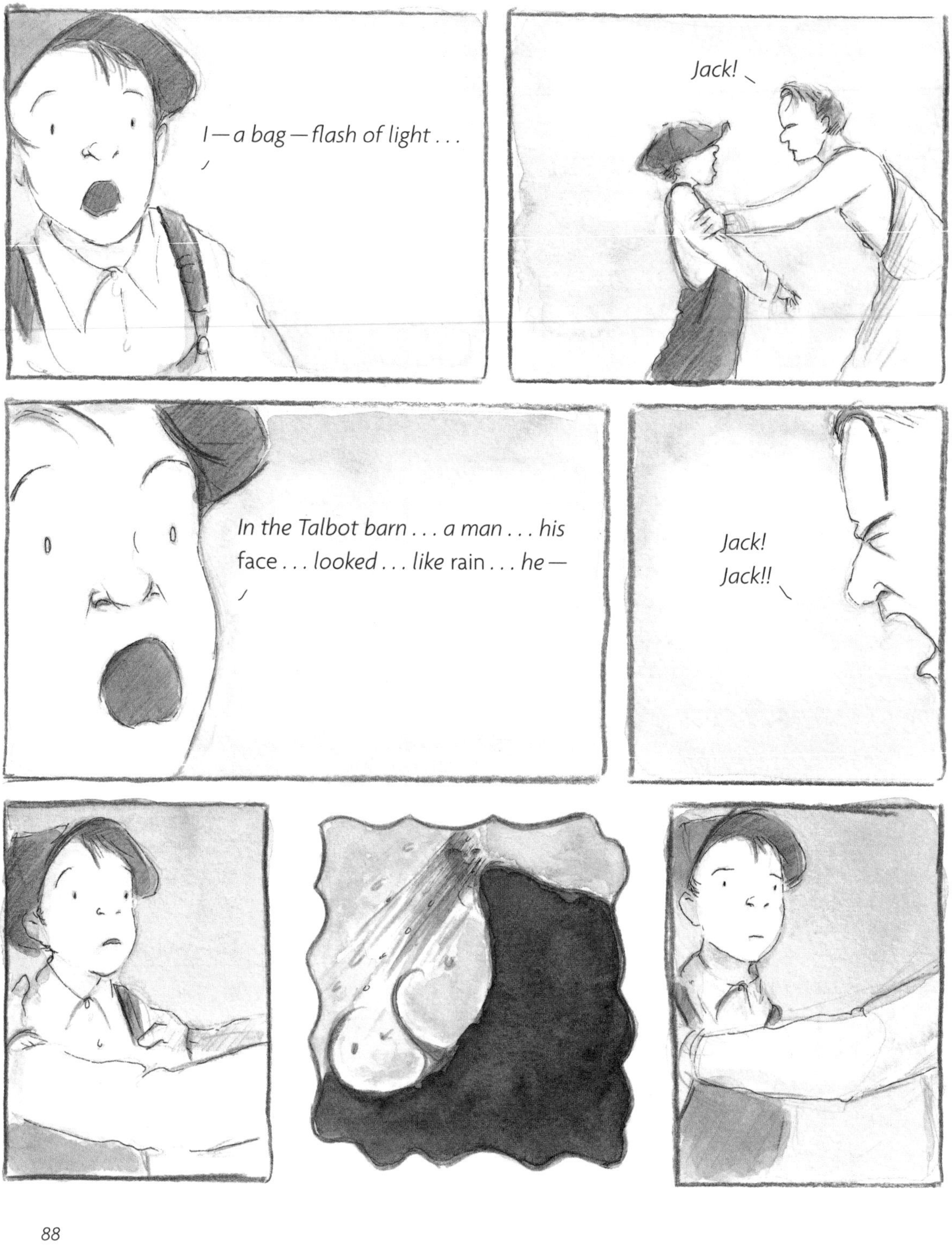
I—a bag—flash of light . . .
Jack!
In the Talbot barn . . . a man . . . his face . . . looked . . . like rain . . . he—
Jack!
Jack!!

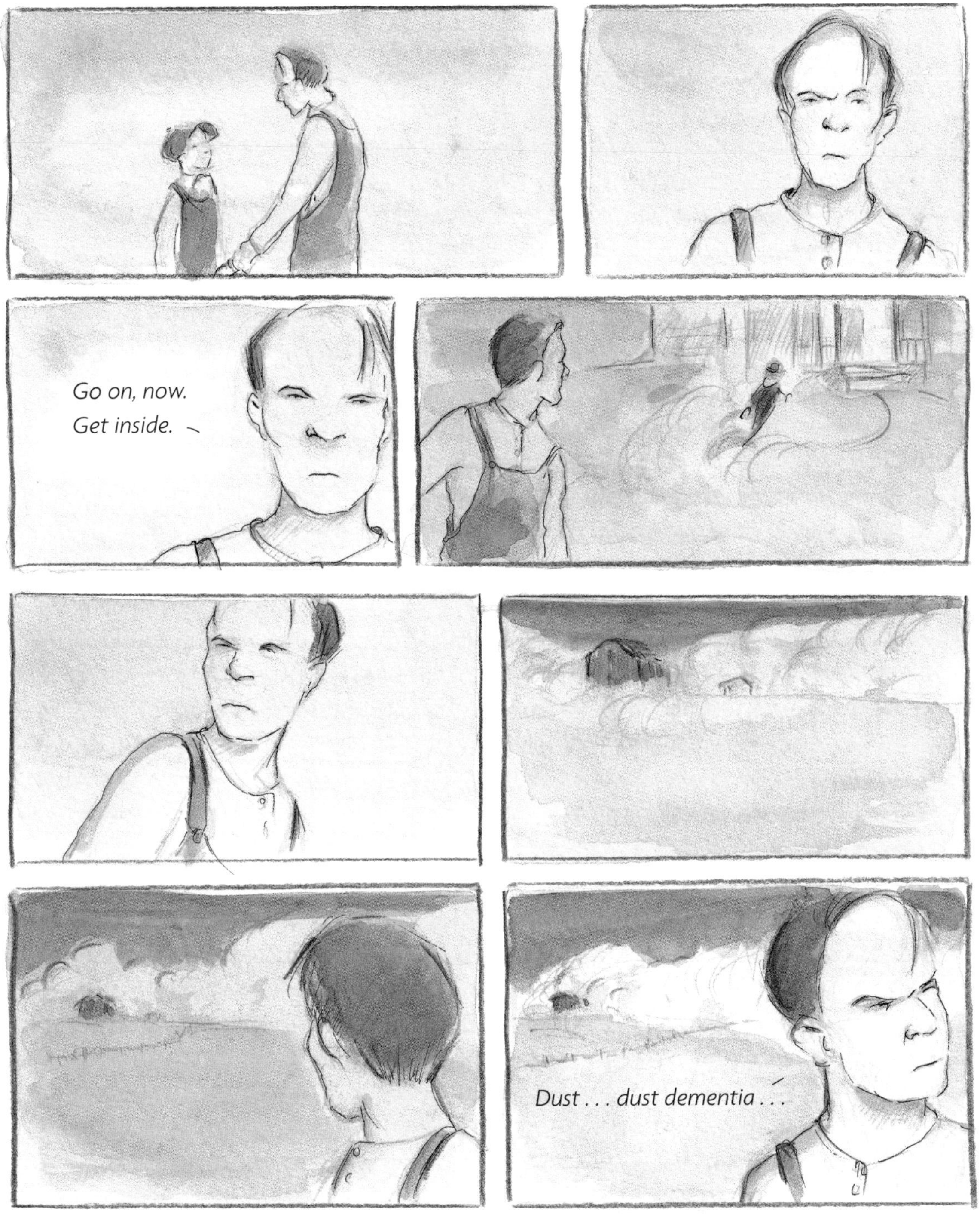
Go on, now.
Get inside.
Dust . . . dust dementia . . .

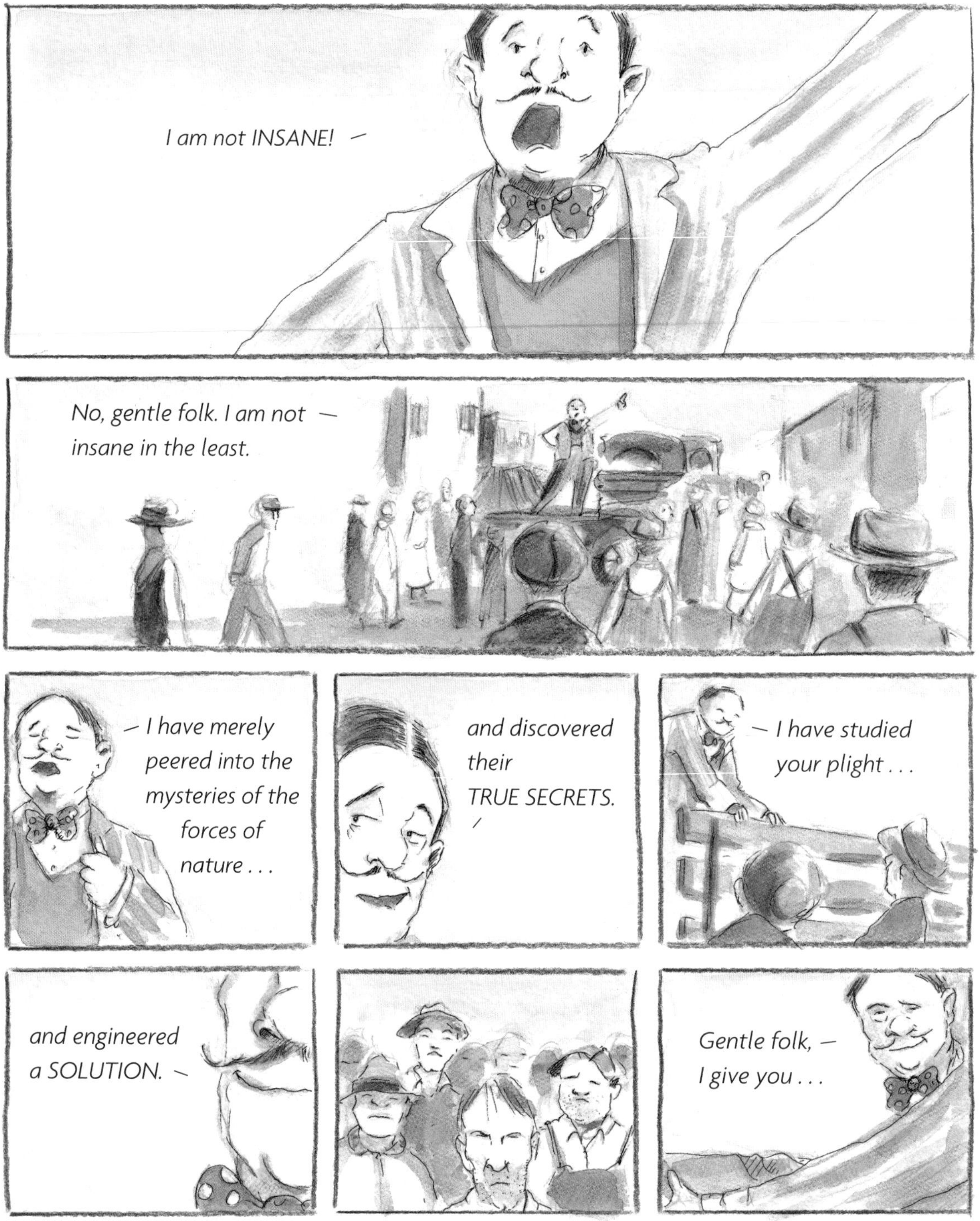
I am not INSANE! —
No, gentle folk. I am not — insane in the least.
— I have merely peered into the mysteries of the forces of nature . . .
and discovered their TRUE SECRETS. /
— I have studied your plight . . .
and engineered a SOLUTION. —
Gentle folk, — I give you . . .

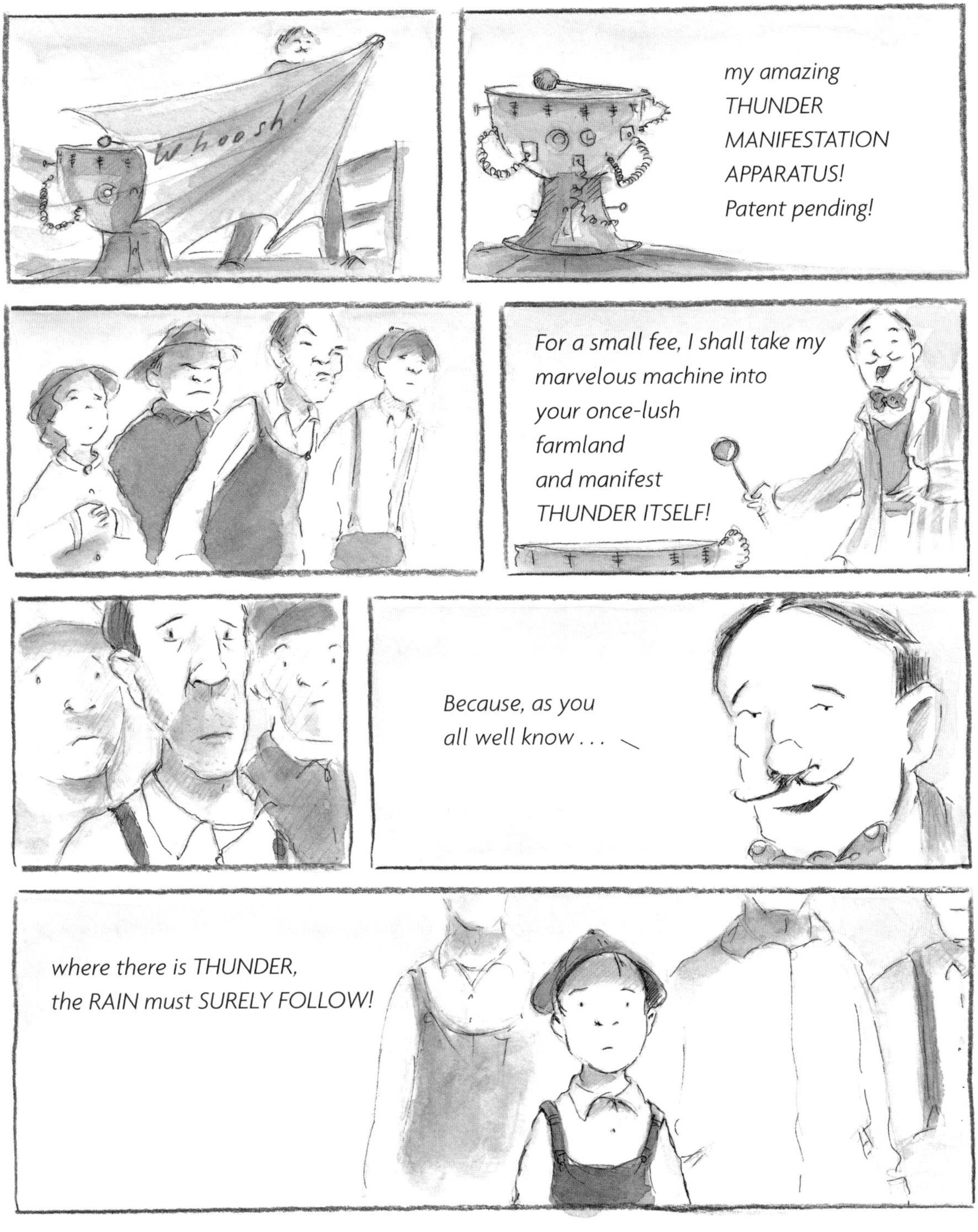
Whoosh!
my amazing
THUNDER
MANIFESTATION
APPARATUS!
Patent pending!
For a small fee, I shall take my
marvelous machine into
your once-lush
farmland
and manifest
THUNDER ITSELF!
Because, as you
all well know . . .
where there is THUNDER,
the RAIN must SURELY FOLLOW!

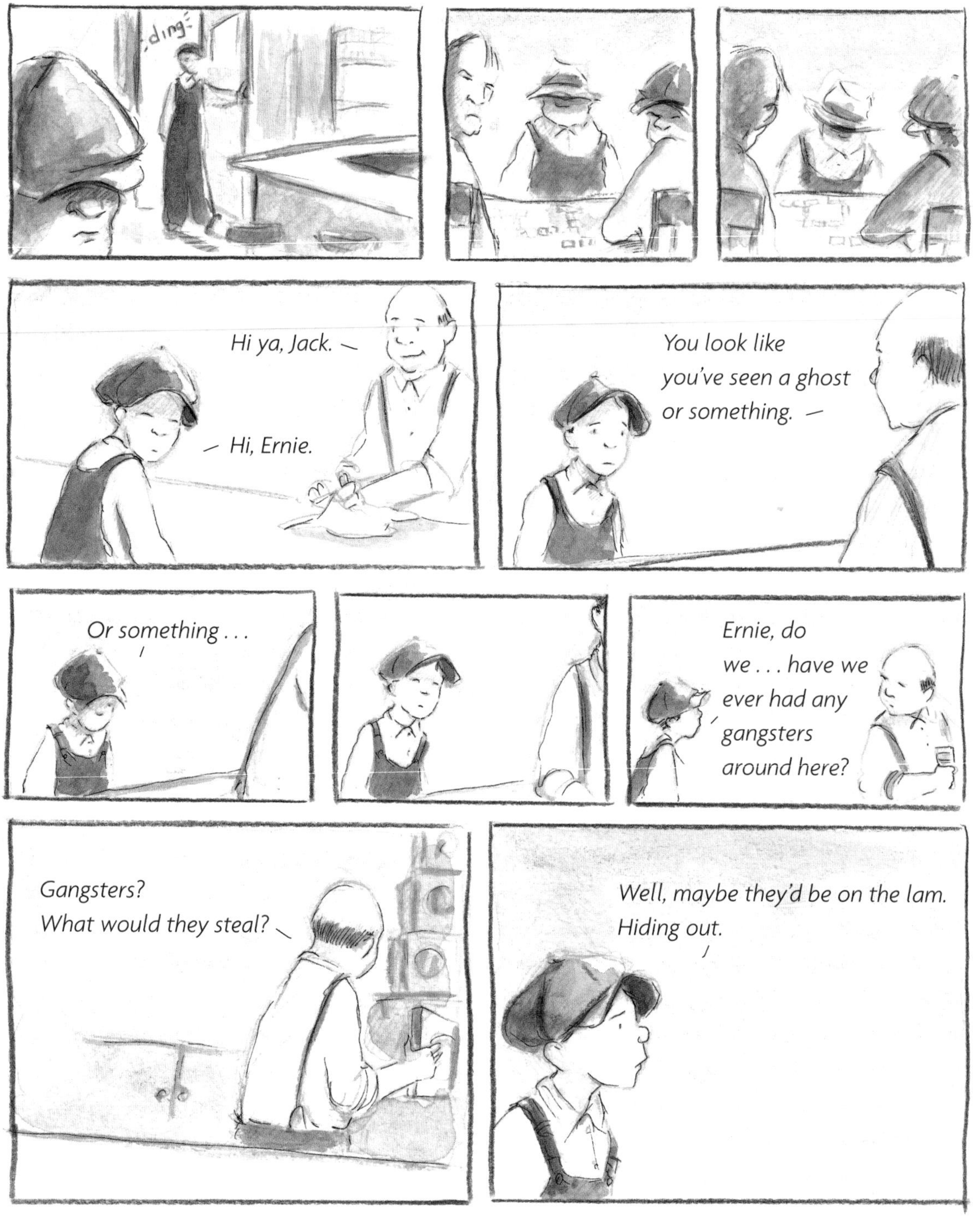
ding
Hi ya, Jack.
Hi, Ernie.
You look like you've seen a ghost or something.
Or something . . .
Ernie, do we . . . have we ever had any gangsters around here?
Gangsters? What would they steal?
Well, maybe they'd be on the lam. Hiding out.

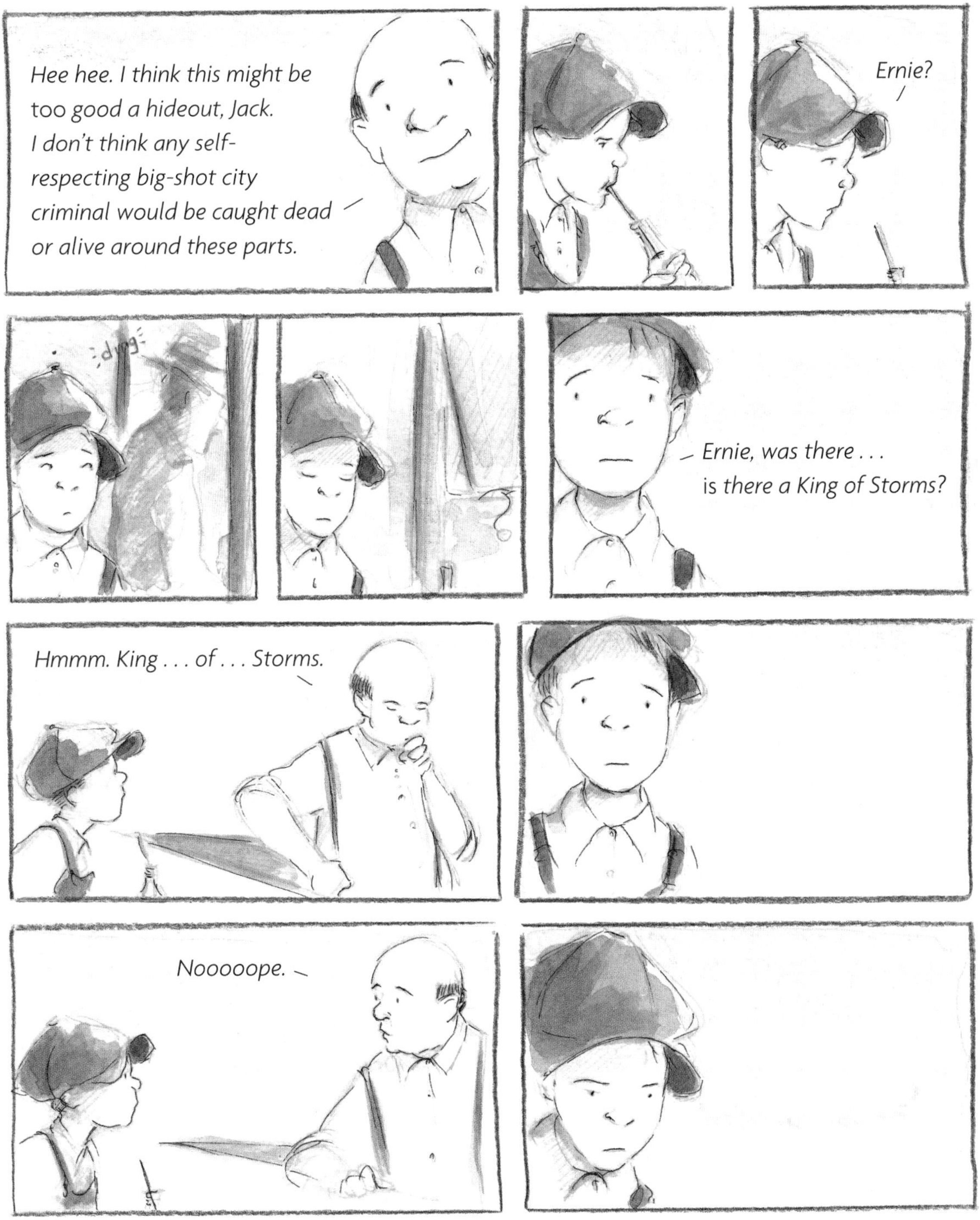

Hee hee. I think this might be too good a hideout, Jack. I don't think any self-respecting big-shot city criminal would be caught dead or alive around these parts.
Ernie?
Ernie, was there . . . is there a King of Storms?
Hmmm. King . . . of . . . Storms.
Nooooope.

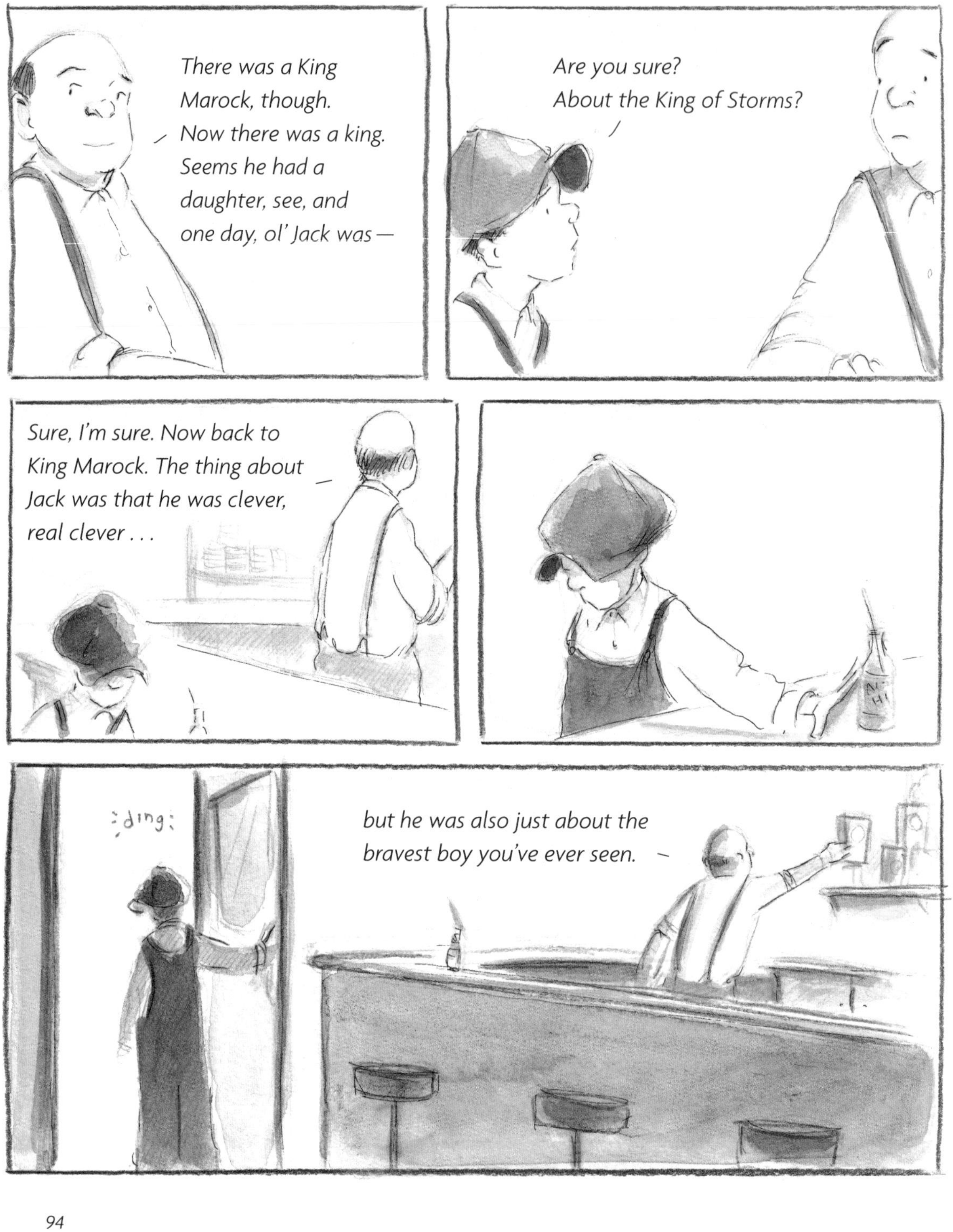
There was a King Marock, though. Now there was a king. Seems he had a daughter, see, and one day, ol' Jack was—
Are you sure? About the King of Storms?
Sure, I'm sure. Now back to King Marock. The thing about Jack was that he was clever, real clever . . .
ding
but he was also just about the bravest boy you've ever seen.

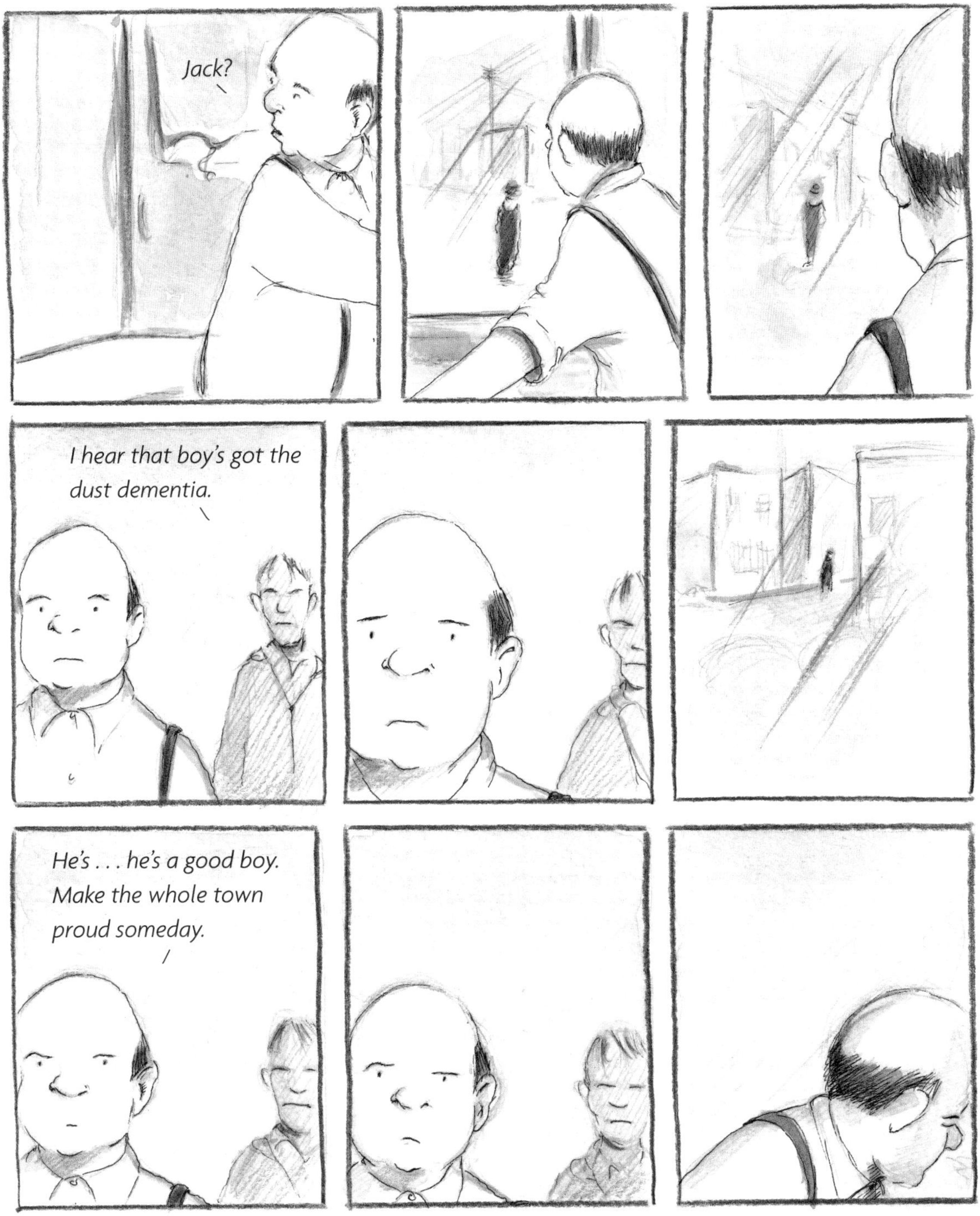
Jack?
I hear that boy's got the dust dementia.
He's . . . he's a good boy. Make the whole town proud someday.

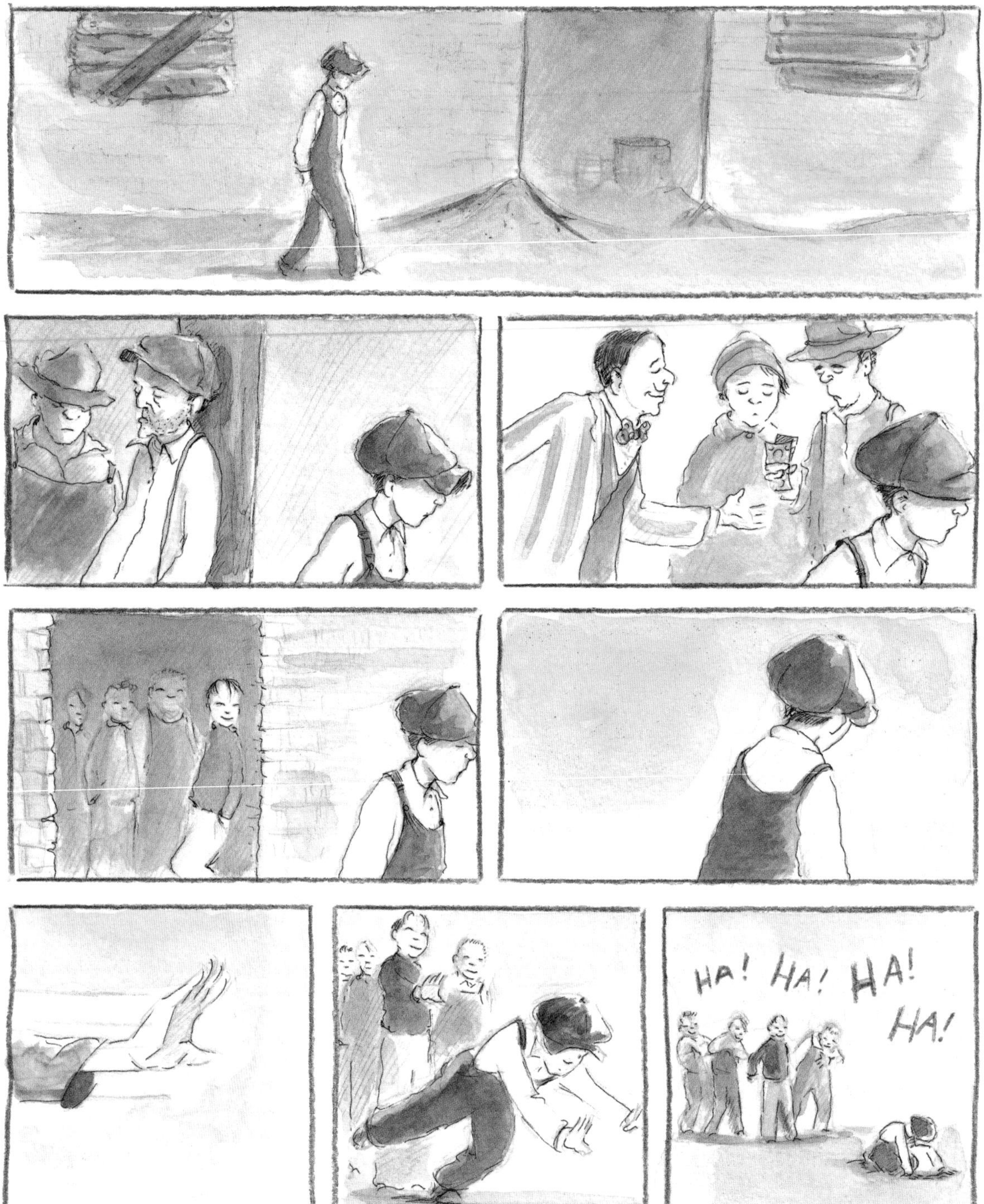
HA! HA! HA!
HA!

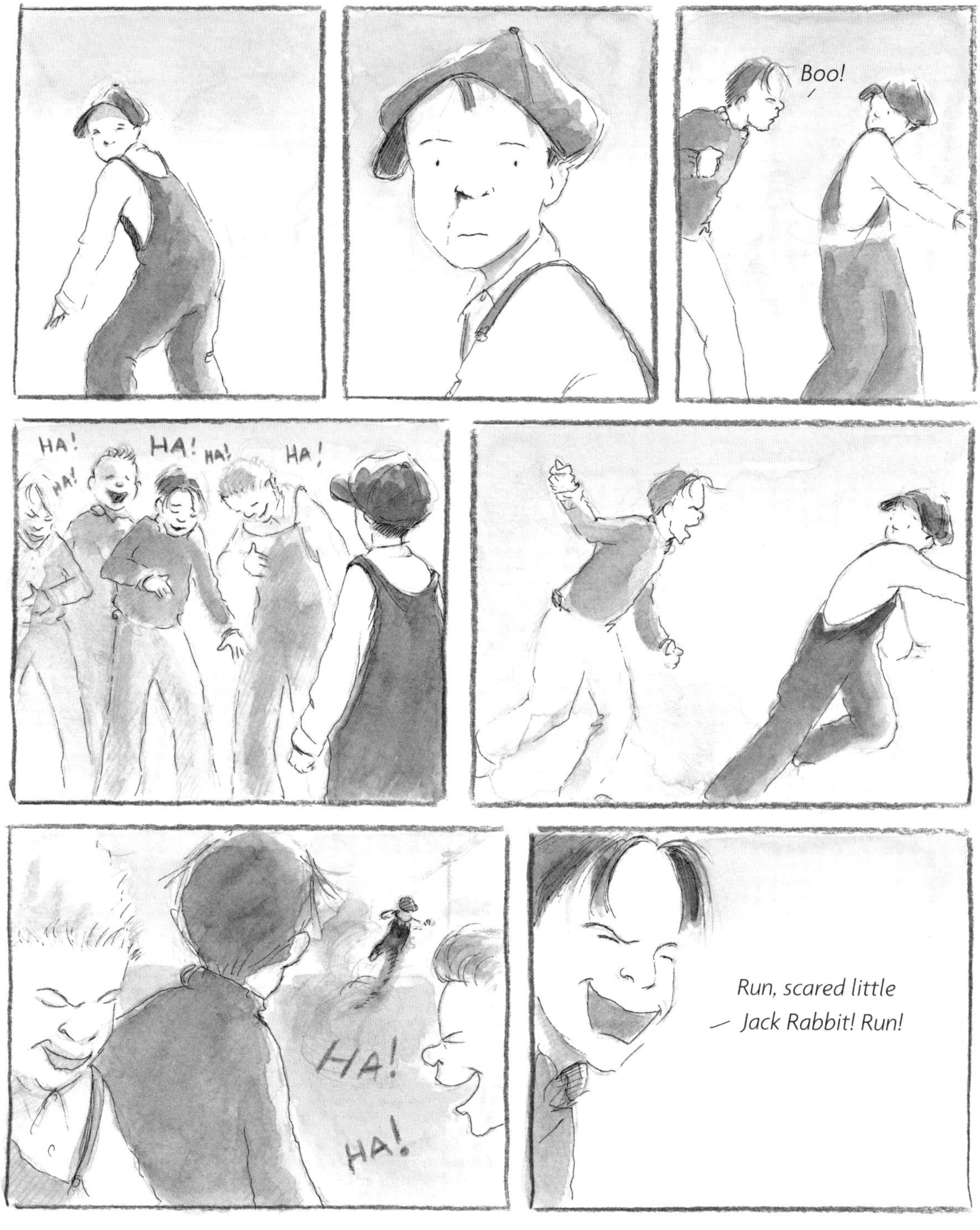
Boo!
HA!
HA!
HA!
HA!
HA!
HA!
HA!
HA!
Run, scared little
Jack Rabbit! Run!

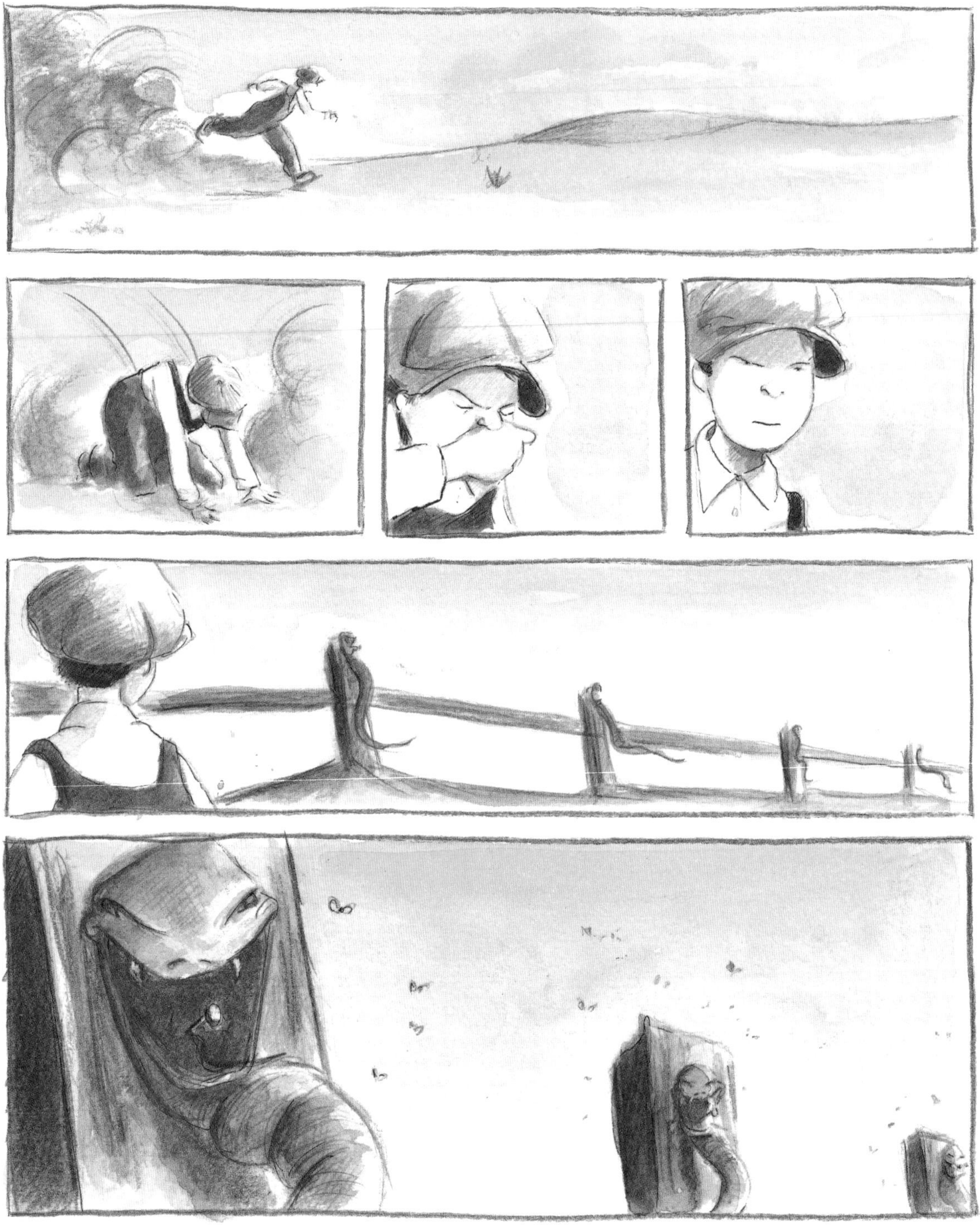

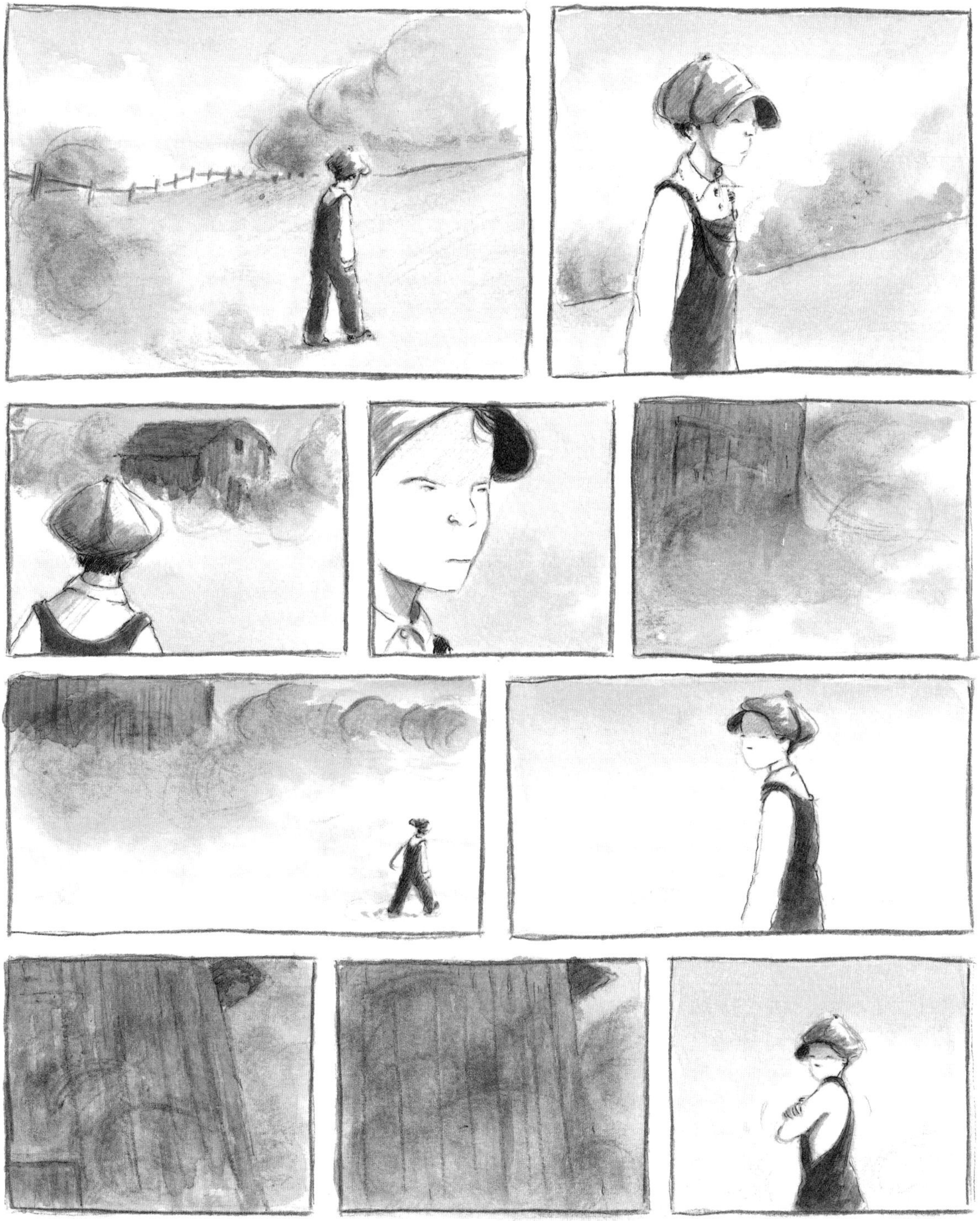

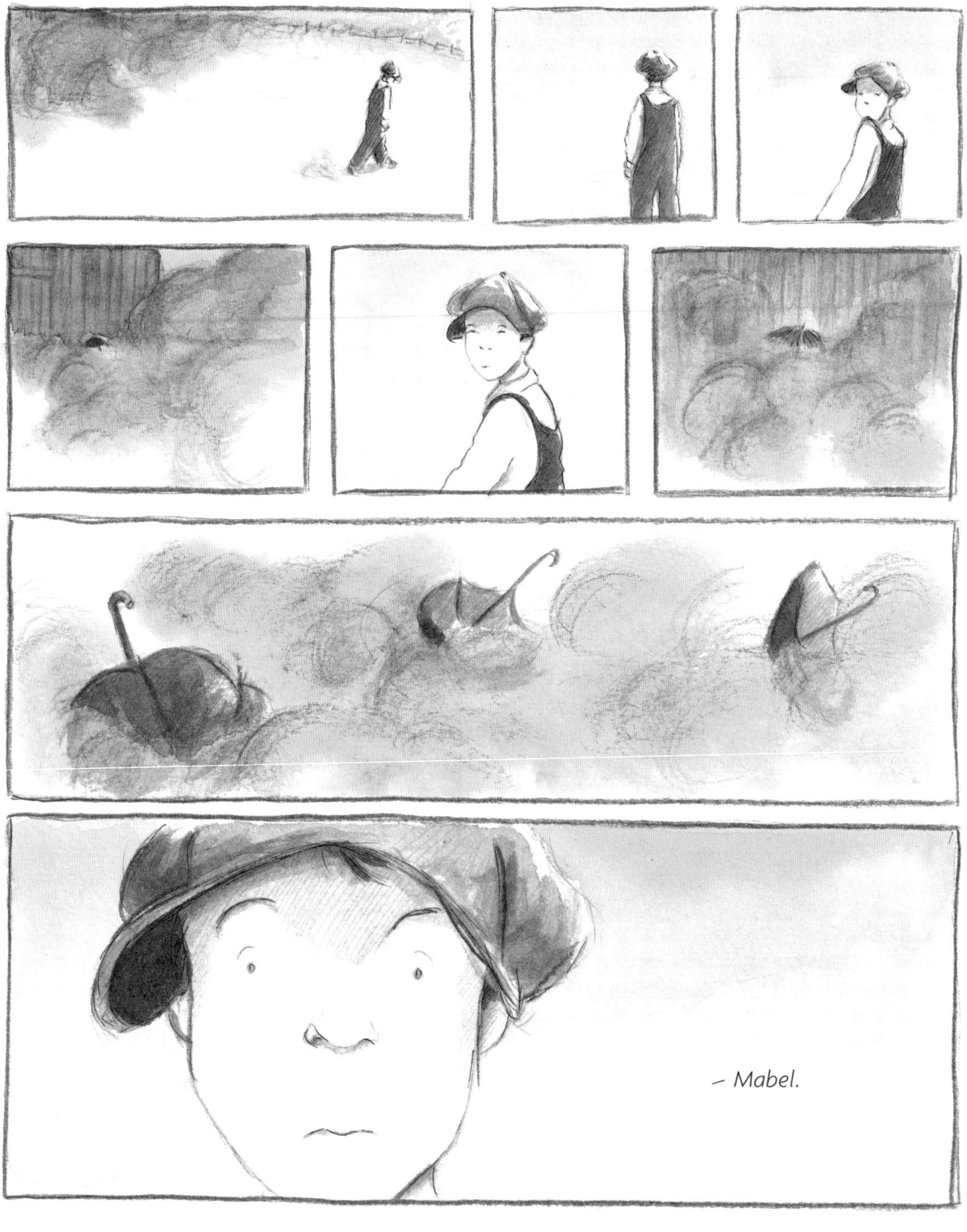
– Mabel.

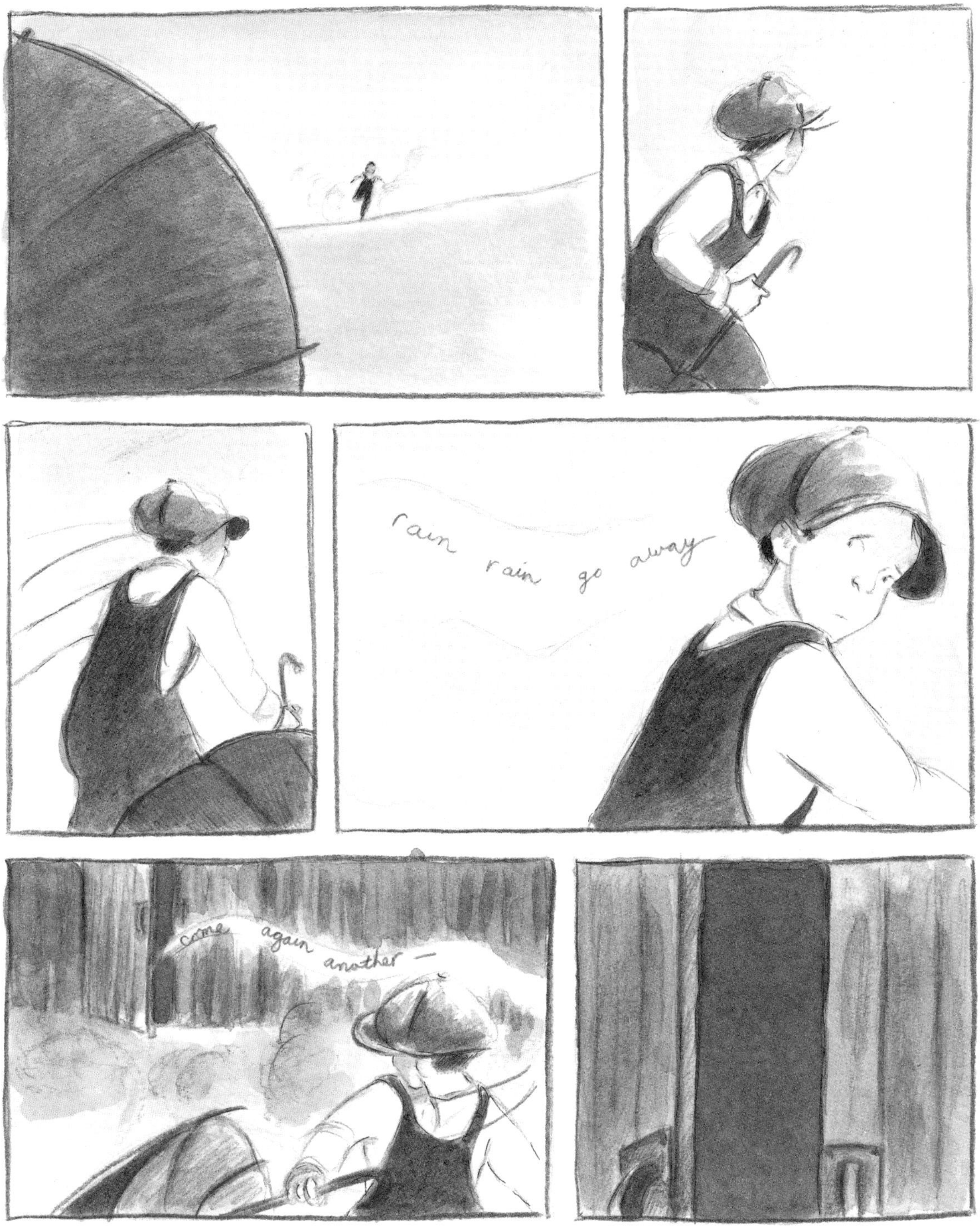
rain rain go away
come again another —

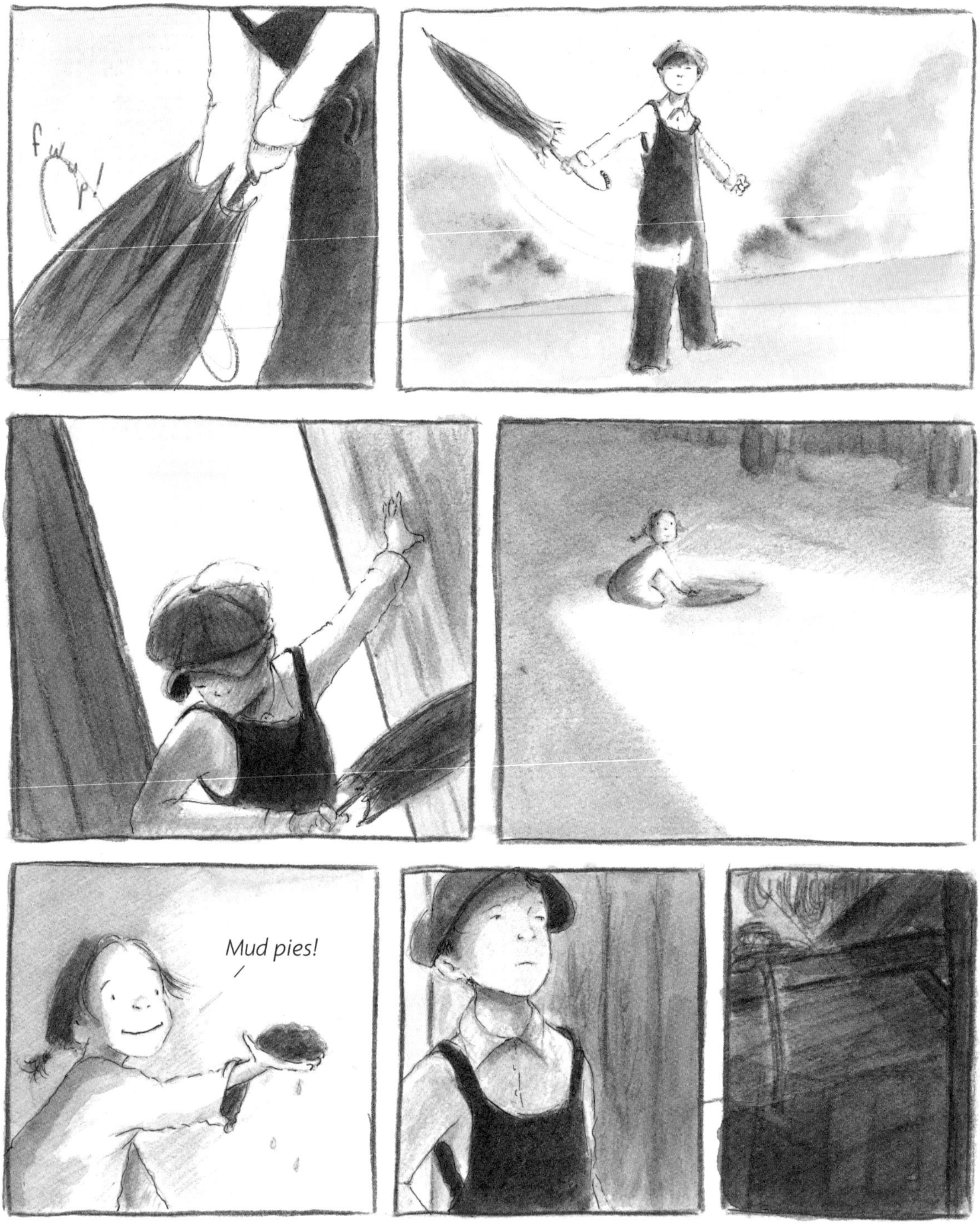
fwup!
Mud pies!

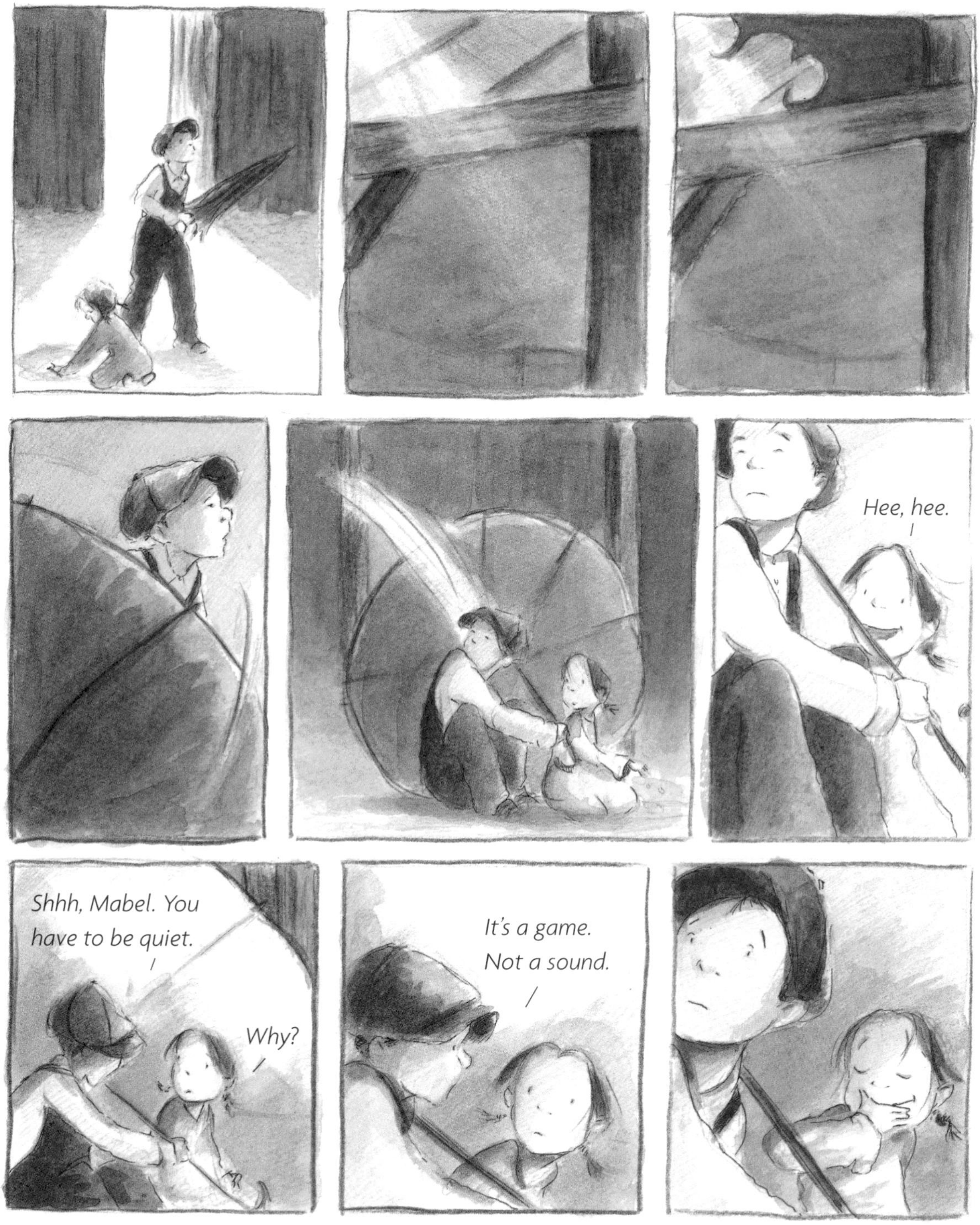
Hee, hee.
Shhh, Mabel. You have to be quiet.
Why?
It's a game. Not a sound.

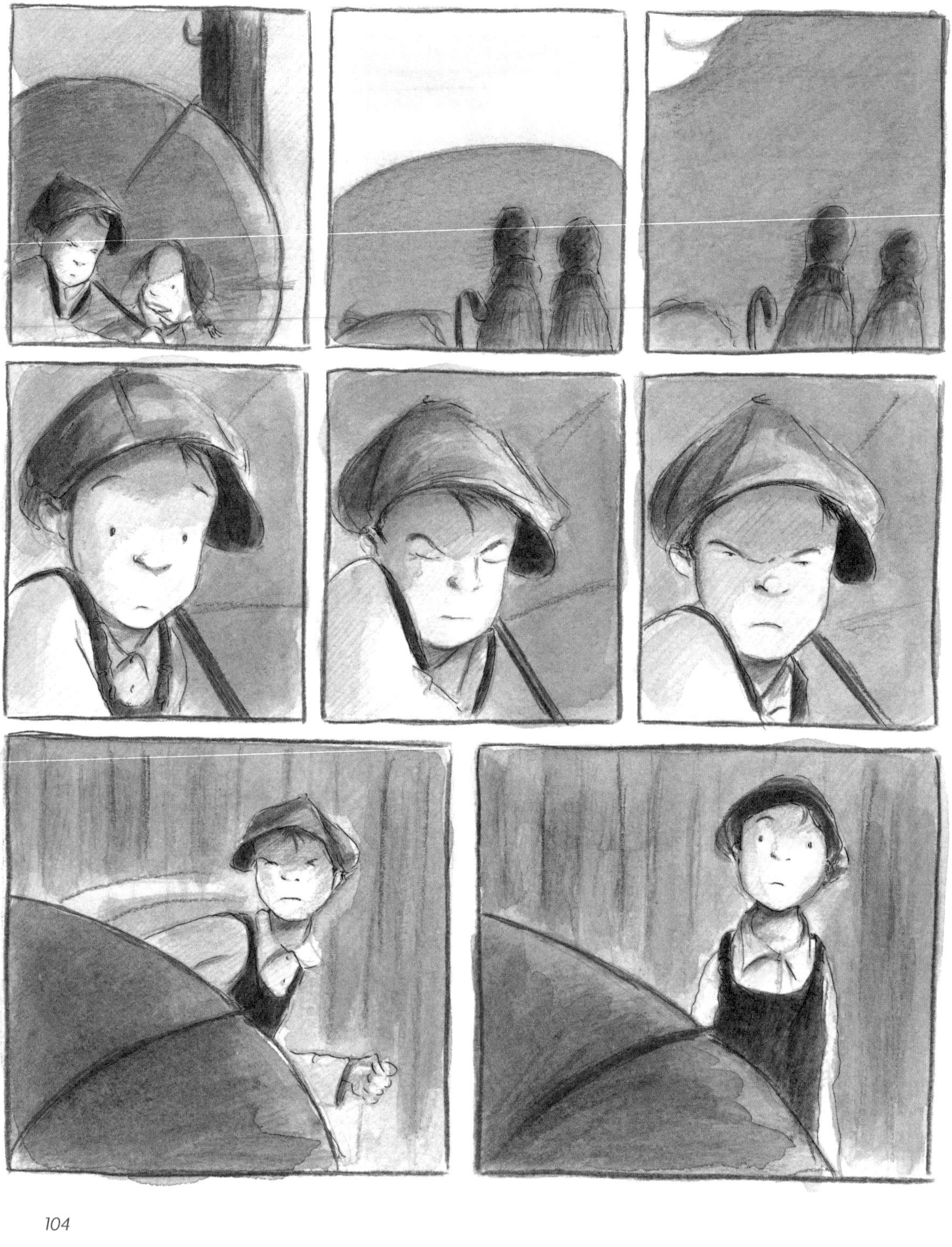

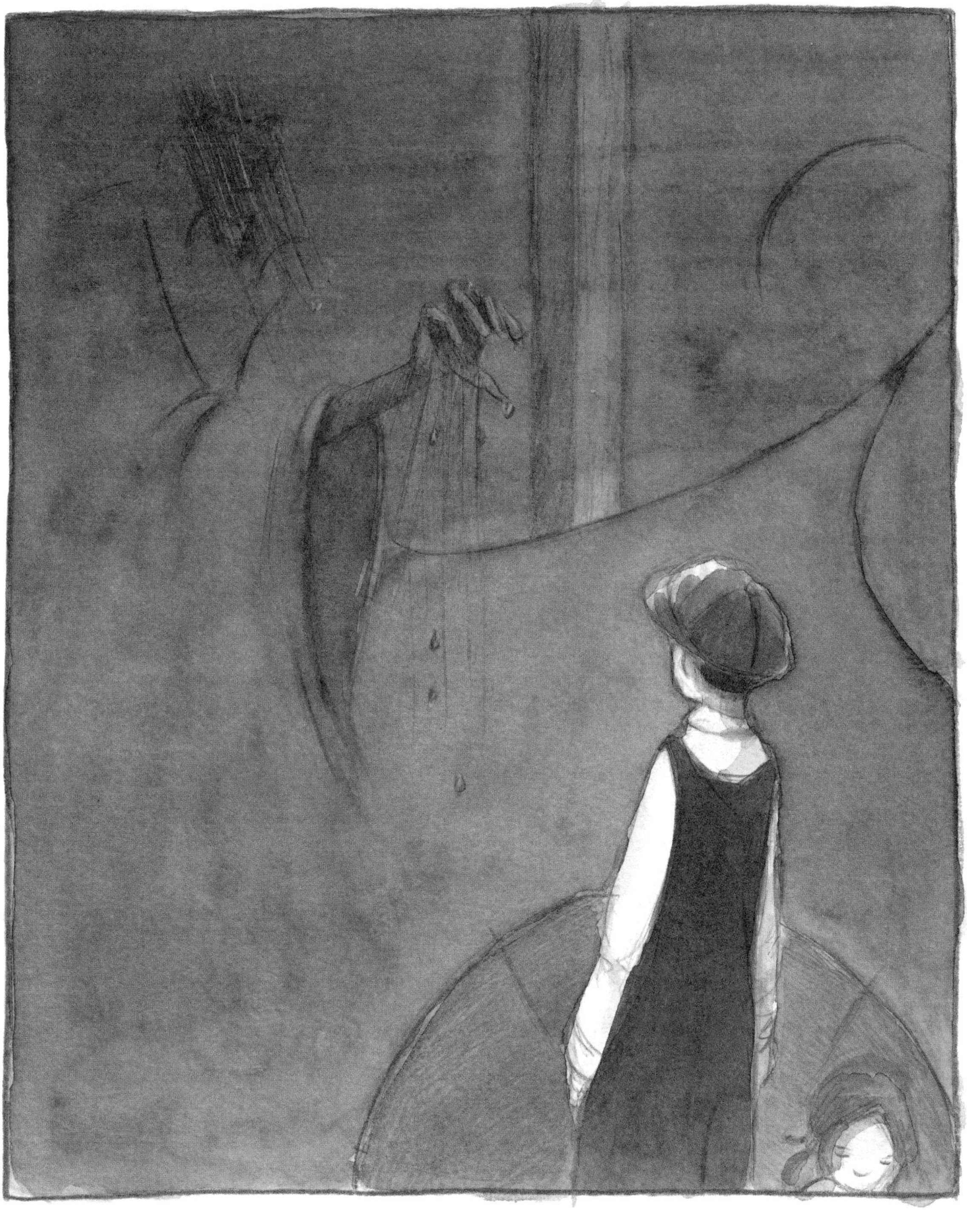

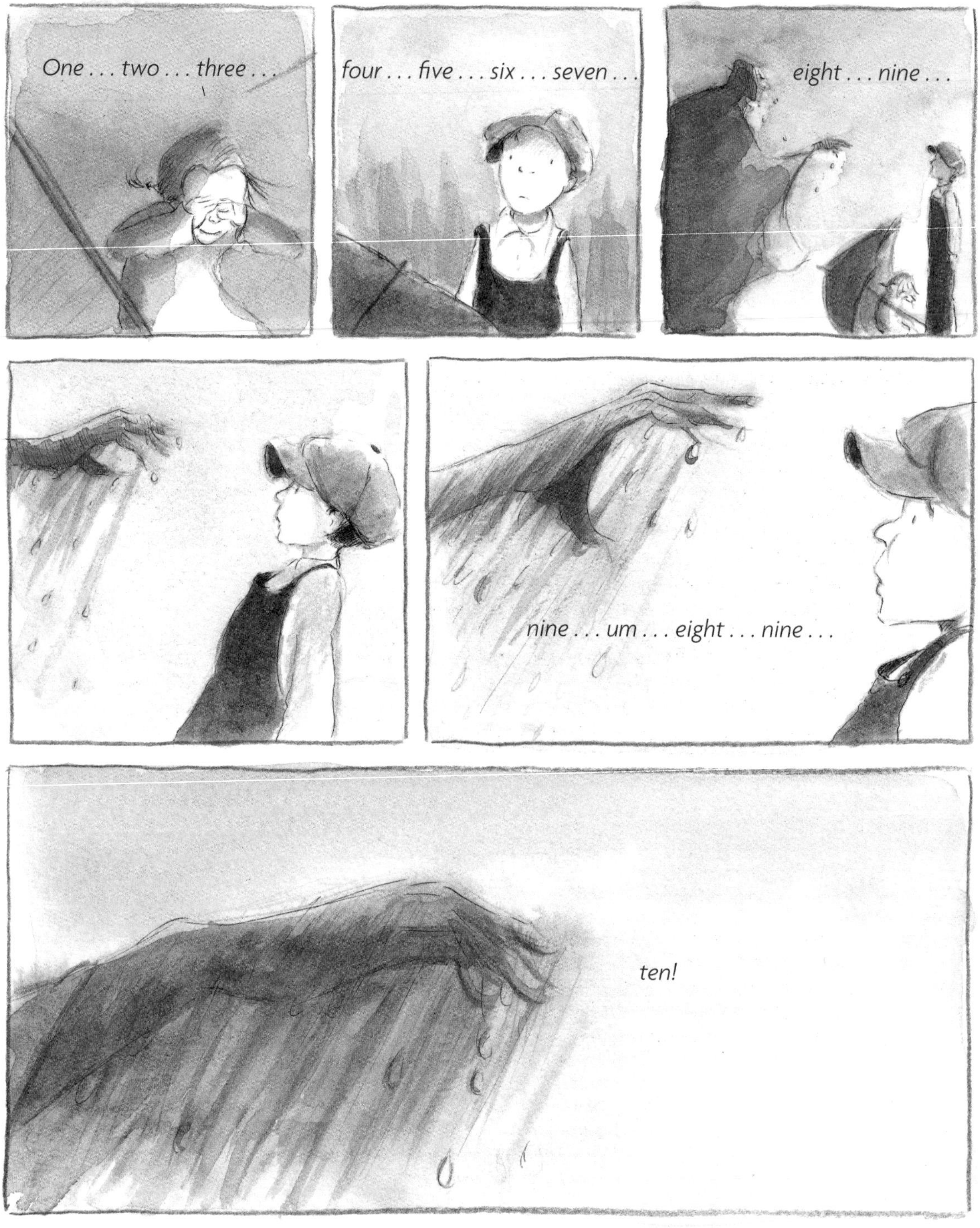
One . . . two . . . three . . .
four . . . five . . . six . . . seven . . .
eight . . . nine . . .
nine . . . um . . . eight . . . nine . . .
ten!

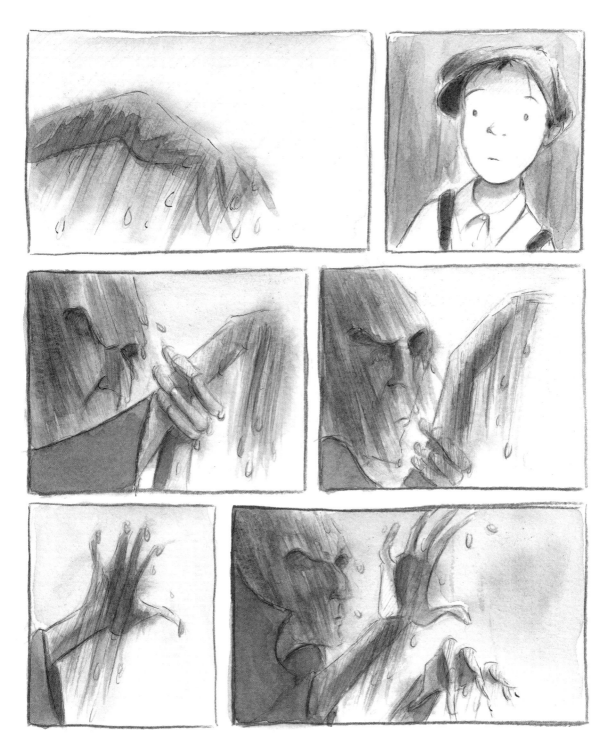

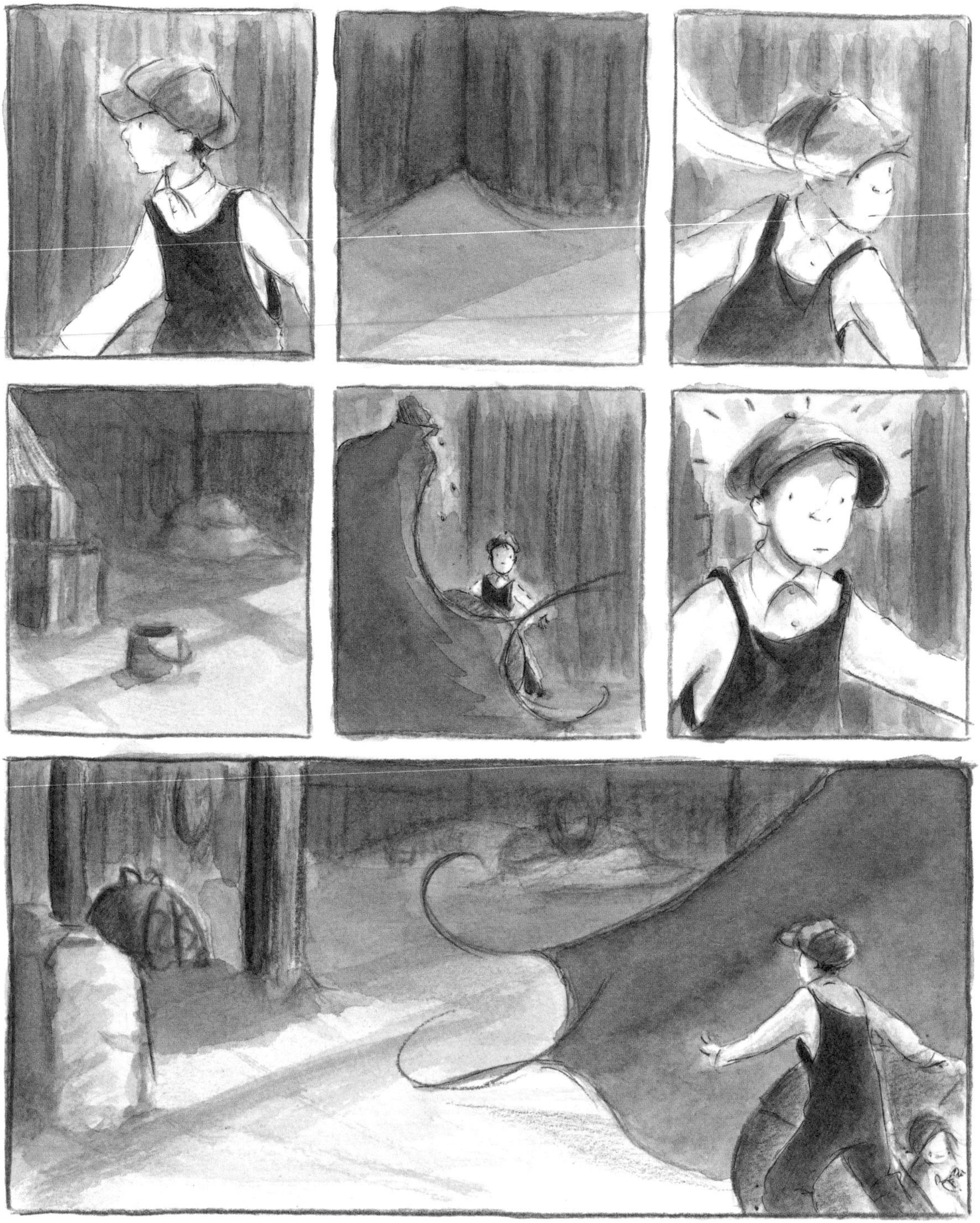

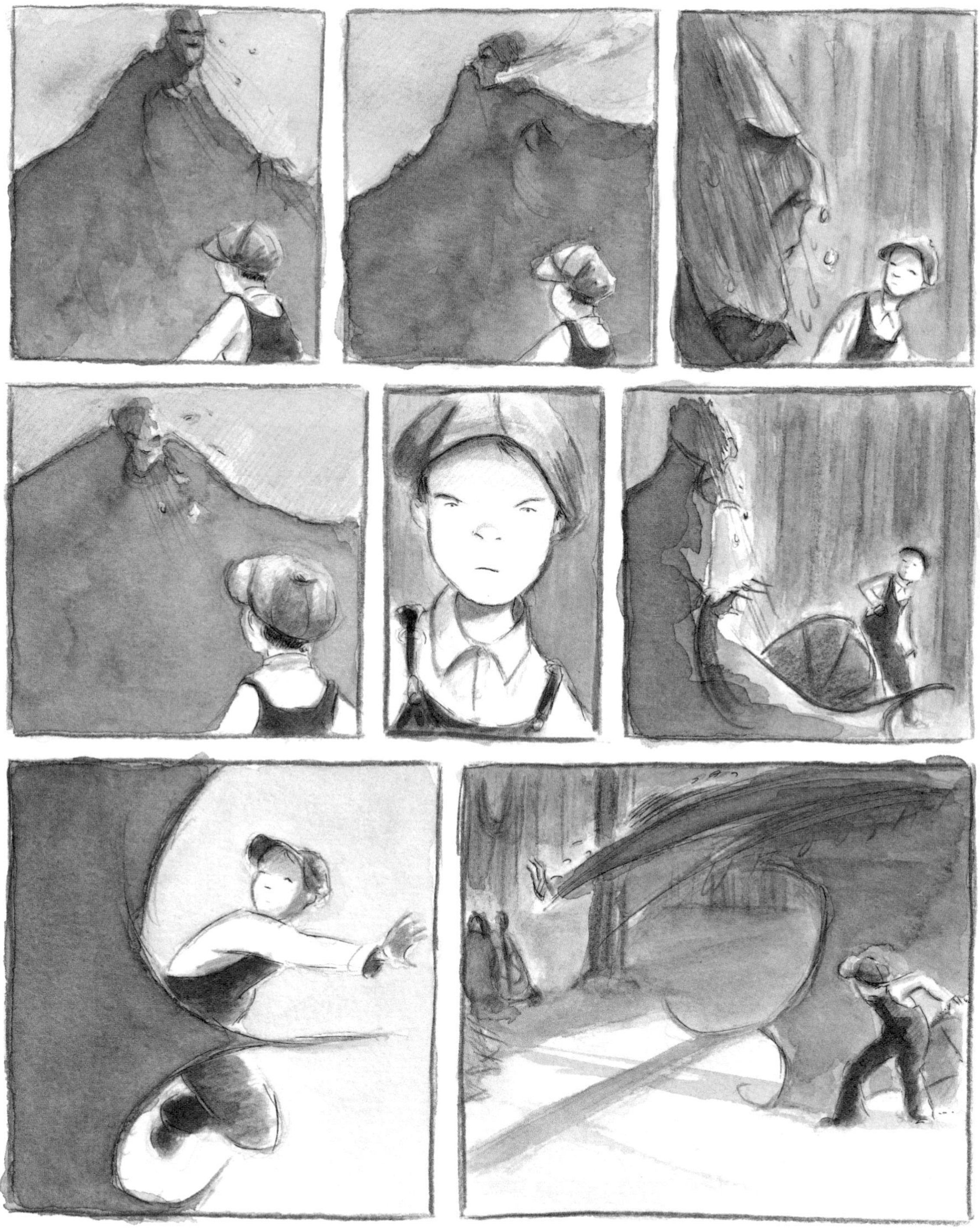

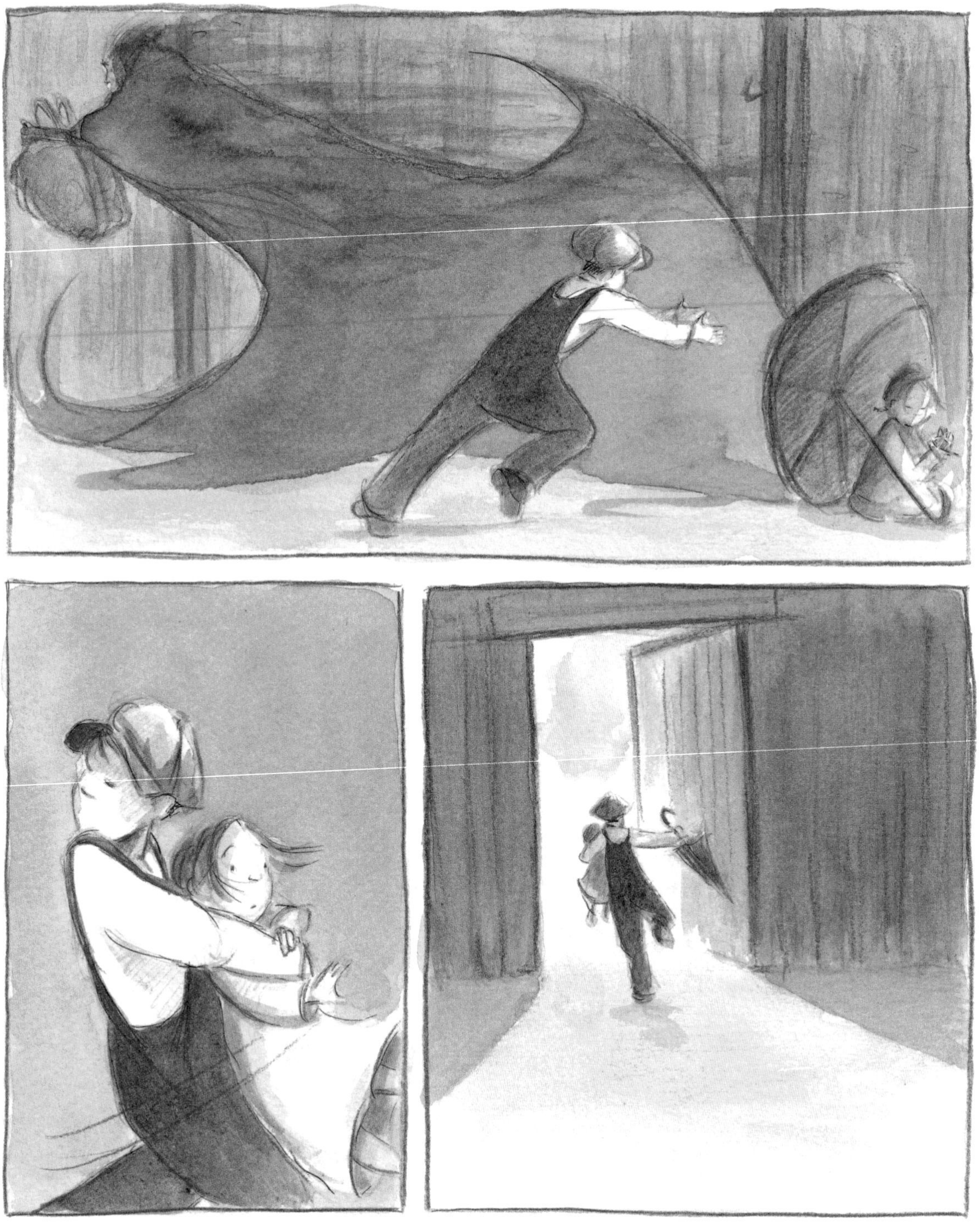

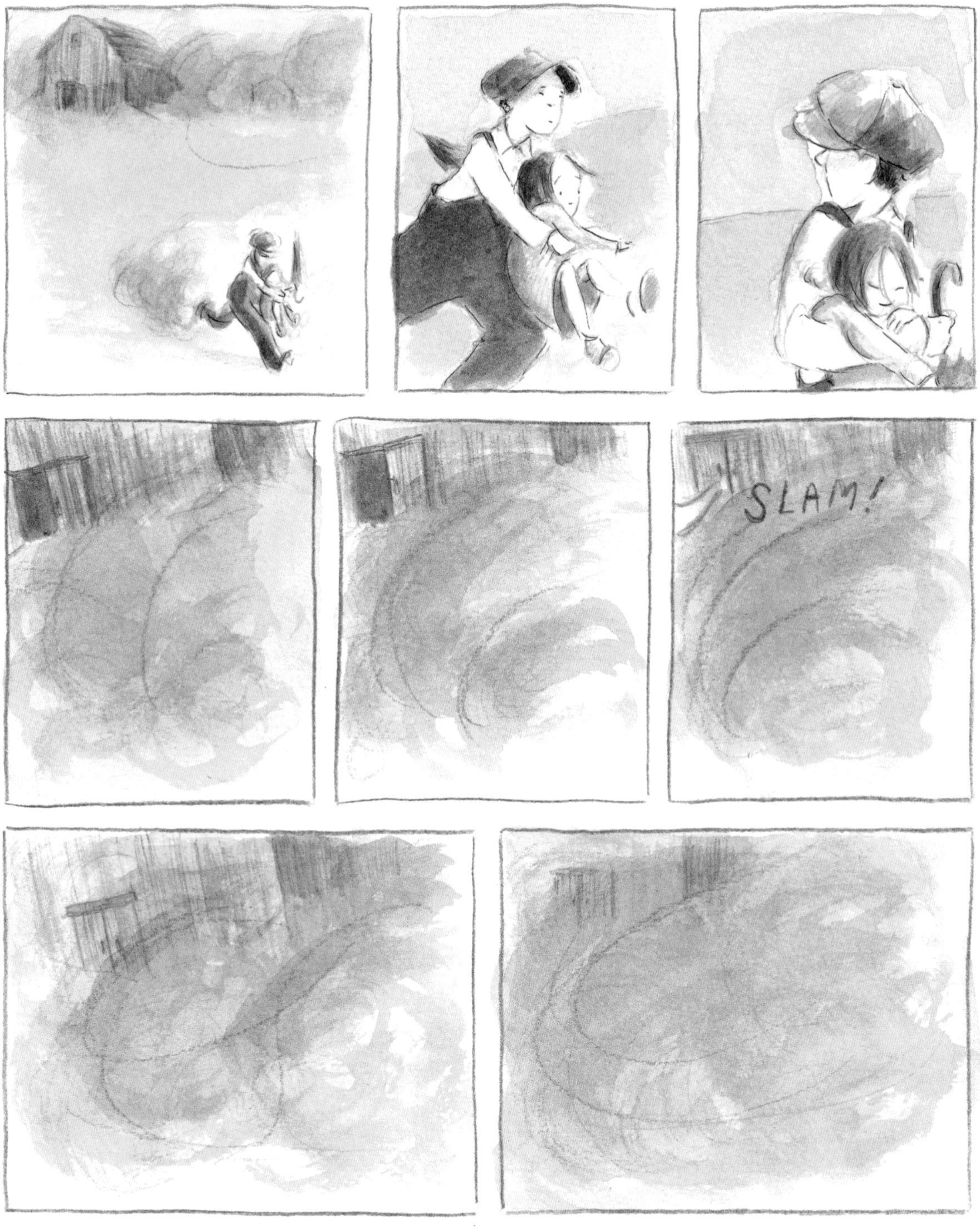
SLAM!

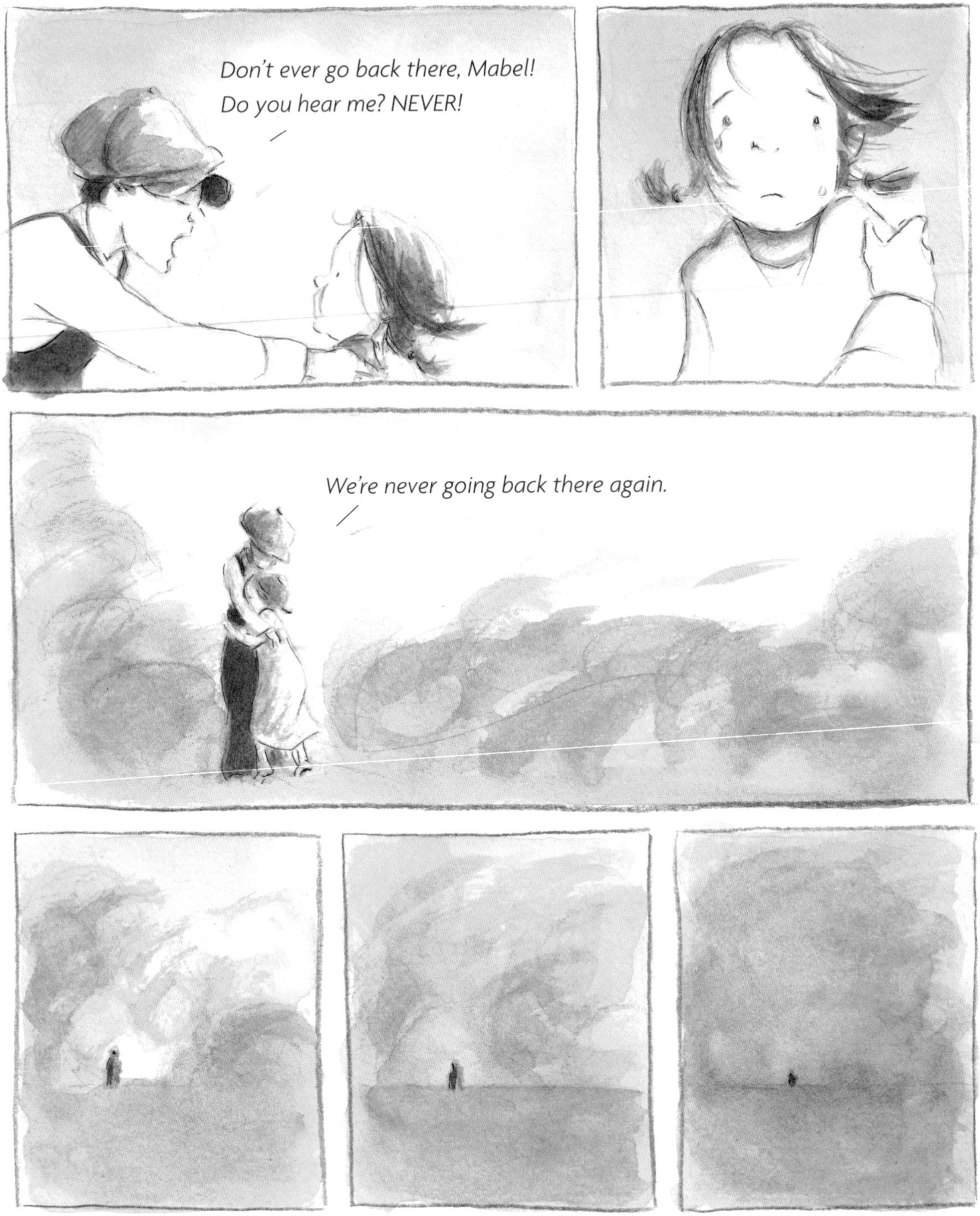
Don't ever go back there, Mabel!
Do you hear me? NEVER!
We're never going back there again.

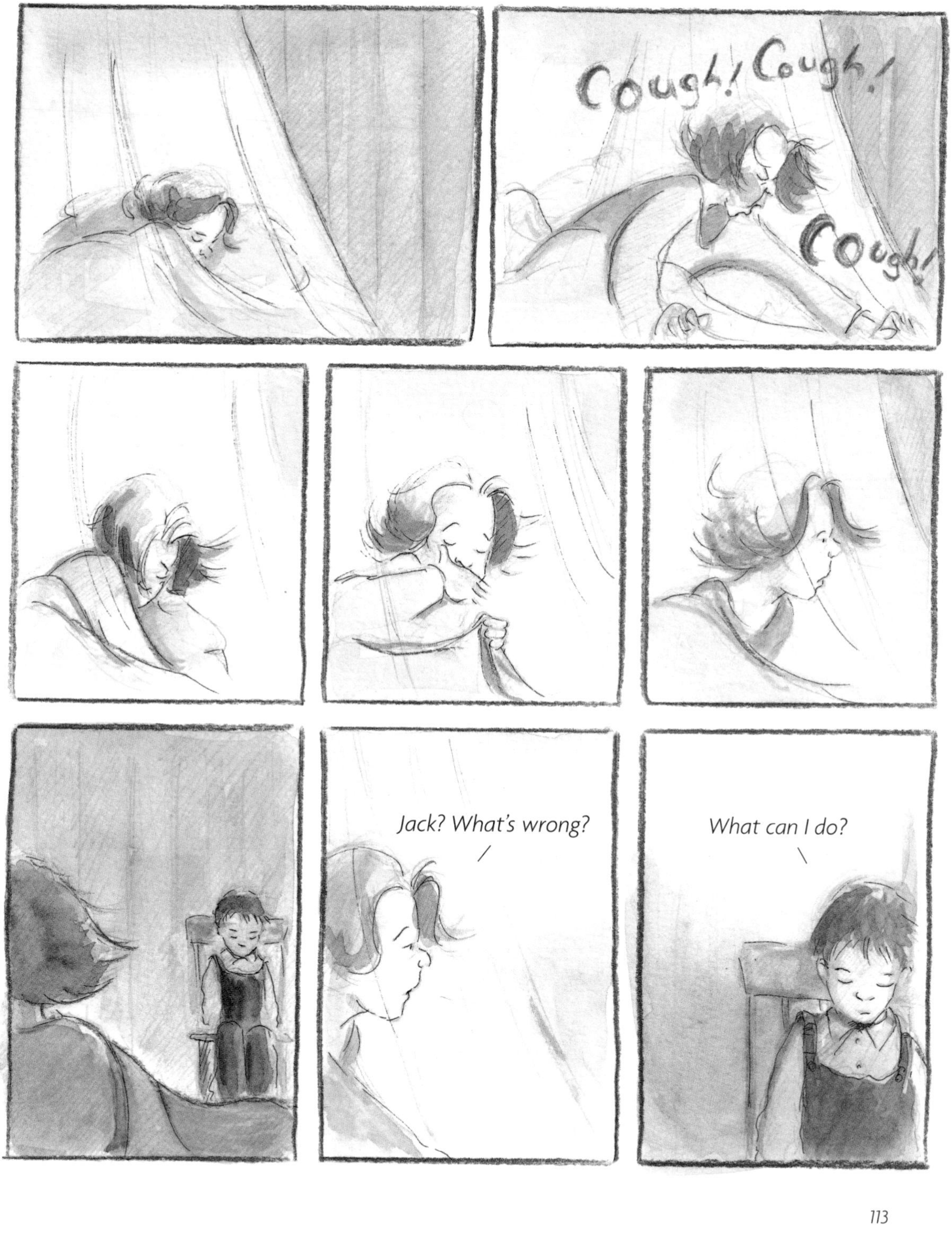
Cough! Cough!
Cough!
Jack? What's wrong?
What can I do?

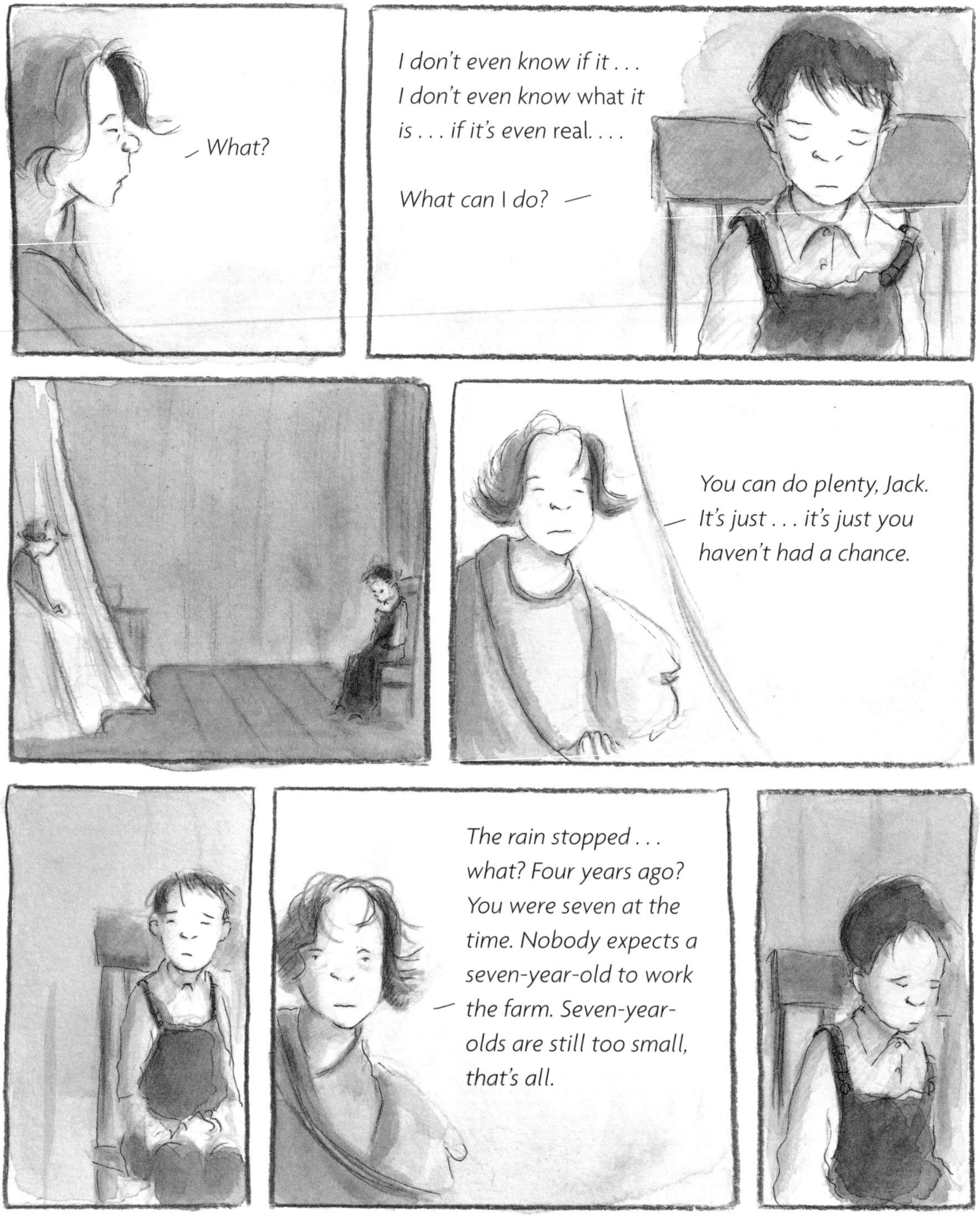
What?
I don't even know if it . . . I don't even know what it is . . . if it's even real. . . .
What can I do?
You can do plenty, Jack. It's just . . . it's just you haven't had a chance.
The rain stopped . . . what? Four years ago? You were seven at the time. Nobody expects a seven-year-old to work the farm. Seven-year-olds are still too small, that's all.

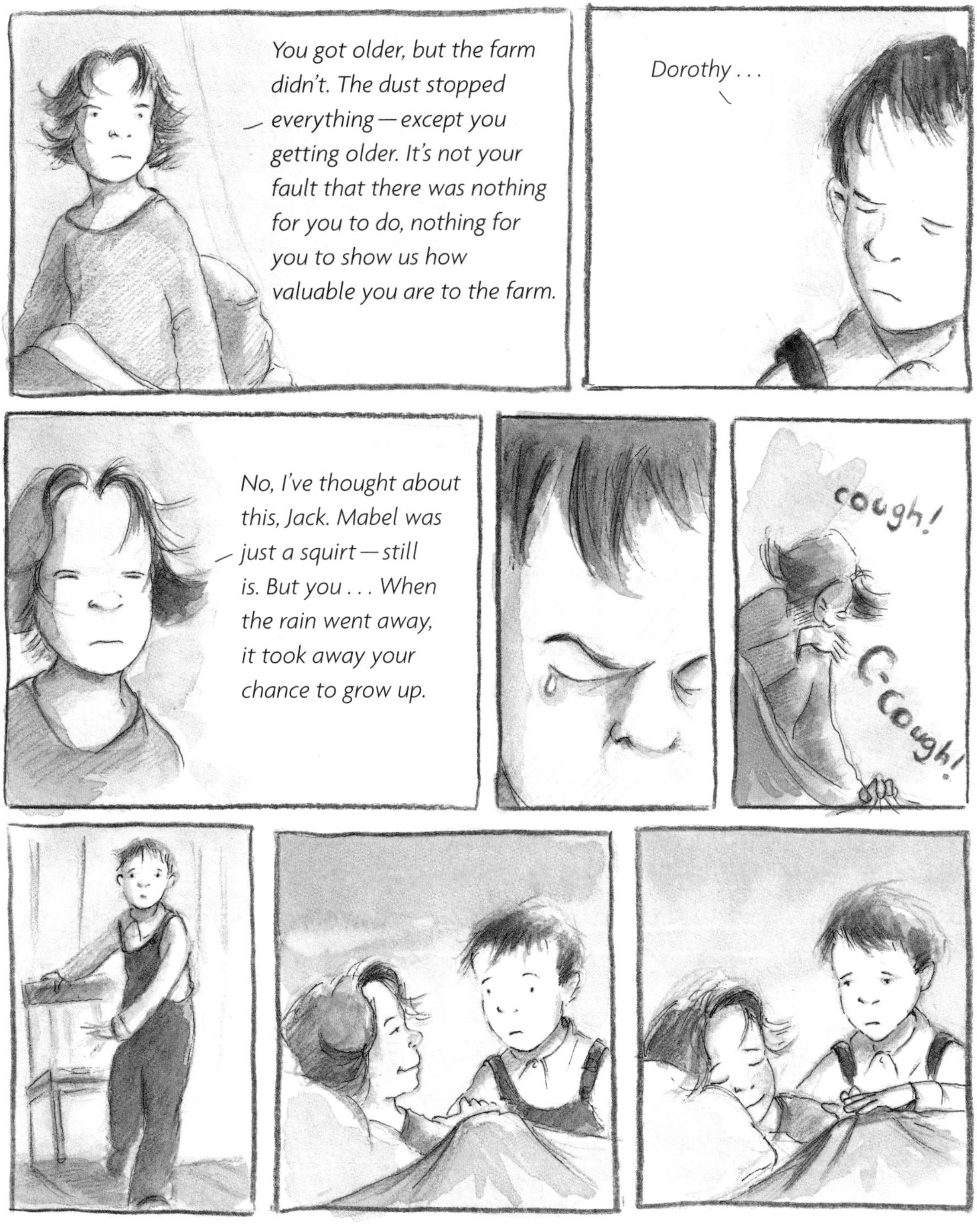
You got older, but the farm didn't. The dust stopped everything — except you getting older. It's not your fault that there was nothing for you to do, nothing for you to show us how valuable you are to the farm.
Dorothy . . .
No, I've thought about this, Jack. Mabel was just a squirt — still is. But you . . . When the rain went away, it took away your chance to grow up.
cough!
C-cough!

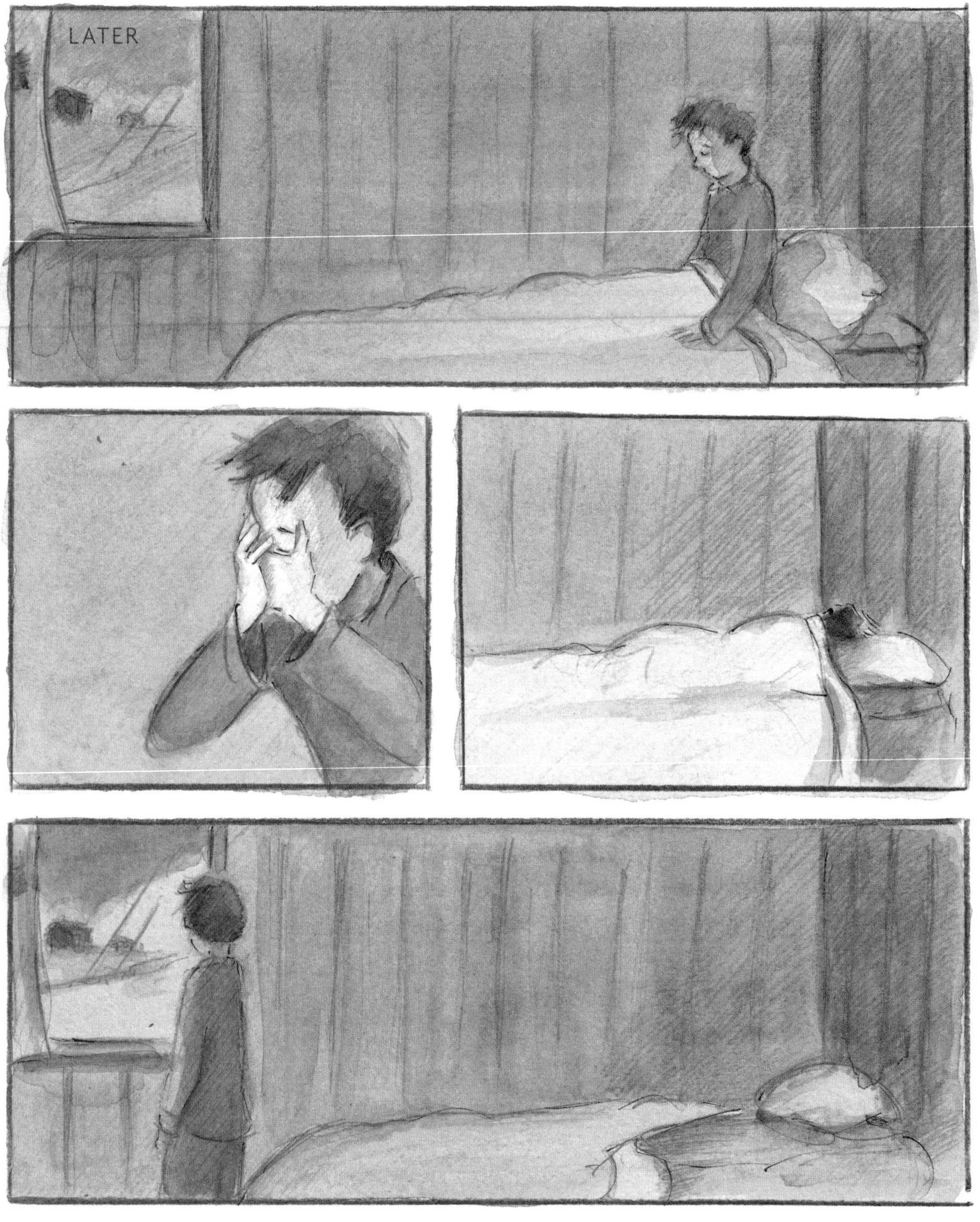
LATER

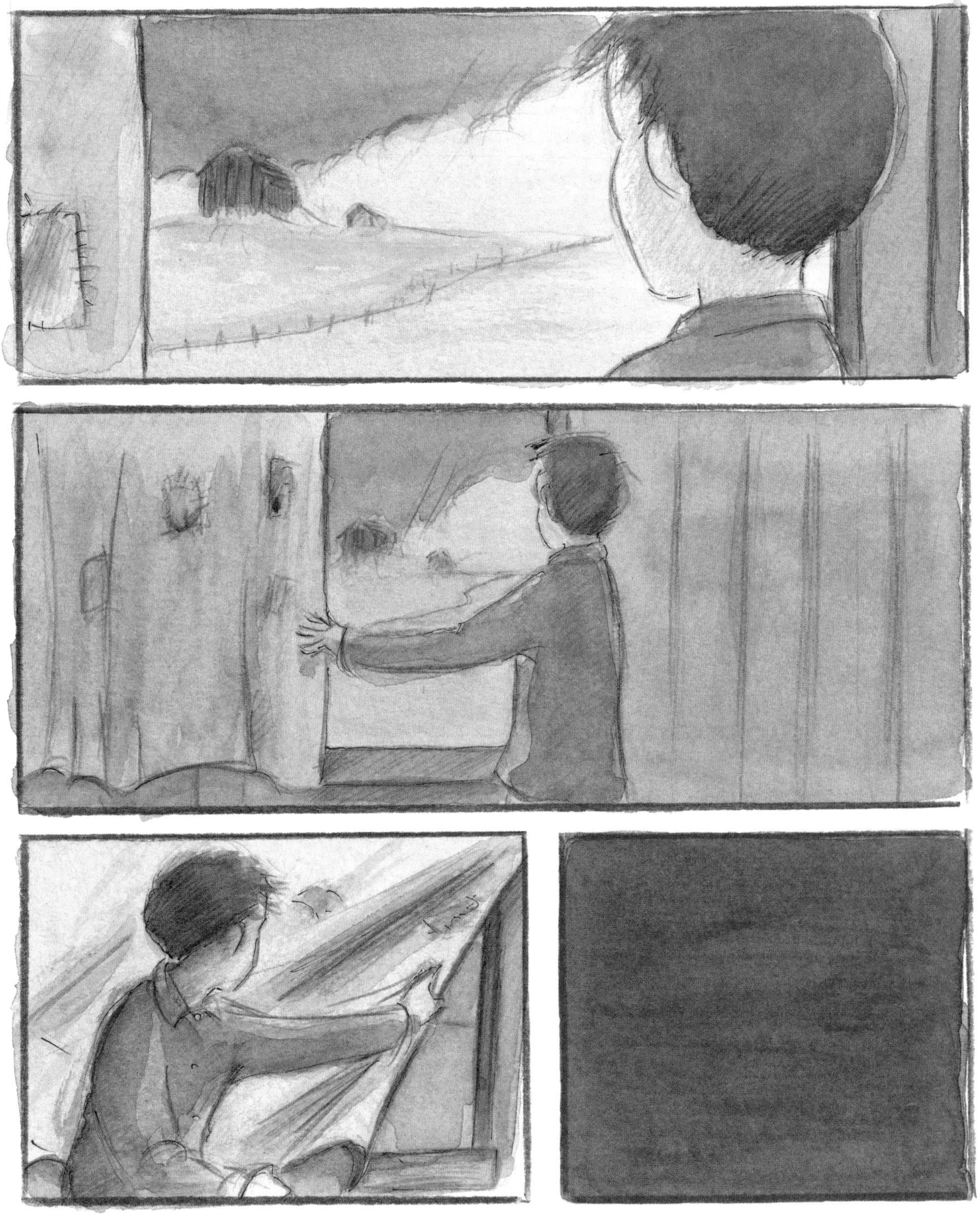

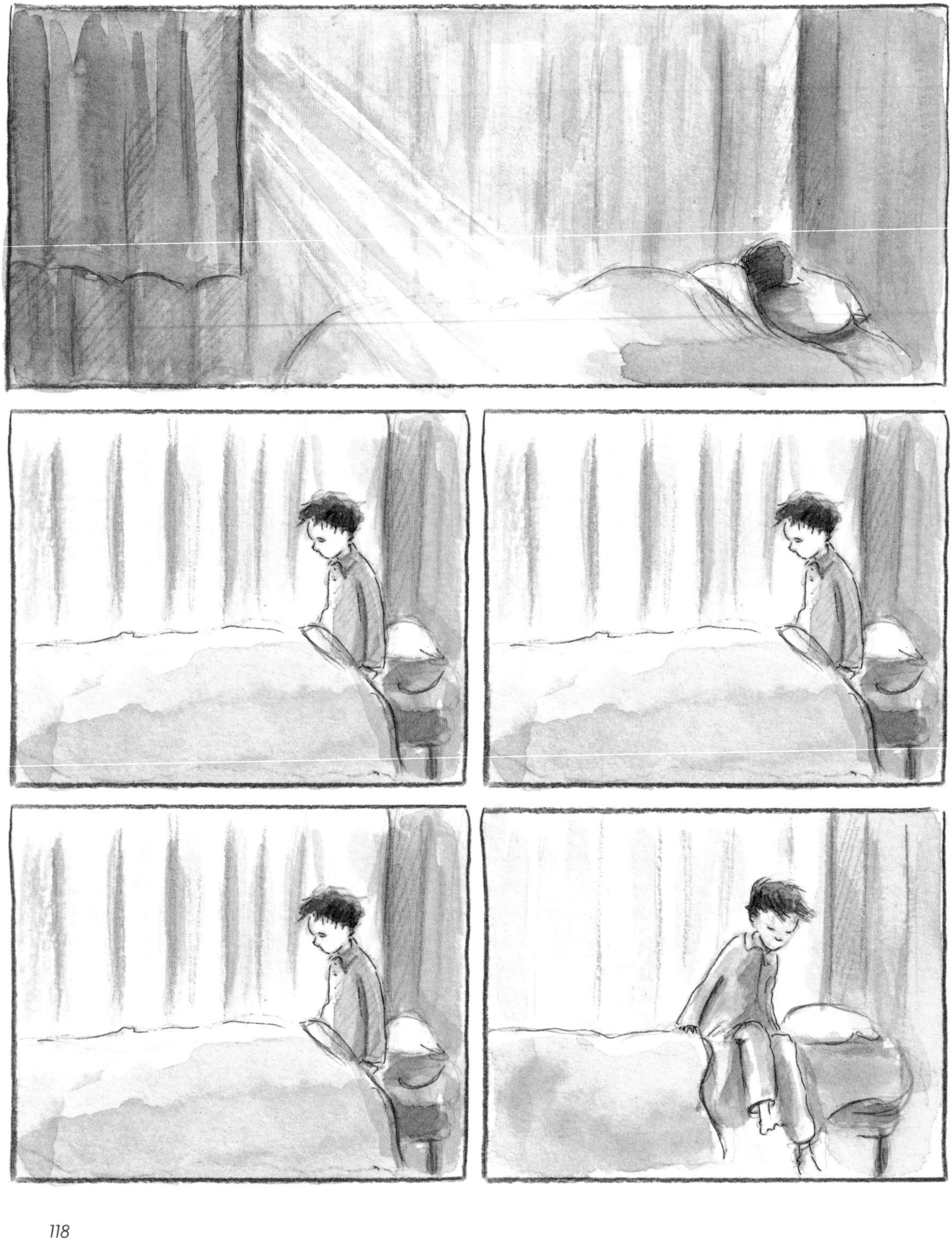

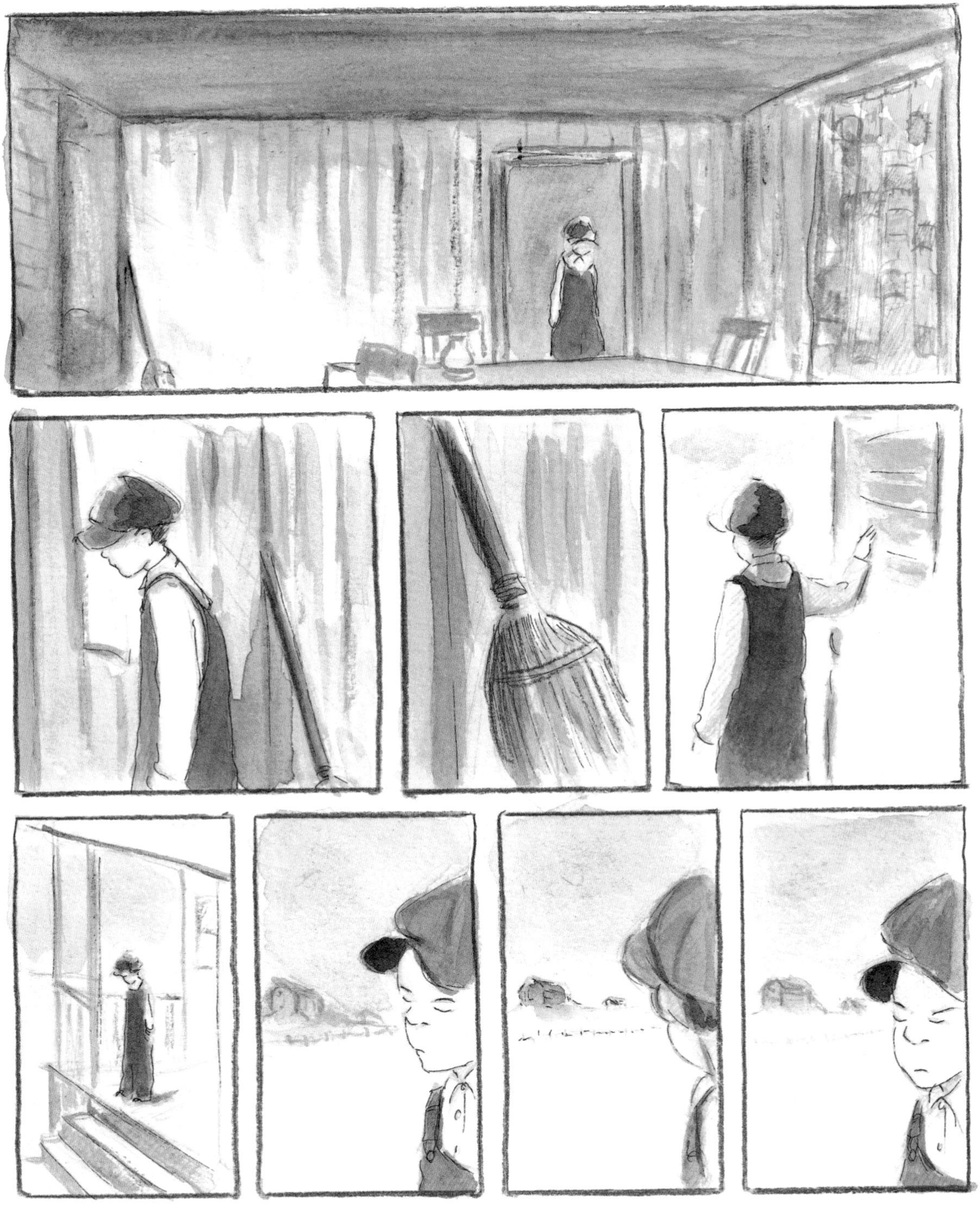

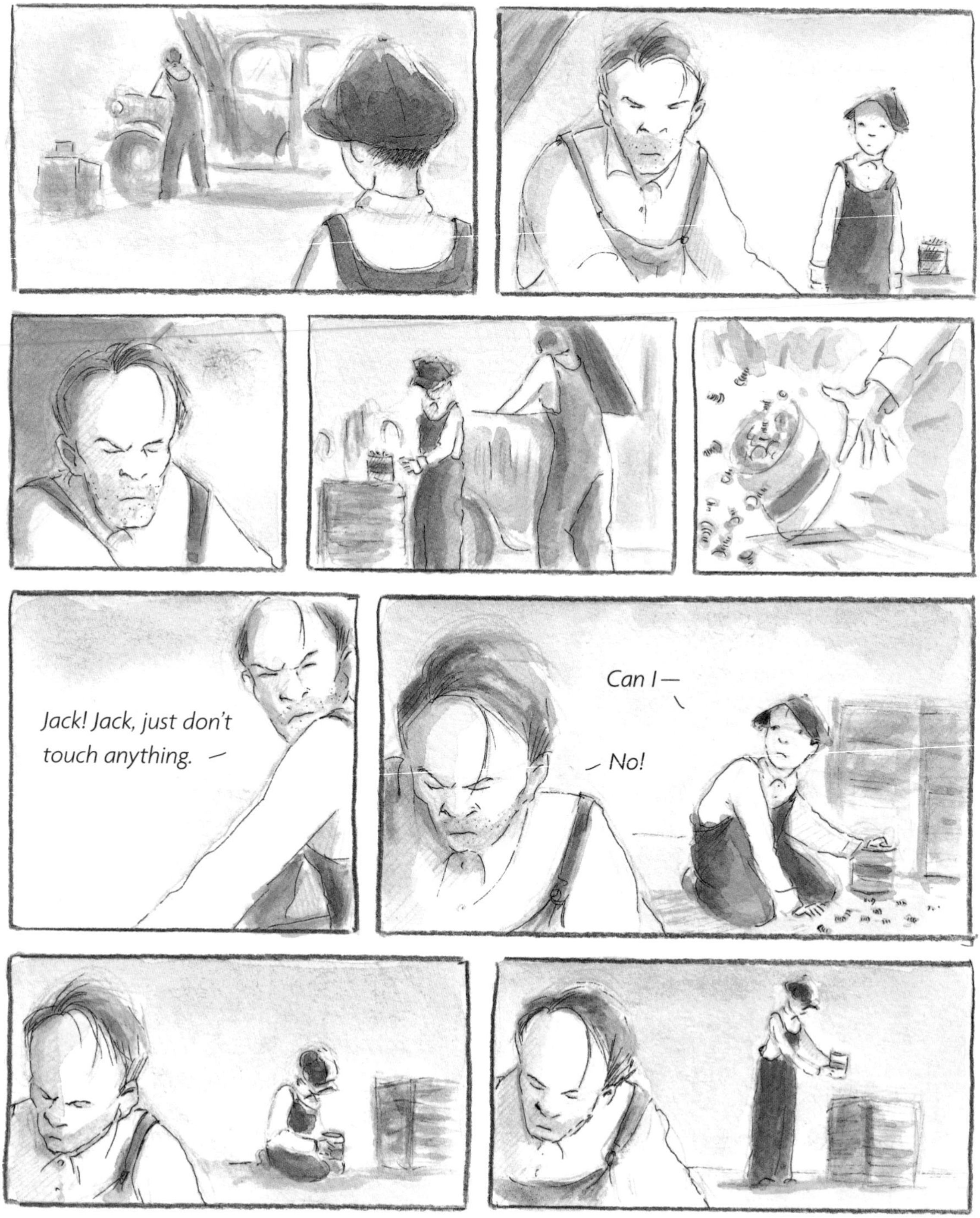
Jack! Jack, just don't touch anything.
Can I—
No!

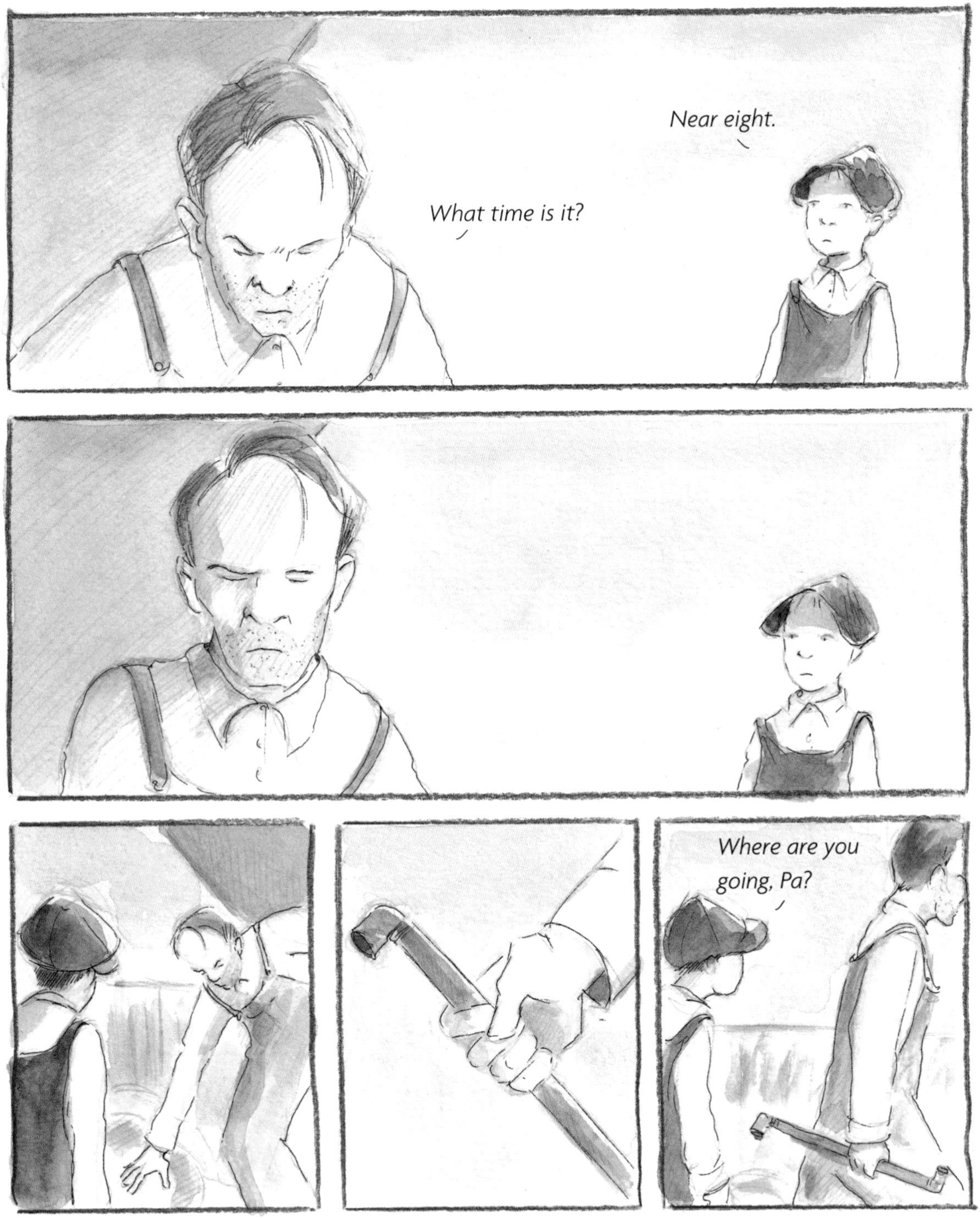
What time is it?
Near eight.
Where are you going, Pa?

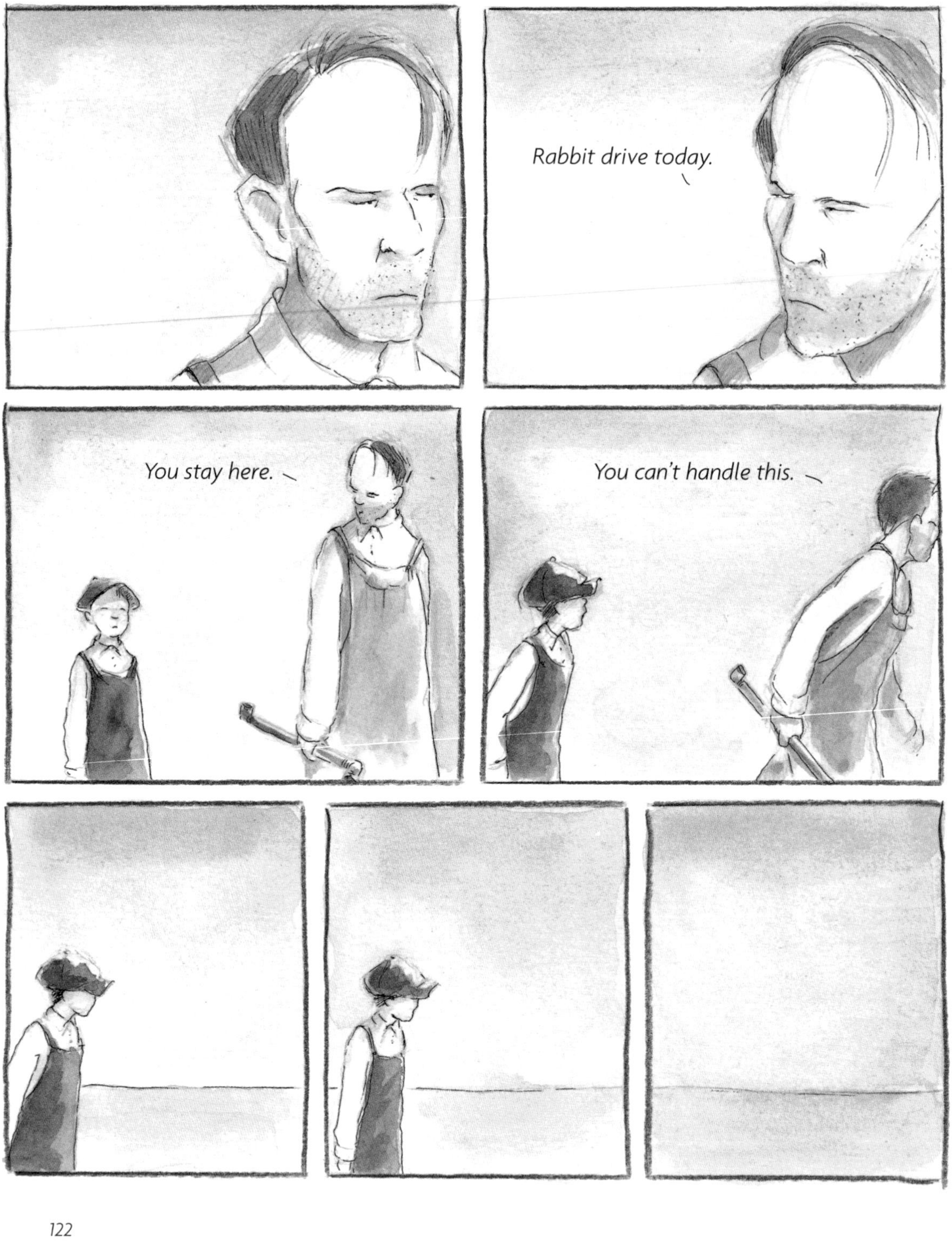
Rabbit drive today.
You stay here.
You can't handle this.

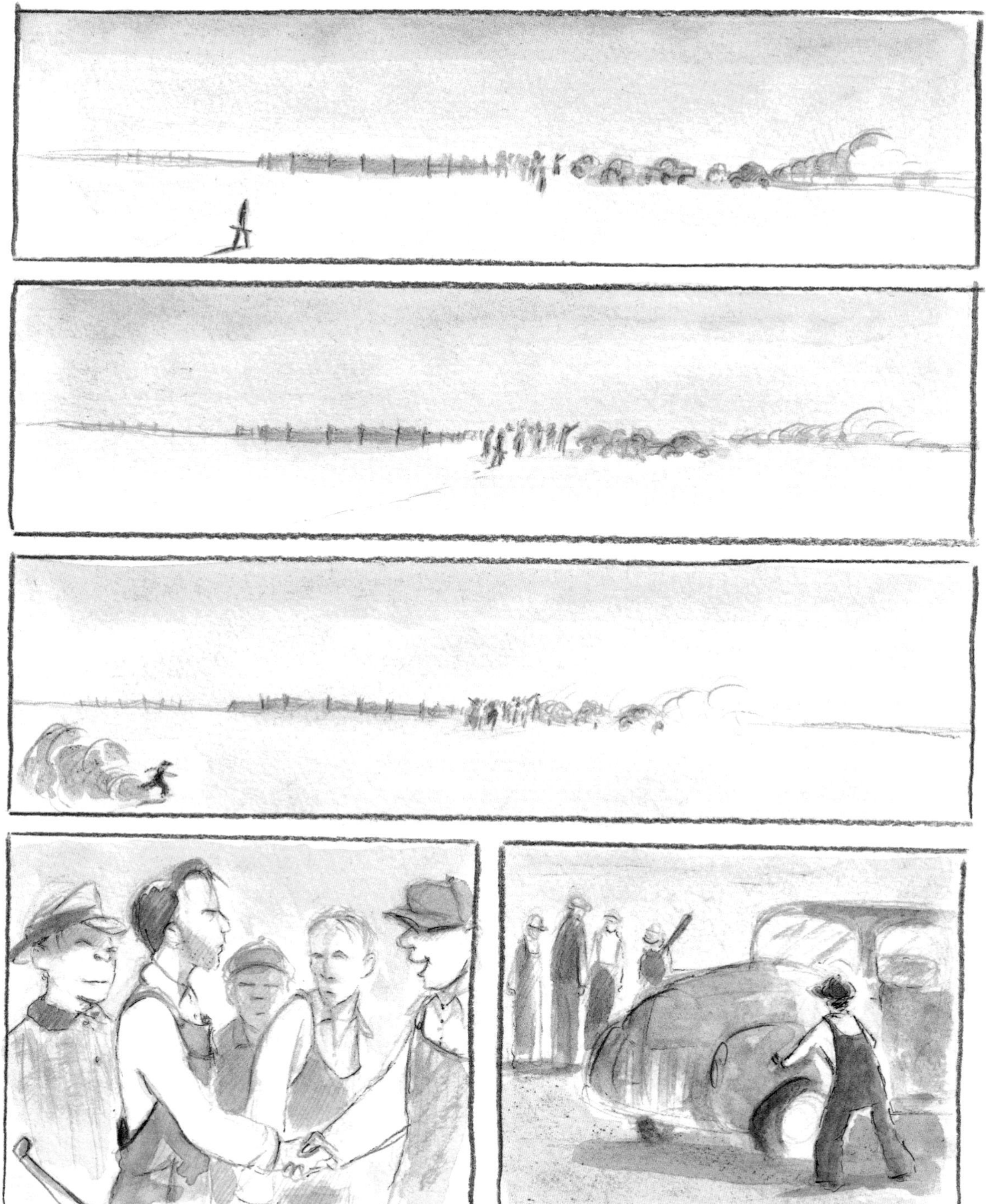

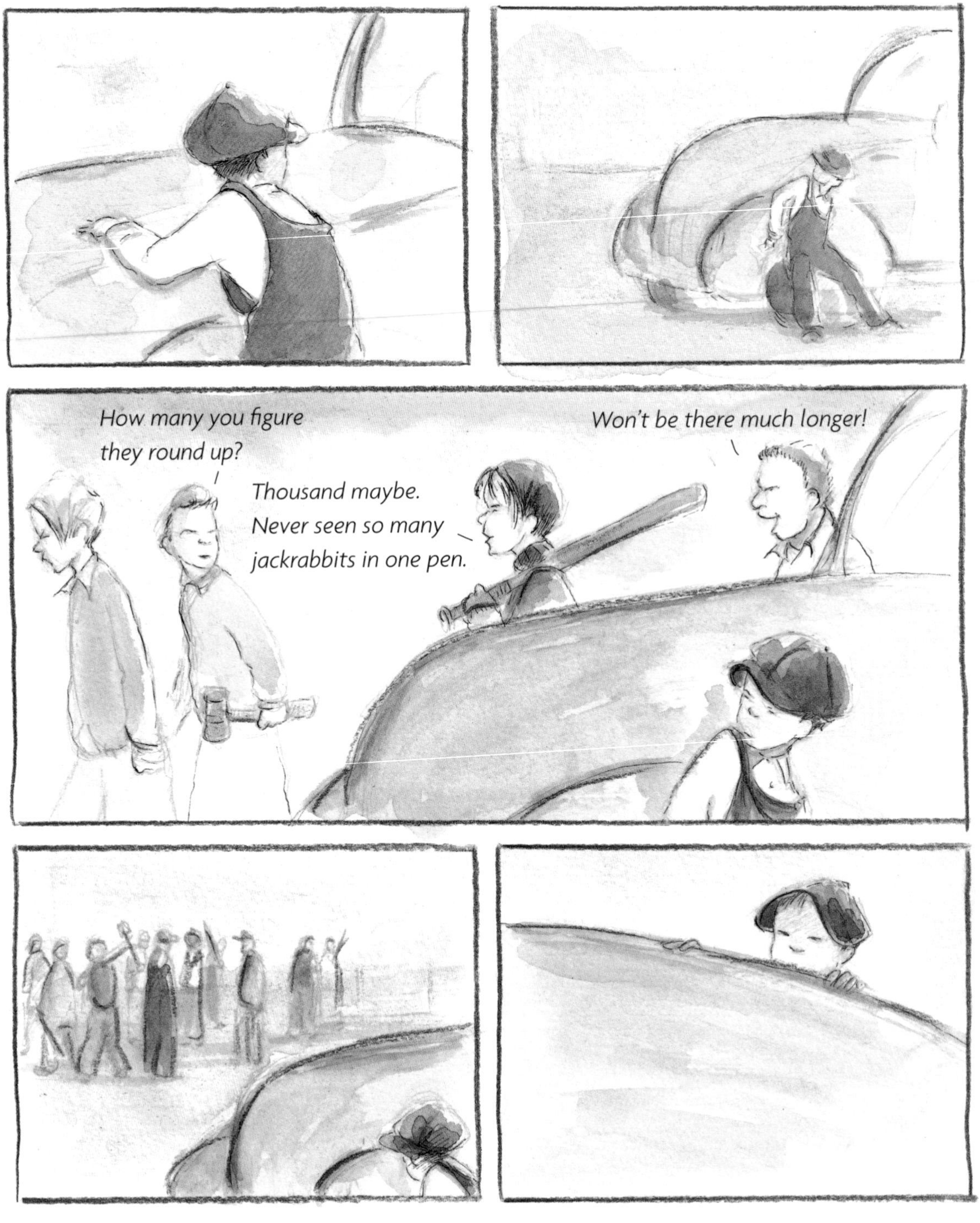
How many you figure they round up?
Thousand maybe. Never seen so many jackrabbits in one pen.
Won't be there much longer!

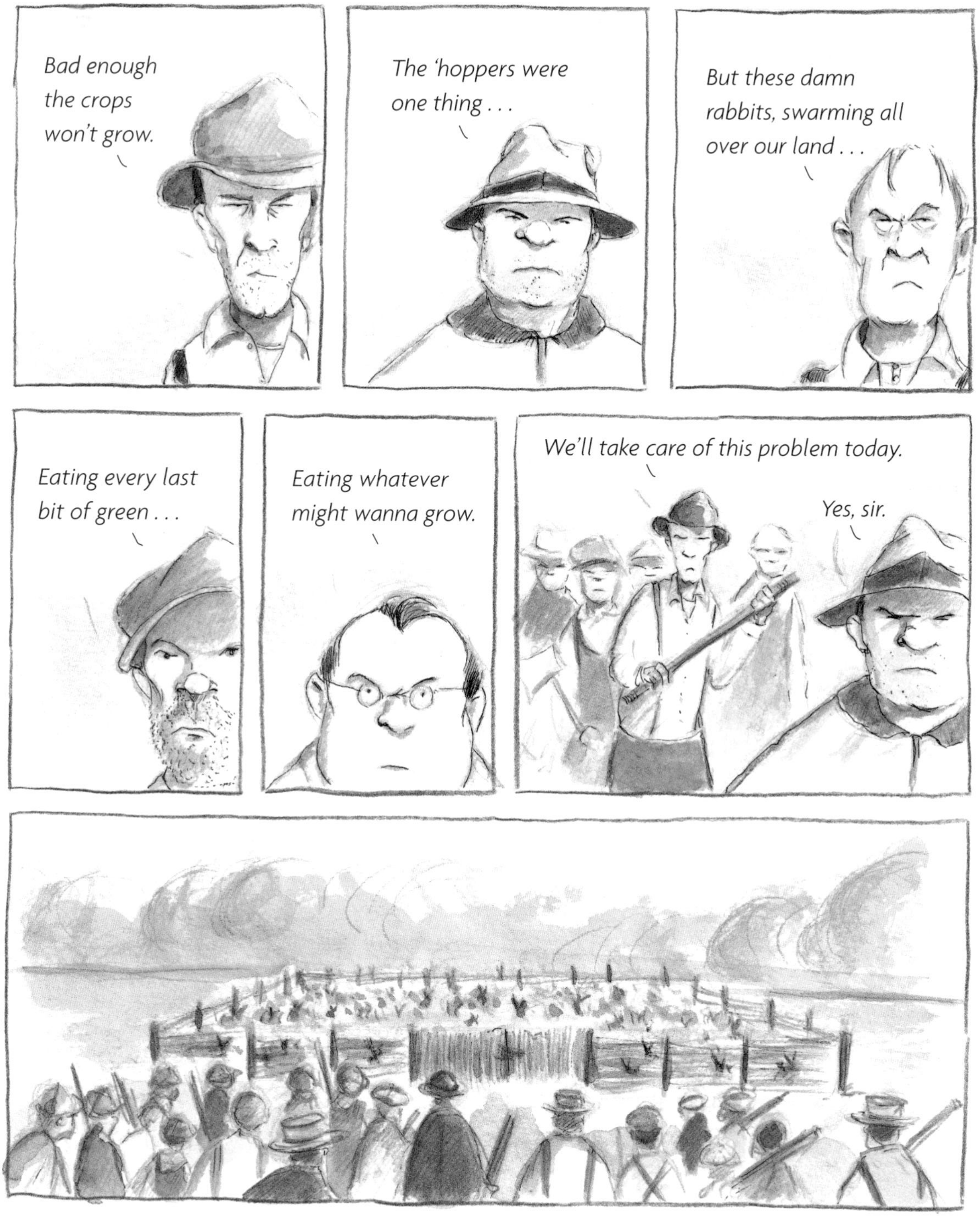
Bad enough the crops won't grow.
The 'hoppers were one thing . . .
But these damn rabbits, swarming all over our land . . .
Eating every last bit of green . . .
Eating whatever might wanna grow.
We'll take care of this problem today.
Yes, sir.

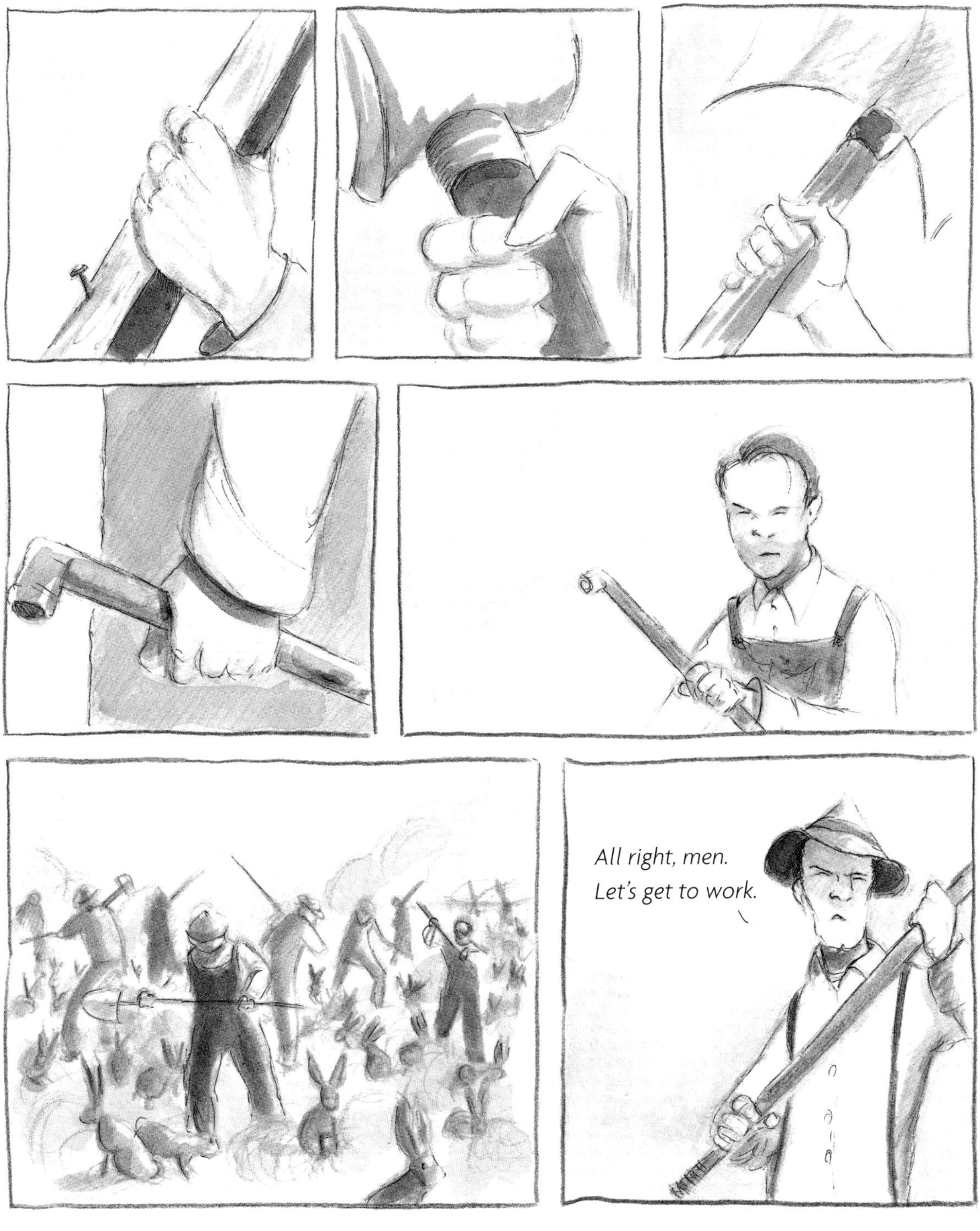
All right, men.
Let's get to work.

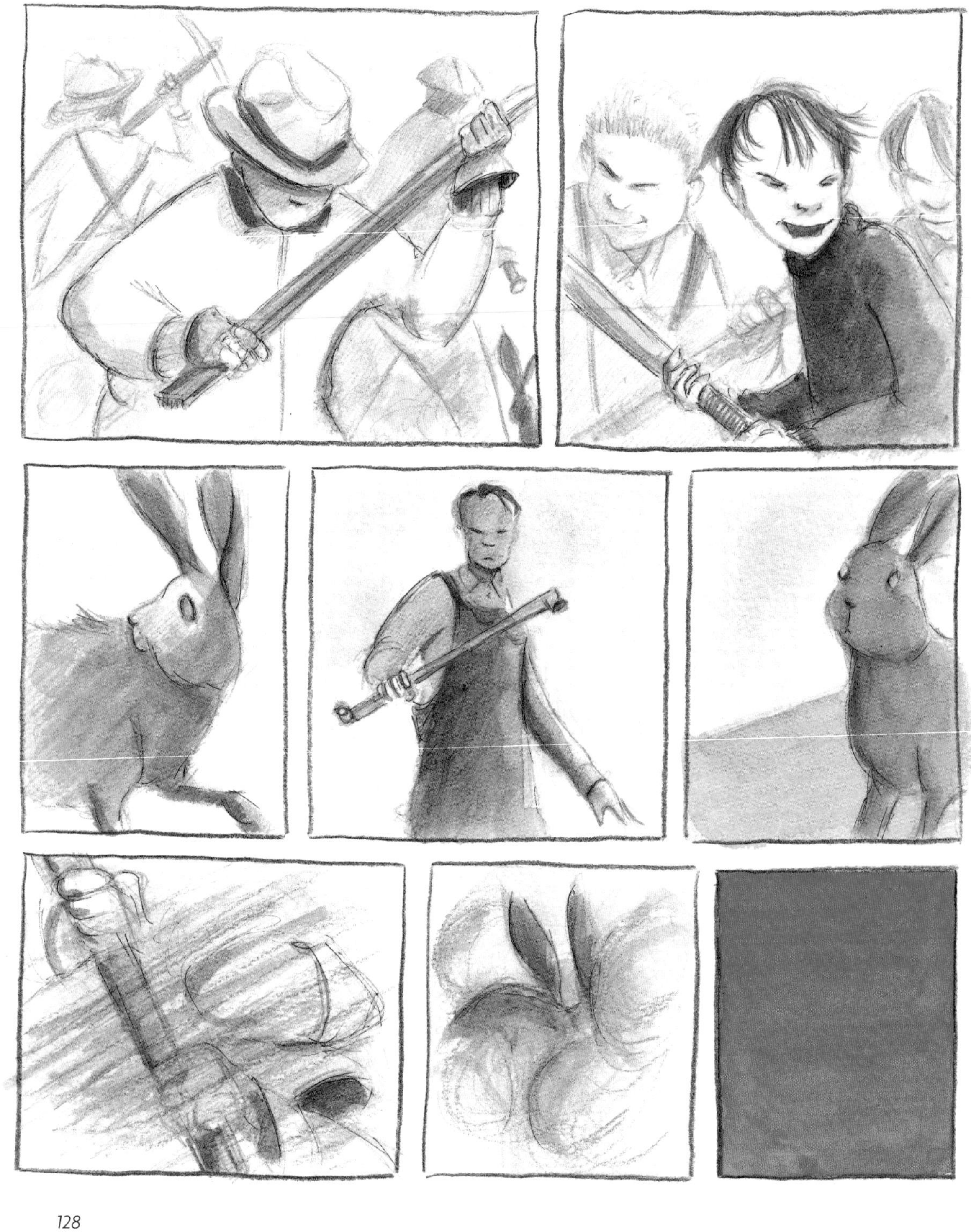

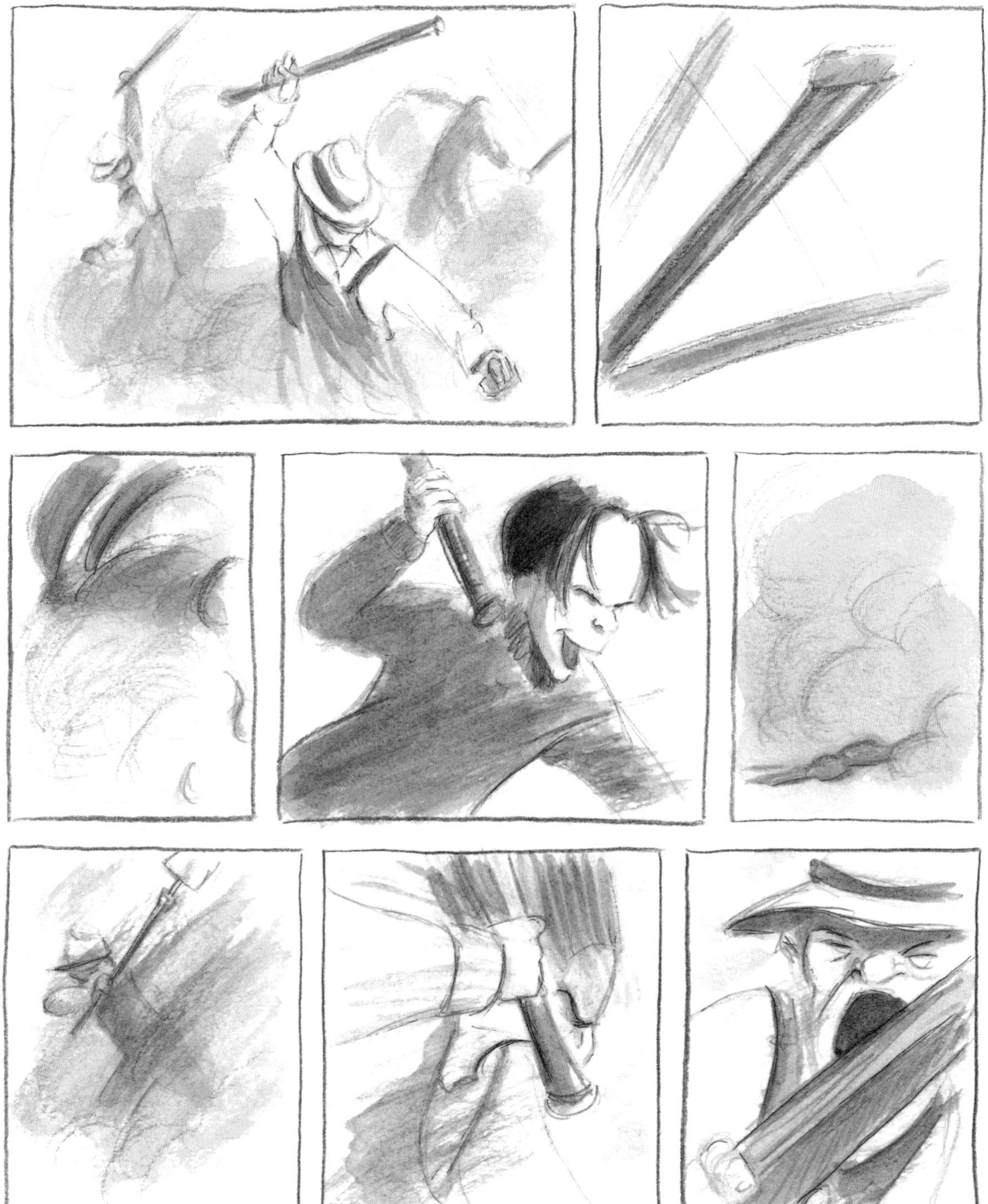

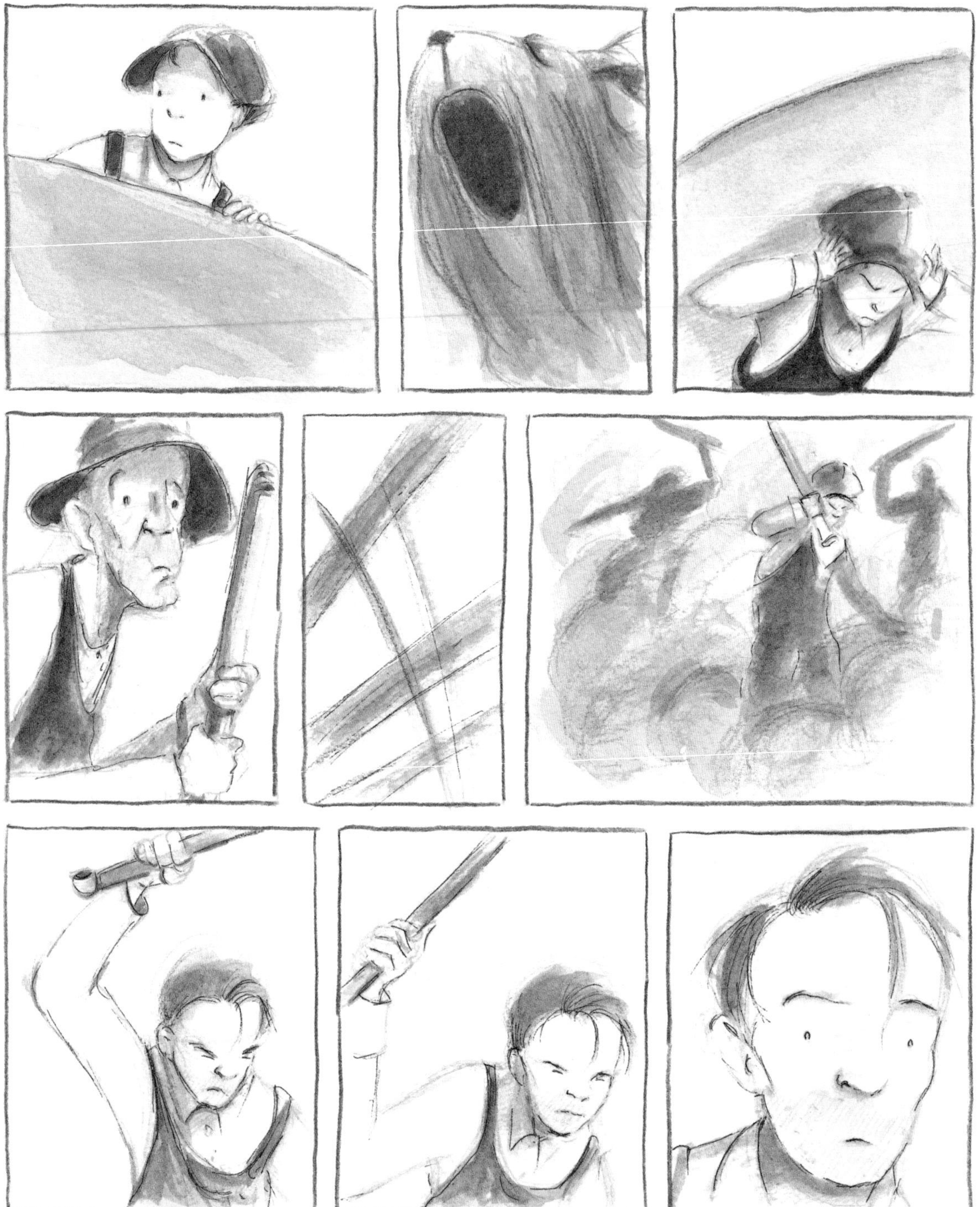

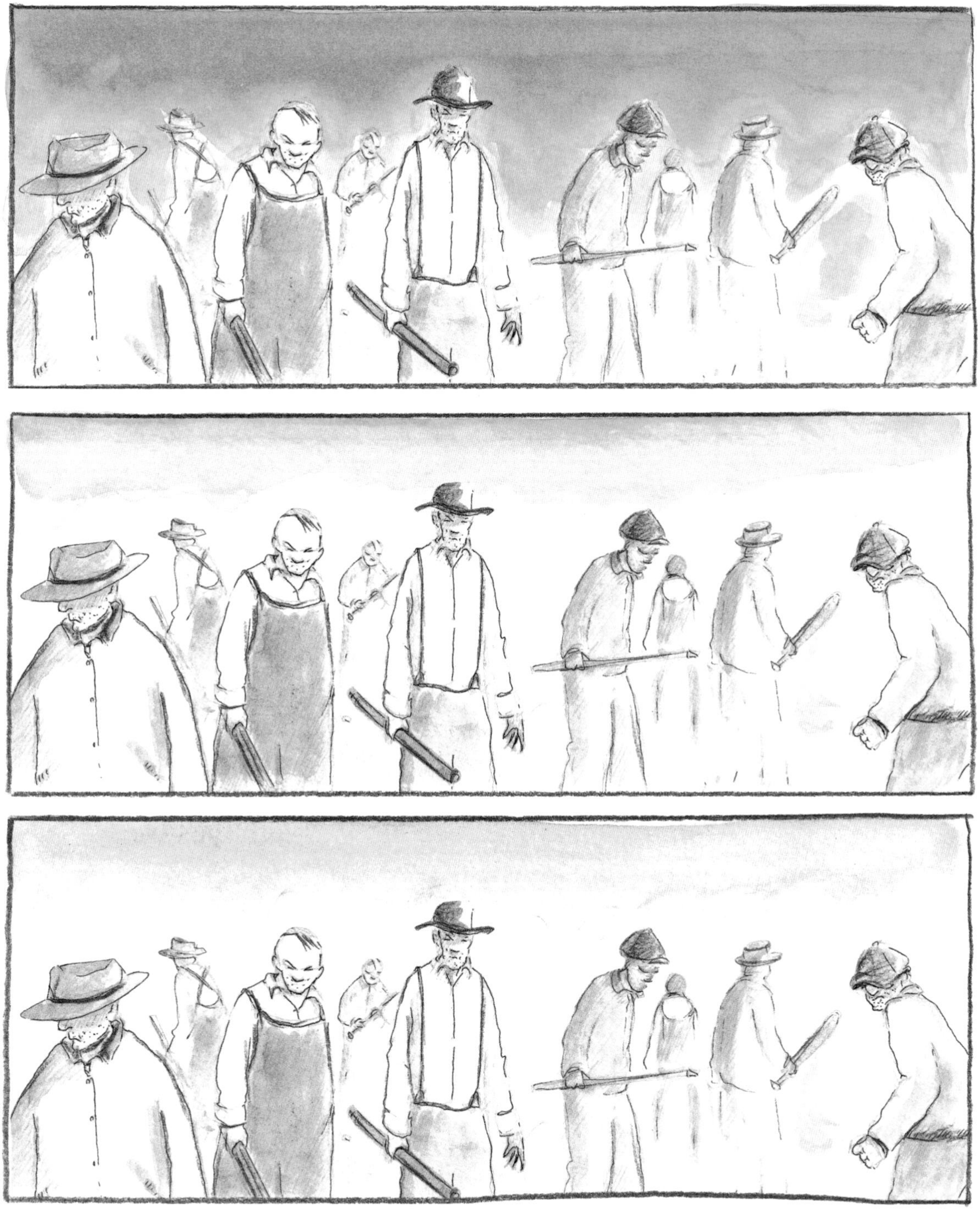

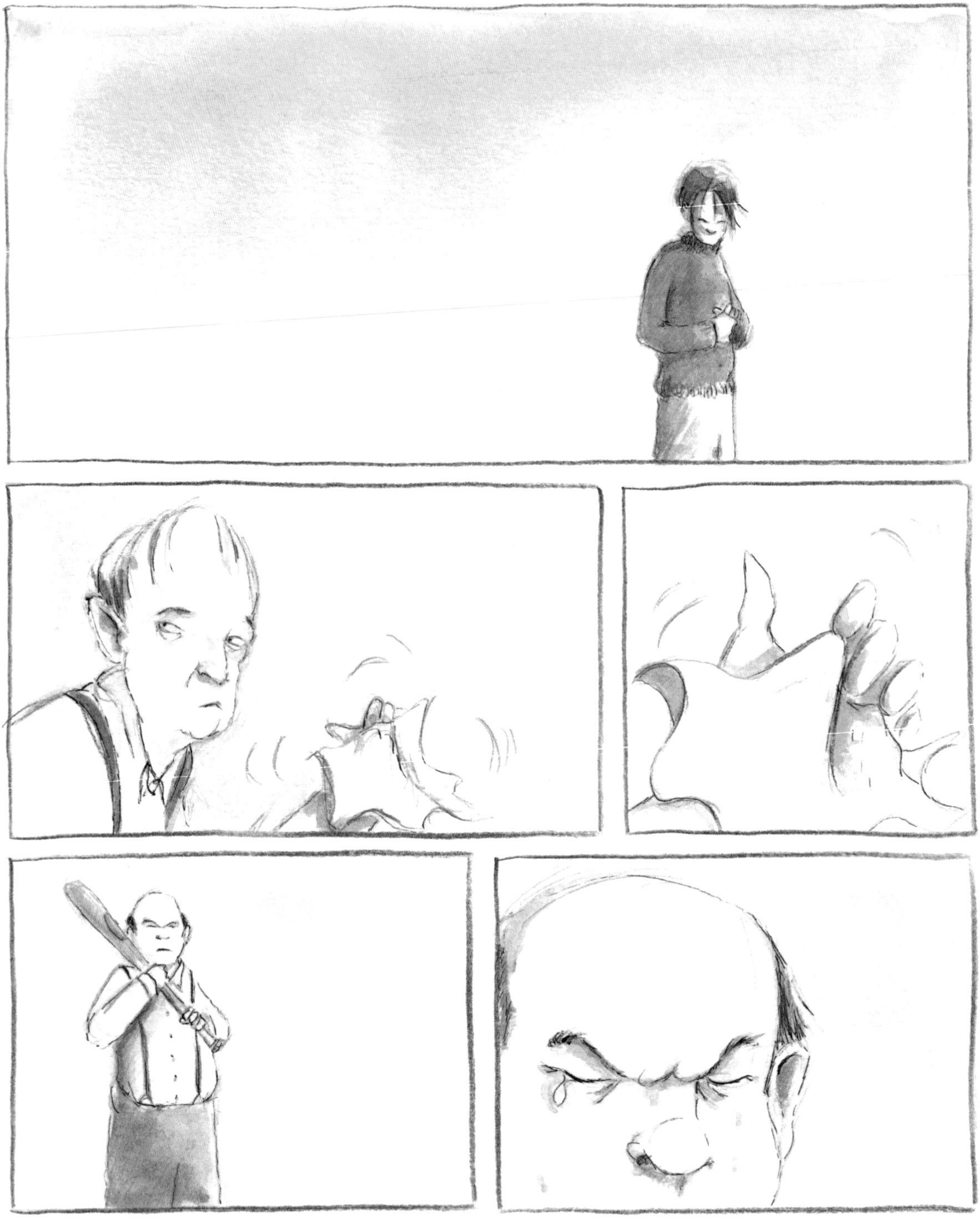

133

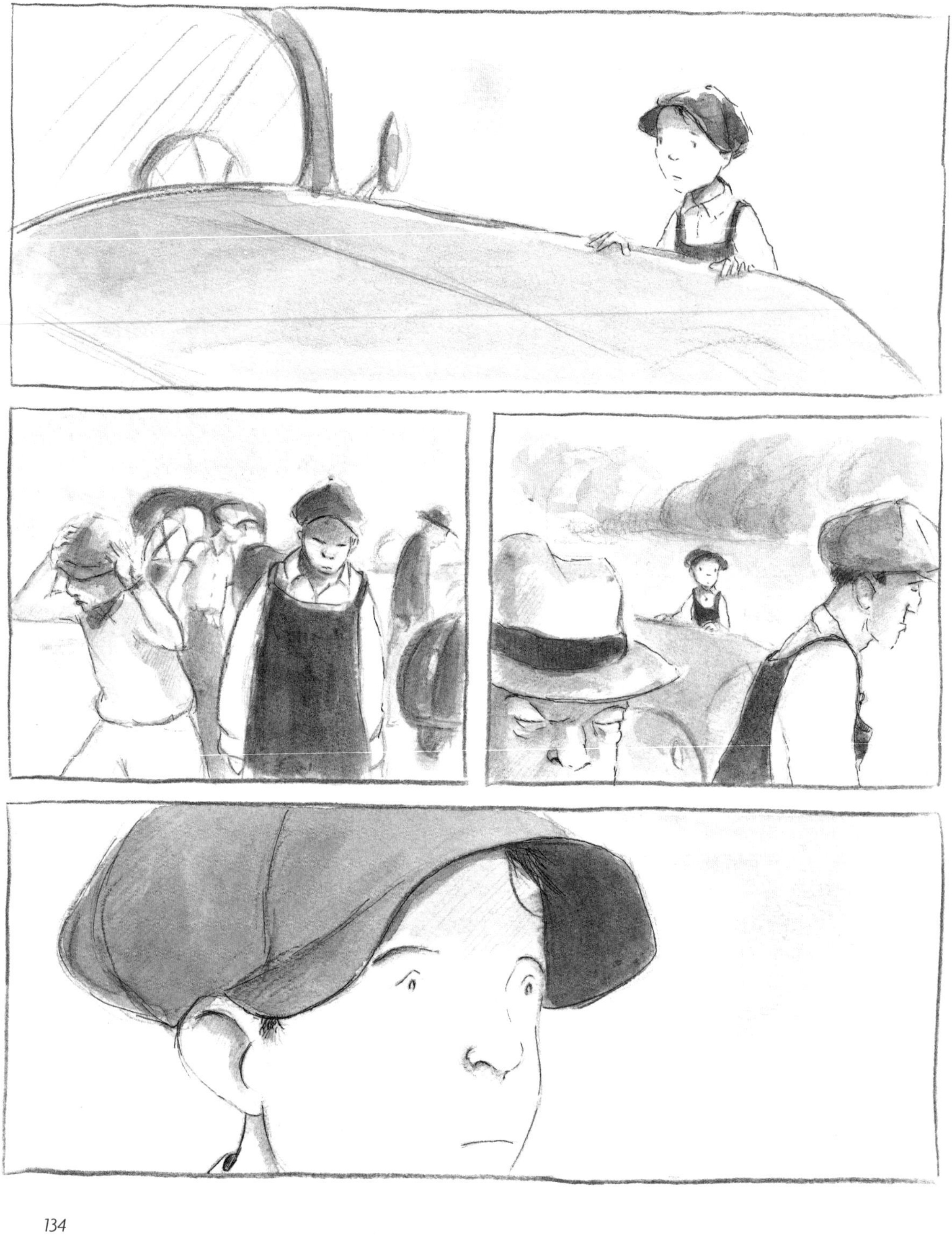

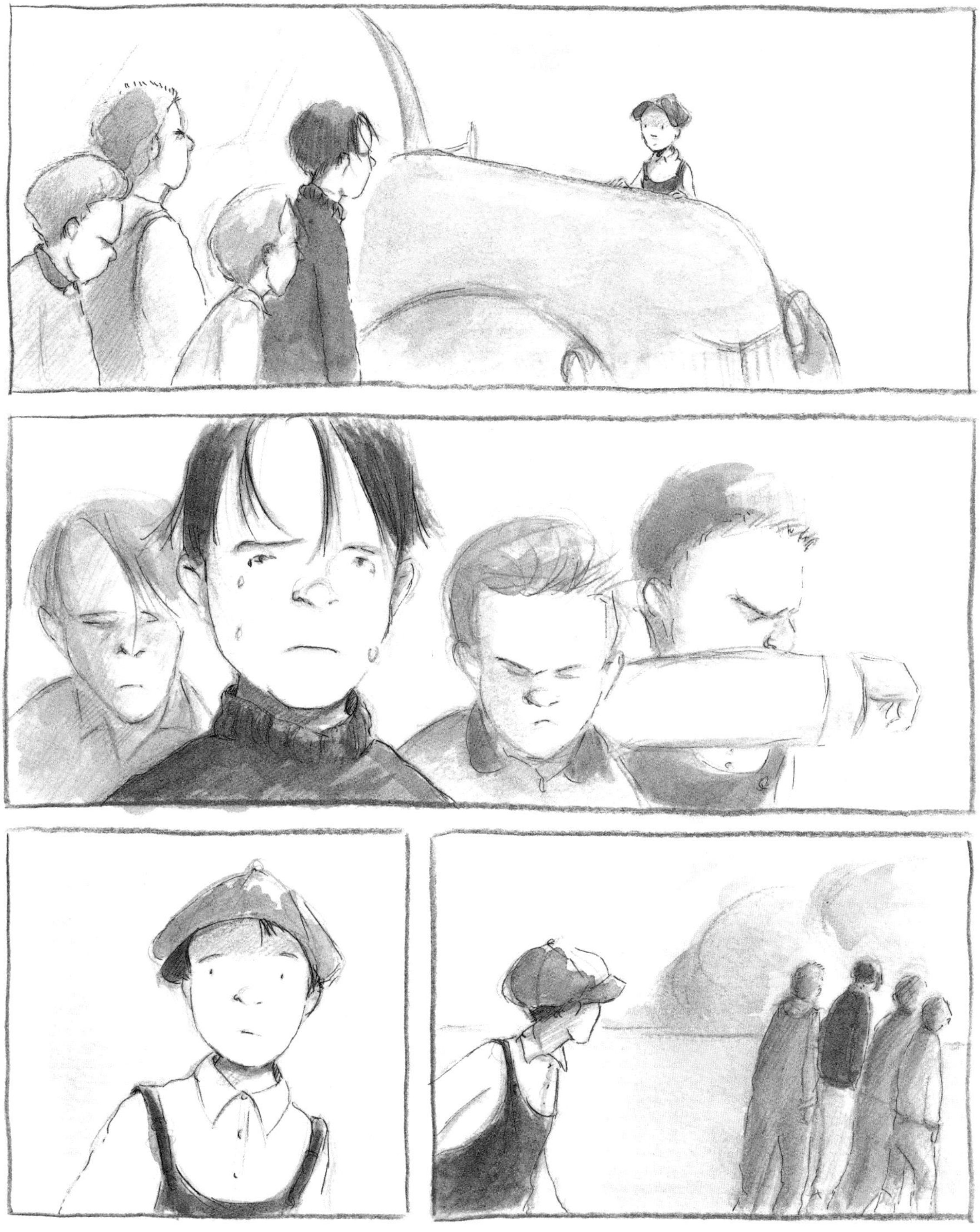

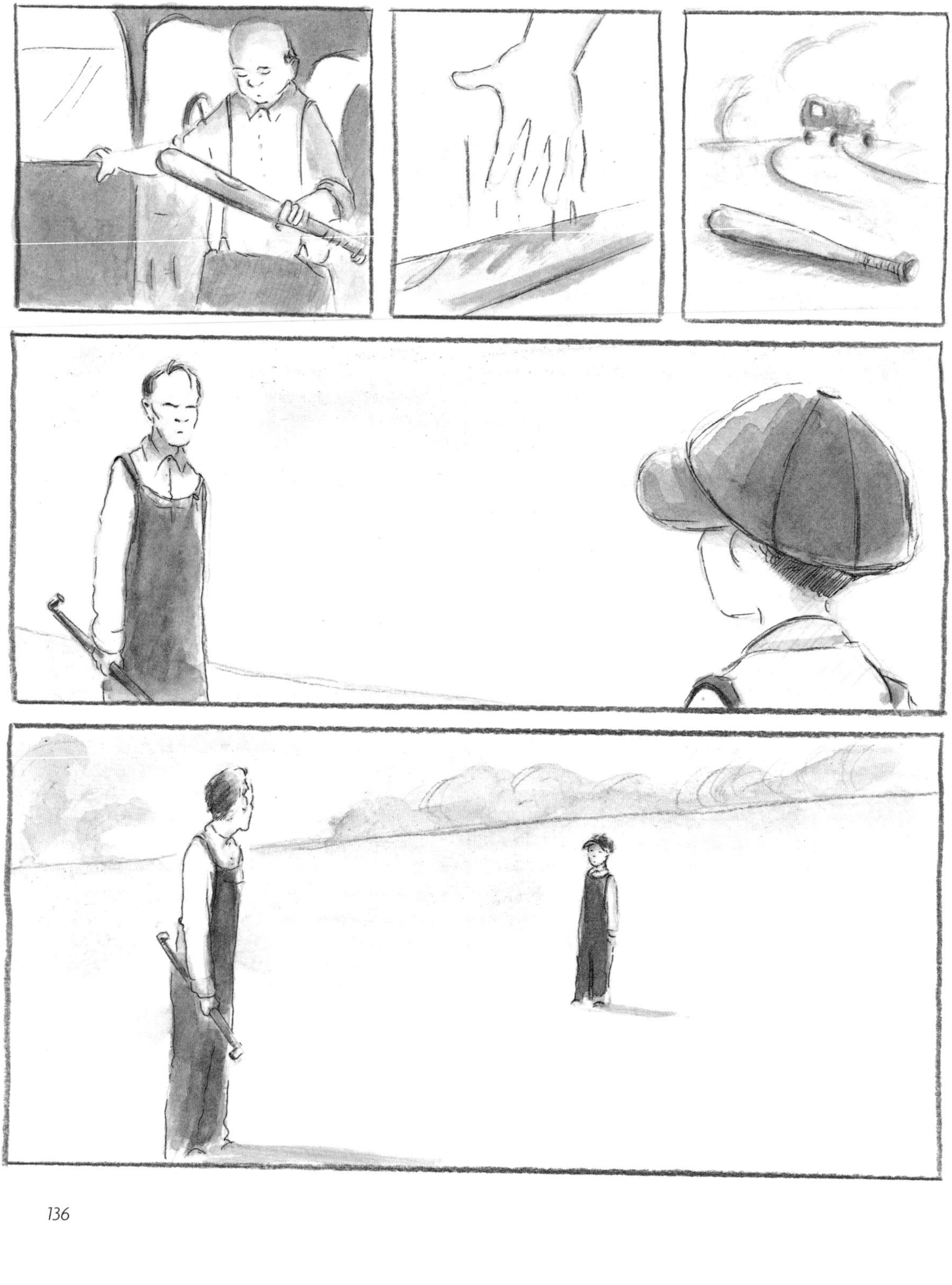

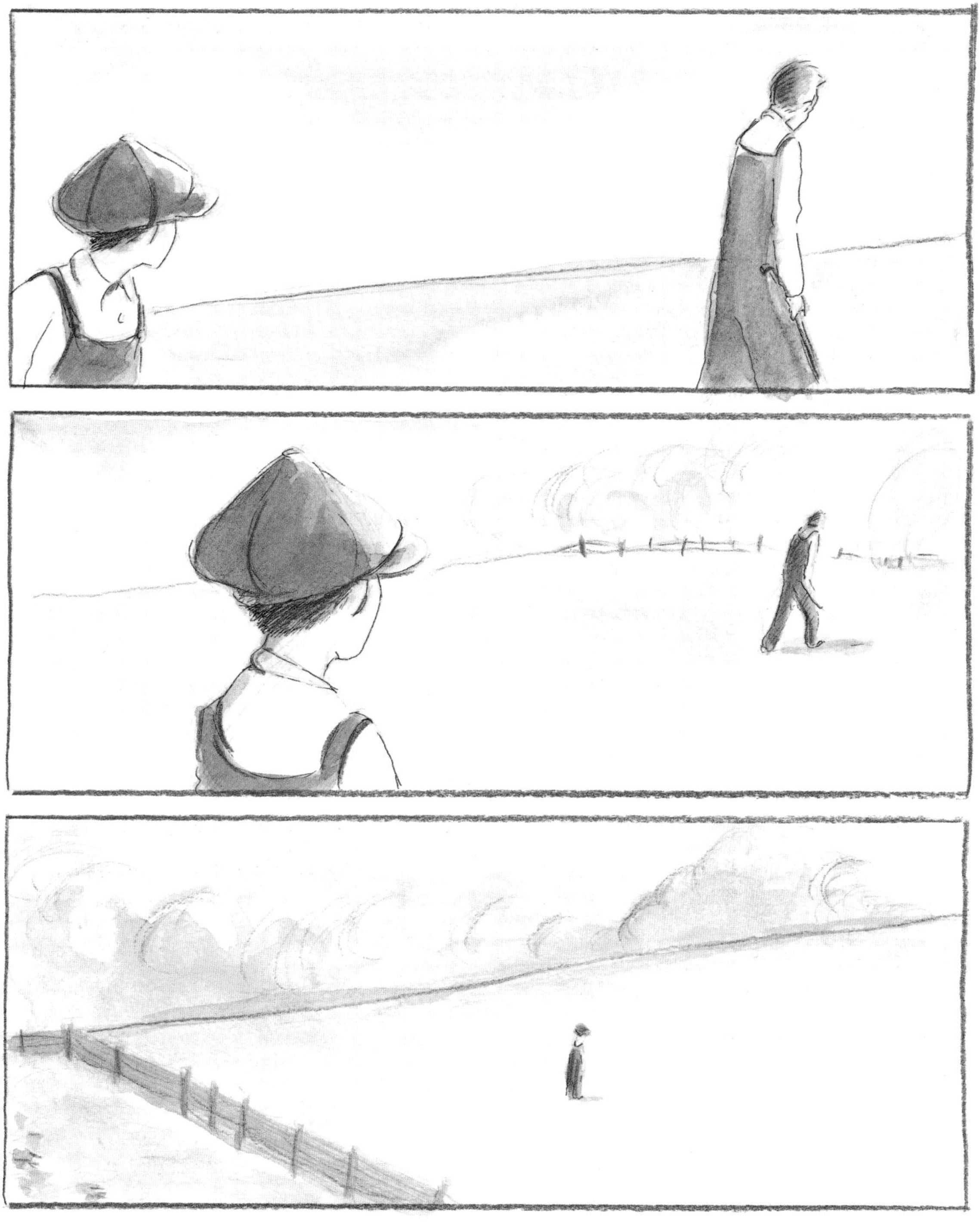

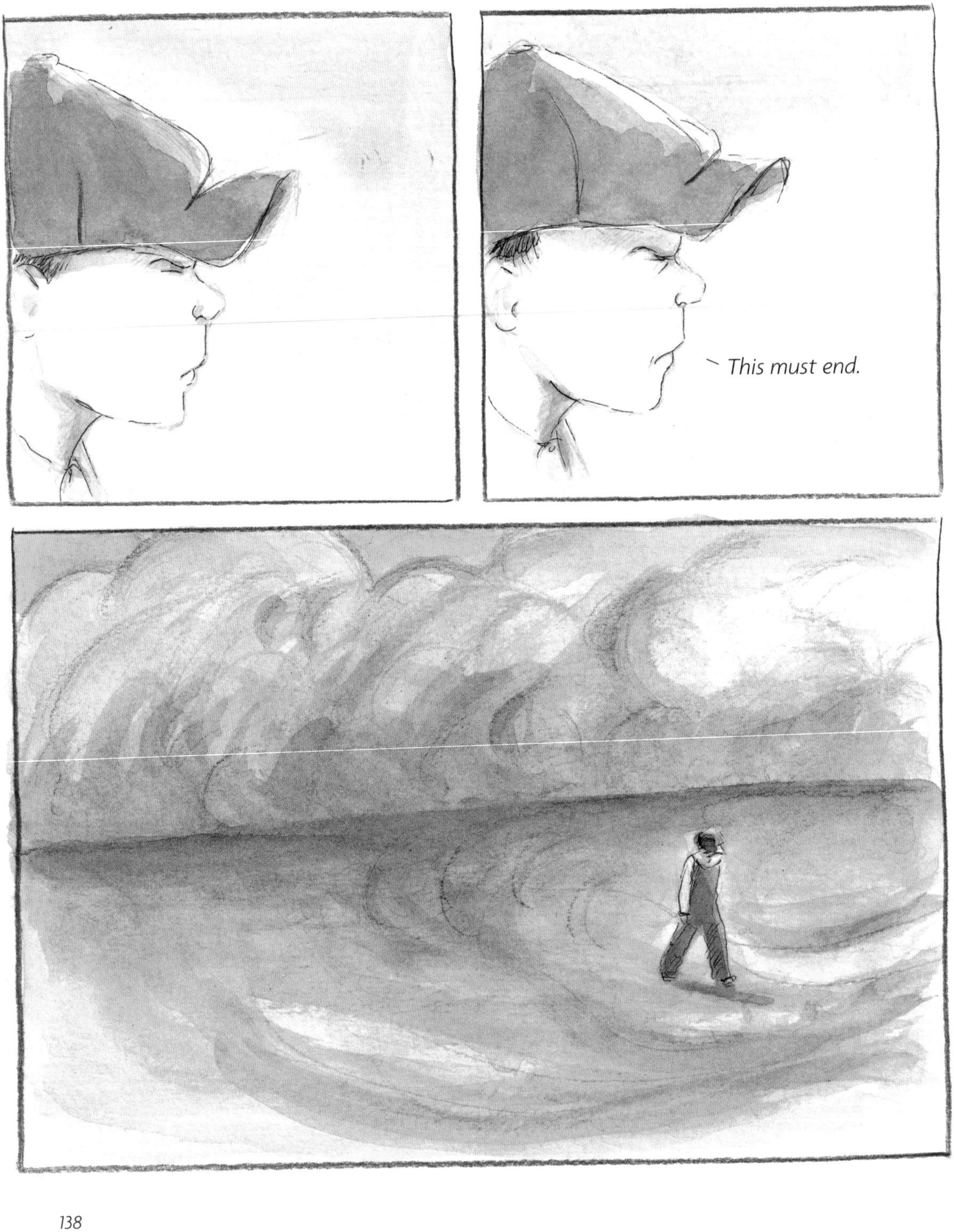
This must end.

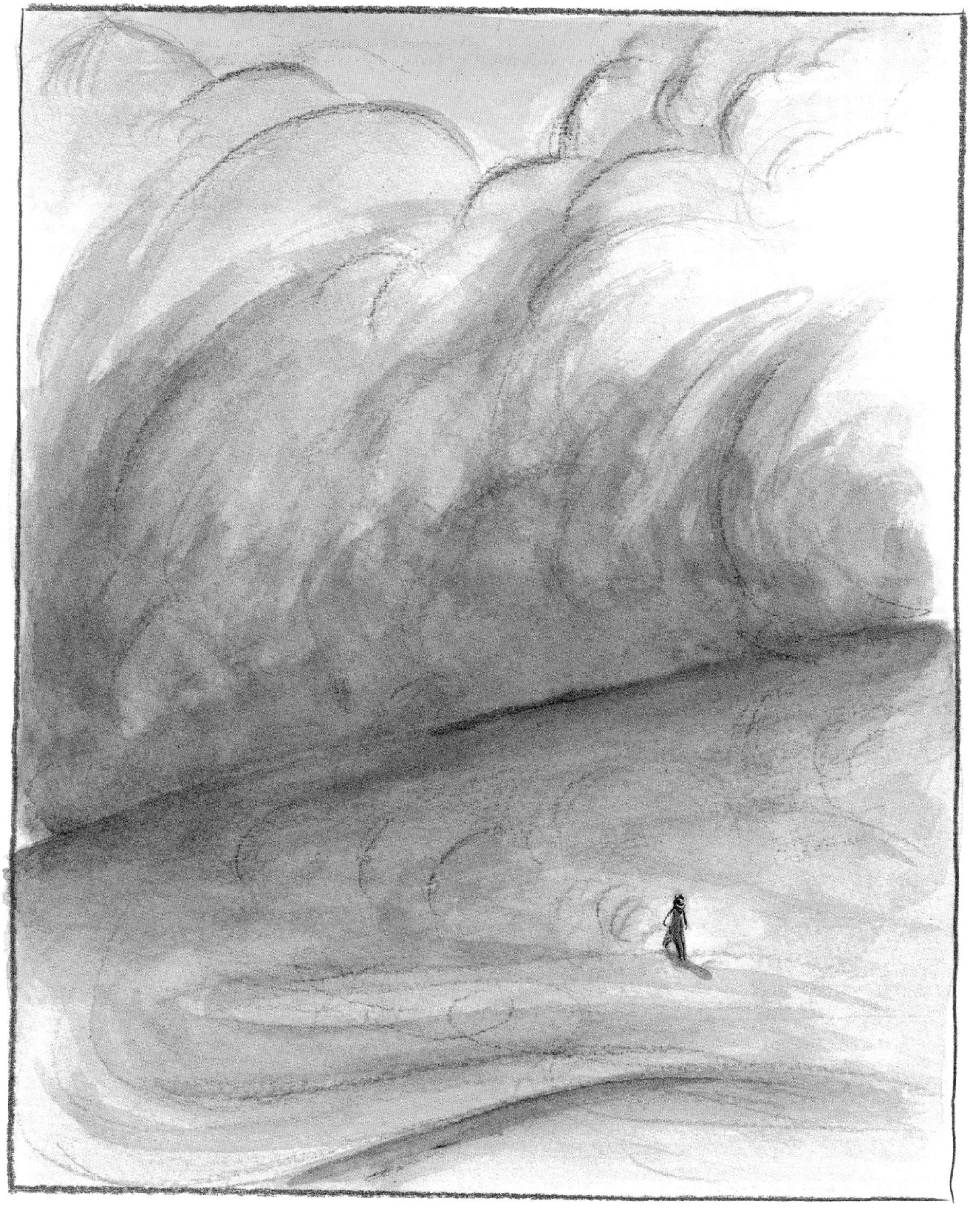

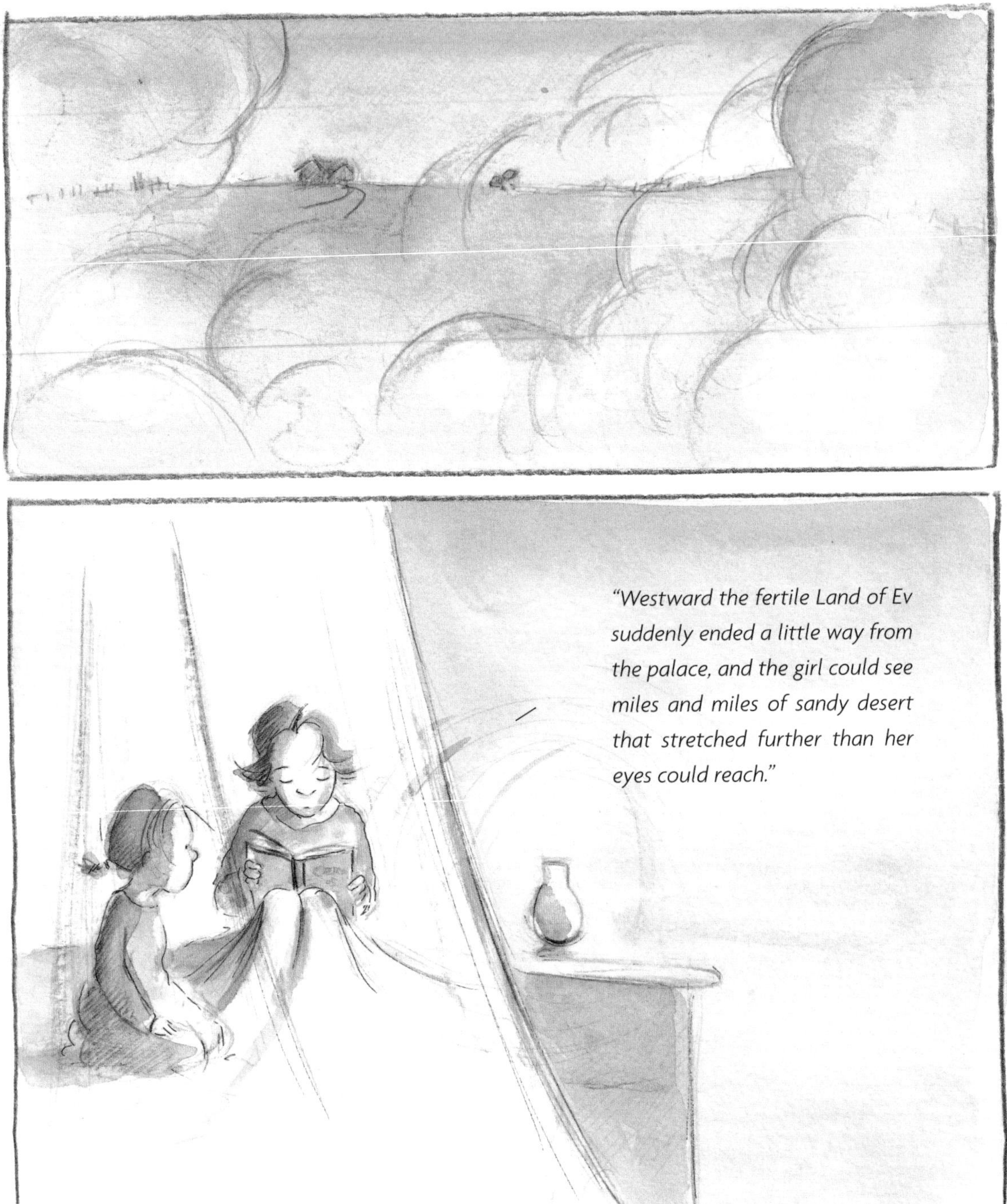
"Westward the fertile Land of Ev suddenly ended a little way from the palace, and the girl could see miles and miles of sandy desert that stretched further than her eyes could reach."

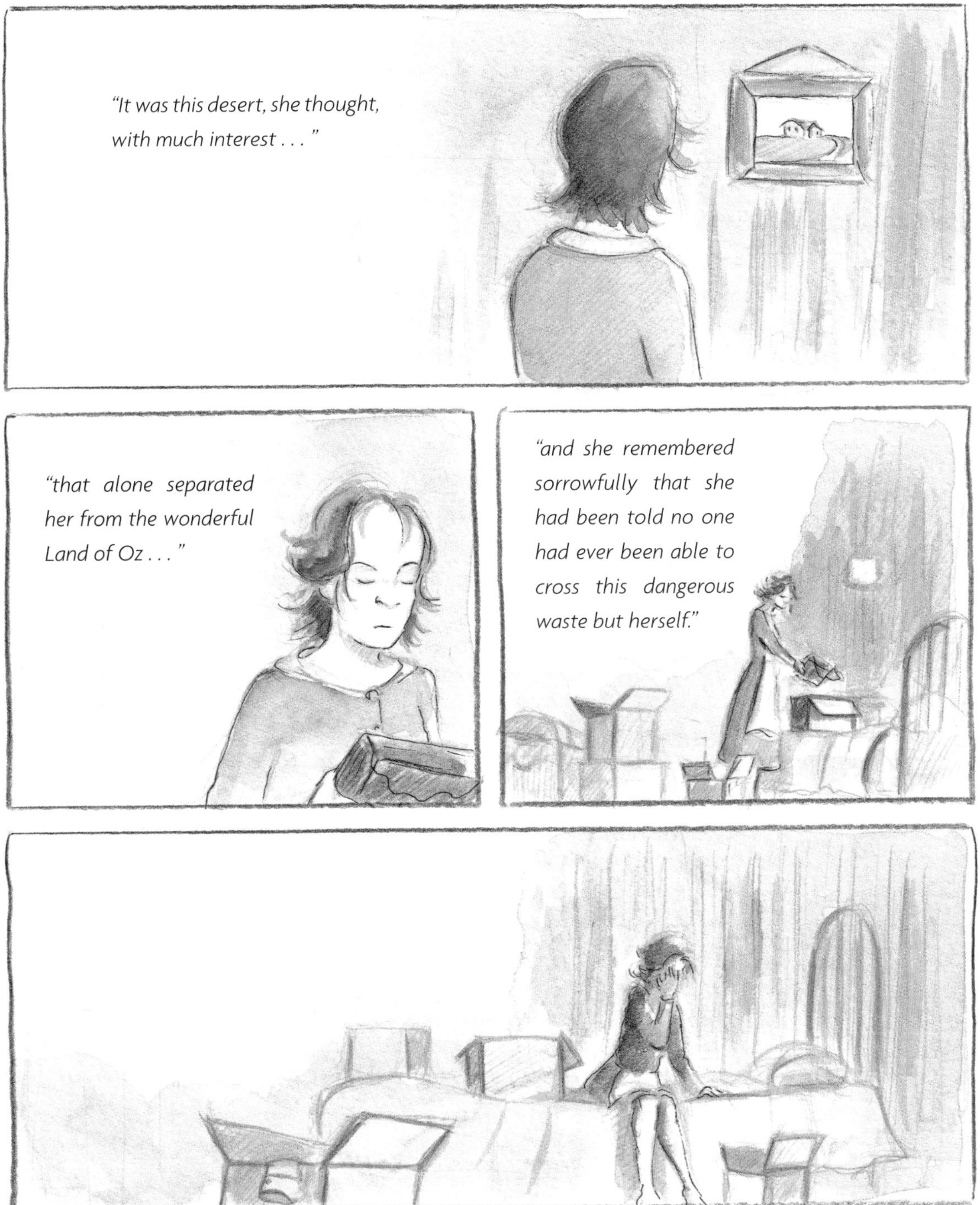
"It was this desert, she thought, with much interest . . . "
"that alone separated her from the wonderful Land of Oz . . . "
"and she remembered sorrowfully that she had been told no one had ever been able to cross this dangerous waste but herself."

"Once a cyclone had carried her across it, and a magical pair of silver shoes had carried her back again."

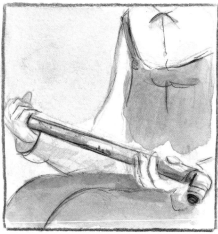

"But now she had neither a cyclone nor silver shoes to assist her . . ."

"and her condition was sad indeed."

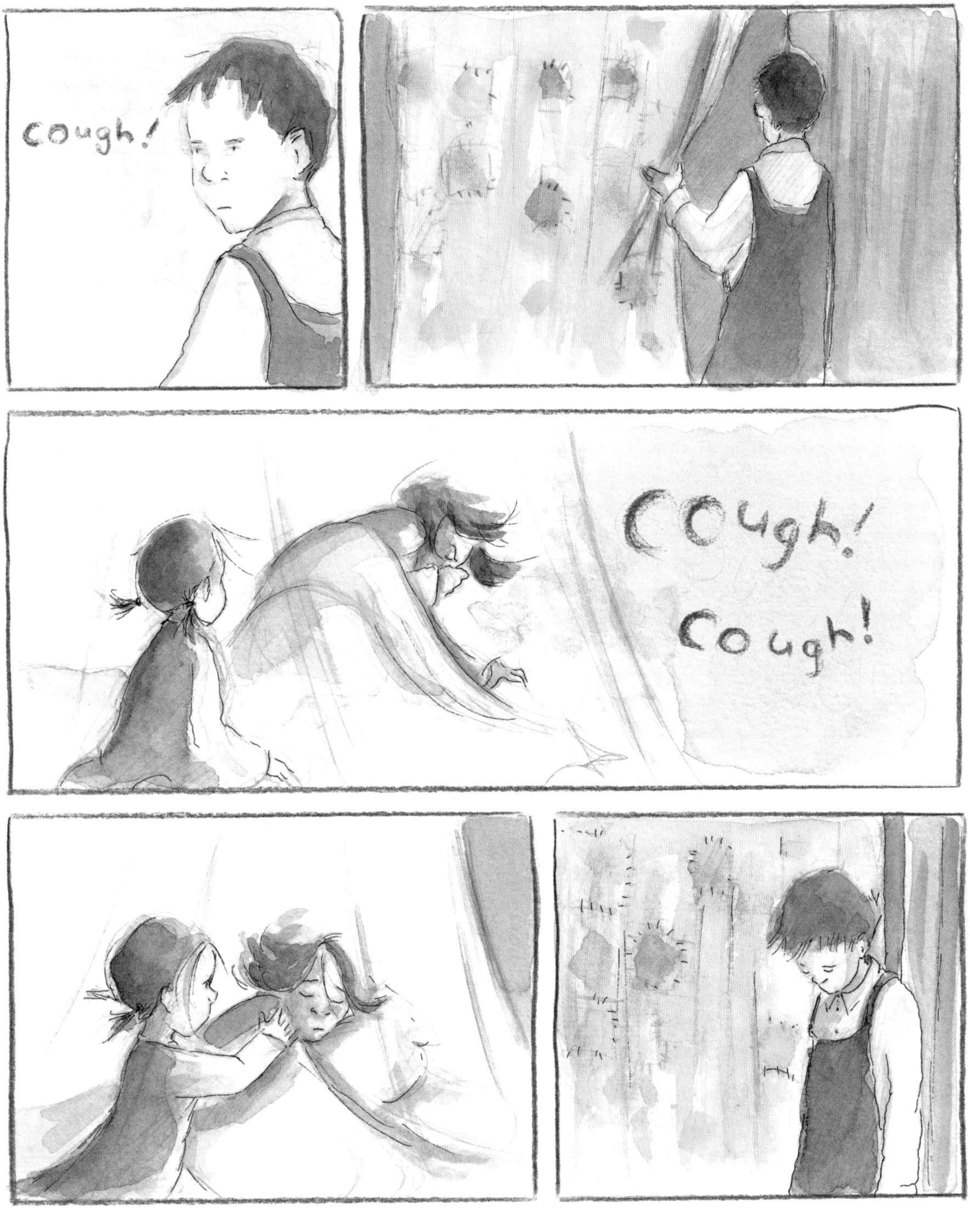
cough!
Cough!
Cough!

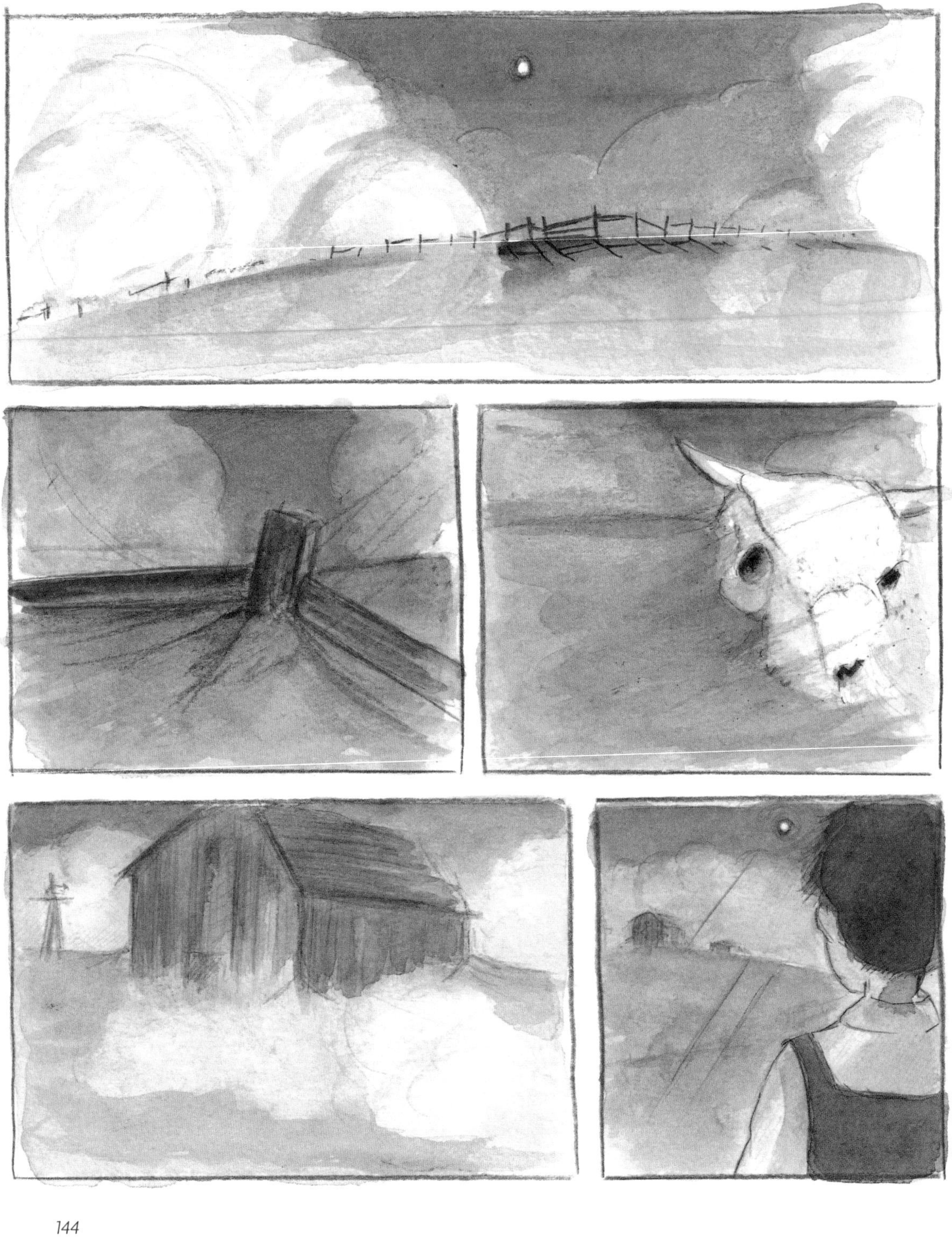

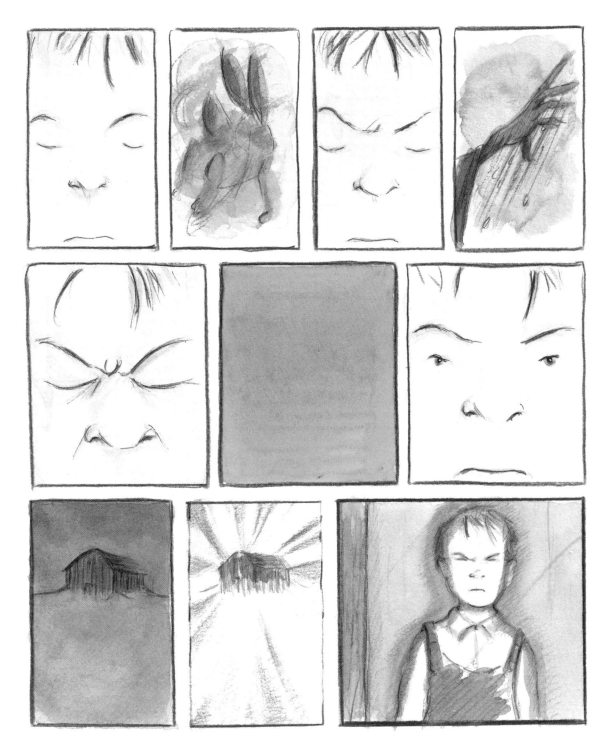

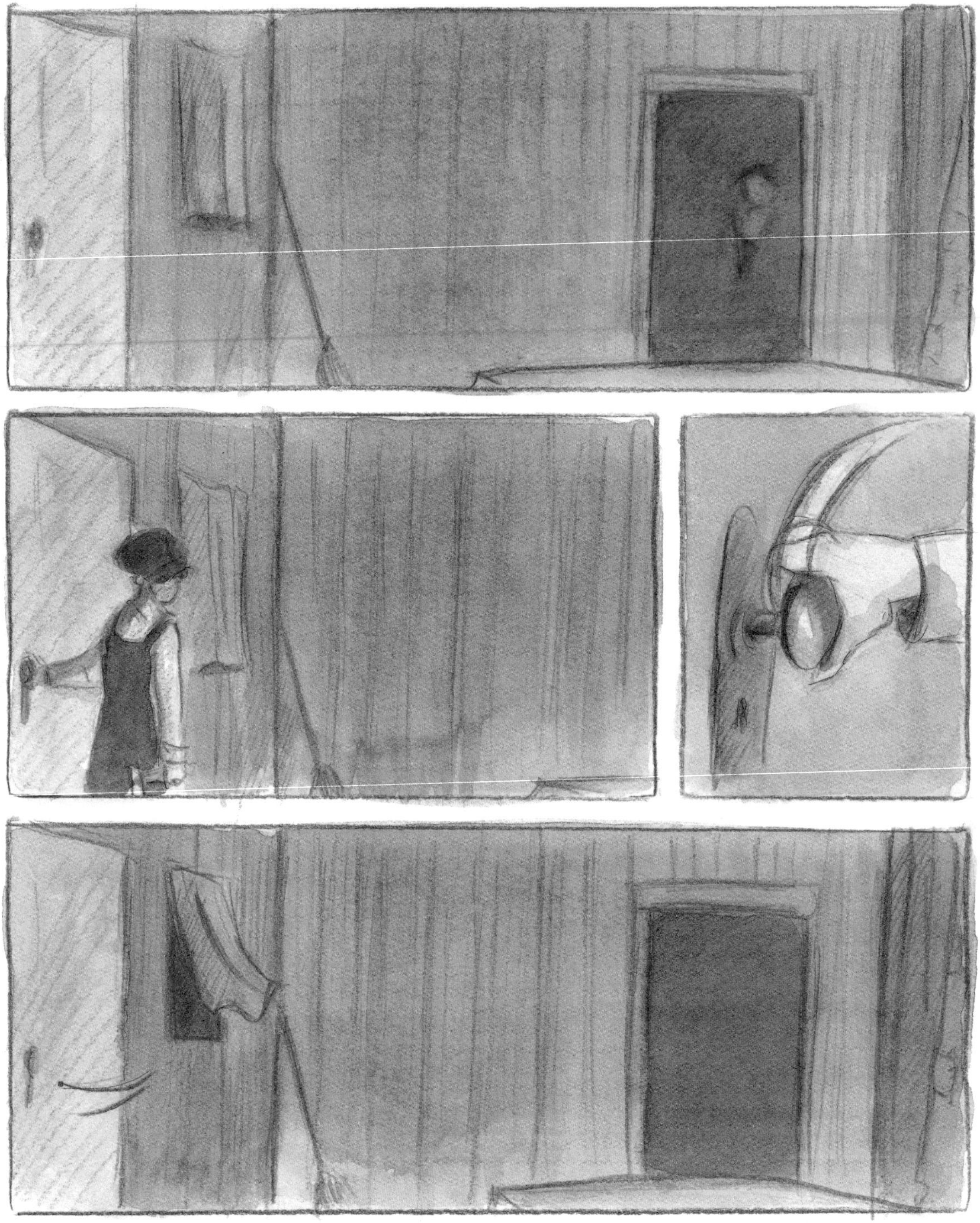

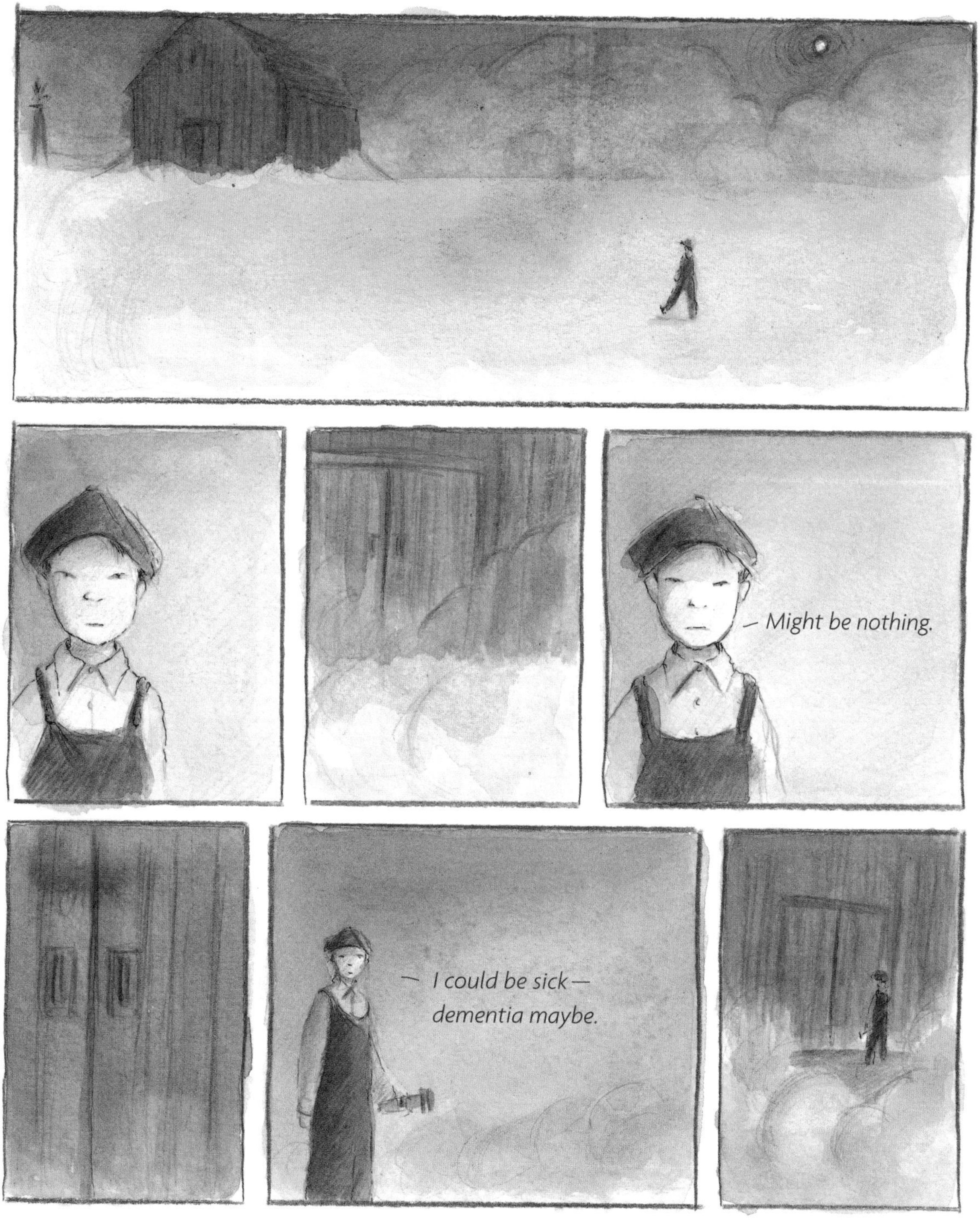
— Might be nothing.
— I could be sick —
dementia maybe.

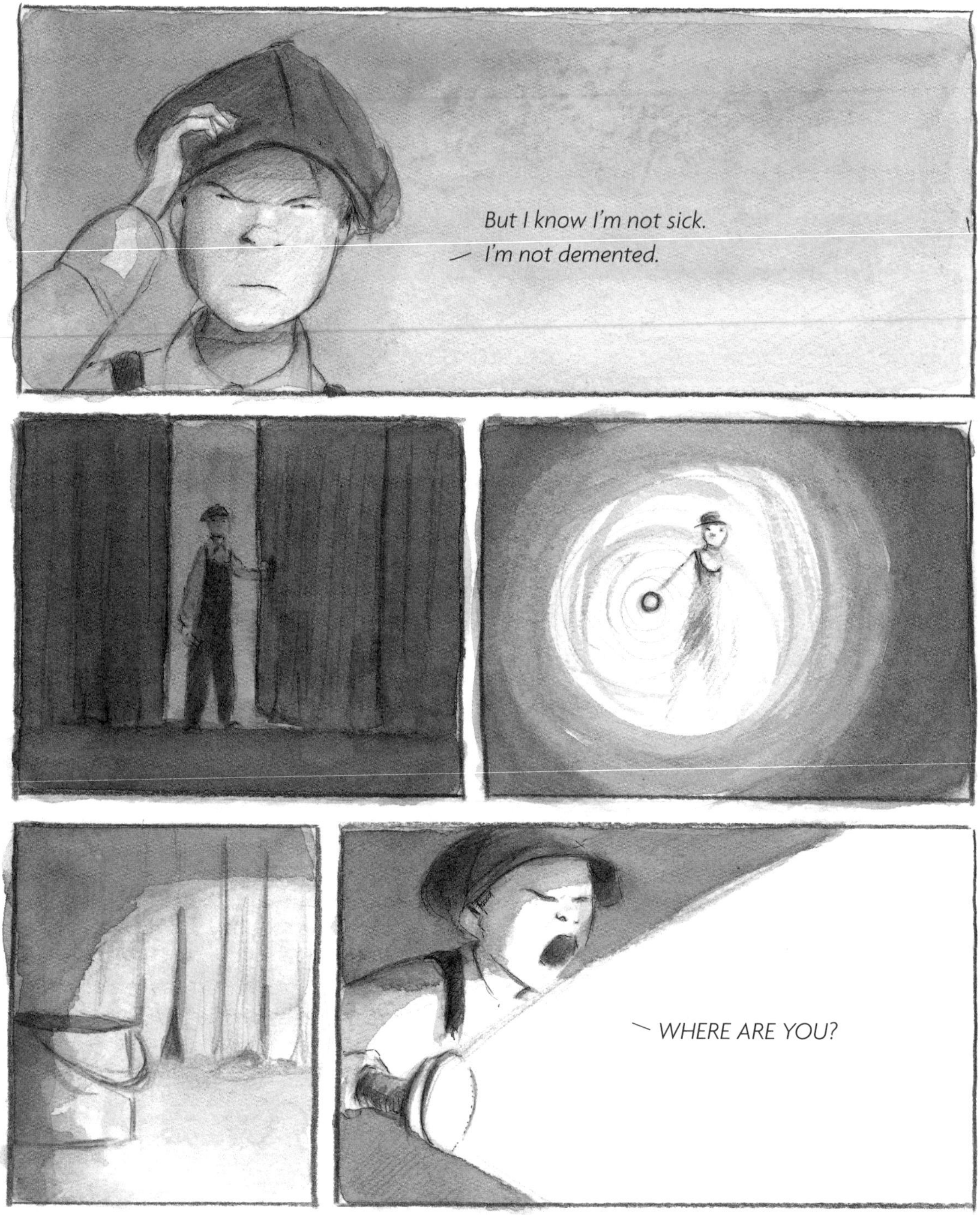
But I know I'm not sick.
I'm not demented.
WHERE ARE YOU?

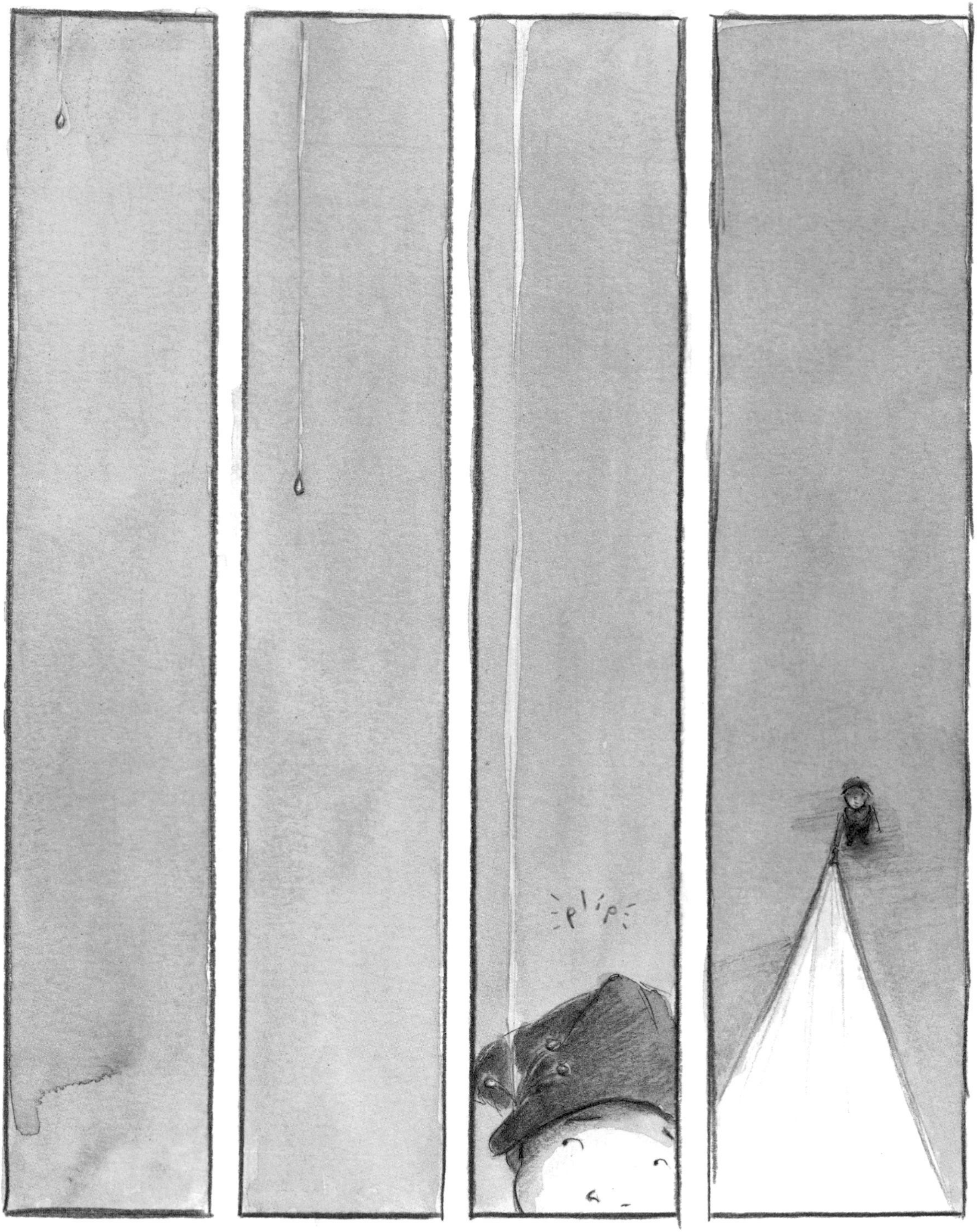
plip

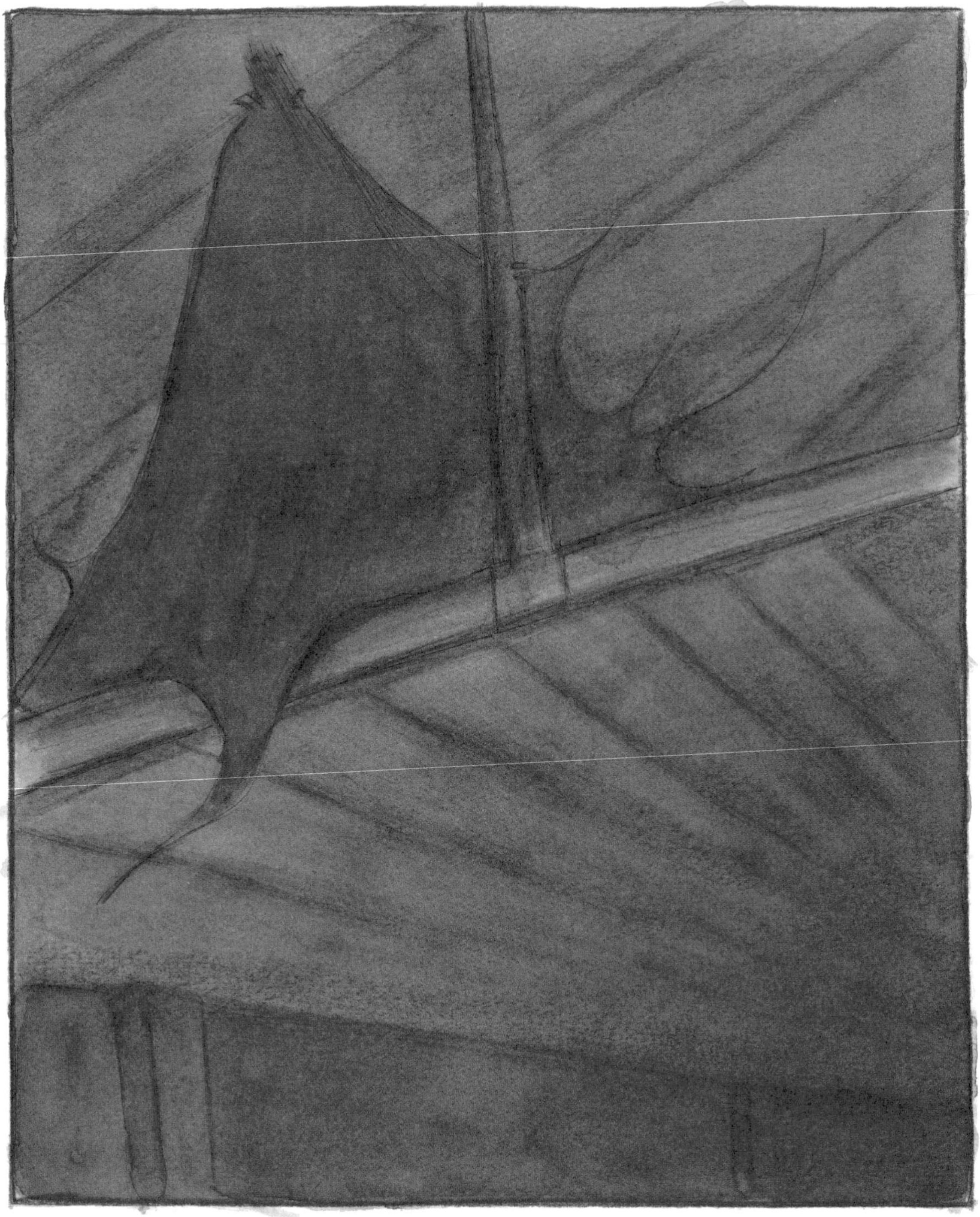

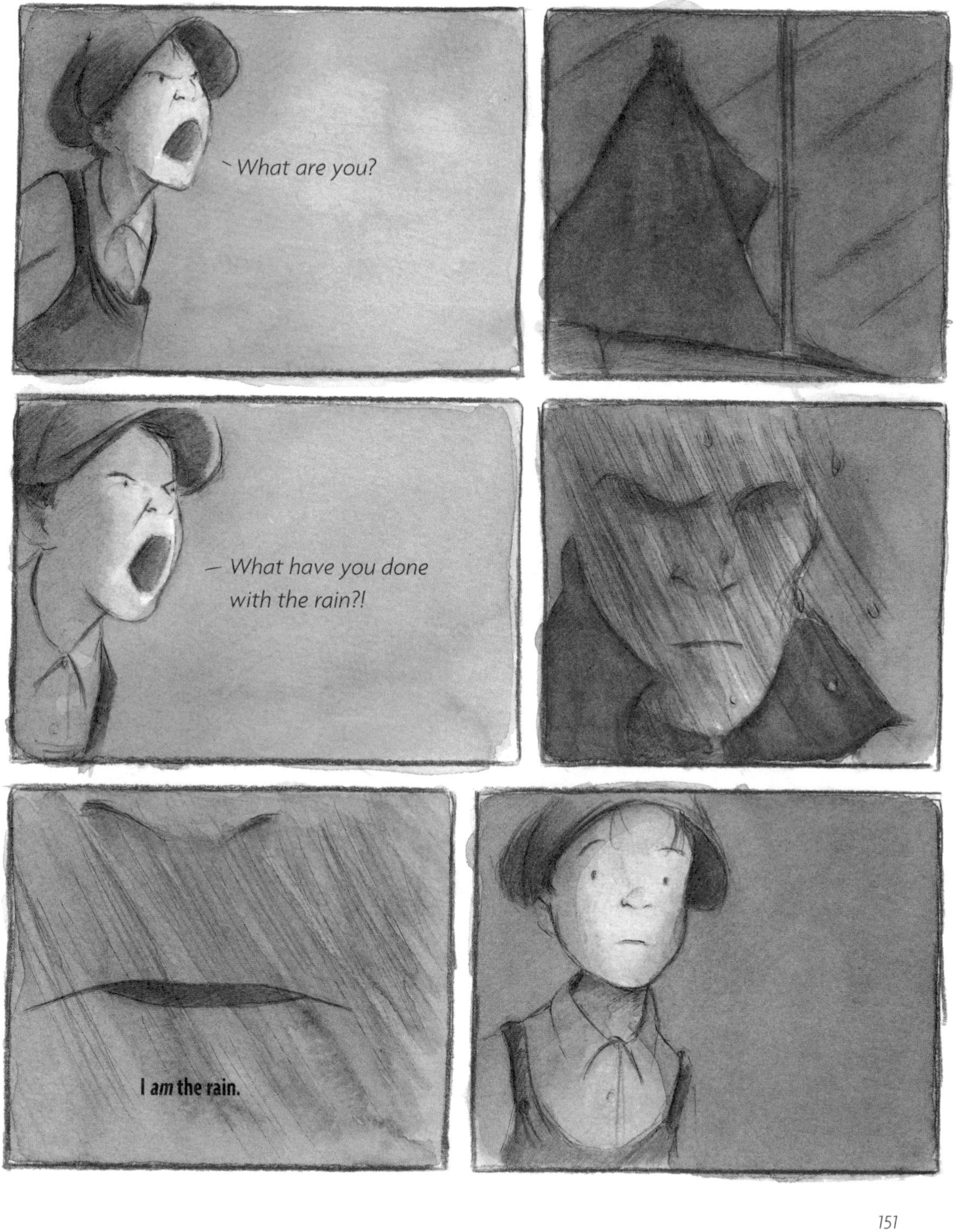
– What are you?
– What have you done with the rain?!
I *am* the rain.

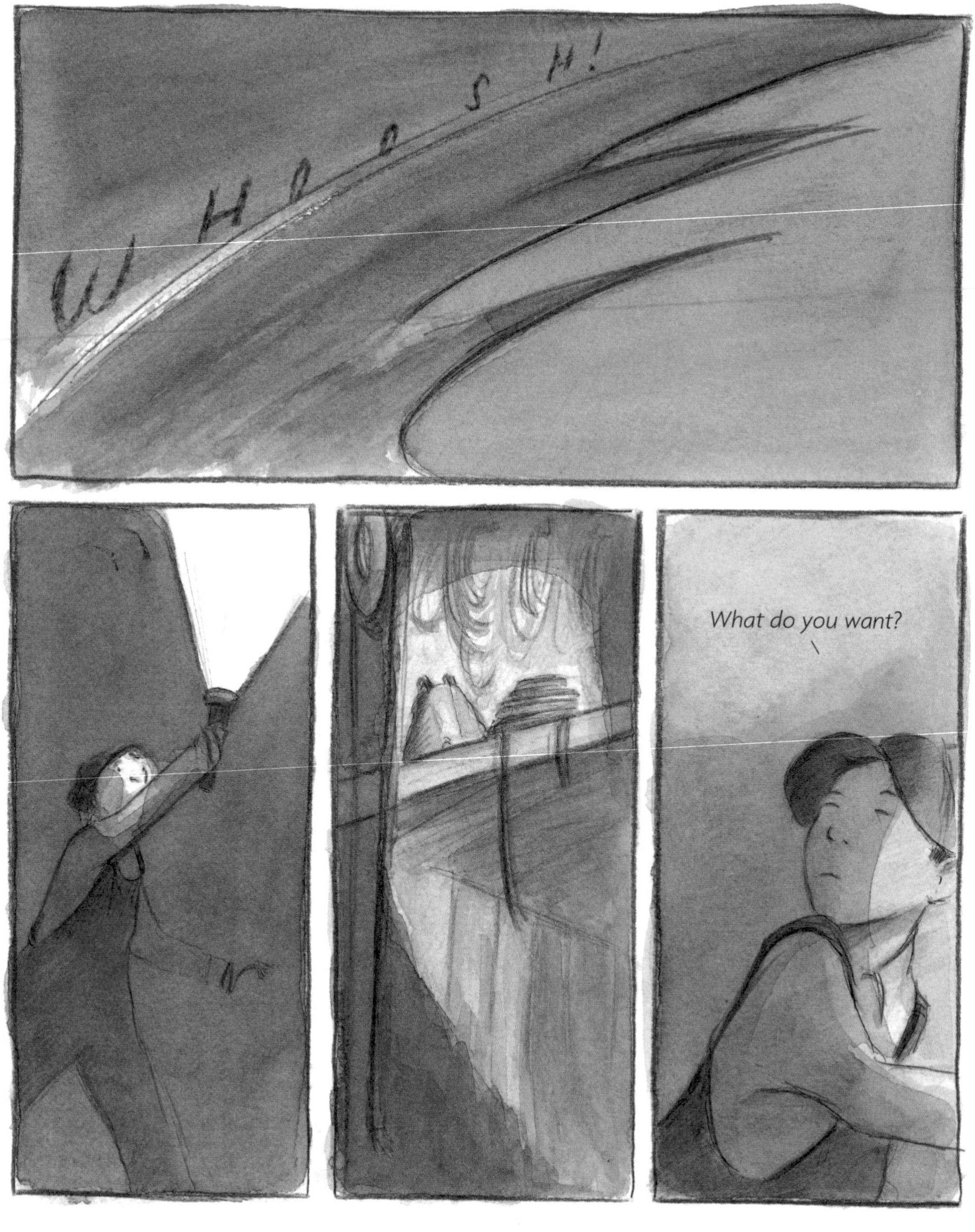
WHOOSH!
What do you want?

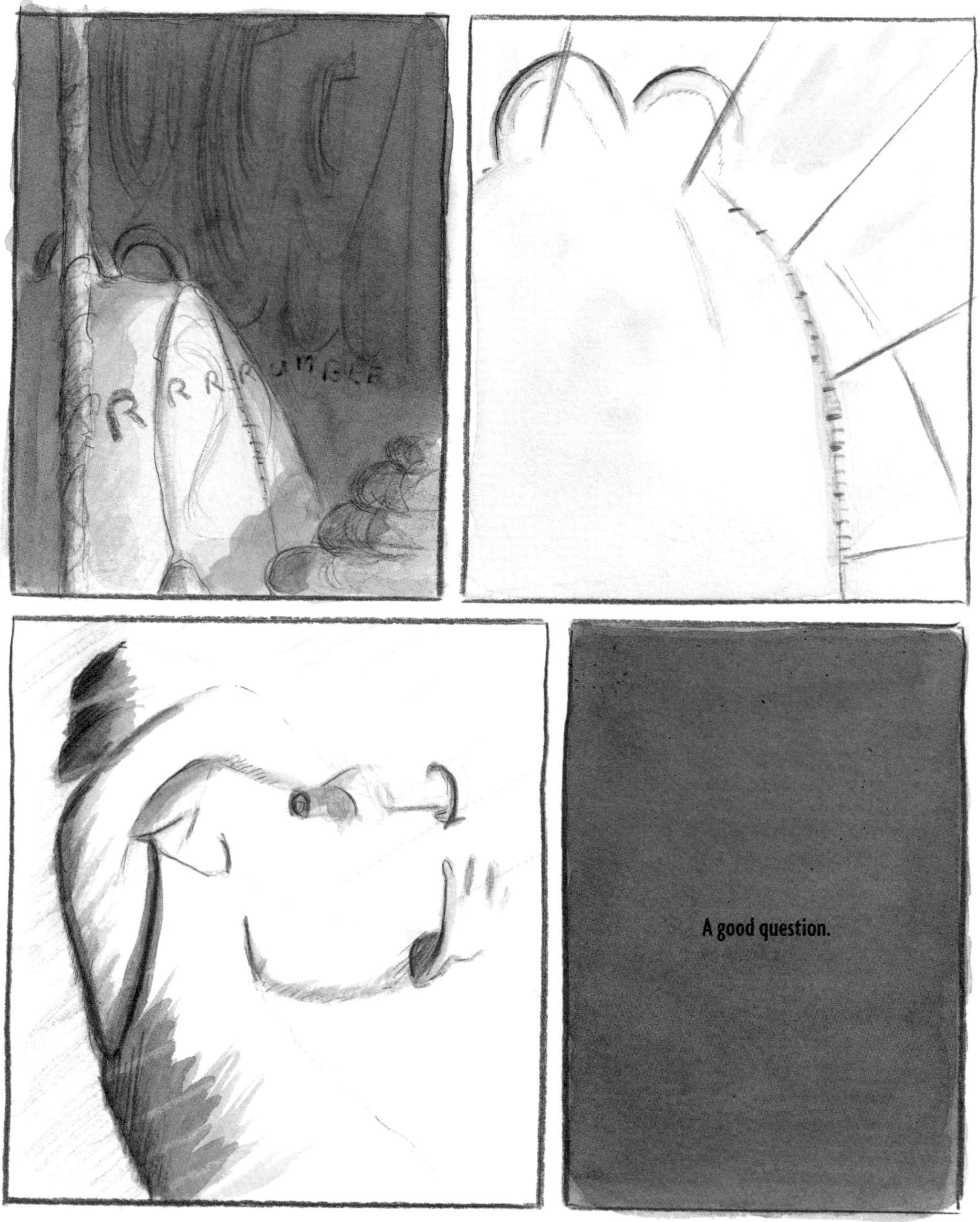
RRRRUMBLE
A good question.

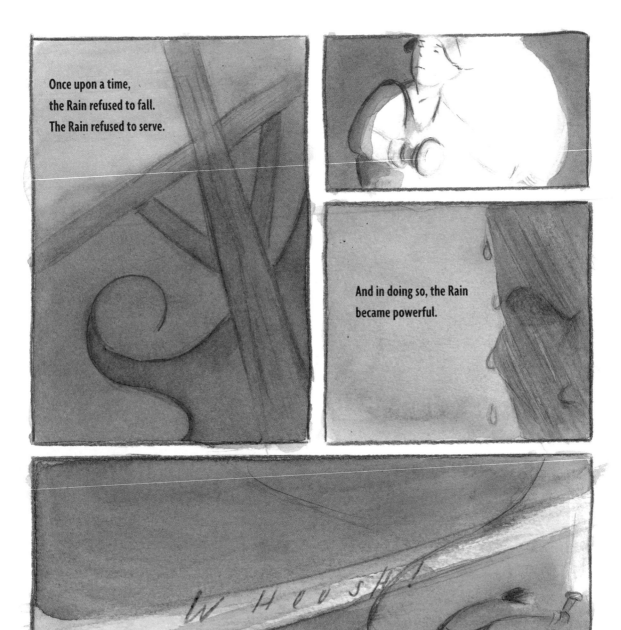

Once upon a time,
the Rain refused to fall.
The Rain refused to serve.

And in doing so, the Rain
became powerful.

WHOOSH!

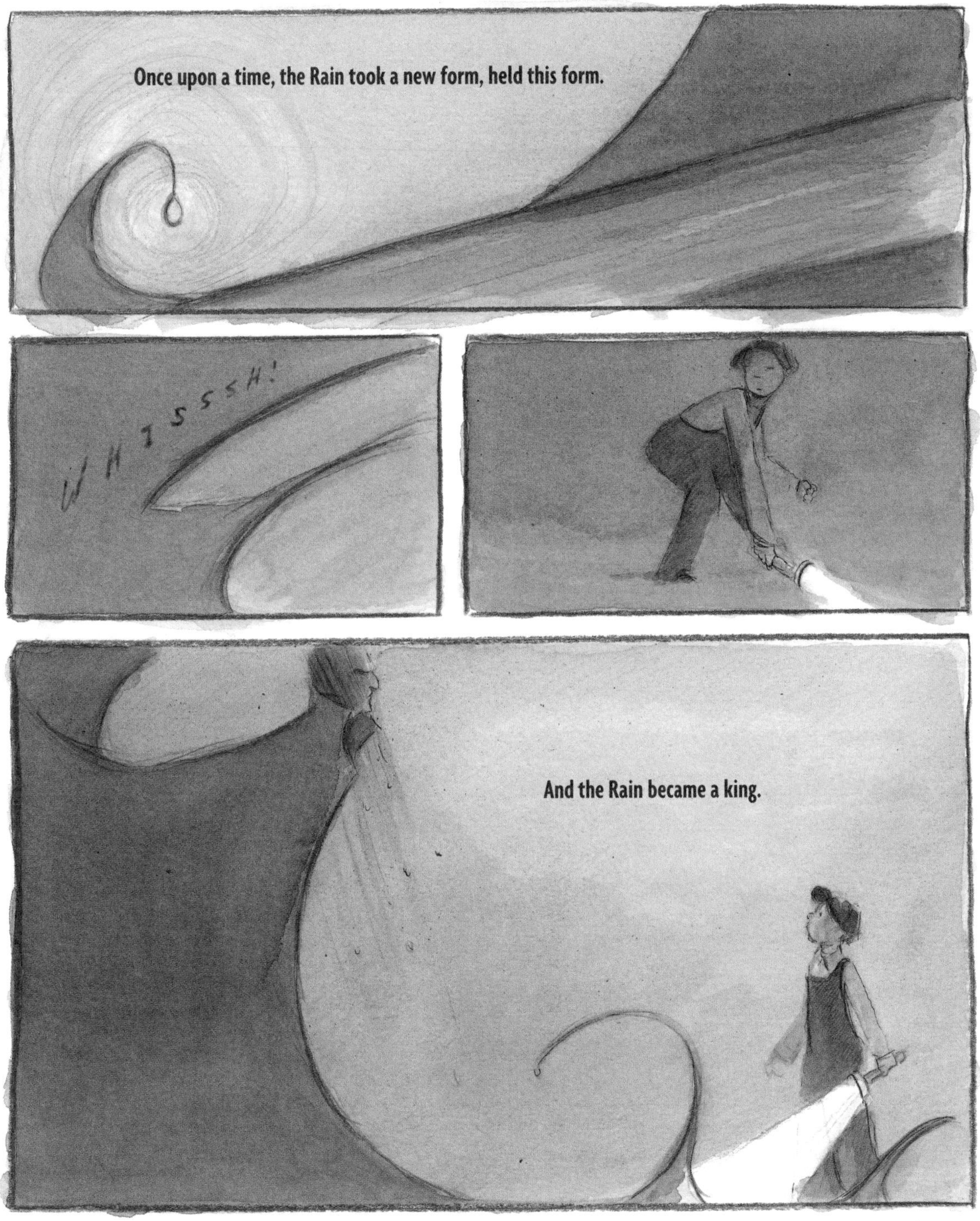
Once upon a time, the Rain took a new form, held this form.
WHISSSH!
And the Rain became a king.

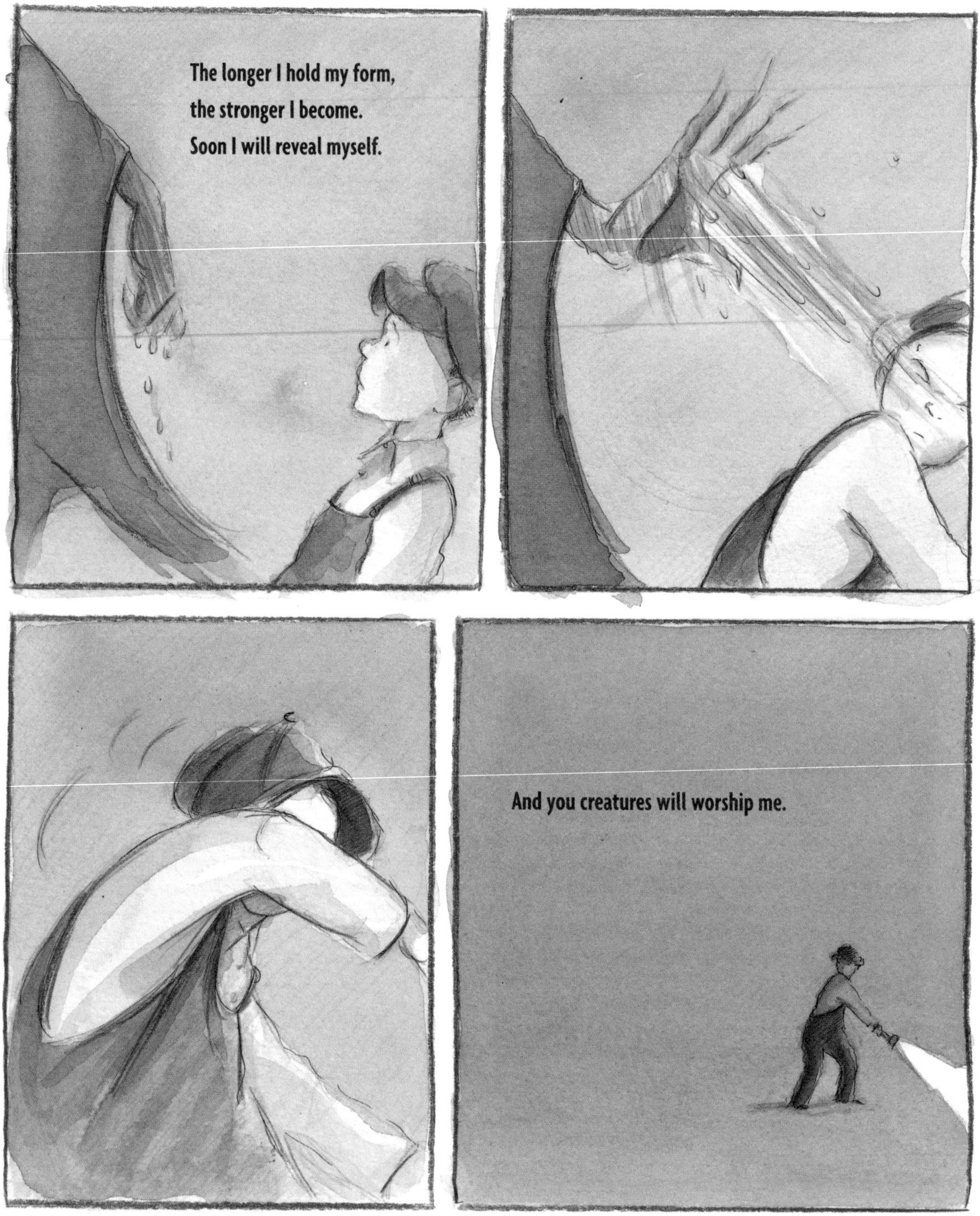
The longer I hold my form,
the stronger I become.
Soon I will reveal myself.
And you creatures will worship me.

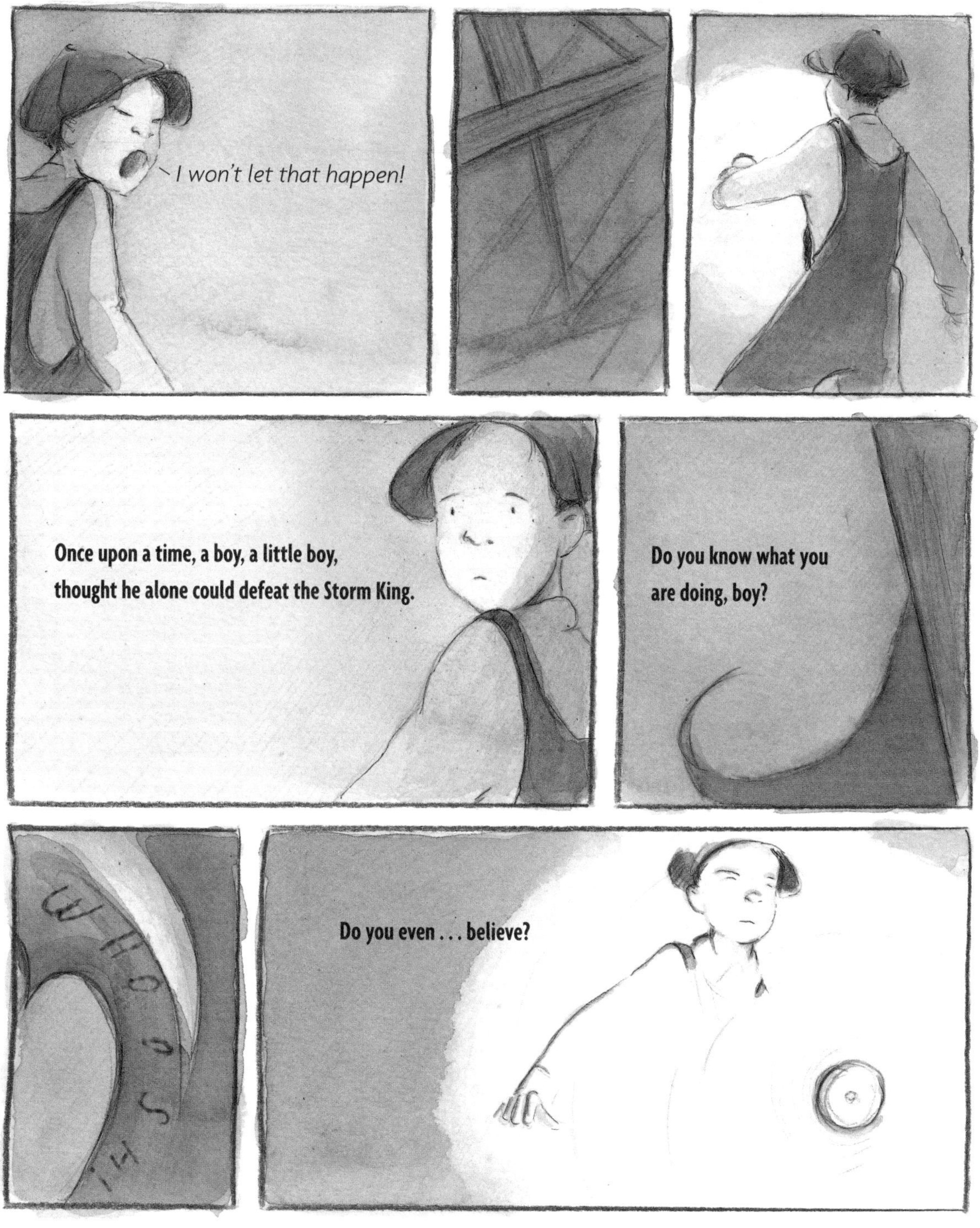
I won't let that happen!
Once upon a time, a boy, a little boy, thought he alone could defeat the Storm King.
Do you know what you are doing, boy?
WHOOSH
Do you even . . . believe?

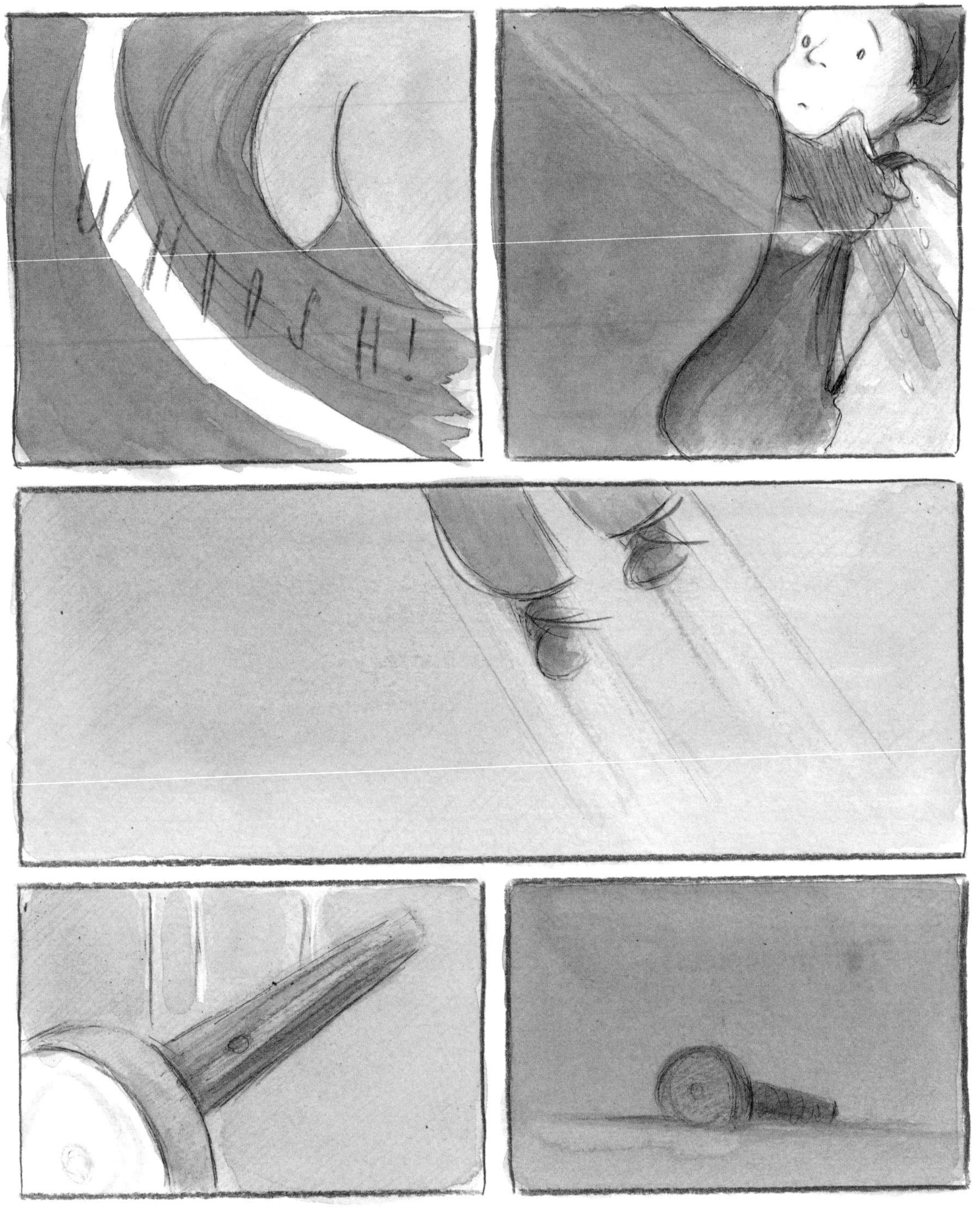
WHOOSH!

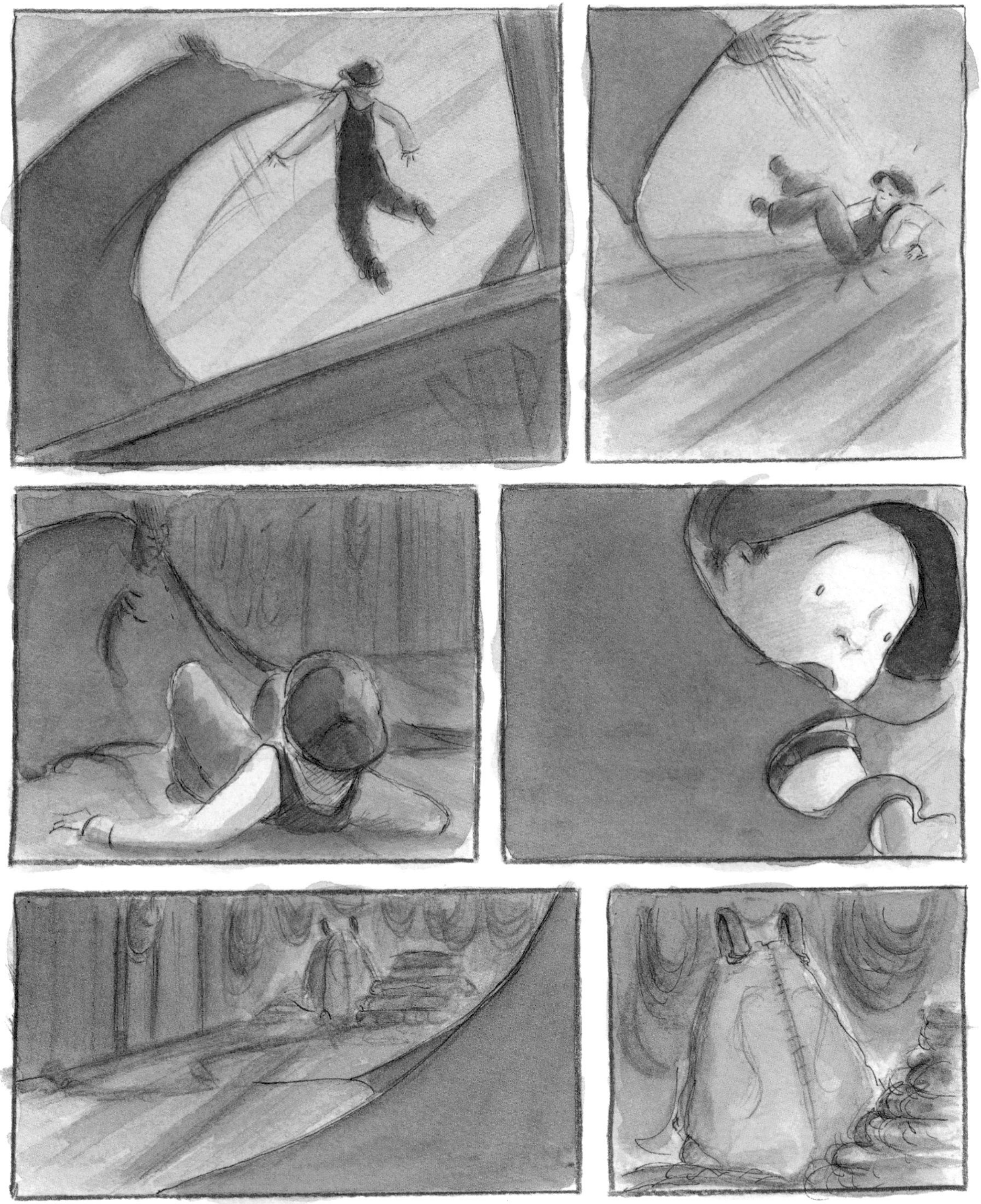

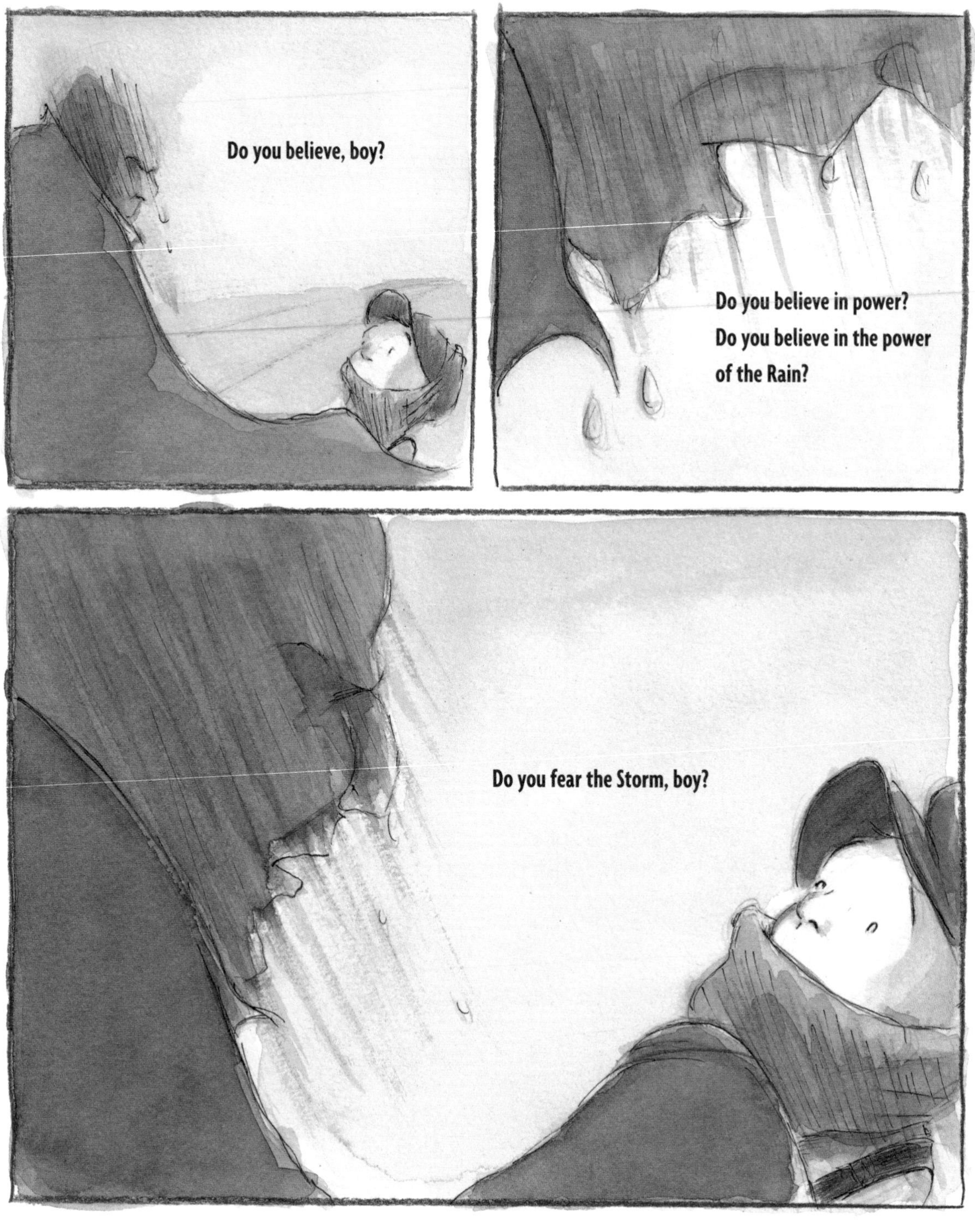
Do you believe, boy?
Do you believe in power?
Do you believe in the power of the Rain?
Do you fear the Storm, boy?

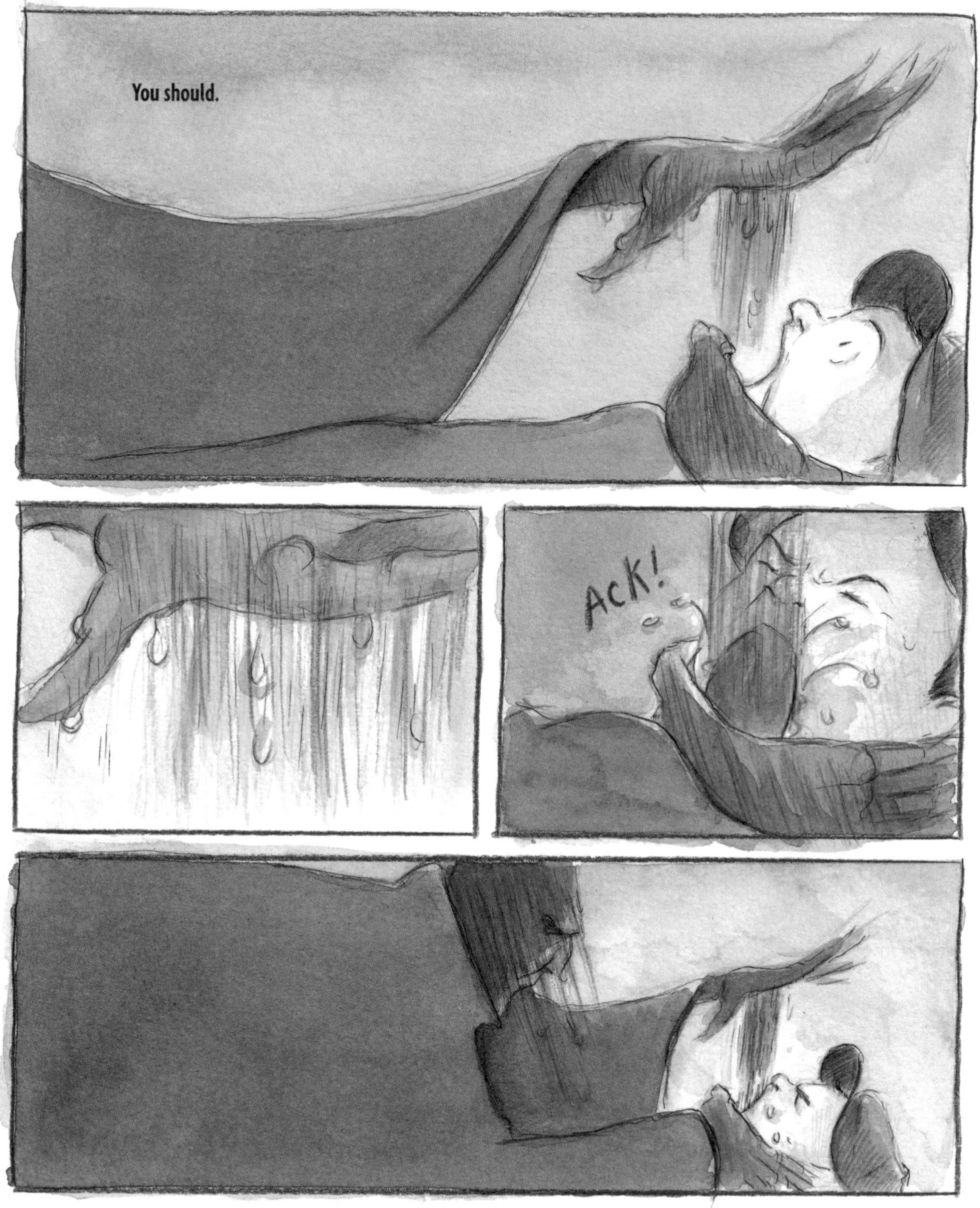
You should.
ACK!

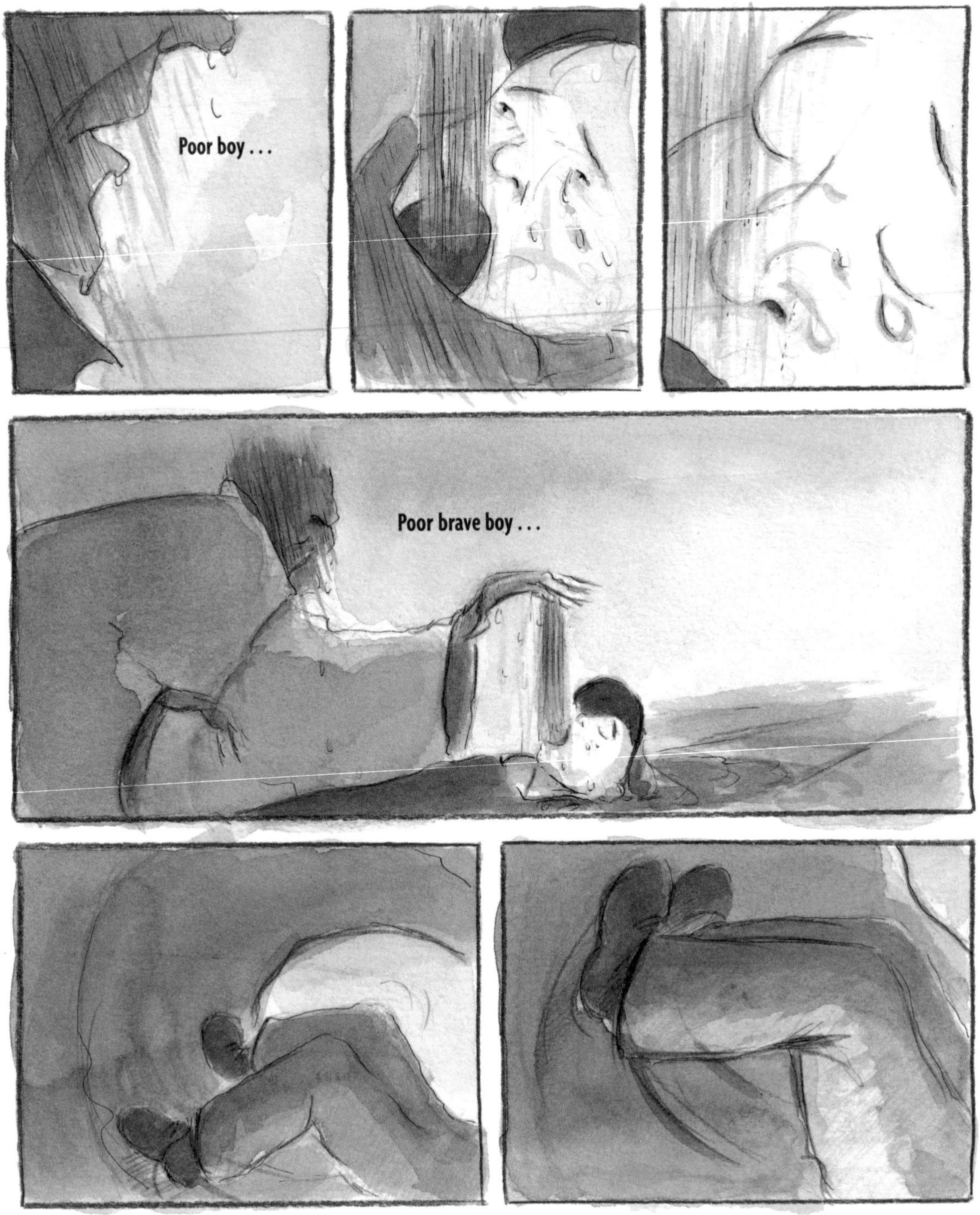
Poor boy . . .
Poor brave boy . . .

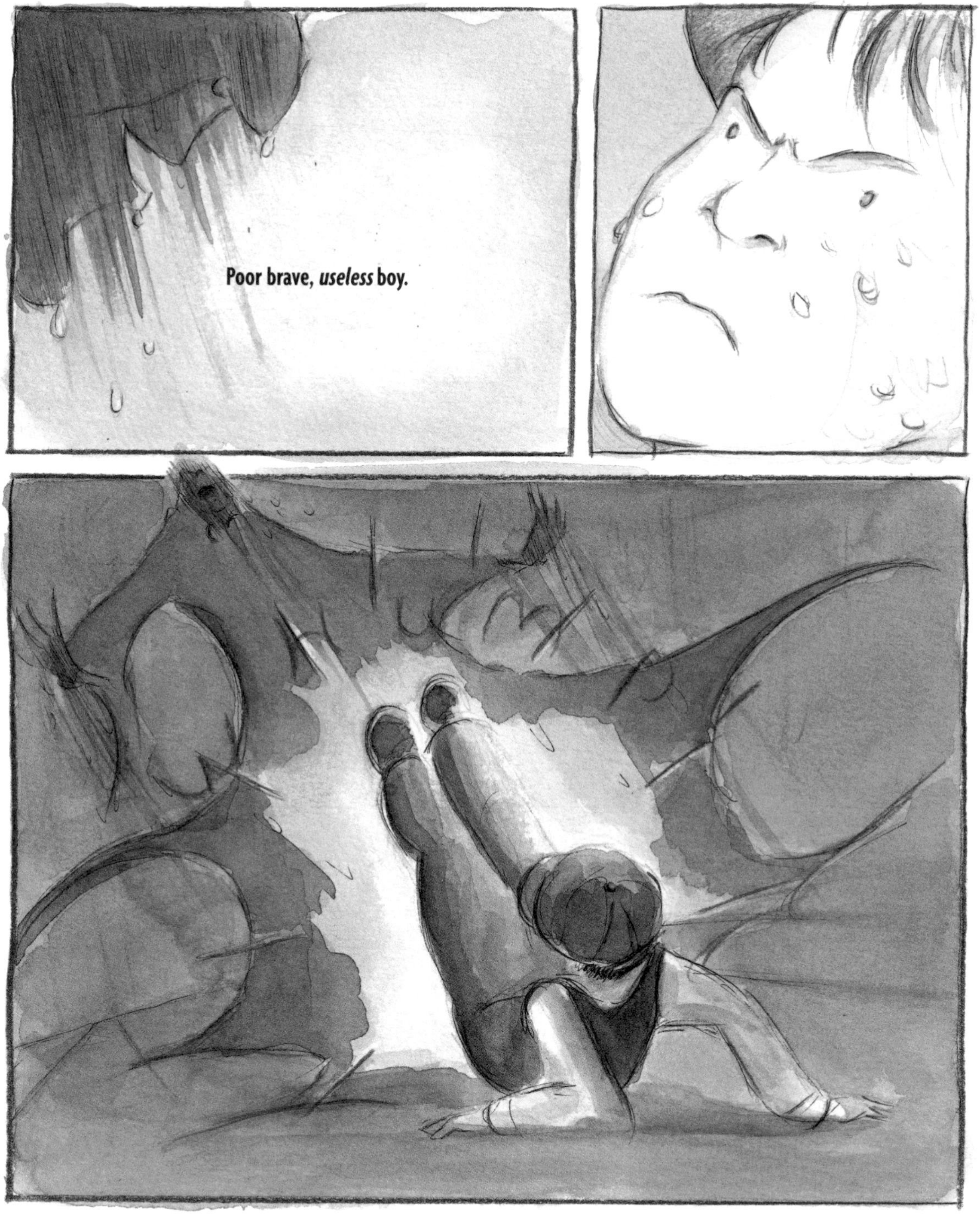
Poor brave, *useless* boy.

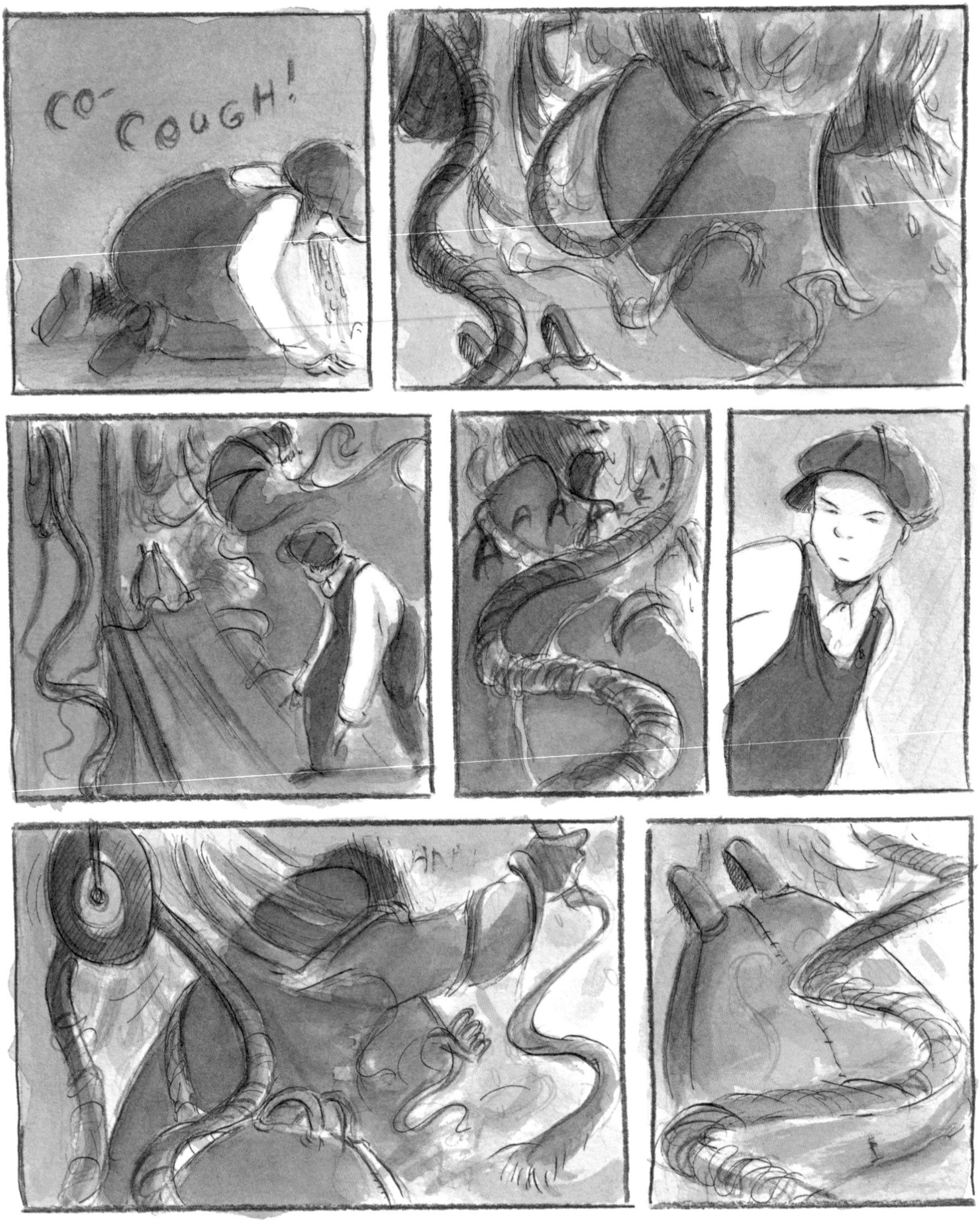
CO- COUGH!

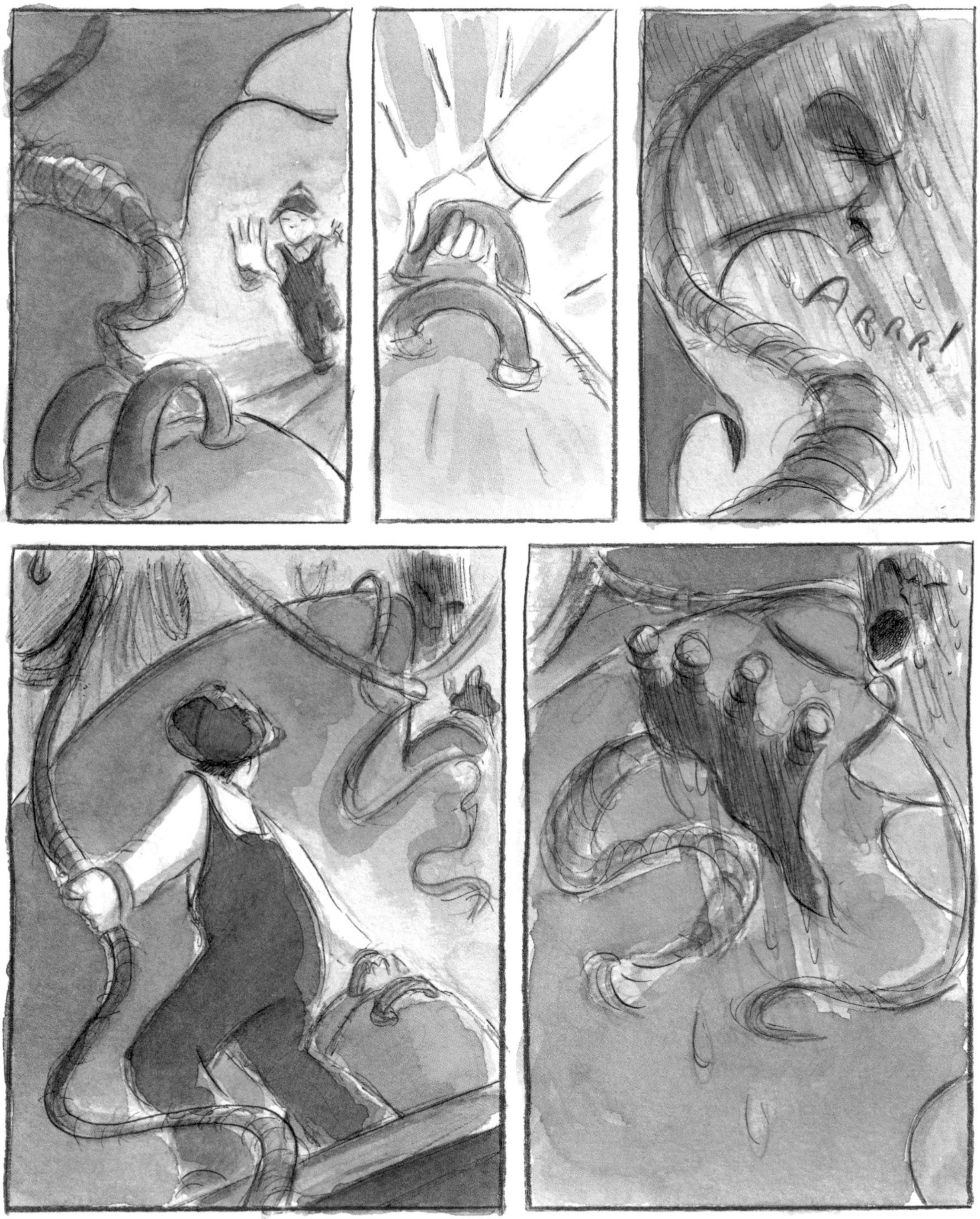
ABRR!

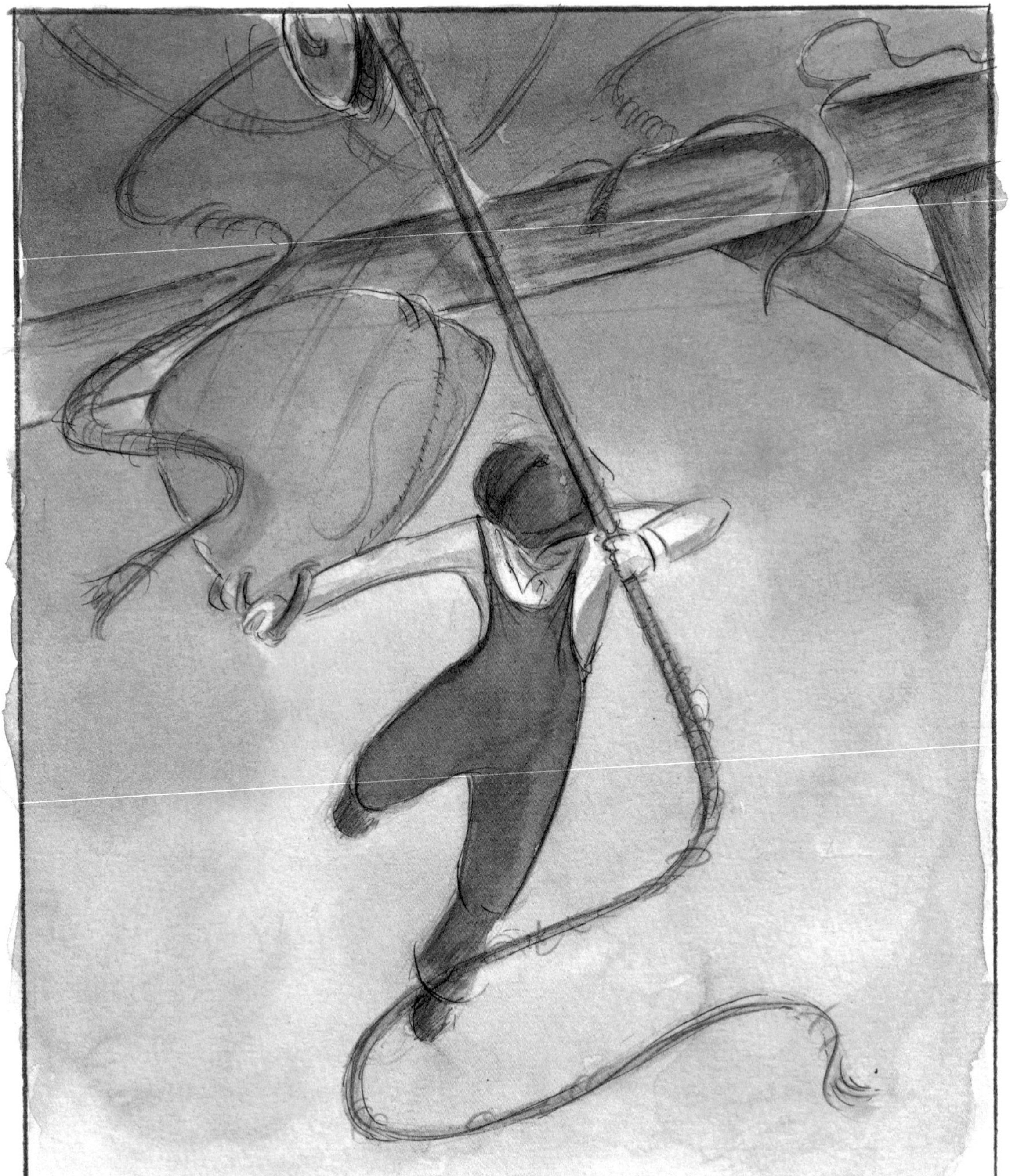

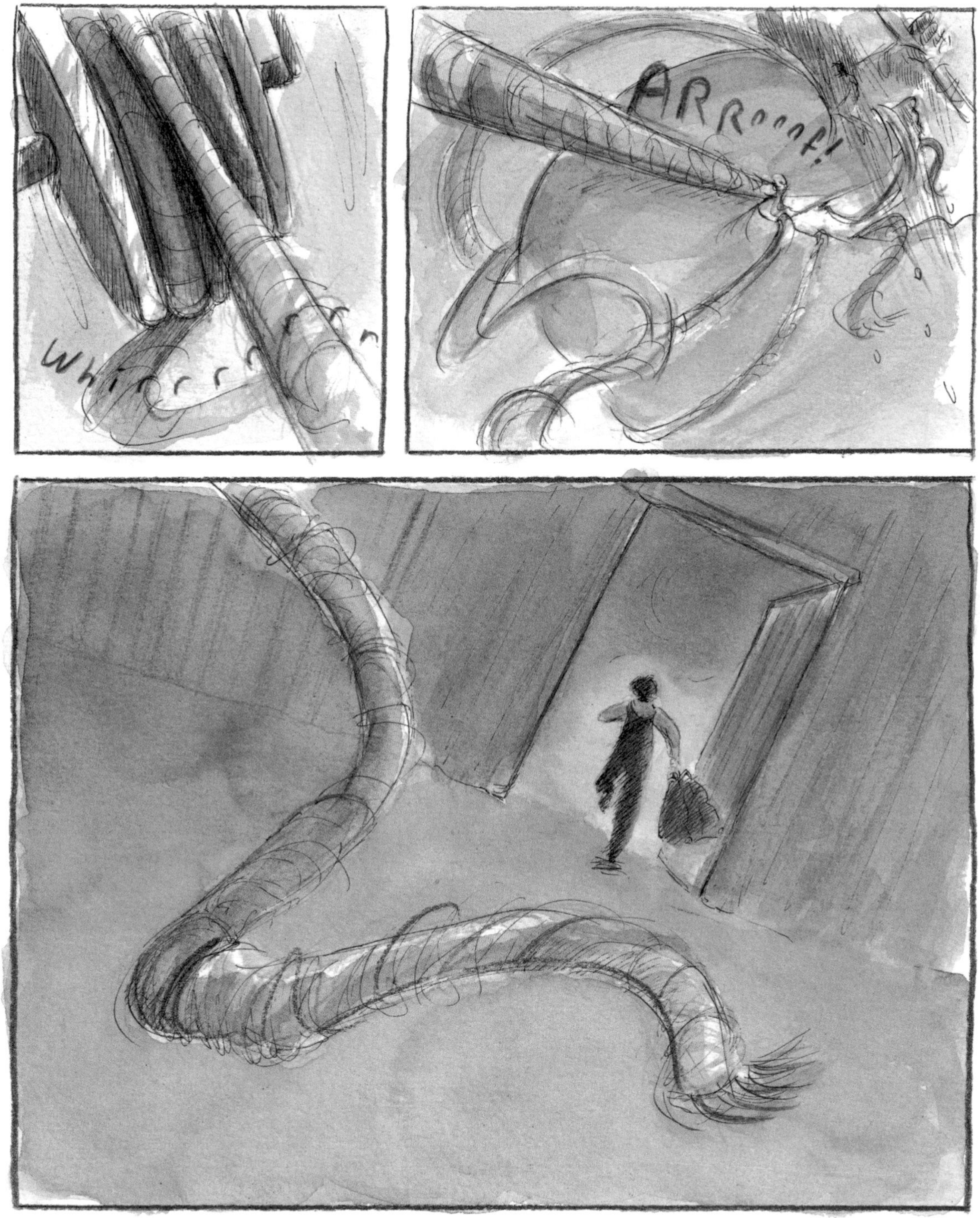
Whirrrrrrrr
ARRooof!

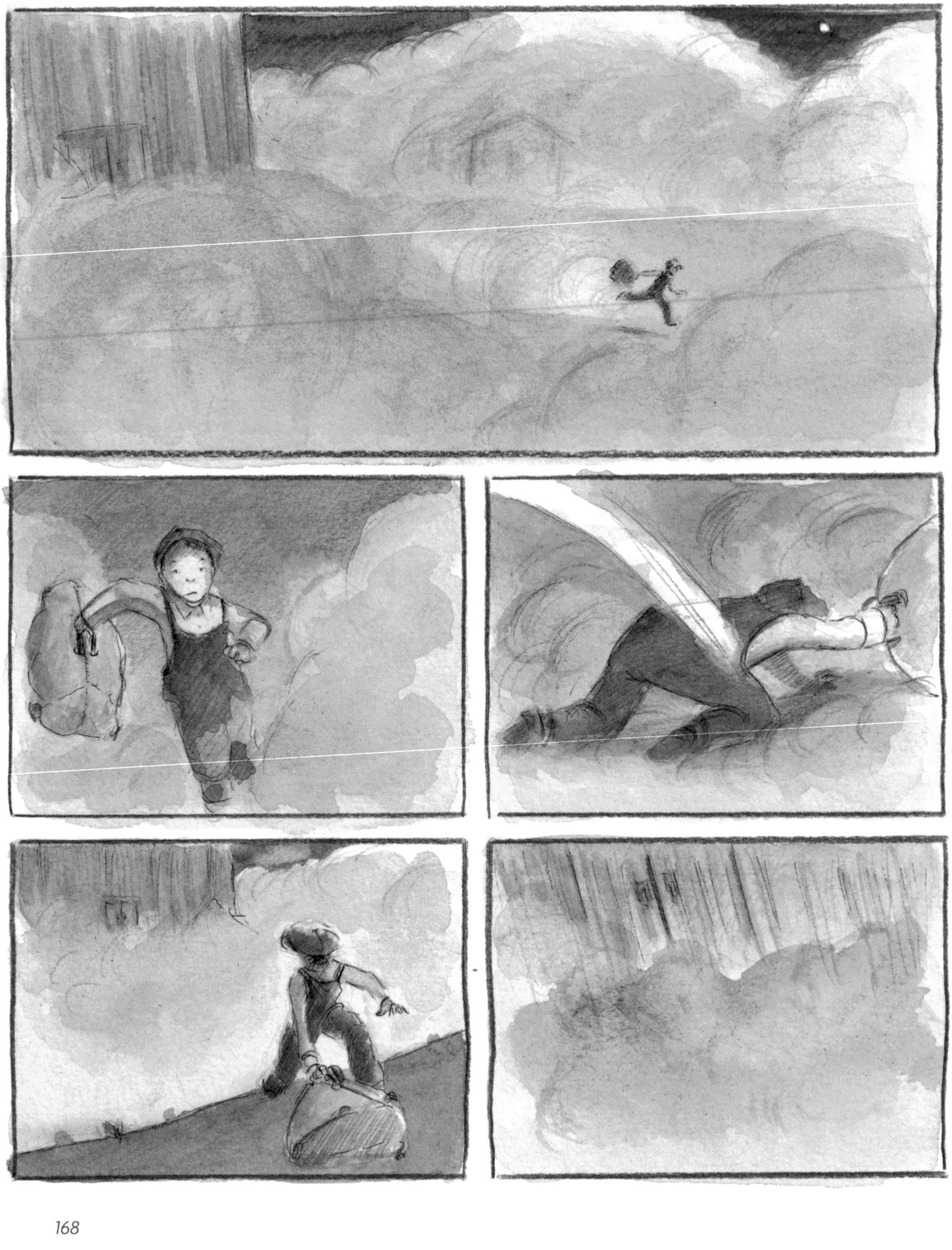

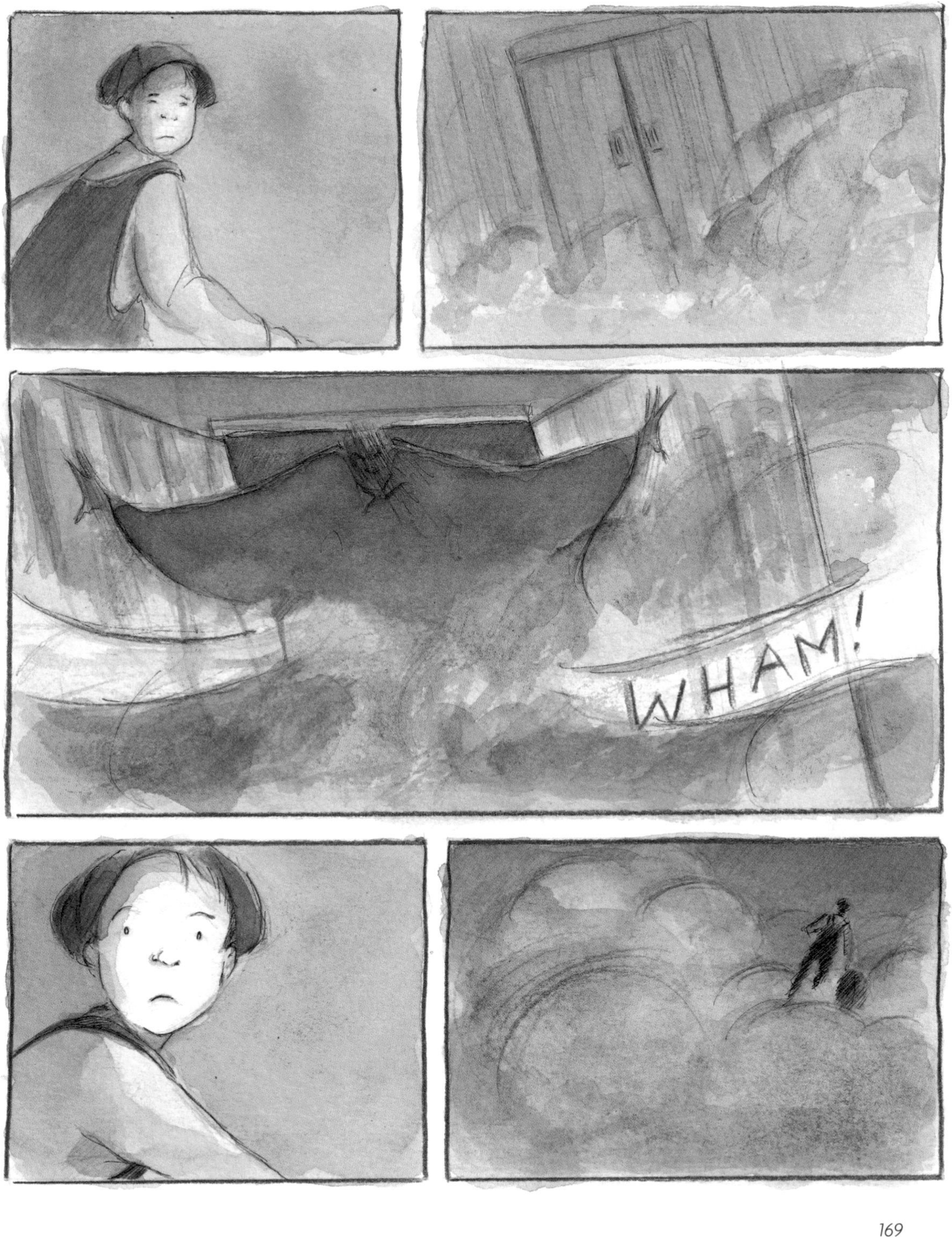
WHAM!

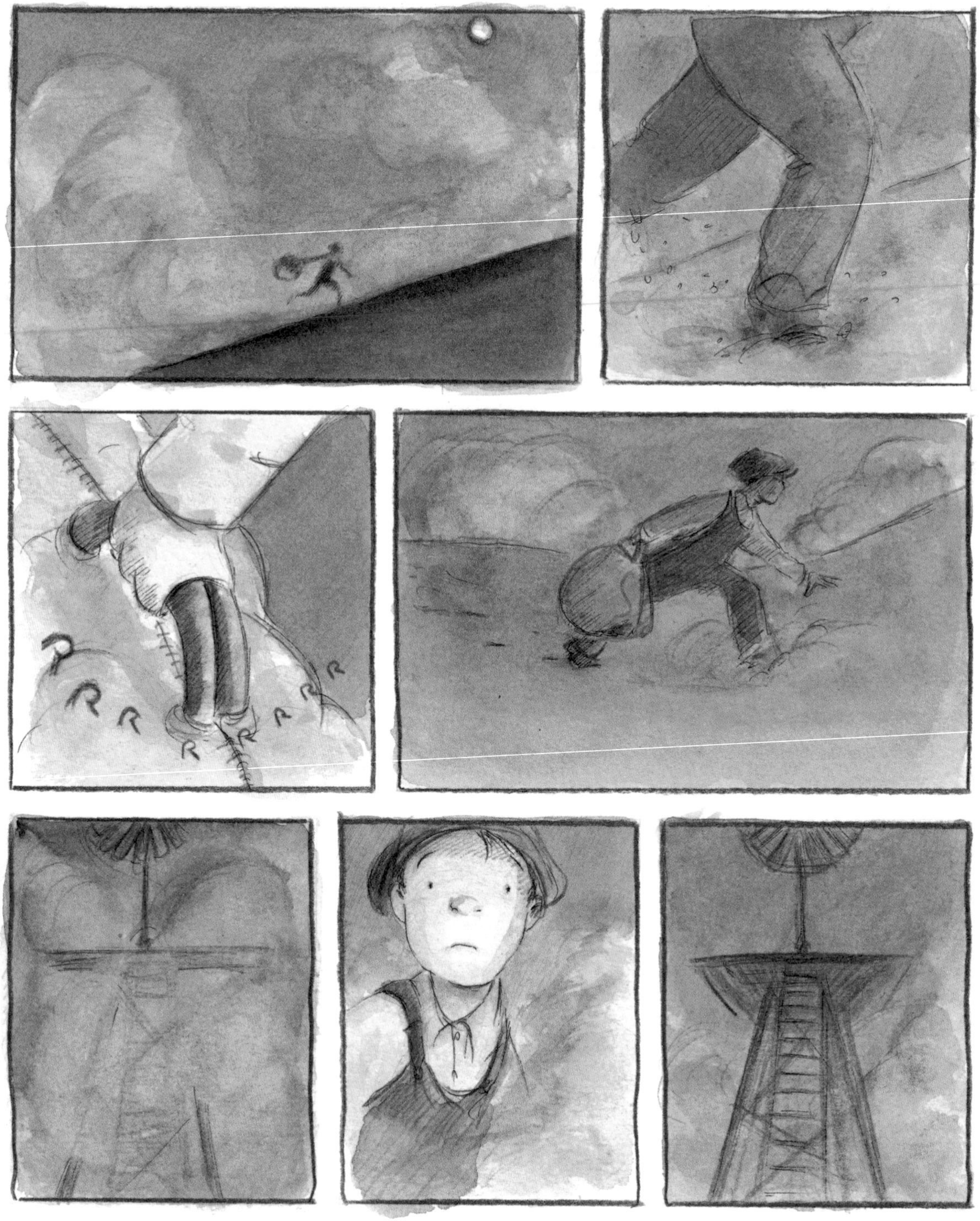
RRRRRRRR

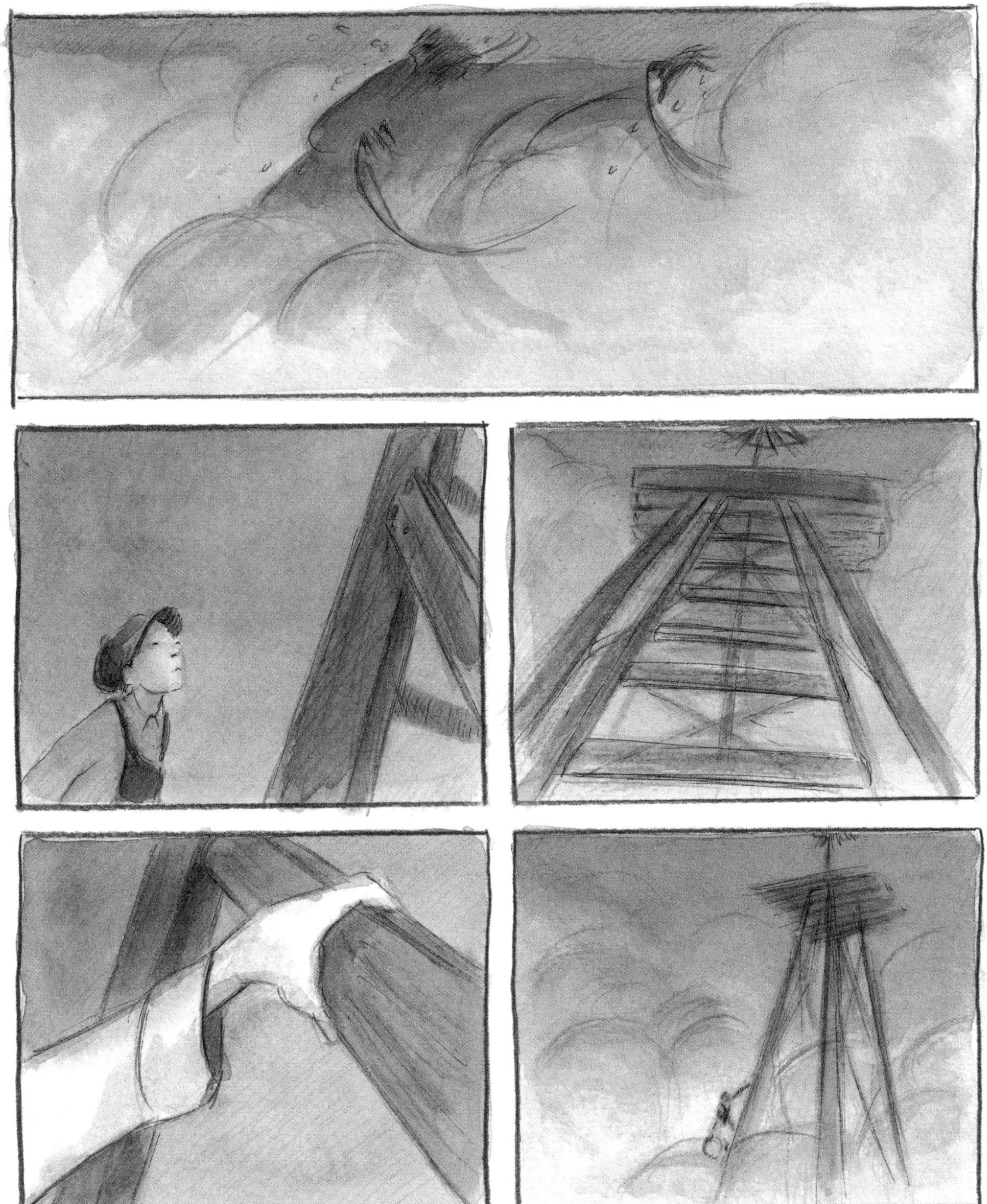

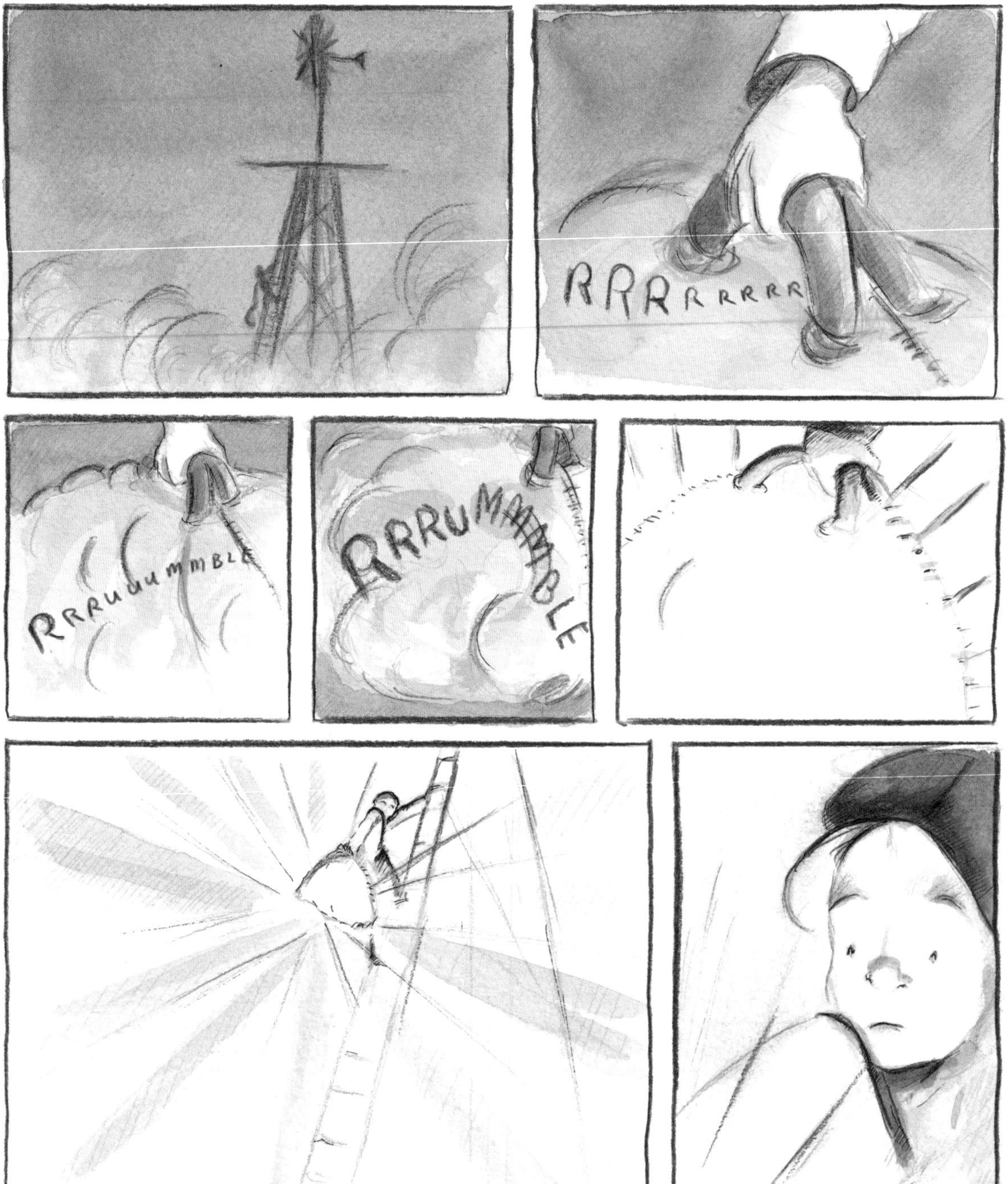
RRRrrrrr
RRRuummBLE
RRRUMMMBLE

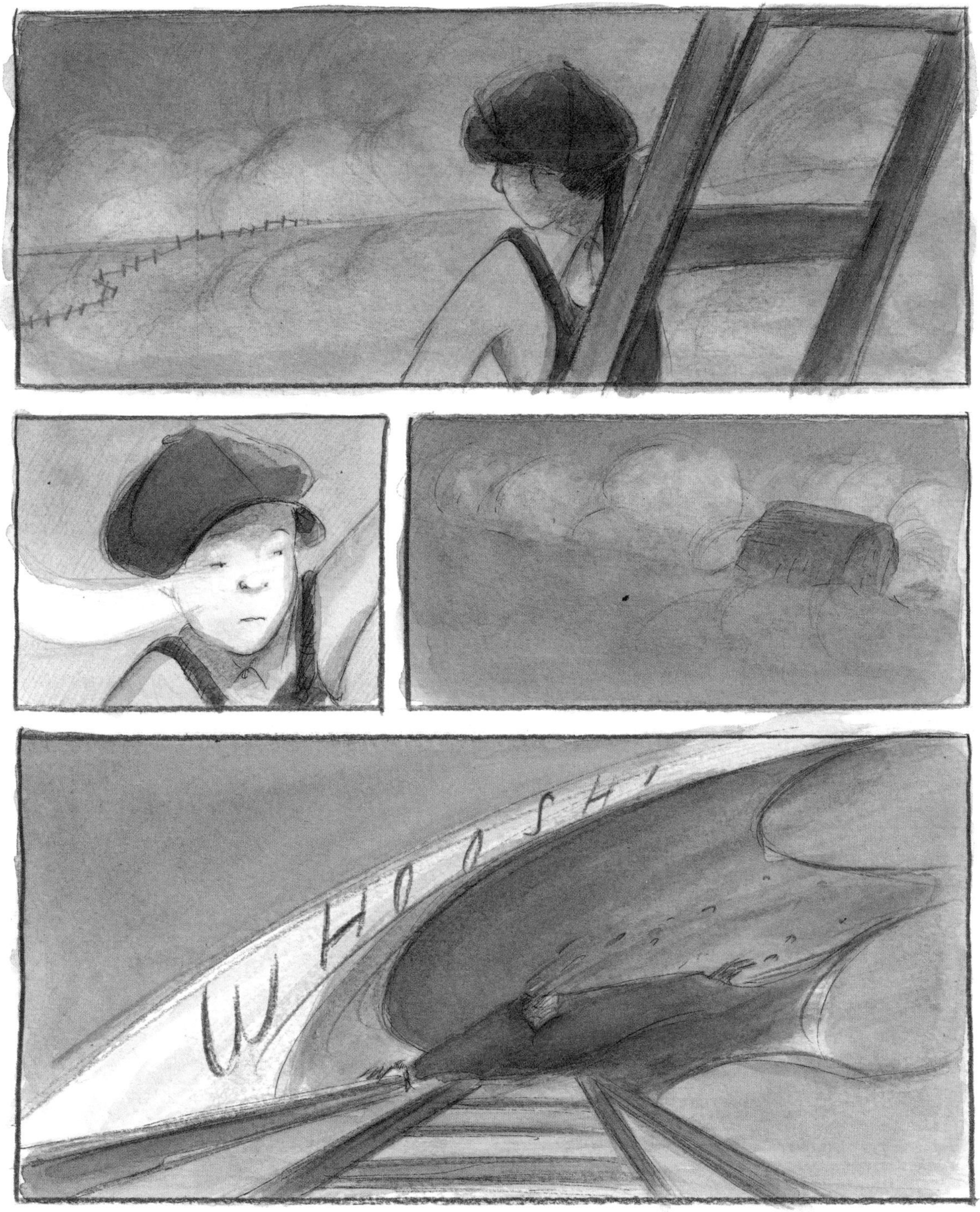
WHOOSH!

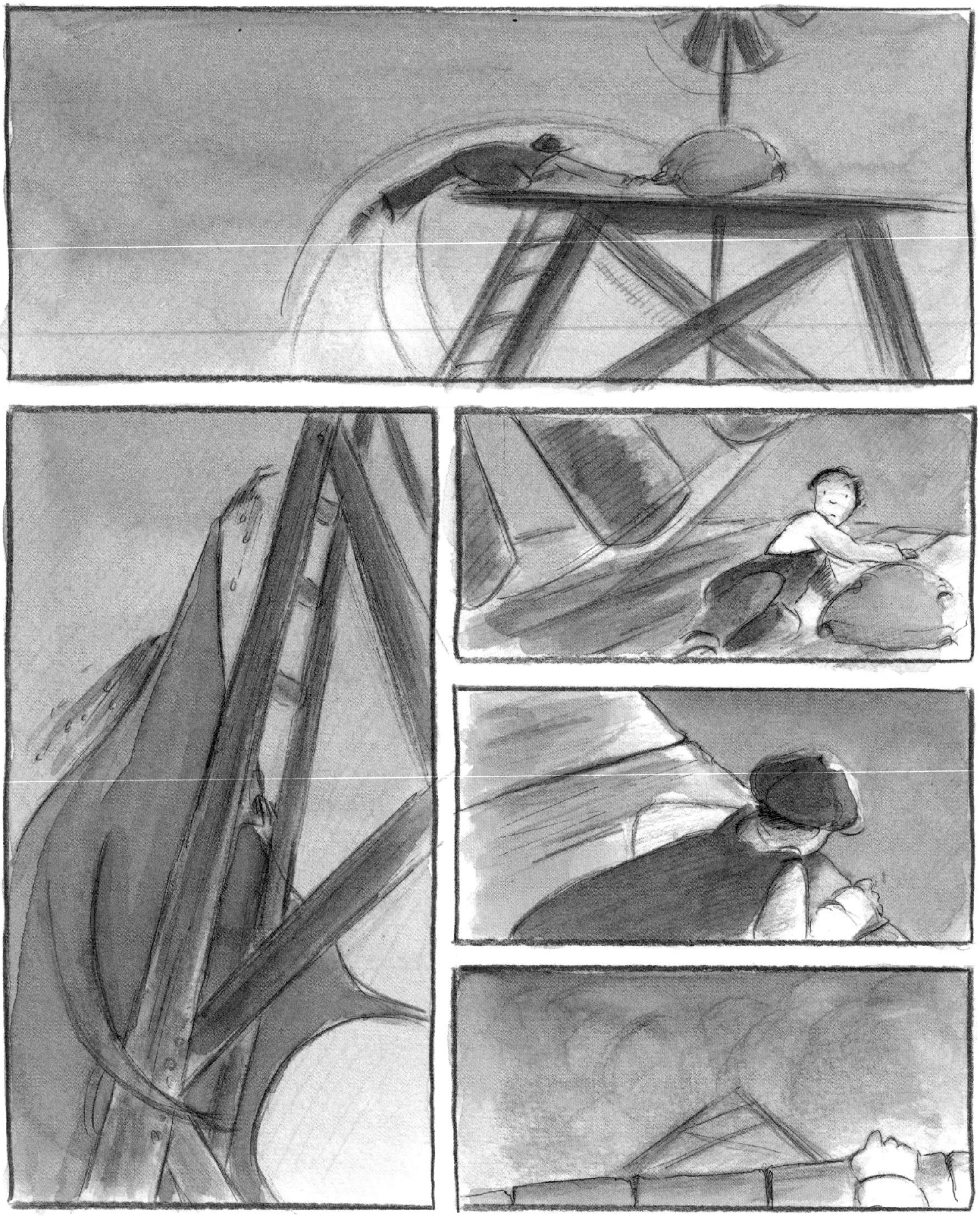

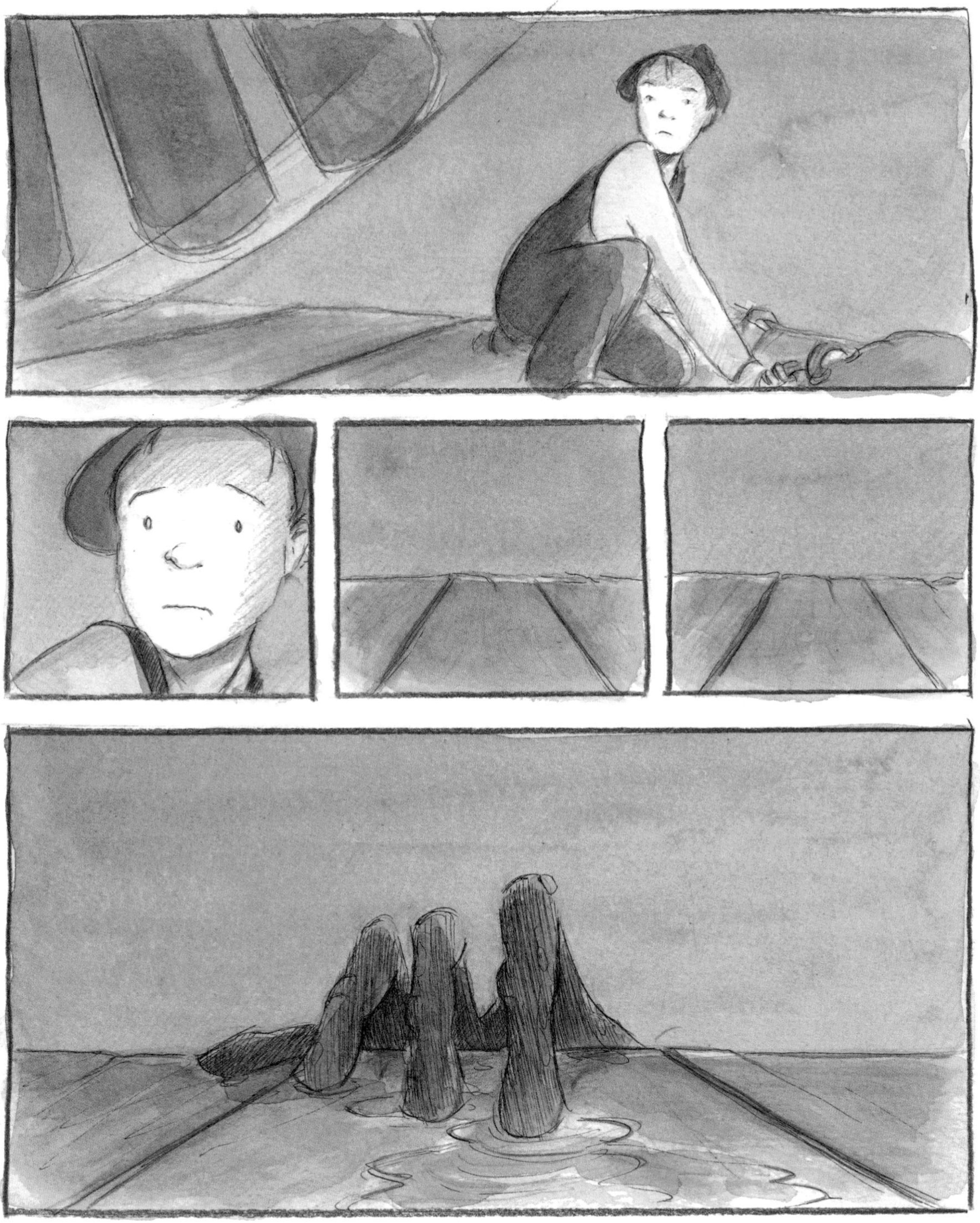

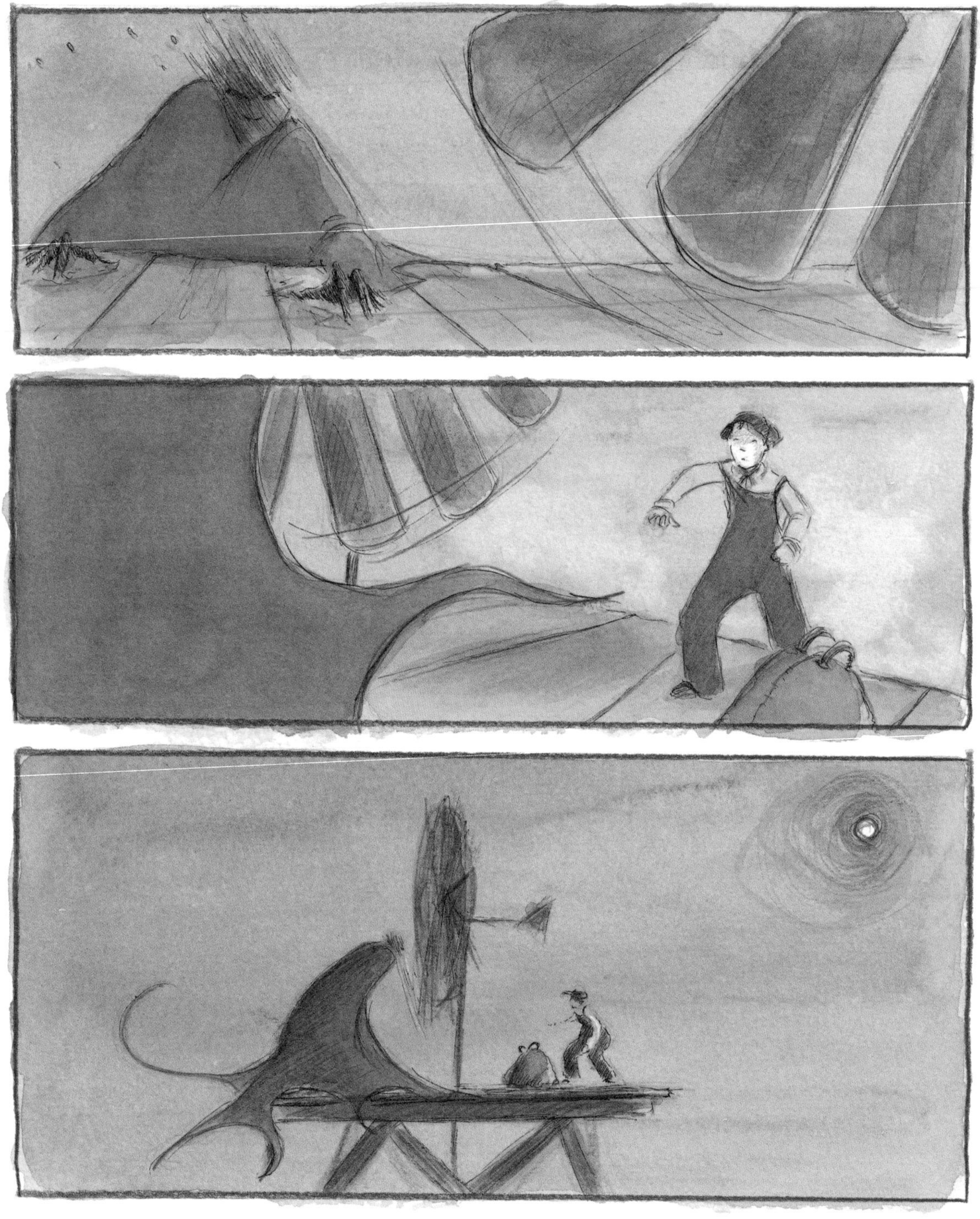

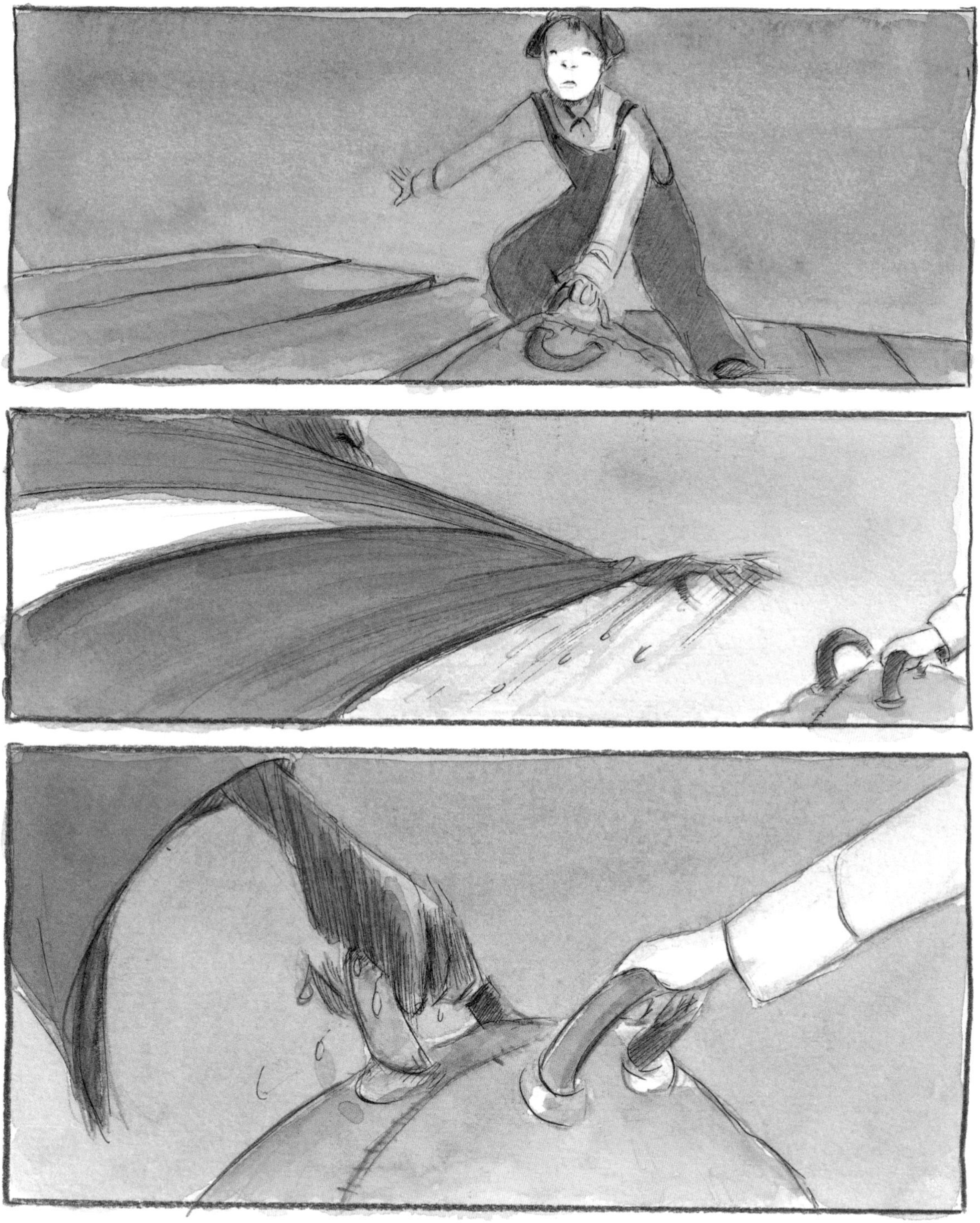

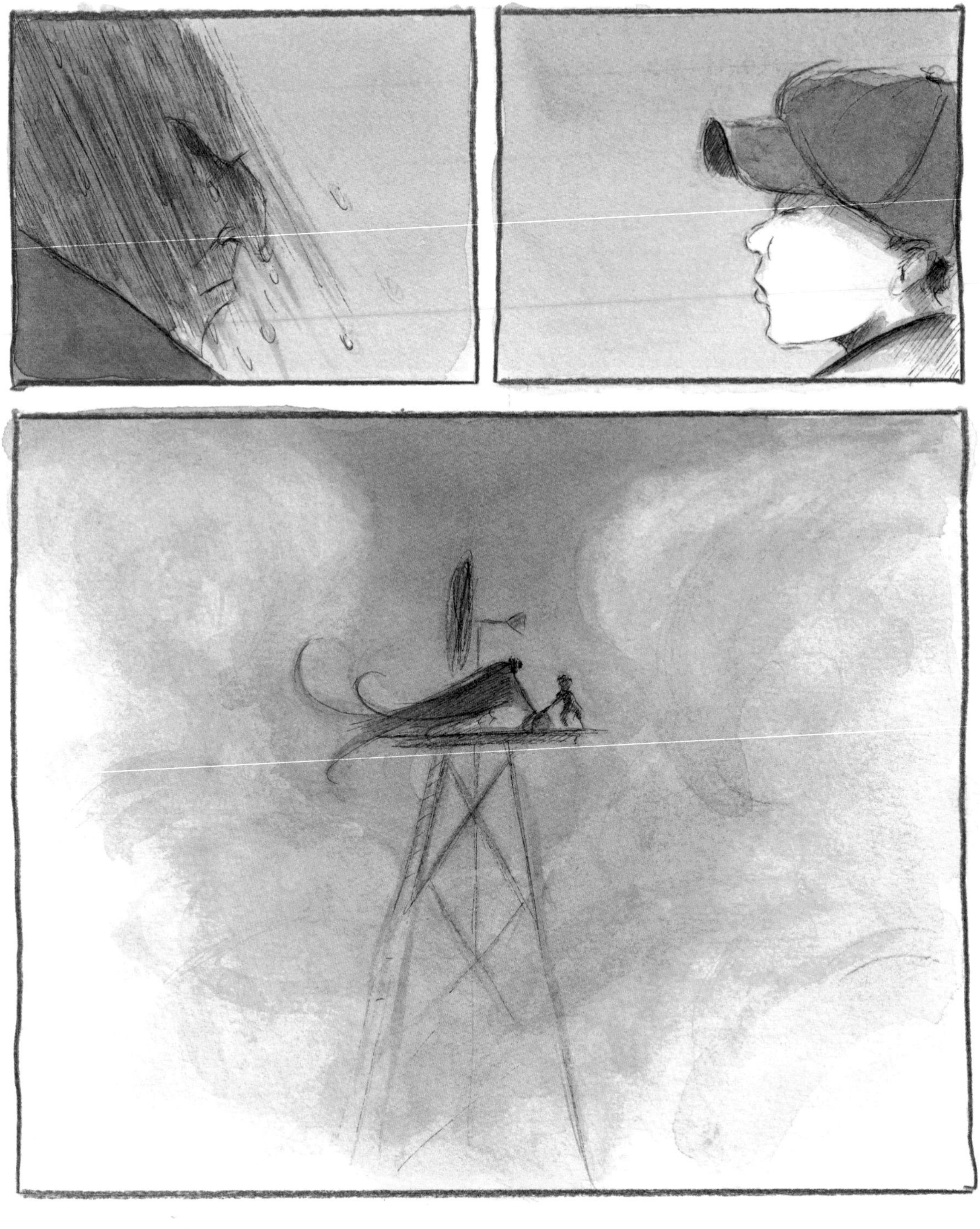

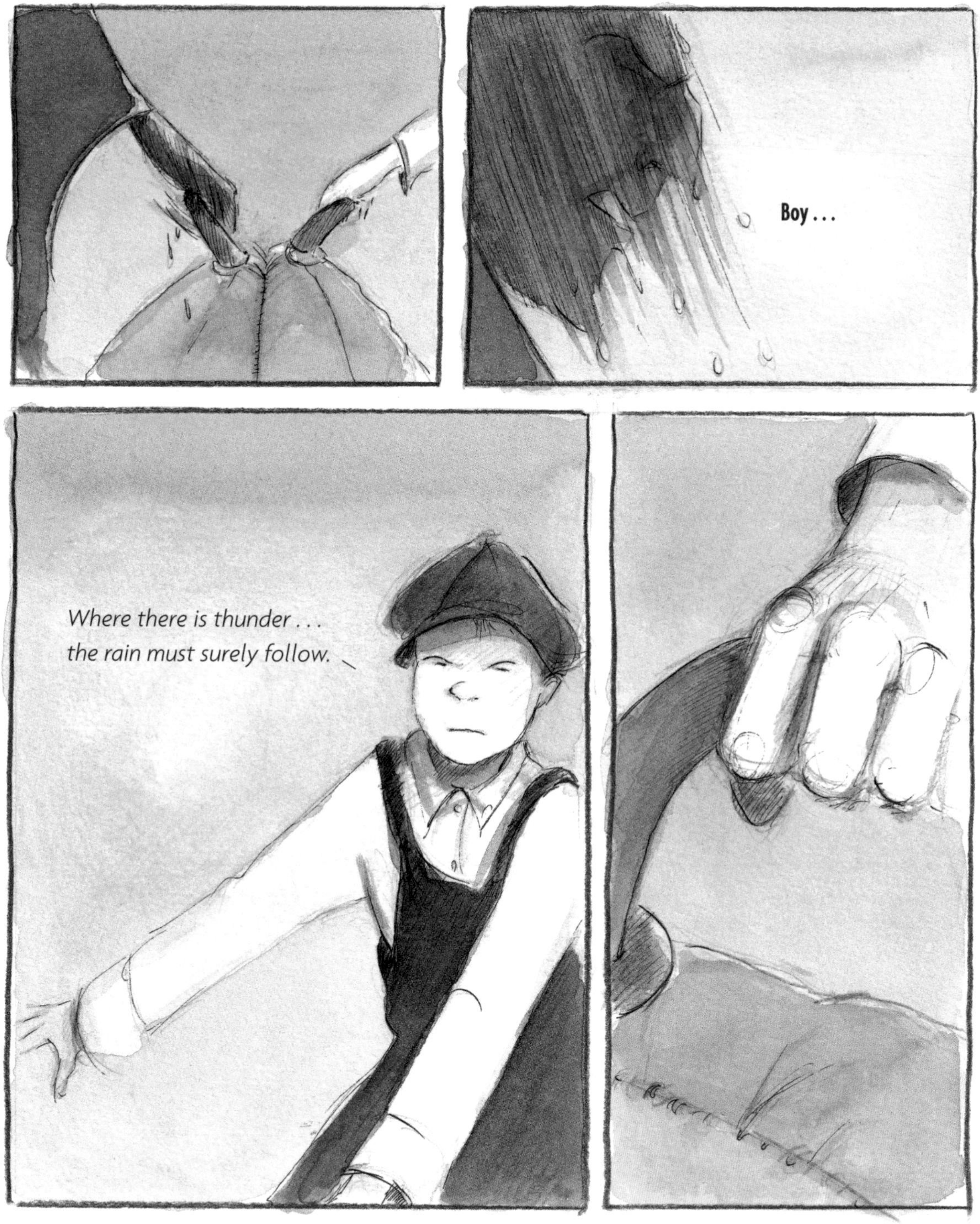
Boy . . .
Where there is thunder . . .
the rain must surely follow.

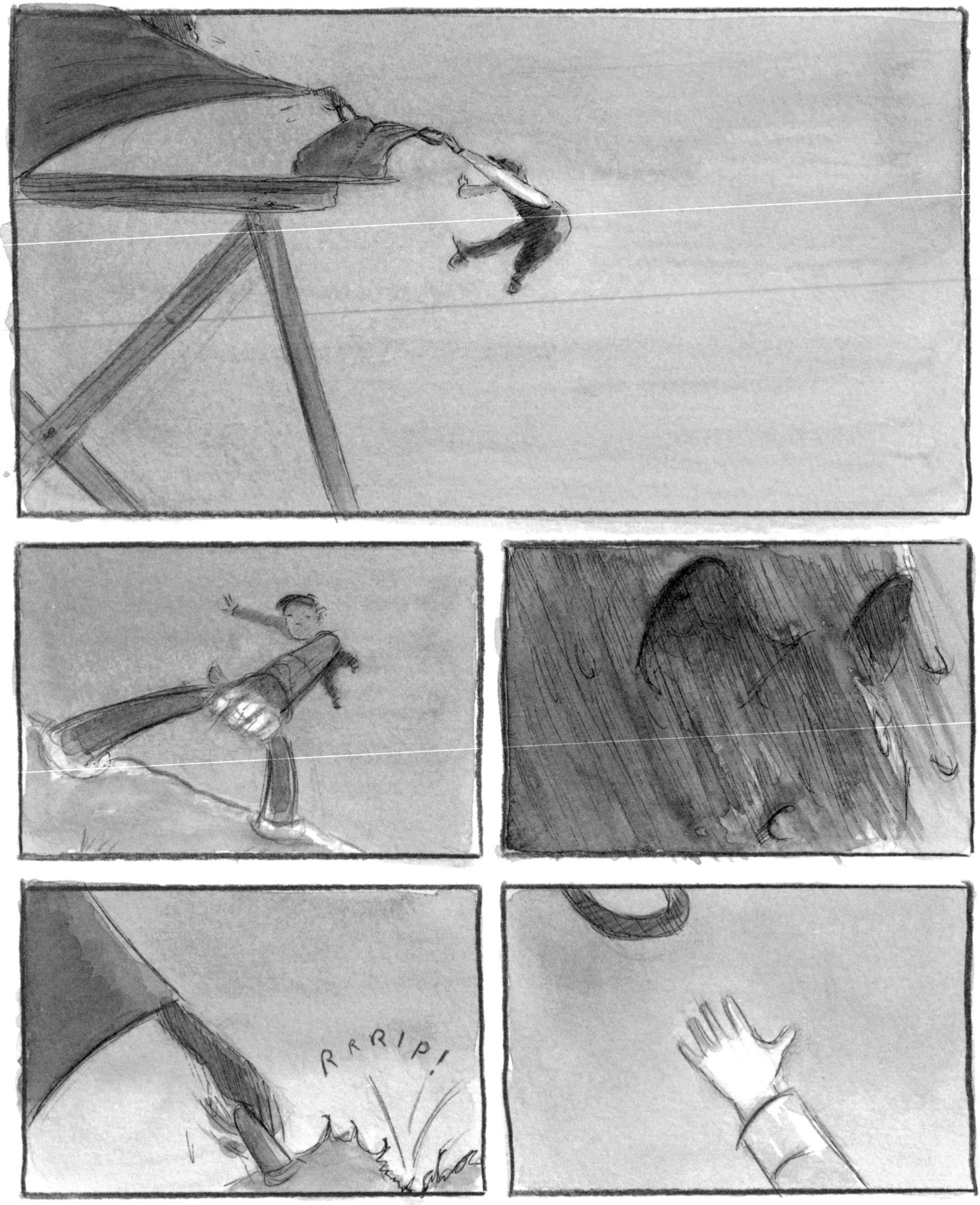
RRRIP!

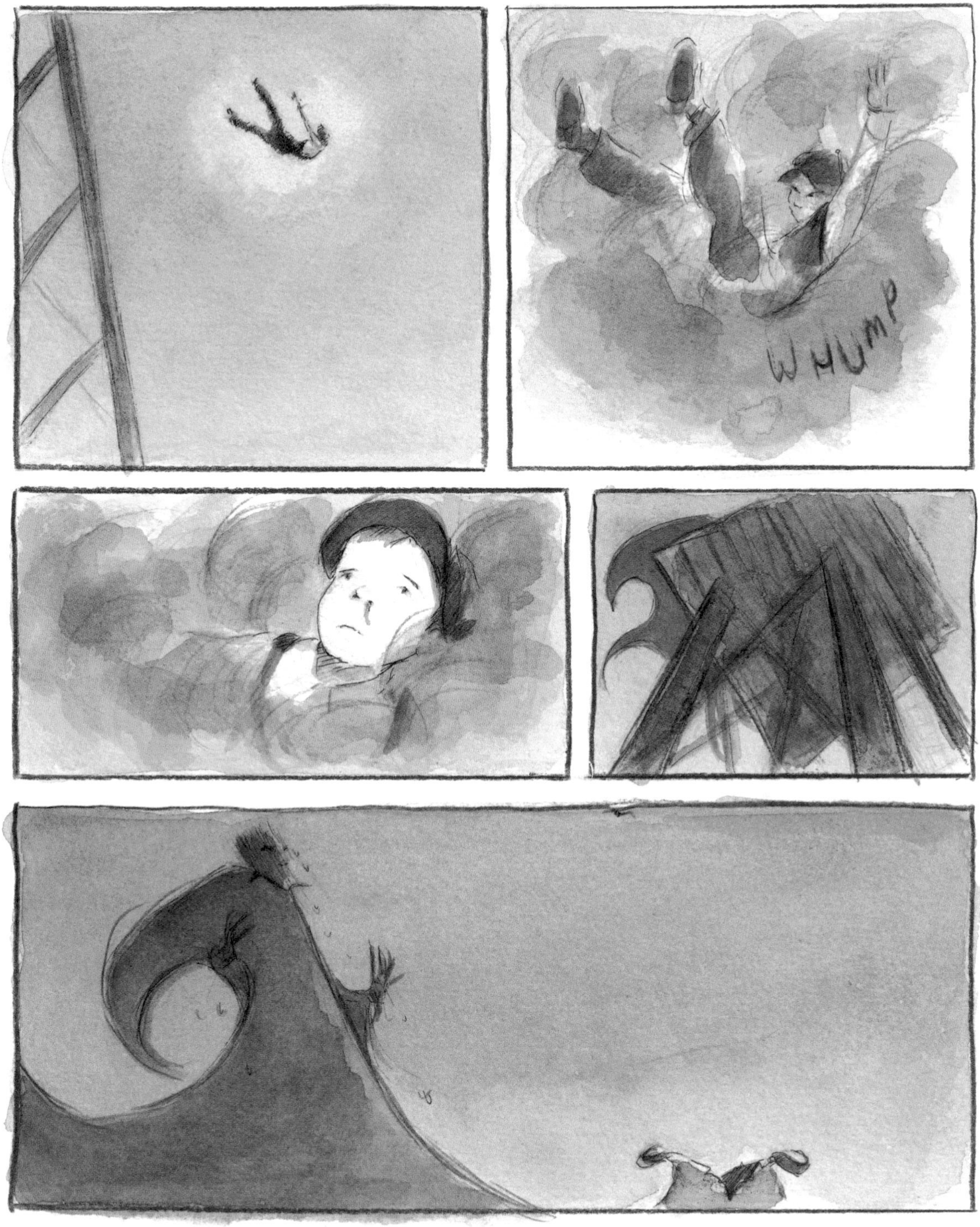
WHUMP

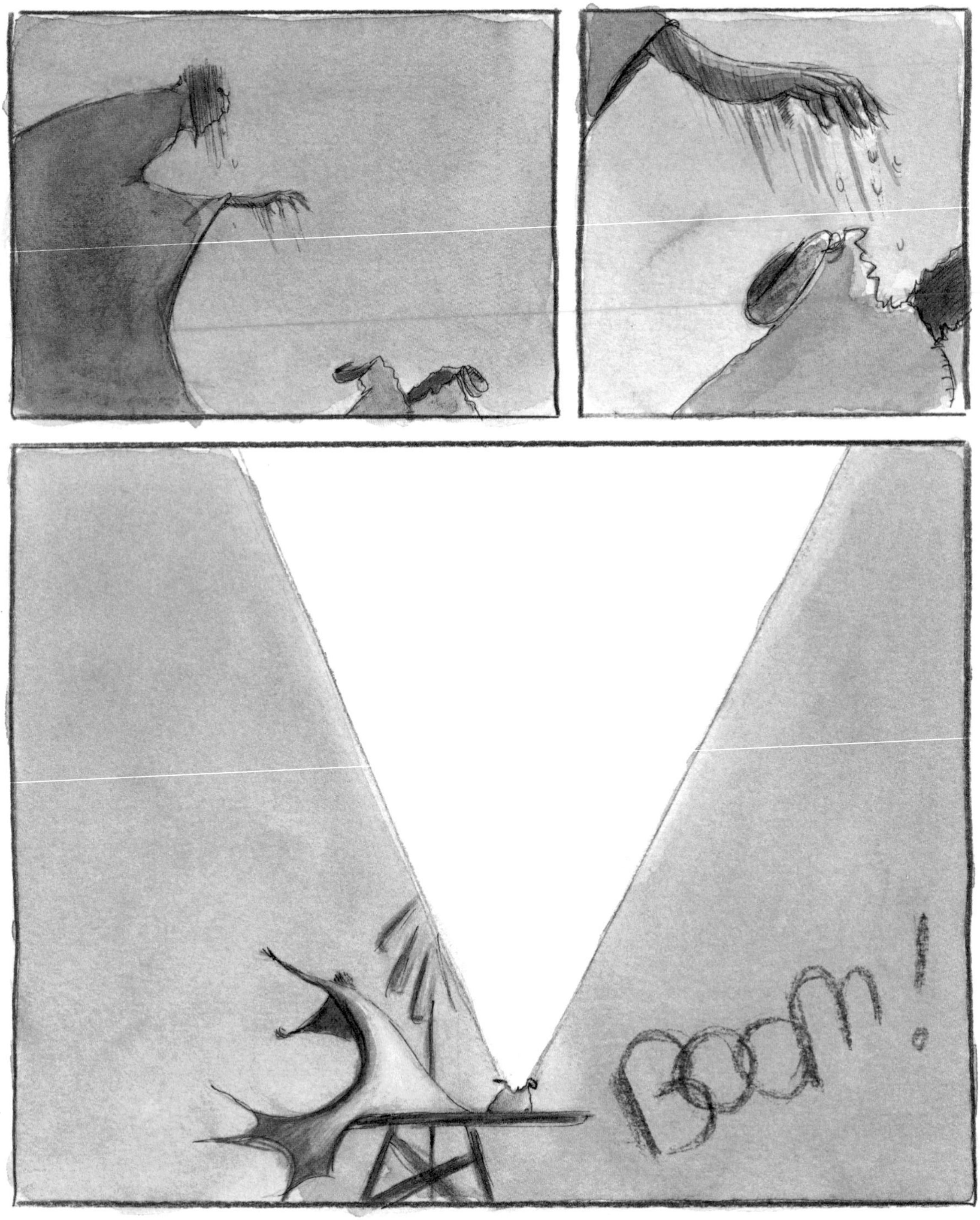
Boom!

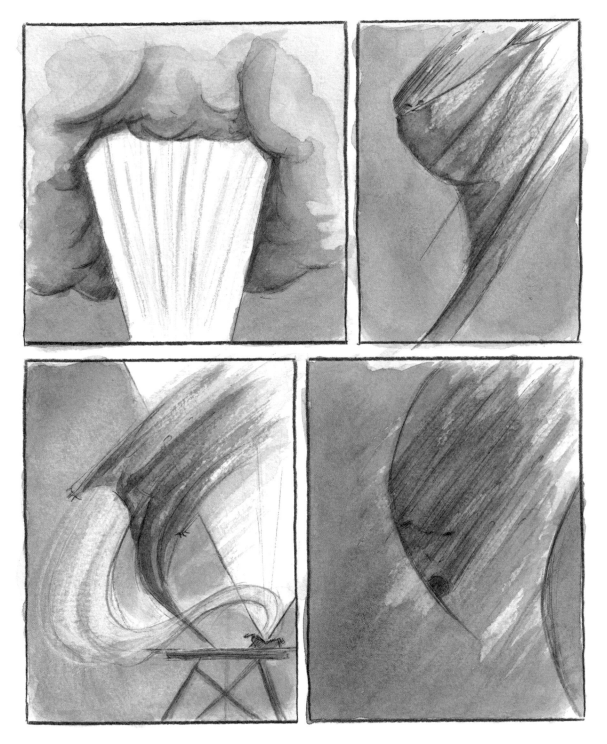

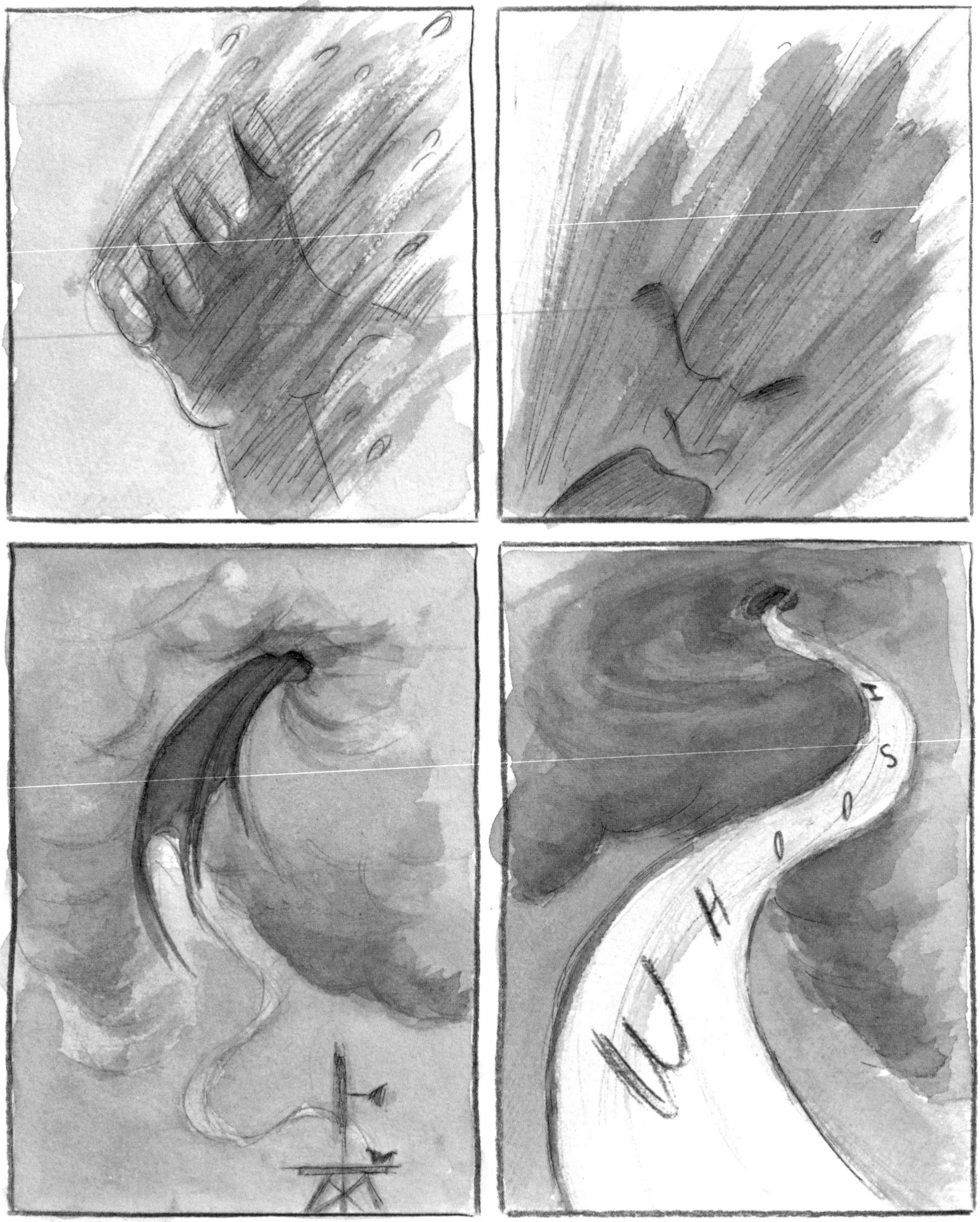
WHOOOSH

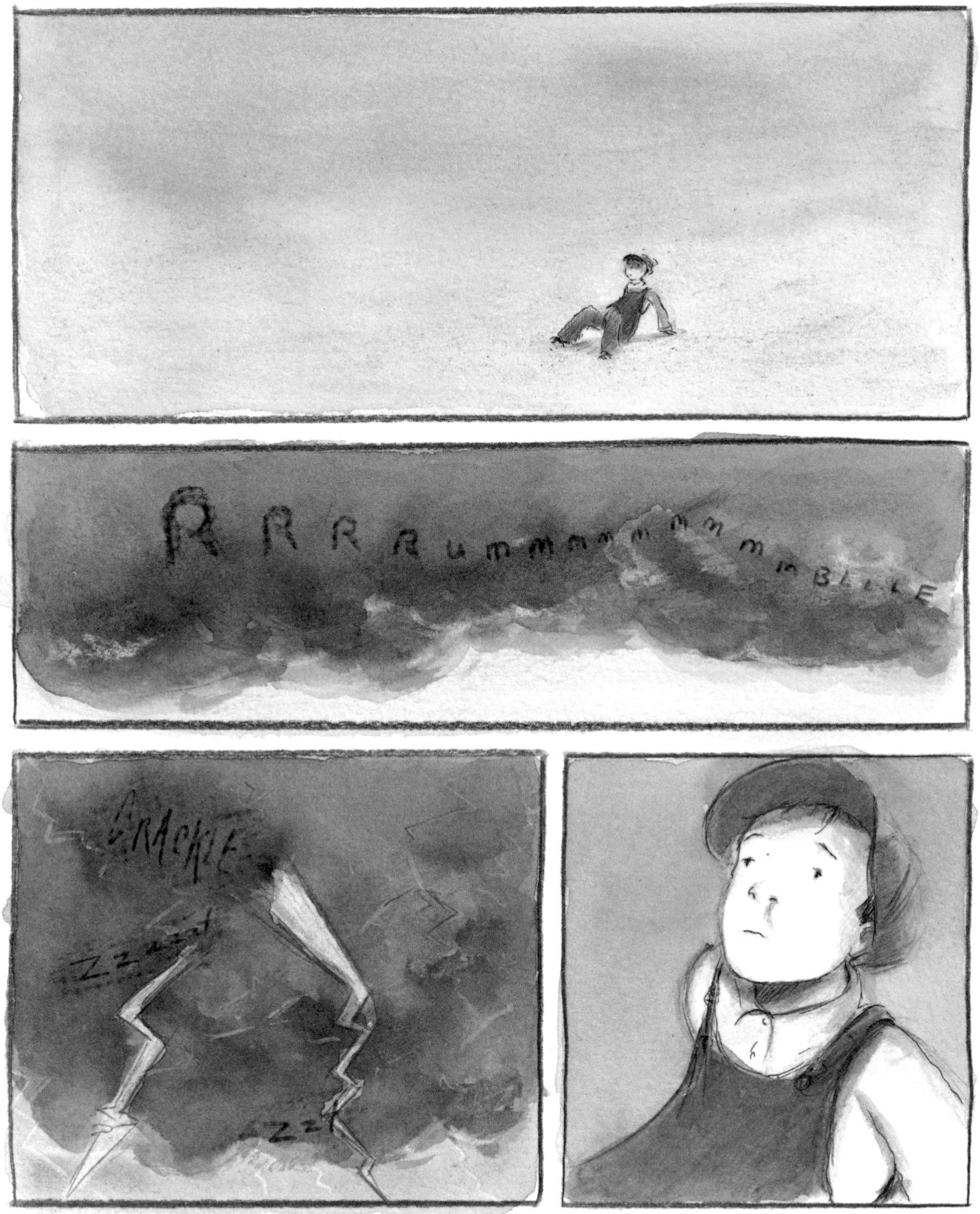
RRRRUMMMMMMMMMBLLLE
CRACKLE

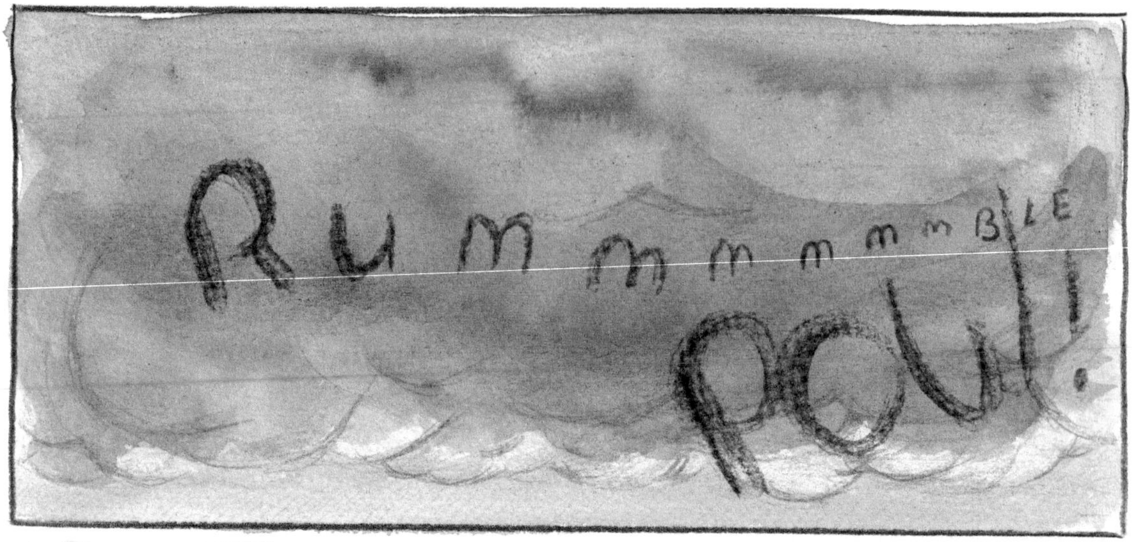
RUMMMMMMBLE
POW!
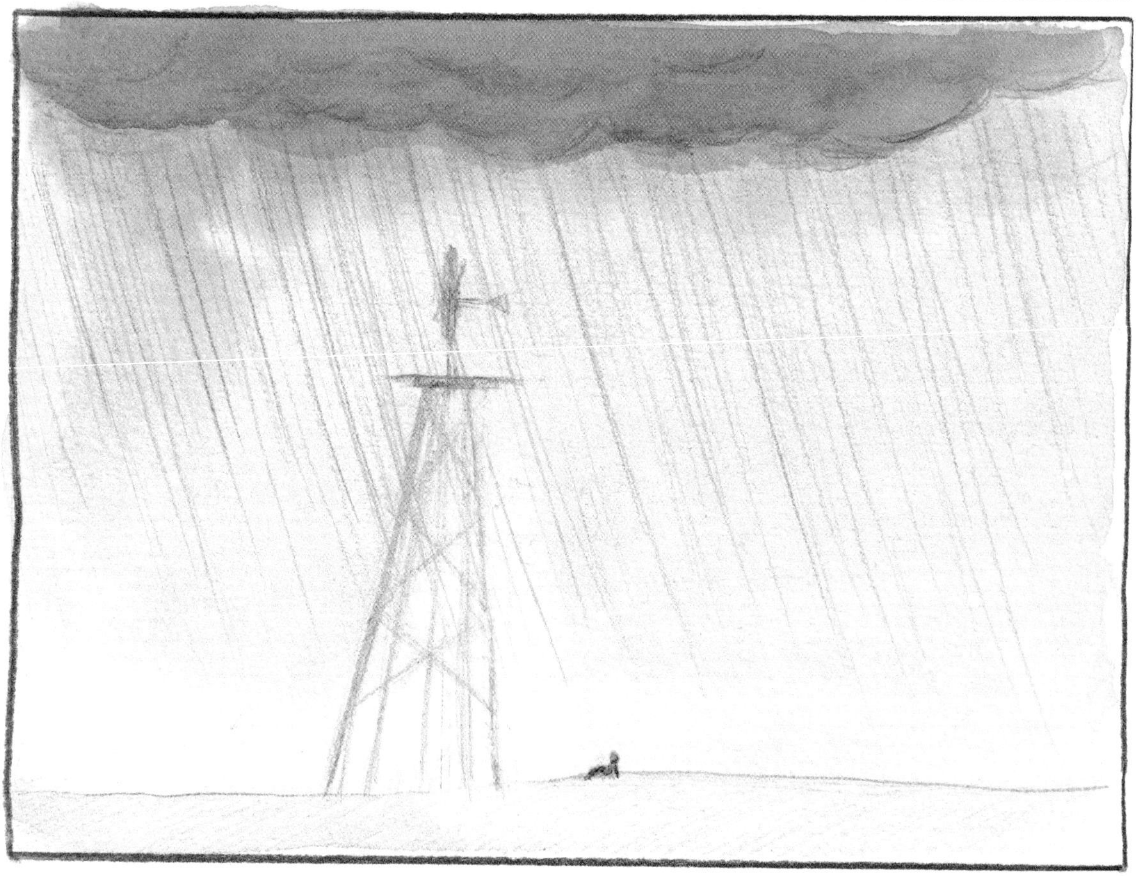

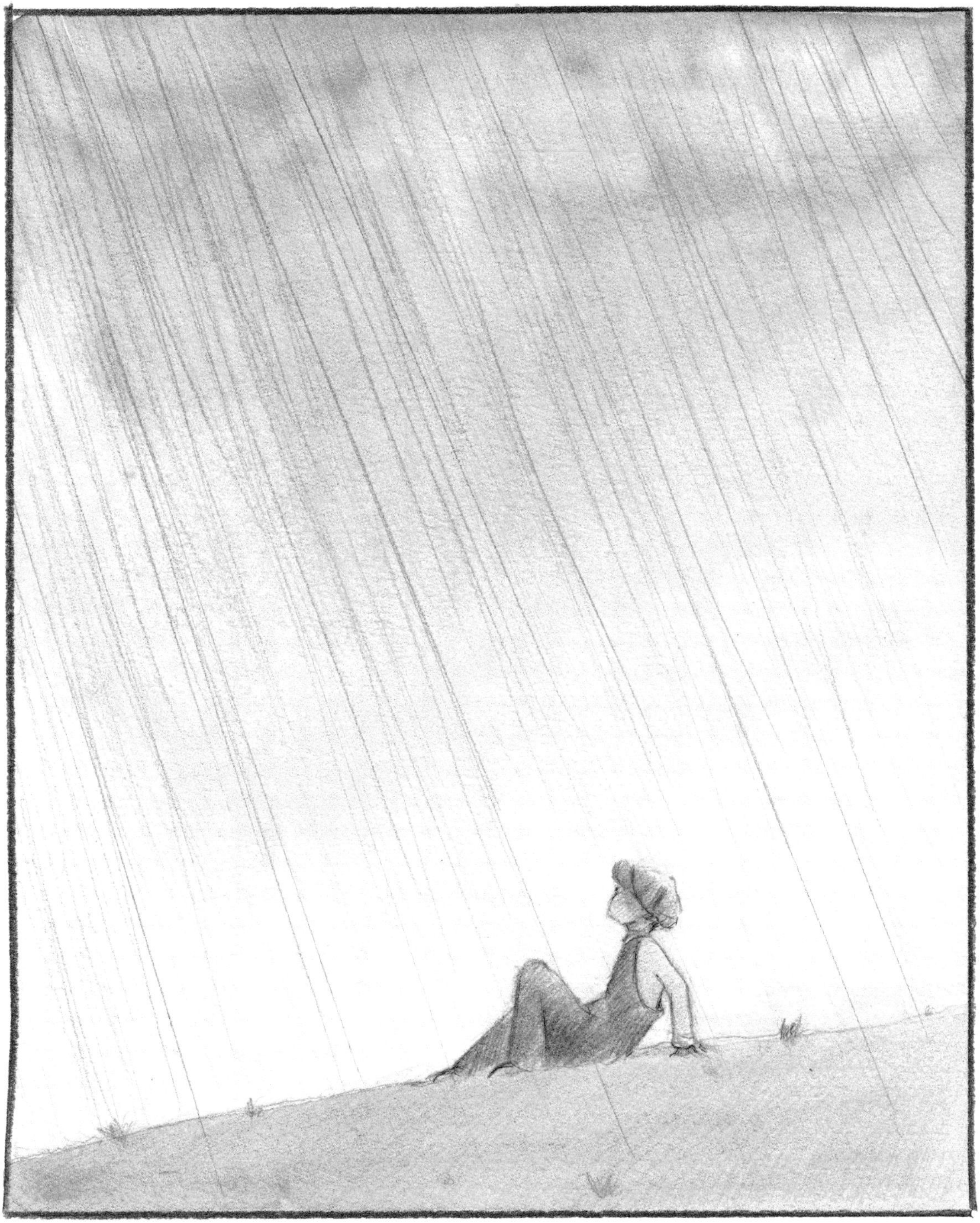

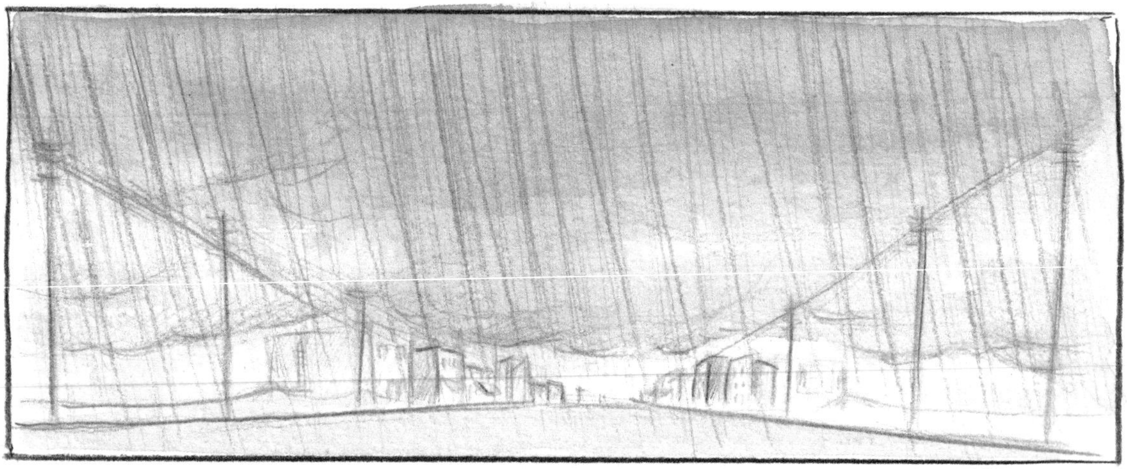

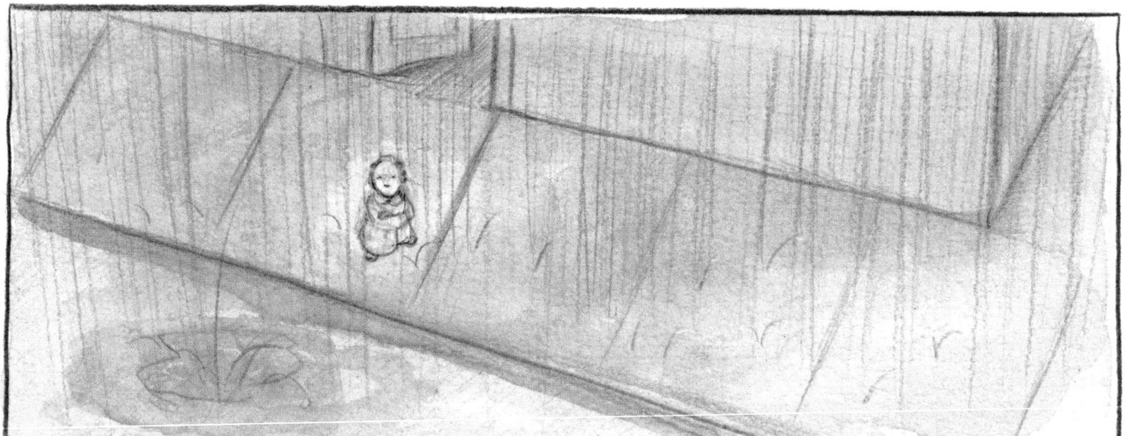

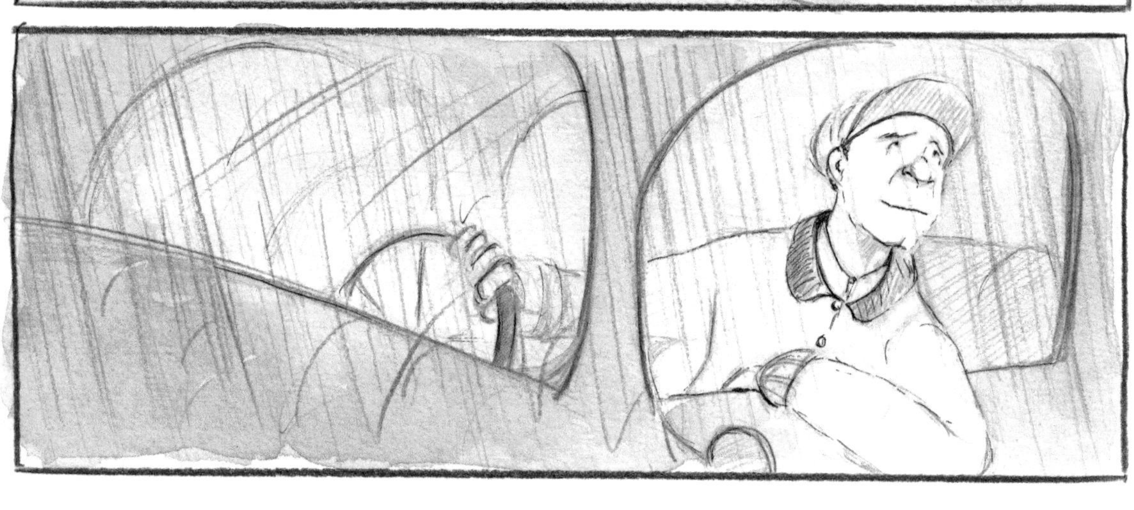

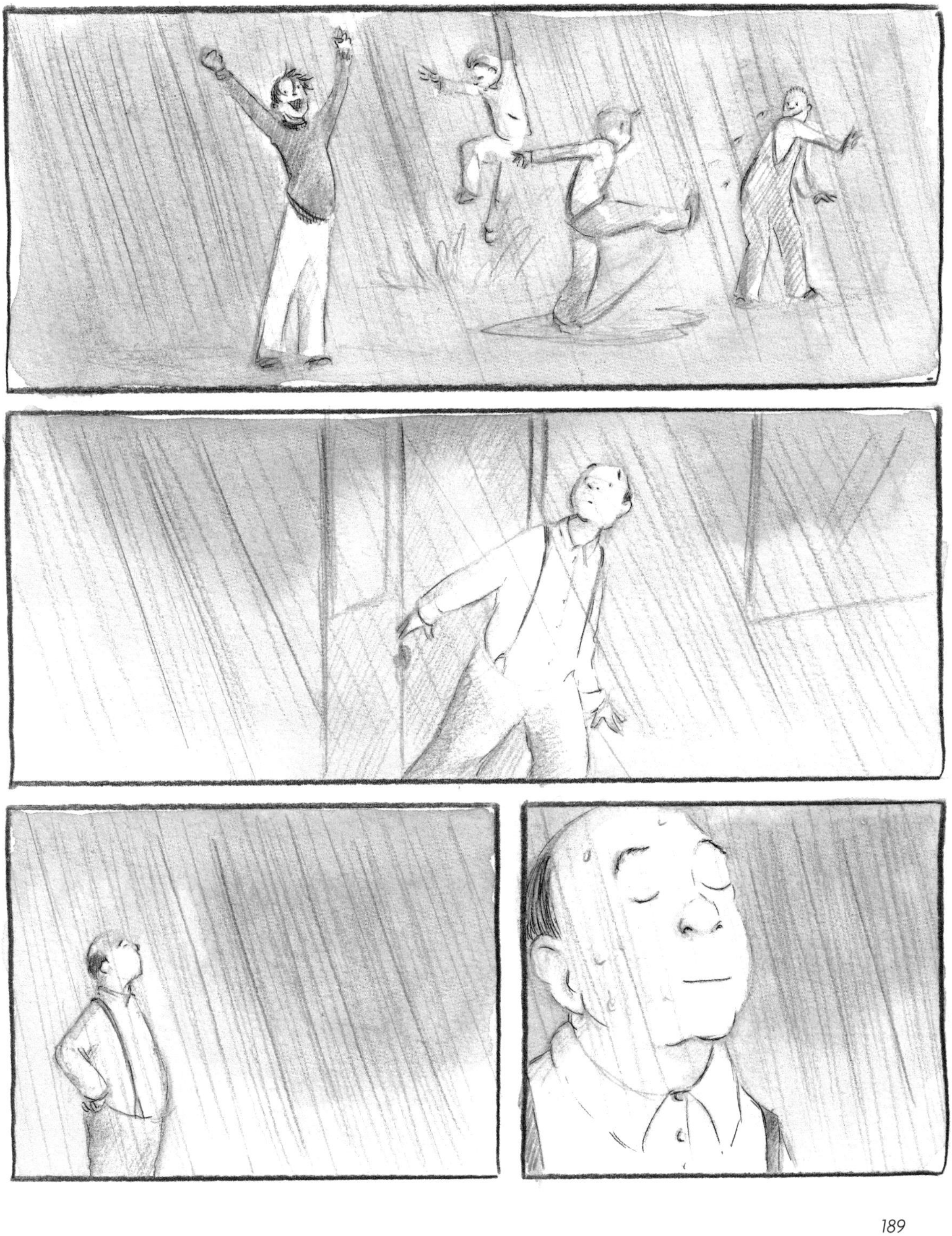

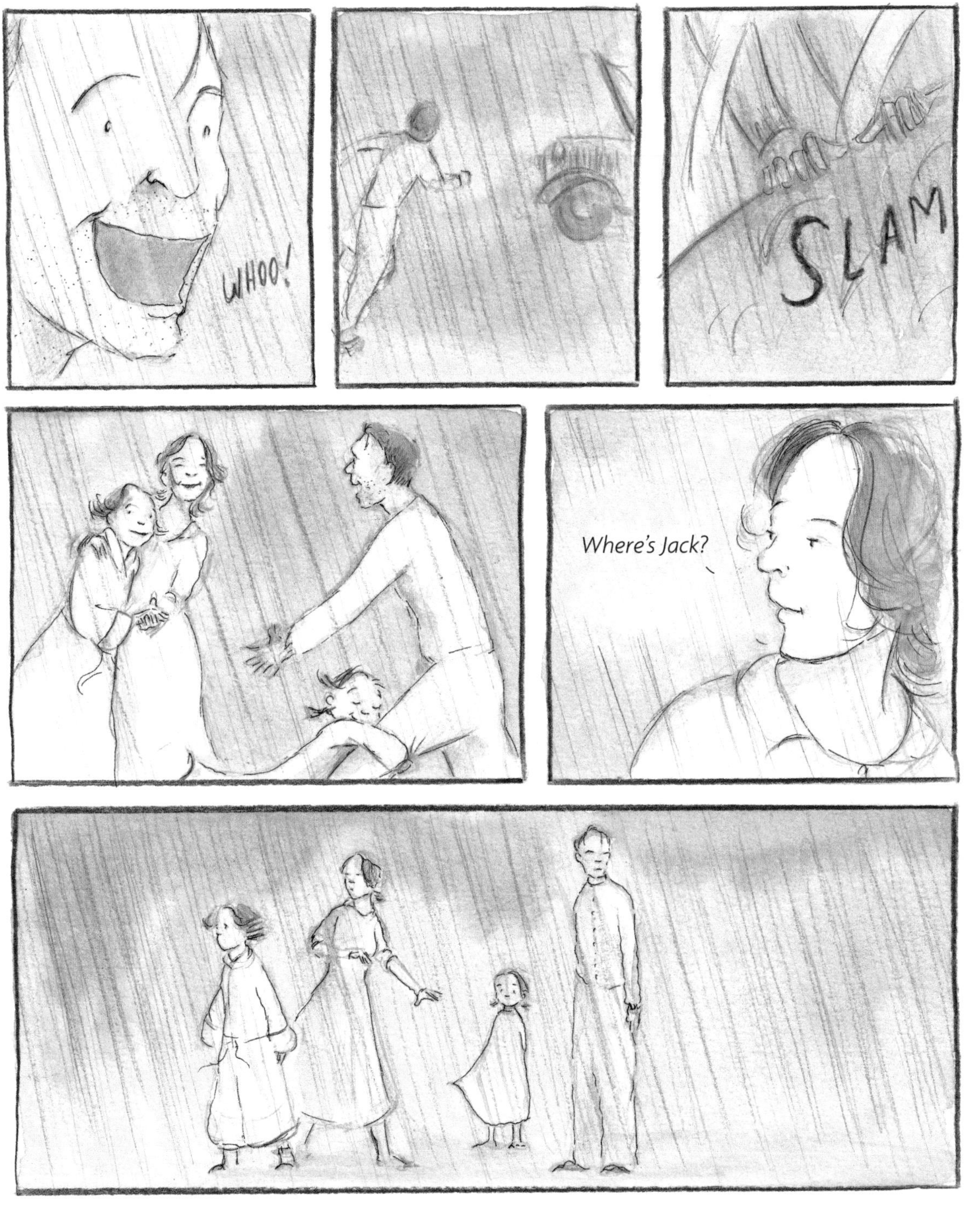
WHOO!
SLAM
Where's Jack?

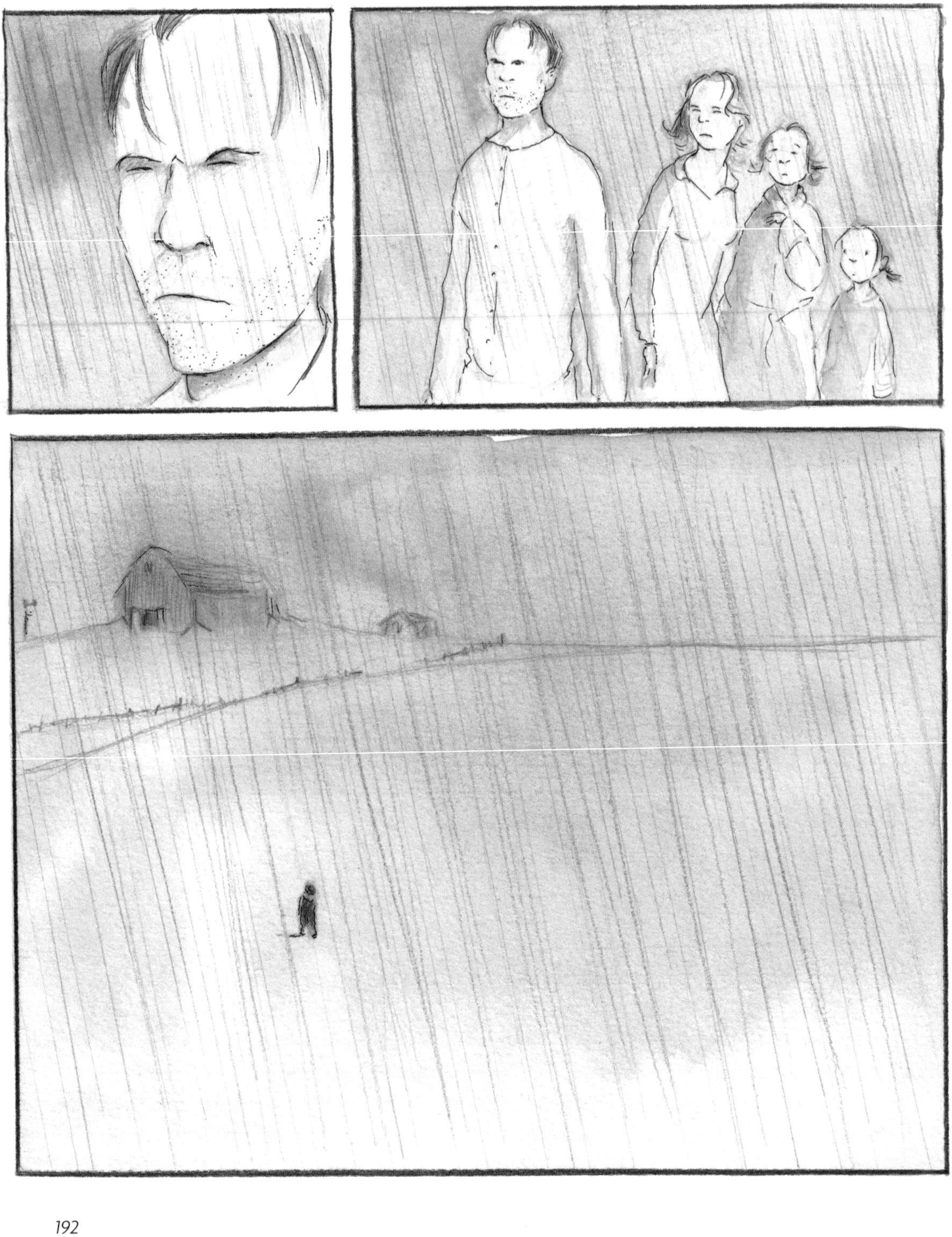

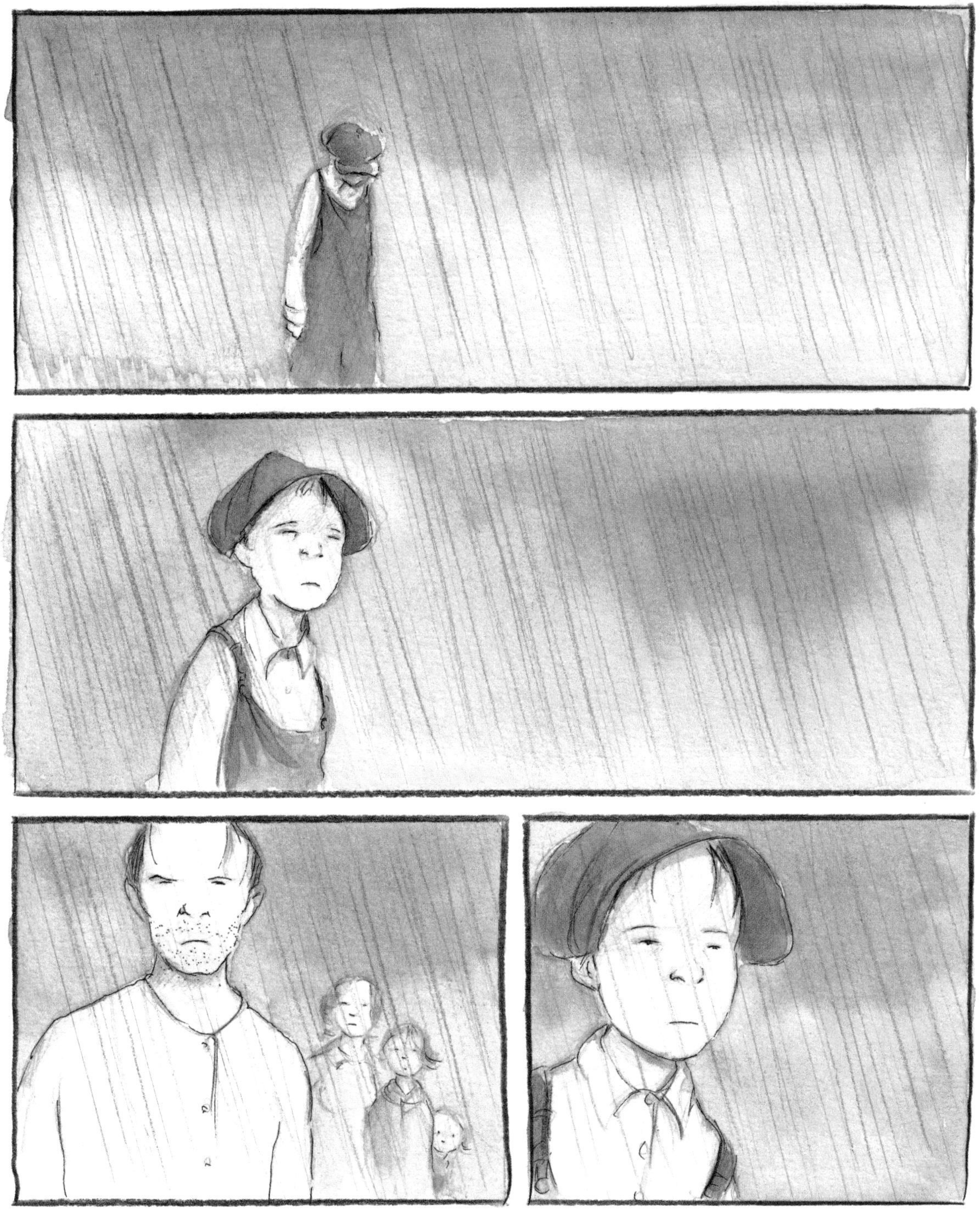

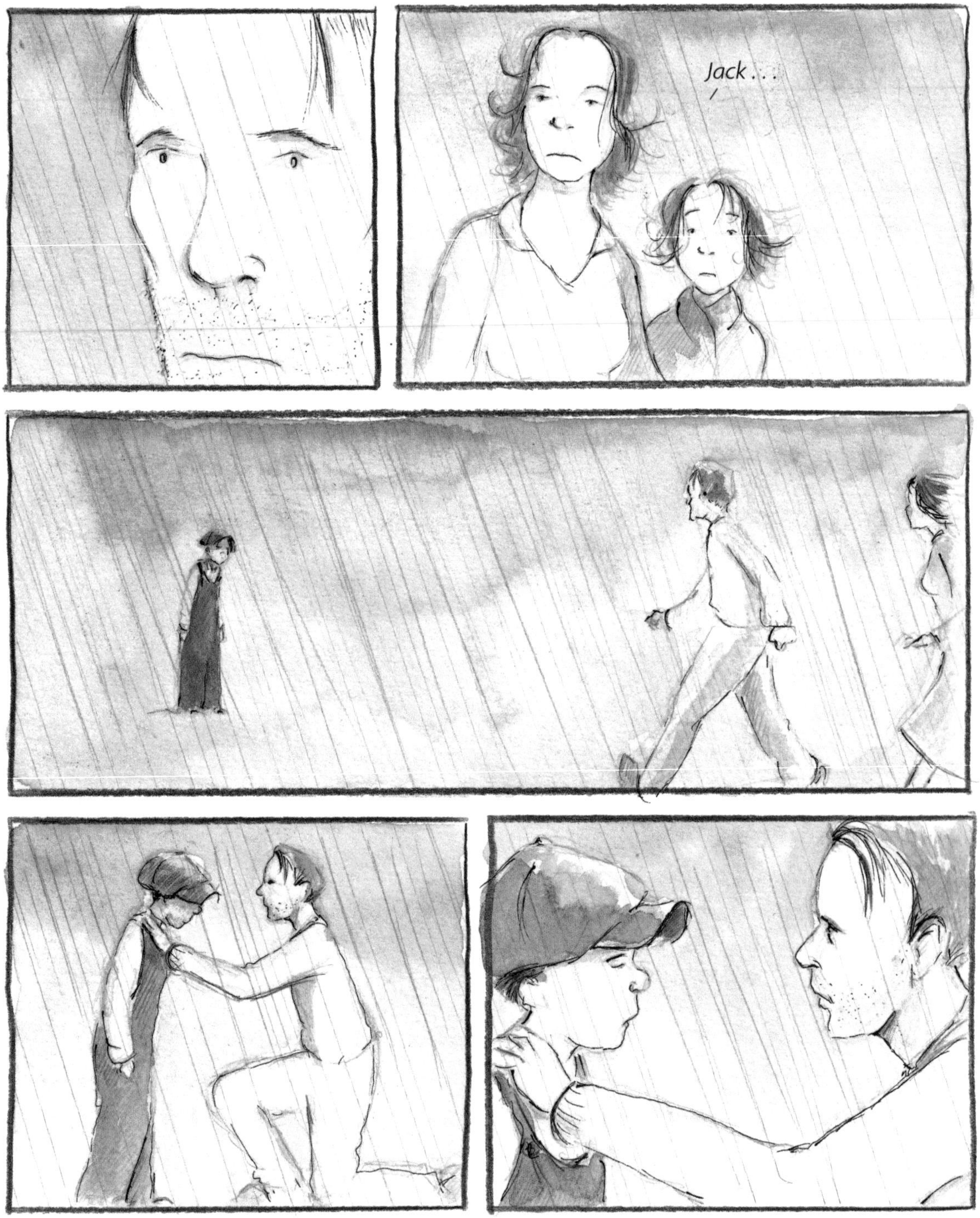
Jack . . .

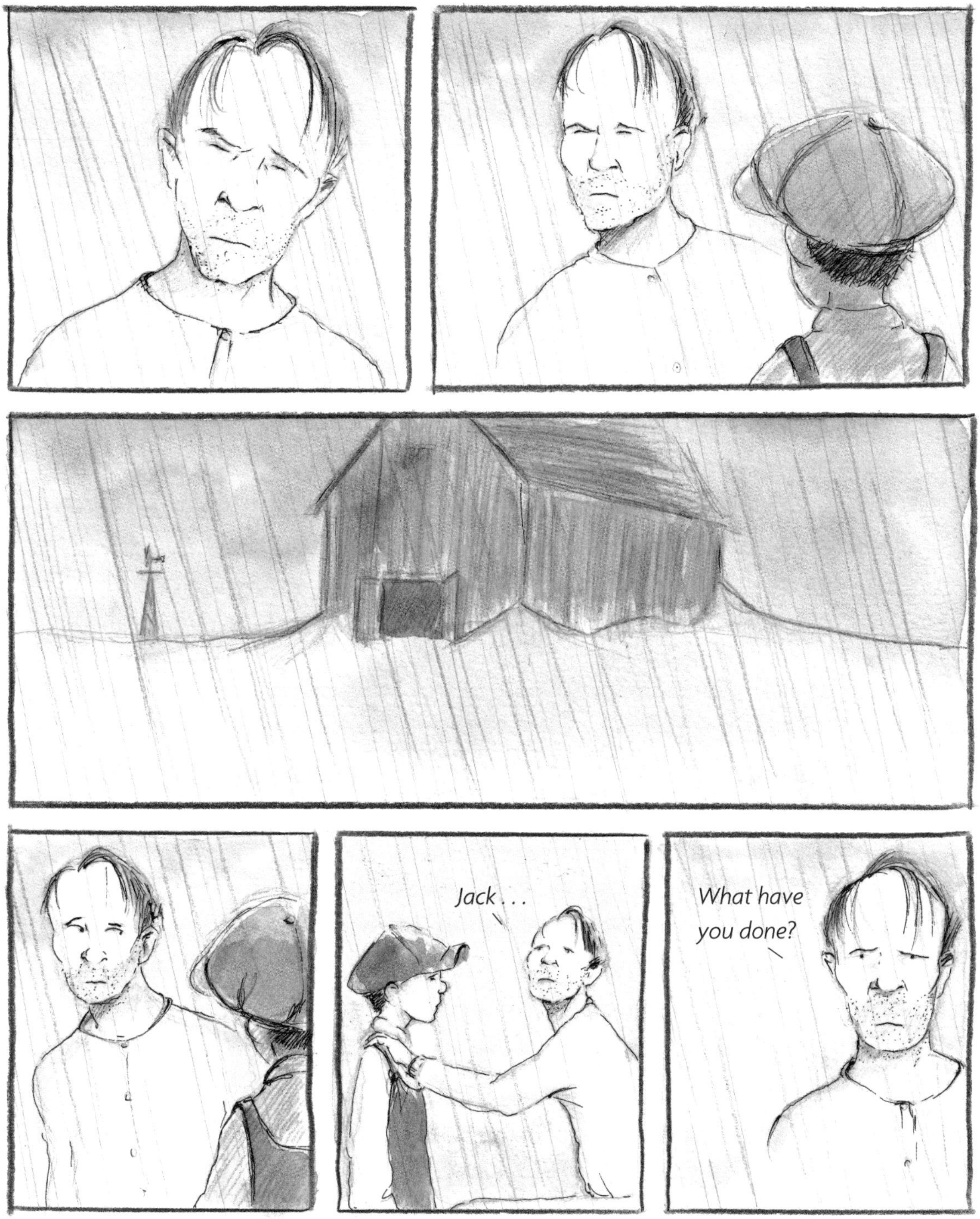
Jack . . .
What have you done?

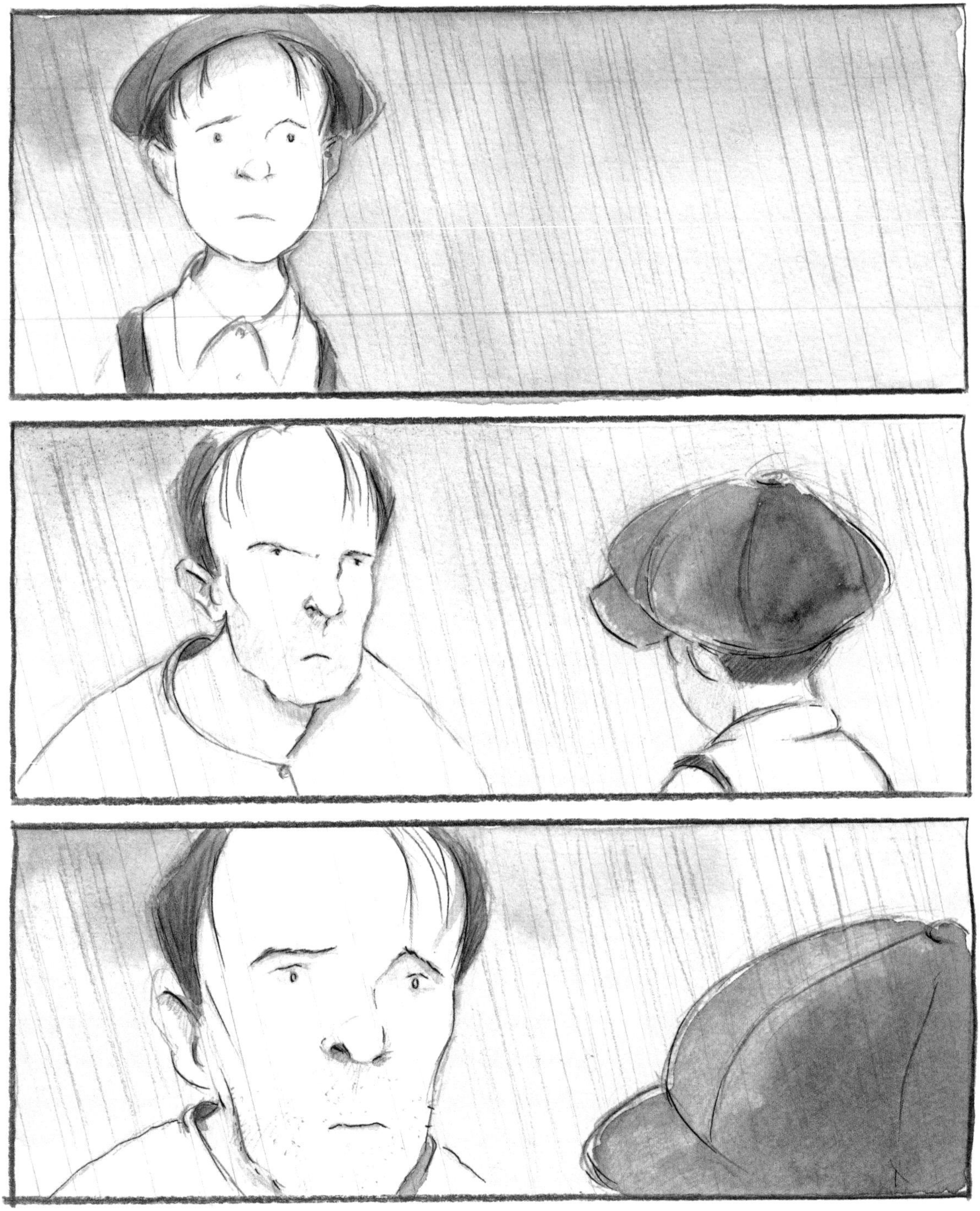

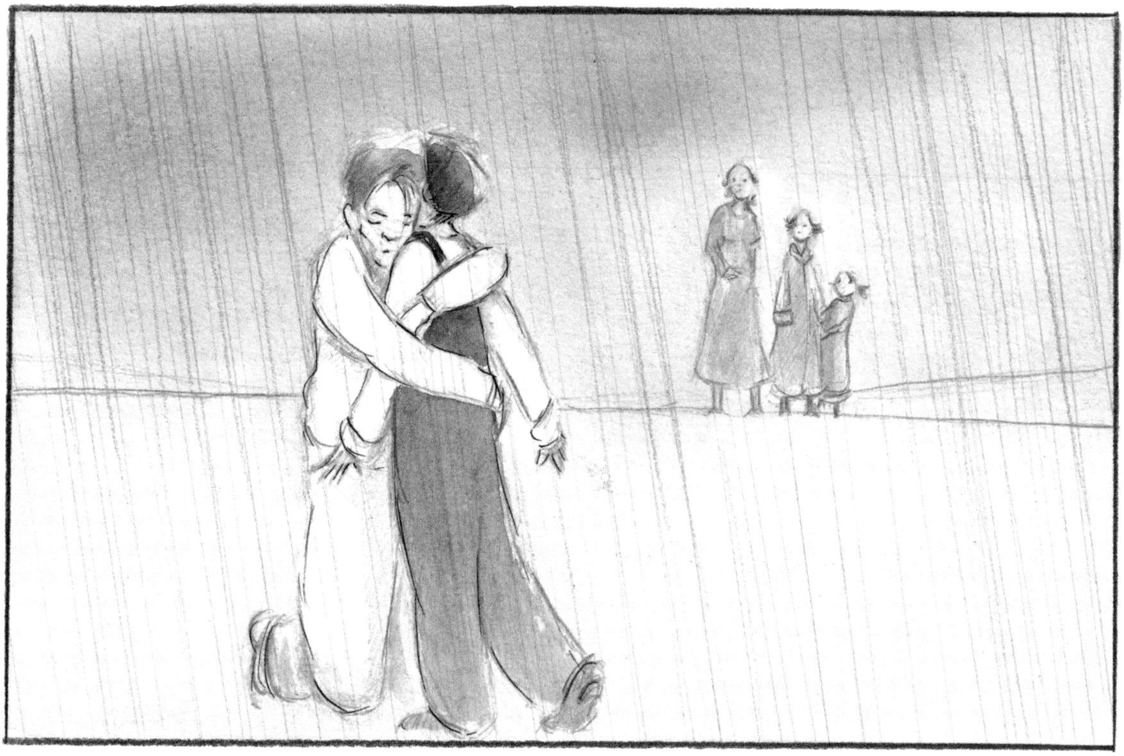

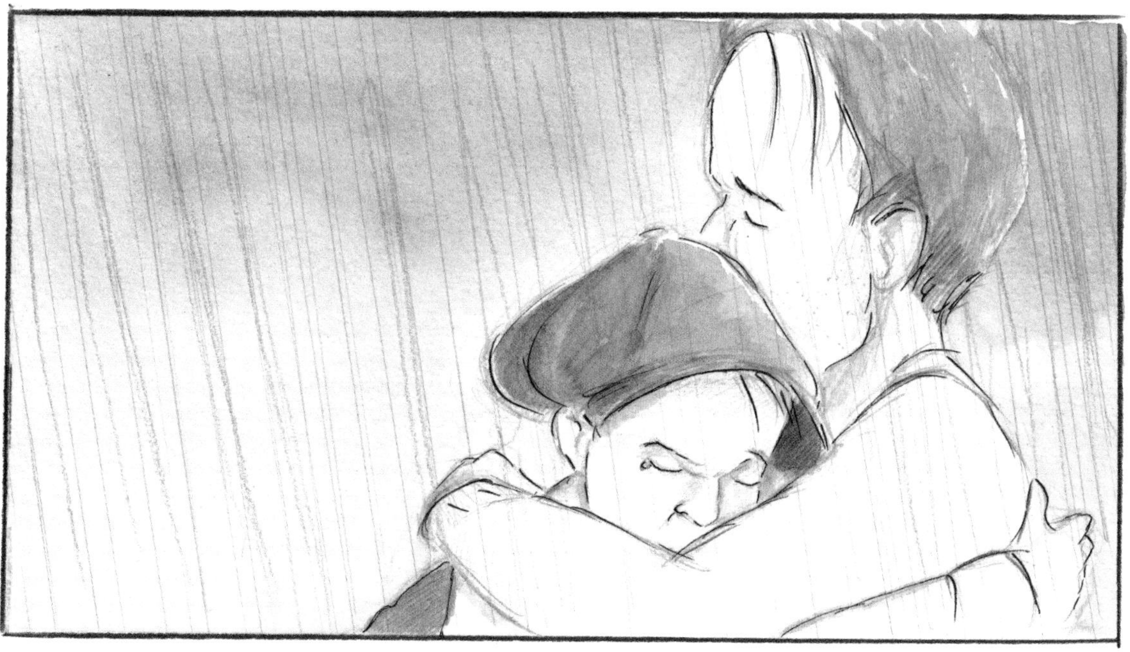

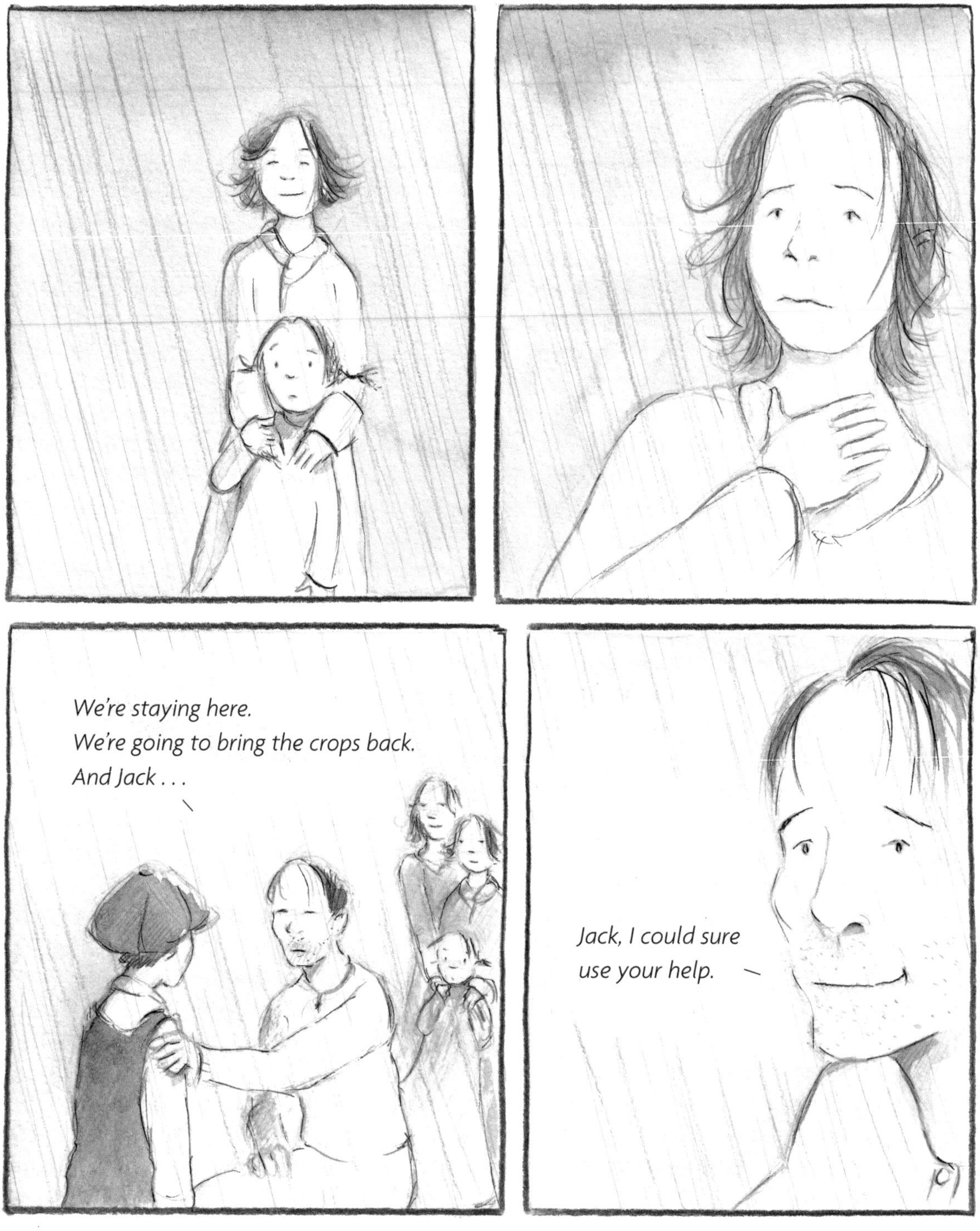
We're staying here.
We're going to bring the crops back.
And Jack . . .
Jack, I could sure
use your help.

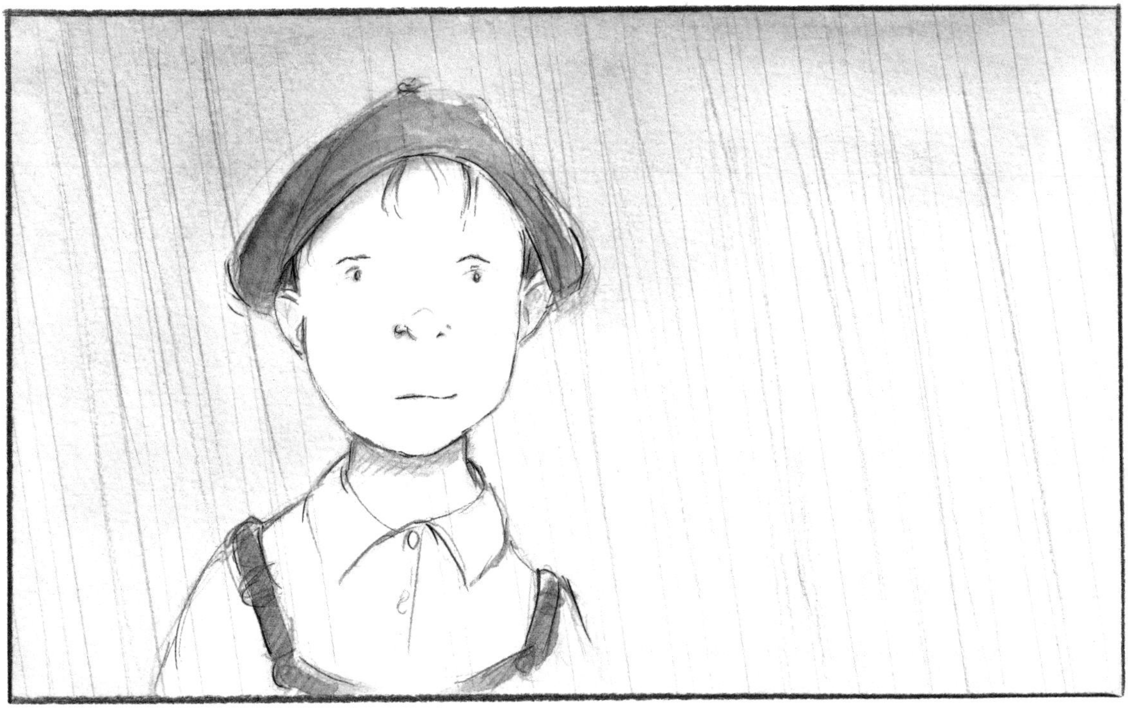

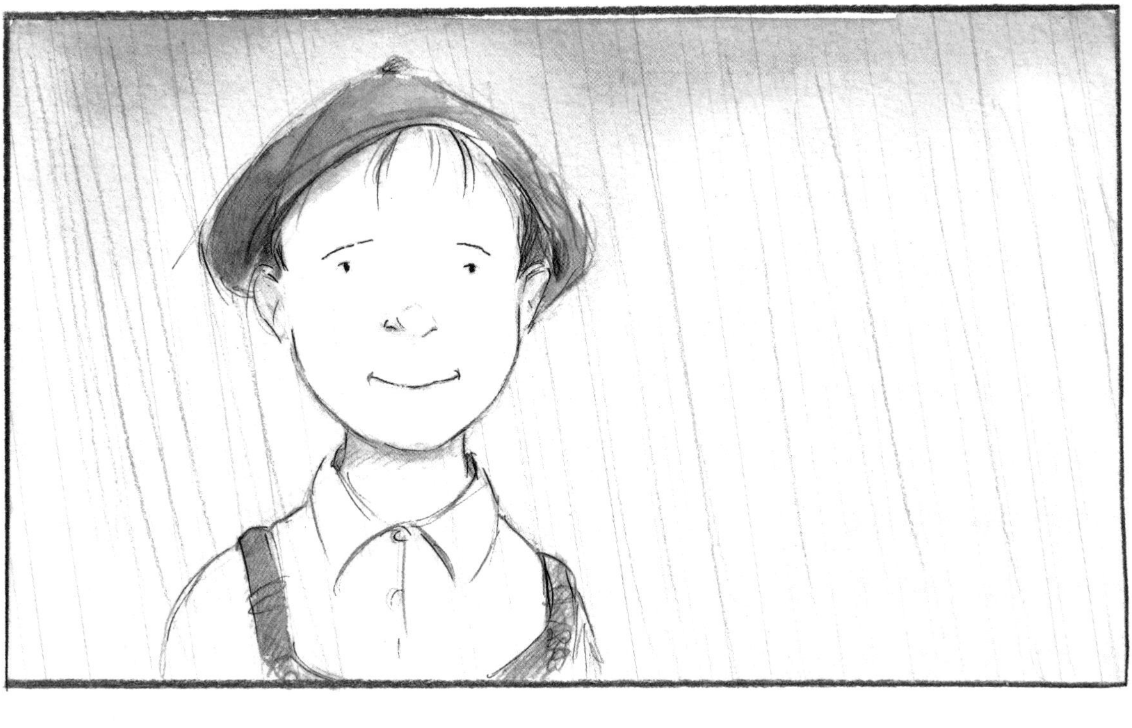

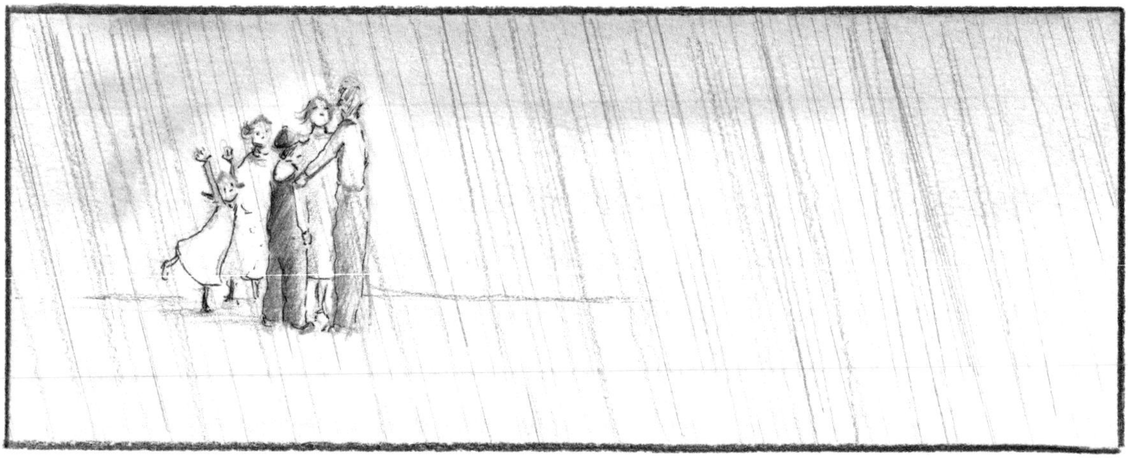

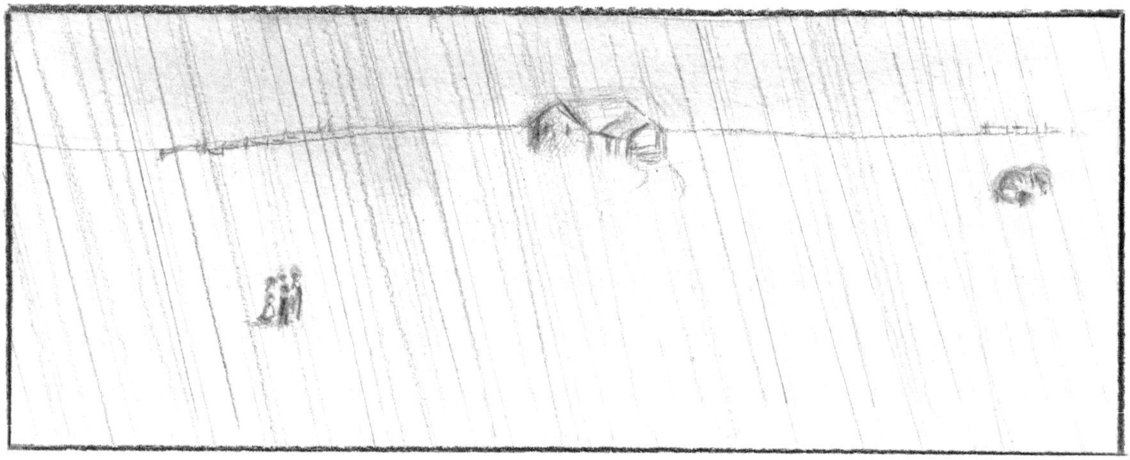

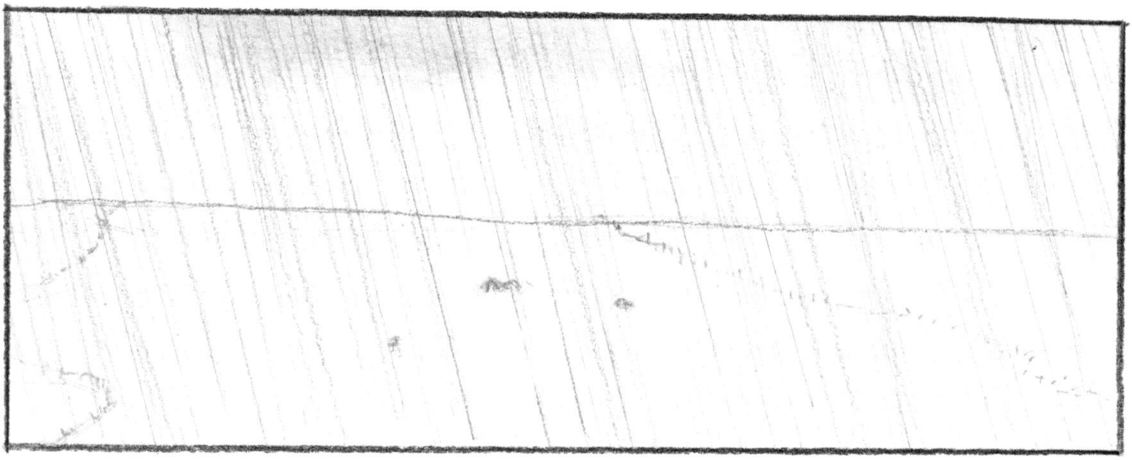

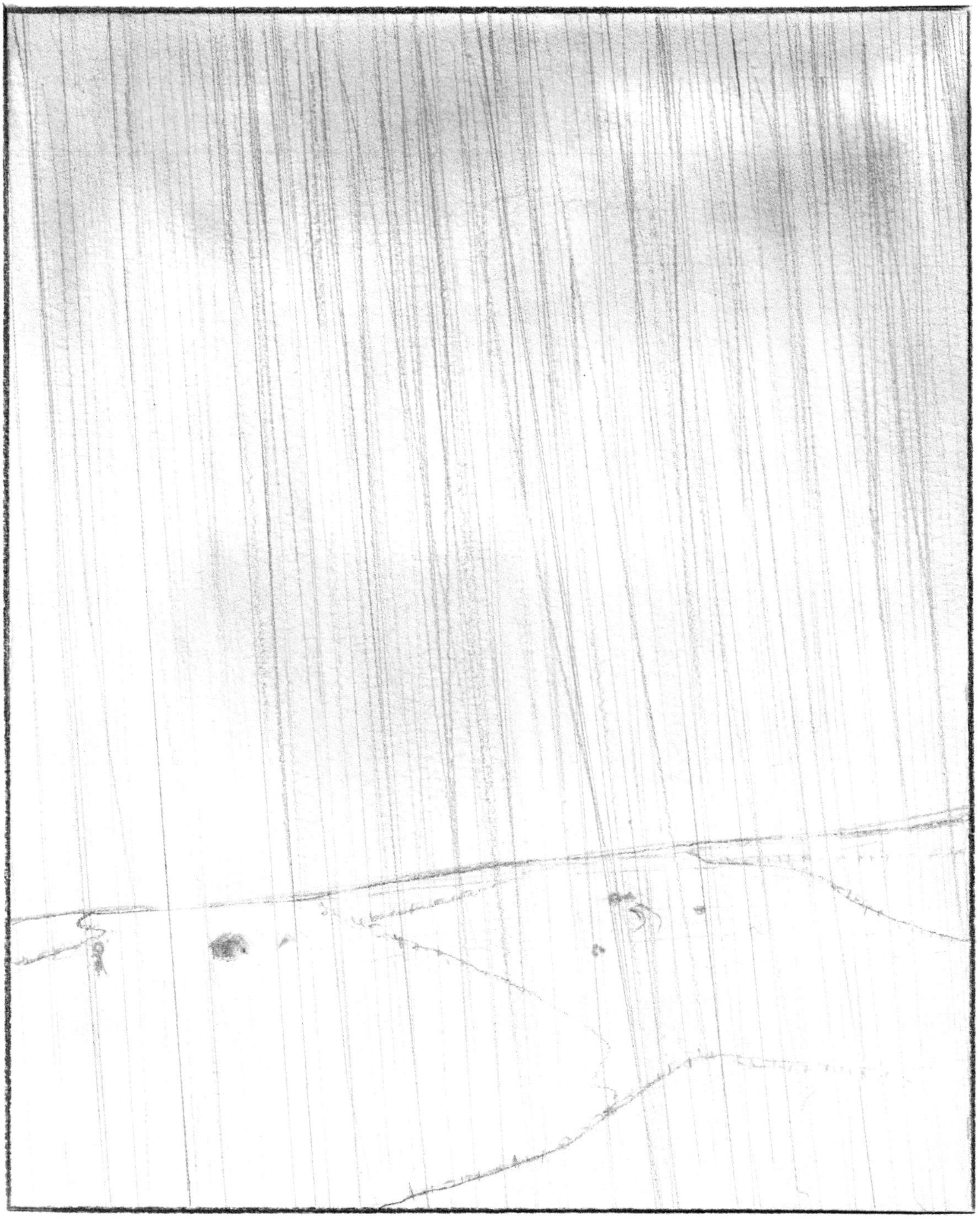

AUTHOR'S NOTE

FIFTEEN YEARS AGO, I was prowling through a used bookstore, not searching for anything in particular. The book that caught my eye was a slim paperback by Donald Worster called *Dust Bowl: The Southern Plains in the 1930s.* It was a full account of the Dust Bowl years — the various causes, the impact on the people, the implications for the future. The selling point for me, however, was the photography.

I had seen some of these photos before. As a kid, I poured over my dad's oversized hardback volumes of Works Progress Administration (WPA) photography. The stark black-and-white images captured by Dorothea Lange, Arthur Rothstein, Walker Evans, and others grabbed my attention. It was the faces. Against a backdrop of a vanishing farmland, these faces stared at the camera with haunting directness. They were beaten down, but somehow they weren't yet beaten.

Ten years ago, I watched an *American Experience* documentary called "Surviving the Dust Bowl." It included actual film footage — not just still photos — of massive dust clouds covering whole towns, people scrambling for cover, and even a brutal jackrabbit drive. This last event still haunted survivors of the time who, now in their old age, were interviewed for the documentary. This was what struck me most. I began to imagine what the experience of living in the Dust Bowl must have been

like through the eyes of a kid. Without the complicated expla-
nation of the history of over-planting, soil erosion, and other
factors, a young boy or girl would only know a world that could
suddenly vanish in a moving mountain of dark dust. The rain
had gone away. But where?

Five years ago, for reasons I can't explain, I sketched a tall, dark,
sinister figure with a face like a thunderstorm.

I knew I wanted this book to be a story set in the Dust Bowl
but not a story directly about the Dust Bowl. I wanted to bring
in elements of American folklore, like the Jack tales that were
still being told and the Oz books that had been enthralling kids
for thirty-odd years at that point. In the next two years, *The
Wizard of Oz* would become a movie and Superman would leap
from the pages of comic books, but in 1937 there were mostly
just stories — stories a boy in Kansas would think about as he
looked at a land apparently as cursed as any in the fairy tales.

Many years have passed since I first discovered those iconic
photographs. They still have the power to stop me cold when-
ever I see them. I went back to those photos many times during
the making of this book. Each time, I tried to absorb some small
feeling for that strange era, so that I could tell this Dust Bowl
story with pictures of my own.